ENTER
THE
META

ENTER
THE
META

COLETTE BENNETT

SOLARIS

First published 2023 by Solaris
an imprint of Rebellion Publishing Ltd,
Riverside House, Osney Mead,
Oxford, OX2 0ES, UK

www.solarisbooks.com

ISBN: 978-1-78108-928-6

Cover art by V.V. Glass
Chapter art by Petitecreme

A CIP catalogue record for this book is available from the
British Library.

Designed & typeset by Rebellion Publishing

Printed in Denmark

FOR MY BELOVED GRANDMOTHER,
WHO ALWAYS BELIEVED.

PROLOGUE

IN THE VILLAGE
OF THE FAITHFUL

November 16, 391 A.D.

THE FIRST TIME the Onyx pillaged our graveyards I was too young to understand what was happening.

Despite all these years that have passed, I still remember the sounds as vividly as if I was hearing them in this very moment. The banging of wood as my mother bolted the door of our bedroom, alone, before dashing outside. The thin shriek of a child. The crackle of consuming fire. The snapping of wood, hastily broken into makeshift weapons in trembling hands. The agonised screams of the men and women of the Village of the Faithful, howls of fear and rage.

And a foetid stink, like a dead cow left to rot in the summer sun.

Also, an even hazier memory arises from time to time, from long before that terrible day: the tension on my mother's face as it hardened the line of her brow, even as I lay in her arms nursing at her bosom. As she nourished me, I drank her strength.

They'll come again, her body murmured to me. *You must be ready*.

The day I turned four, my mother sat with me at the stone table where we ate our meals.

"Son," she said, "it is time for you to know the face of our enemy."

Her eyes stayed steady on me as she told the story of the Onyx. She never once tried to soften it, make it palatable for a child. She spoke as if I was a man sitting across from her. Perhaps that's how she saw me that day. Not a four-year-old boy, but the man I would one day become. Or maybe she needed me to be that man sooner rather than later. Because if I wasn't, we would be robbed of everything we Jiu'sho stand for. She needed every person in our village to fight back, no matter how young, foolish, or unprepared we might be.

I didn't learn where they came from that day. No one knew that, although many had their ideas. But that wasn't important. There were only two things that mattered when it came to them: the wretched stink of their skin and the squeals of their creaking knees. These were the things that let us know they were drawing near. If it wasn't for that they could have dug up our graveyards in the night at their leisure, leaving us to wake and discover they'd taken our most precious treasures.

But because their bodies were ruined and horrible, as I imagined their souls to be in those long-ago days, we learned to use that against them. We grew attuned to inhaling deeply when we rose in the morning, before sleep in the evening, and every time we walked outside or past an open window. We were always waiting for the moment when that rancid smell would announce them in the air, all life in between no more than an uneasy pause.

The Xi'sho have followed the same practices for the last thousand years. When one of our elders leaves this world, the Matriarch—in our case, my mother—performs a ritual to seal the wisdom and experience from their time in this life into a Shard. We wrap their bodies in the leaves from our trees as an offering to the True Spirit, and we place the Shard inside their mouths.

I followed my mother every morning at dawn to pay homage to their graves as their souls journeyed to the next realm, thanking them for the paths they walked and the lessons they left to us. I learned that by guarding the places where their bodies rested, we honoured their lives across the centuries. It was our duty to make sure they could rest long into eternity.

Until the Onyx came to dig up their bodies and steal the Shards from their mouths.

I'm not sure when they came, how long after my mother traded my childhood innocence for the horrible truth of reality. But I know it didn't feel like long at all.

Saneif, the man who'd been on watch that night, fell asleep. He was too old to be out on watch, but we'd needed every warm body, no matter how frail or ill prepared. Like every other Jiu'sho in the village he wanted to do his duty for his people. So, he sat at his post and waited. Perhaps he dreamed of rising up to defeat them when they invaded, striking their bodies down with a rage I could not have understood then, but know all too well now.

The Onyx were clever that night. They could have sent an onslaught, but they knew we'd learned to prepare for their coming. So instead of sending an army, they only sent one. A'janna, the woman who found it, told us it'd wrapped its knees in gauze to muffle their horrible sounds. Since Saneif was dozing, no one was awake to notice the stink. But A'janna awoke cold in her bed with the scent in her nostrils and her stomach heavy as a stone. She dressed, put on her boots, and went to check on the graveyard to find something that brought her to her knees.

I'll never forget the shrieks of grief that awoke me that day, long before dawn. Terrified, I ran outside and followed them to their source in the village graveyard. I found my mother on her knees next to my grandfather's grave, choking on her sorrow as it struggled up her throat. My heart broke over and over as she clutched his body in her arms. The mouth lay open, skin torn at the edges and left bloody as if gnawed by a rat. The head lolled on its shoulders, so I couldn't see the eyes. But I had seen enough.

They not only took his Shard but chewed the dead flesh off his bones.

MY PEOPLE ARE Jiu'sho, known as the faithful tribe, which is why our home is known as the Village of the Faithful. While we may not be as proud as the Wu'sho or as clever as the Ba'sho, we still carry the weight of our history on our backs everywhere we go. We believe in the wisdom of the old gods and pray for their blessings so they will watch over us. Every day and night of our lives begin and end with that ritual.

I wouldn't even think of falling asleep without giving thanks to the ones who give us life. When I see the sky every morning and the stars above me at night, I know every breath I am allowed to take in this world is a sacred gift.

Some say this makes the Jiu'sho too soft. These days, despite my pride, I think they might be right. When I think back on how we believed the gods would send us a miracle, how the other tribes would one day join us and we would all fight the Onyx together, I see how our faith and our shock mingled and numbed our sense of reason. We imagined only good and evil. We forgot all the places one could stop in between.

My mother sent messengers to the other tribes after the first attack, long before I was born. When no replies came my people assumed the worst: that the others were already dead. We had lost many who tried to fight back in the beginning without knowing what the Onyx were really like. It was easy to imagine the same had happened to our fellow Xi'sho and we were the last ones standing. At that point, the fight had gone on for nearly seven years.

Mother told me that in the early days of those first attacks panic blocked her mind and that of the villagers.

"The forethought required to pause, observe, and form a strategy is the furthest thing from your thoughts at first," she told me one day. "We were in shock for a long time, just reacting as quickly as we could to defend the ancestors, our hearts numb with terror. We made many mistakes, and we lost many lives. But with time, as terrible as it sounds, we were able to adjust, to learn to react accordingly. They've adapted, too, as they realised we were learning their strategies. The

Onyx may seem slack and unintelligent, but they're not. There's much more to them than we know."

She was proven right the day a woman from the Wu'sho tribe approached our village. I was six years old, and I remember it was the first time I'd ever seen anyone from the outside. While I did not recognise her elegant facial markings at first, I learned later that they were a symbol of pride for the Wu'sho, who were better off than any other Xi'sho tribe. The thickness of her garments was also strange to me as I'd never seen its like before. The little clothing Jiu'sho wear is thin since our fibre crops tend to be feeble and sparse. I wondered what it must be like to have the luxury of wearing clothing that hung so heavy on the body.

To me, a boy uncomfortably made to be a man too soon, she was strange and beautiful. The fine lines that curled up her jaw and cheekbones were like the tendrils of mysterious plants that crawled and sprouted. Her crimson hair was shaved high on the sides but hung long from her scalp to the small of her back, and her lips were full and proud. Cool green eyes watched me as I told myself she looked that way because of all she'd seen. I marvelled at her long robes, the tall leather boots she wore which were nicer than any object in our entire village.

"I am Ayshe of the Wu'sho. I seek your help," she'd said.

"Of course," my mother replied, opening the door of our cabin and motioning for me to add more wood to the fire.

I was mostly quiet that night as the woman told my mother how it had been for her village when the Onyx first attacked. Her story was much like ours:

dozens killed, countless graves pillaged, and Shards lost. Her people were desperate to understand what they were collecting them for. Or who.

As awed as I was by Ayshe's beauty, something about her presence stirred in my gut and left me on edge. She had been through as much hardship as we had, if not more. But in the midst of all that, somehow she managed to dress herself as finely as a diplomat going to represent the rank of her kingdom. I didn't know a lot about the Wu'sho, other than they had the most distinguished bloodlines in all the land. But my people had long forgotten to bathe or dress well. How could we, when every part of the lives we lived was constantly in danger of being torn away from us?

My mother listened as the fire burned and dimmed and the crickets sang their evening song. I didn't understand everything I heard, but I listened as well. We drank the tea my mother made, and I savoured the taste of the dandelion roots. When the hour grew late, she offered Ayshe a place to sleep. She was always willing to help someone in need, a habit I one day would gather for myself.

She came to our room that night, sword in hand. She hung it next to the door with care, then came to sit down next to me on the edge of the bed reaching out to stroke my hair.

"This is the beginning of a great alliance," she said. "Her people will help ours. Together we have a better chance of defeating the Onyx and taking our lives back."

Her eyes held a hope I had never seen before. I thought of telling her about the feelings I had around the fire, those flickers of misgiving about Ayshe's

13

appearance. But the idea of seeing the glimmer drain from her eyes was too painful. I wanted her to have that. I wanted her to be right.

You're worrying for nothing. Let her be.

That night, I fell into a thin, restless sleep, punctuated by periods where I lay awake and stared at the ceiling. The house was quiet. I was drifting back to unconsciousness when a scent prickled my nostrils and jolted me fully back into reality. The stink. Rancid, like the chicken eggs when they'd gone bad. My hand went to my mother's arm and squeezed hard as a bolt of panic surged through my heart. If she had been fast asleep a moment before, you never would have known it. She stood up with the precision of a soldier, grabbing the sword as she ran out of the room. Still disoriented, I pulled my training bow and its quiver of arrows from a hook on the wall and chased after her.

She shoved the wooden door of our house open and stopped short in the entryway. I was running after her so quickly I crashed into her back and dropped my bow on the floor. I felt her body when mine collided with it; she'd grown as still as stone. My heart felt tight and hard. Gathering my bearings, I moved to her side so I could see the same thing she was seeing.

Ayshe stood some twenty paces away as Onyx spilled past her, first three, then half a dozen. One stopped to speak to her and for the first time I realised our enemy spoke a language: clicks of the tongue followed by single syllable grunts. Before this we'd never heard anything except their battle cries.

Ayshe nodded, then spoke back to the creature standing by her side in the same tongue. What felt like freezing water spilled from my shoulders to my wrists as goosebumps rose on the flesh on my arms.

"She... she..."

I remember myself unable to finish the thought, my words choked by the blaze of fury climbing up my throat. As I grappled for control of my emotions, my mother strode across the land towards the woman who I had thought beautiful only a few hours ago. In the darkness her hair had turned the colour of old, long-spilled blood. I watched as my mother grabbed a handful of it, pulled Ayshe's head back with a rough jerk and cut it off her shoulders with a single stroke. My mother, the kindest person I knew. My mother, the warrior.

The cold leaked down my armpits and over the rest of my body as she returned to me with the gored blade in one hand and Ayshe's hair in the other. The decapitated head dragged behind her through the snow. The woman's stately face was frozen in an expression of alarm—the last moment of feeling she'd had time for before my mother ended her life. Surely there were other secrets hidden there, but we'd never know them. The most important of them—the one she betrayed our people for—was already out in the open.

"My son," she said to me that day as her voice cracked. "I have led you astray. I was weak. I wanted so badly to believe that our fellow Xi'sho would come to help us. And now I know that fantasy must be laid to rest."

She knelt to look into my eyes. I see hers every time I close my own, even today, shot through with threads of pulsing red and wet with tears. Her mouth opened, then closed again, pressing back against some invisible force. My own fear dissolved into tears as well. I wanted to be strong for my mother, but I hated seeing her suffer with all my heart. To think this creature with a spirit of steel could believe she had failed me was more than I could take.

"Mother... I..."

"Listen to me," she said, taking my arms in her hands. Her grip was firm and strong. "Do not trust them, no matter how hurt they seem. The gods told me to watch for a sign. I chose to interpret it through my own desires—to believe the sign was that someone would come to help. But this is the real sign. Now I know the truth."

I wanted to tell her there was no way she could have known. Still today, I regret I could not do this, that the words were far beyond my child's mind on that terrible day. All I could do was sit mutely, my heart felt sodden with a dangerous rage.

I wanted to kill them myself. And not just the ones that came that day. All of them. Every single one.

"They will always come for us, Rin. And we must always fight. Never forget that."

I nodded, and she stood up.

"Bring your bow and come with me. There is more killing to be done before sunrise."

I followed my mother into the night holding my vengeance close as a newborn, mesmerised by its heat, its whispers.

Satisfy me, it murmured. *Or I will eat you alive.*

That was the night I became a warrior.

PART ONE: JUNE

CHAPTER ONE
THE WORLD OF
ANCESTRAL

April 6, 2030

"JI-SOO, GUARD THE right! They're too close!"

Lissa had barely finished her sentence when Ji-Soo darted past her in a blur of red and white, her cape cutting a bloody swath through the air. The rising sun painted the chrome wings that sprouted from her shoulder blades with a menacing gleam. As dawn crested in the Village of the Faithful, hungry ghouls poured forth, eager to crack the graves of its dead.

Lissa ran to the far side of the village without a single thought in her head. Just impulse, reaction. The tiny passage on the edge of the map, that constant pitfall she tried to fortify every time, spouted Onyx like a bottle shaken for too long and mistakenly uncapped. She hated this map for this very reason. Hammering the dash key, she went for the creature closest to her.

Ji-Soo threw her cape back and sent a blast of lightning in the direction of the invaders. It cracked and spread, stopping two in their tracks and slowing the ones behind it. Onyx might be a pain, but they were also stupid. Or their AI was, anyway. After all, they were just buzzing flies, not the real threat.

Lissa's eyes flicked to her power circle. She'd hoped to buy time before the next onslaught to recharge it for a Transcendence, but it wasn't enough. Her resources were low—and the fact she hadn't timed it well could cost them the match. But Ji-Soo's Transcendence was much closer to being ready, and in the next few seconds, they were going to need it.

"Death Flight! Cast Death Flight!" Lissa shouted into her mic as she used Dark Rush, dashing through the horde in a flash with both arms extended, daggers jutting out. The heads of the Onyx she moved through tumbled gracelessly to the ground in her wake, their clenched fists going limp and useless as their misshapen bodies collapsed alongside their severed heads.

More were coming, but Lissa had a moment to think. They were Raging, their health icons bursting with fire. Raging Onyx were strong enough to overcome the two of them—easily—and she knew it. They could easily penetrate the graveyards in this state. And with Jae-Jin and Zio down, they would need to be clever.

"I don't have enough Essence—" Ji-Soo said, her voice thin and frantic.

"When you CAN," Lissa said, regretting her harshness even as her fingers flew over the keys. She ducked to avoid a line of spinning blades and obliterated an Onyx coming in on her left. If they could just flatten the last of these, they could focus on the rebel Xi'sho—the real threat. But the match was too close, and as always, she lost her calm.

Devon always told her that her impatience was a double-edged sword, both a weakness and a strength. Confusing, but when it came to *Ancestral* she knew one thing about herself for sure—she would take any advantage she could get.

She flipped backward, her eyes darting towards her partner's ability gauges. Death Flight, Ji-Soo's most powerful spell, was a hair away from being ready. If she could survive those few precious seconds, they might be able to win this. But Raging Onyx surged forward with horrible speed, nearly atop her despite the speed of her jumps. Fire leapt from the gaps in their crooked fangs.

"Ji-Soo! Help!"

"Casting now!"

The world around them slowed. Sh0uj0, Ji-Soo's avatar, bowed her head in prayer, hair like ink shining in the light as her wings unfurled to their limit. With an elegant stroke, they drew back and then forward, releasing a mighty gust of wind. The remaining Onyx staggered as their bodies blew backward, disoriented by the attack. In that second, the feathers of her wings split into sections, revealing themselves for what they were: swords. She reached to her shoulder blades and returned with a gleaming bundle of blades in each hand. Her arms flew, spraying blood and dismembered parts across the battlefield.

"Close," Jae-Jin said as he respawned a few feet away from them. A generous hood covered his avatar's face, and black robes billowed around his slender frame, interrupted only by a low-hanging belt with animal skulls dangling from it on long strips of leather. The blood-encrusted axe in his hands would have looked more at home in the hand of a man twice his size. He'd only been down for fifteen seconds—the time it took to respawn—but they'd come within a hair of losing.

Without another word, he darted up the passage that had been choked with Onyx only a few moments before. Ji-Soo followed, casting a protective spell in his wake to boost their defences. Lissa was about to give chase when she noticed Zio respawning a few feet to her left.

While magnificent antlers were the most striking thing about Zio's avatar, they were far from the most interesting. From the waist up, Weavers could easily be mistaken for a clan's most virile warriors. A necklace of teeth, all of differing sizes, lay atop a bare male chest, and vines wrapped tight around his arms from bicep to wrist. From the waist down, sparse fur thickened over his broad thighs. These tapered into mighty legs that ended in cloven hooves black as nightfall.

"I am going to eff that dude up," Zio snarled as she came back to life, firing a vine attack at no one in particular. Fronds uncurled from her arms with a vicious speed.

"Salty," Ji-soo said, giggling.

"Whatever!" Zio said, digging at the ground with her hooves and sending poofs of dust into the air. "Let's go."

"He's north," Lissa said, reactivating her shields. As the two headed in the direction their friends had gone, a kill notification hit the screen.

✦SISTERFERRARI HAS BEEN
ELIMINATED BY JAEBOMB✦

"Looks like he found them," Zio laughed.

"Damn, Jae," Lissa said to her mic. "Leave someone behind for us to kill!"

"If you weren't so slow, I would!" Jae-Jin's voice was unruffled.

"Cold," Zio said. "At least no more Onyx though. Now we have the Turned to deal with."

While the match could be easier once the Onyx hordes were dead, they were far from safe. The Turned were those from clans that chose to side with the Onyx for reasons no one knew. While the Onyx were a part of the game's living world, its players got to choose whether to be a Devoted or a Turned. Today they'd matched with a team of all Turned—meaning their opponents wielded dark attacks and darker intentions.

They had seemed slow to react once the match had started. Zio and Jae-Jin had picked two of them off within a minute while Lissa strategically thinned out the Onyx, careful to use crumbling houses long ravaged by the horrid creatures to stay out of sight as she crept closer. It had gone so well she'd gotten reckless as she darted from one area to the next, and for a few moments, she thought there would be no challenge at all.

She knew it was always a bad idea to assume the opponent was weak. She'd had some humiliating losses thanks to those momentary flights of fancy, and this very nearly could have been one of them. Could still be. Not to mention, she'd do just about anything to avoid one of Jae-Jin's lectures on every tactic she could have used to play the match better. Damn know-it-all.

"Stay tight," Lissa said as she bounded around the houses in the middle of the village. She glanced at the straw-thatched roofs and crudely carved fences, thinking as she had many times before: *these people never had a chance*. Then again, one of the things she loved most about playing *Ancestral* was that it was a MOBA—or Multiplayer Online Battle Arena game—with a truly memorable story. She'd had more than enough of cutesy character designs and showy skill sets. This was a dark, threatening world, one that felt like the lives of its people mattered.

She found nothing hiding around corners waiting to snipe. In fact, it had gone too quiet, especially for the late end of a match. She looked at the mini-map and found her team members exploring the south, west, and east parts, where the village trailed off into uninhabited grassland.

"Zio? Jae?"

"No one," Zio replied. "They must be hiding, I just can't figure out where."

Lissa frowned at her monitor.

"Ji-Soo?"

A few moments of silence went by. Lissa's heart was picking up speed, her anxiety beginning to go off in little flashes of light. She breathed through her nose, focusing on the quality of her inhale to steady herself and counting to five. As she counted the last number, Ji-Soo finally replied.

"No one. Is it a bug?"

Lissa stared at the map, at the dots that represented her teammates. She'd never seen a bug like this, but as young as the game still was, it certainly was possible. They'd lose points for the match and their team ranking if they forfeited. Lissa had been called stubborn in the past, and in this case it was spot on. She did not intend to give up this match unless there was no other option.

A red dot—the enemy—flashed and vanished before her eyes in a fraction of a second. If she'd blinked, she would have missed it.

"They're cloaked," she said, moving fast towards the location where the dot had been. "Did you all see that?"

No response.

"Zio—"

"I know," Zio said, her voice determined. "I'm ready."

Their team's graveyard lay at the southernmost part of the village. In each match, it was each team's goal to keep their opponents from gaining access to it and stealing the Shards. Lissa had seen the dot right inside the perimeter of it, meaning they had precious little time to stop the one remaining player from making its way to the sacred graves. The moment one of those was cracked open, the game was over.

There wasn't a soul living or dead to be seen as Lissa and her teammates approached. She kept her eyes trained on the map, waiting to see that pinpoint again. Nothing came, but they were vulnerable and she knew it. She moved constantly, fingers hovering over her shields to recast the moment they ran dry. Her heart thumped in her throat. Just one more and the match was theirs. One more.

✦ZIO2GO HAS BEEN ELIMINATED BY WRAITHX✦

"What?" Lissa growled, shaken as she read the notification and spun around. Just a moment ago she'd heard Zio's footfalls behind her, but now she was nowhere to be seen—and there should have been a corpse at the very least.

"Zio? What the hell?"

No one replied. This was insane. A one-hit kill? What weapon would allow someone to do that? Especially with Zio's ironclad defences? She swung the camera wildly now, her hands shaking as she tried to cover all her blind spots at once.

"Jae-Jin?"

Nothing. Lissa's pulse thrummed in her right temple. She jabbed a button to open the mini-map to full size and saw him up on the far left. It made no sense. Jae-Jin was always in the middle of the fight, there before she even thought to call out a command. He had to have heard her when she said she'd seen a cloaked opponent.

As Lissa watched, the blue dot that represented his character pushed against the edge of the map over and over, a ball bounced against a wall again and again. It seemed like a hiccup in the game, but somehow Lissa knew it was not.

"Jae-Jin? What are you doing?"

Silence. Lissa felt an irrational stab of fear. She'd played *Ancestral* every day since it came out ten months ago, thousands and thousands of matches. But never once had she experienced this feeling of *wrongness*, like something massive had crept onto the field and swallowed them all, leaving her alone to die. It triggered some deep and unmasked terror in her gut, and she hated it.

The screen flashed as it unrolled the blue banner that every *Ancestral* player hated—or loved, depending on your team—to see.

✦JAEBOMB HAS BEEN ELIMINATED BY WRAITHX✦

"WHAT?" Lissa yelled, unable to control her fury. "What is happening?!" Anger bloomed across her chest, pluming up into her throat as a sourness pooled in the pit of her stomach.

I won't lose this match. I won't.

✦SHOUJO HAS BEEN ELIMINATED BY WRAITHX✦

She ran north towards where she'd last seen Jae-Jin, scanning all the hiding spots she knew so well as her heart thumped in her throat like some horrible foreign object. She still had no idea what was happening, but if it was legit (and it certainly seemed to be), this game would be over in seconds if this player got to her. And that couldn't happen. Couldn't.

A flash of movement registered just barely on the edge of her peripheral vision. She spun around, her arm swinging as her dagger cut through the air. At its furthest point she saw the edge catch something invisible for a fraction of a second. A surge of adrenaline shot through her veins, fuelled by pure desperation. This was her last chance, and every second would count.

"Come here," Lissa said through clenched teeth. She dashed towards the spot where her dagger had caught and triggered Dark Rush. Her speed doubled, the trees at the edge of the village blurring in her peripheral vision like streetlights glowing through a rain-soaked windowpane. If she'd noticed, she'd have found it beautiful. But her vision had narrowed to a pinhole with this faceless enemy at its end. All she could see was the kill in front of her, that victorious moment, her status inching one step closer to being the player she wanted to be.

She could almost taste the vicious delight as her avatar collapsed. Blood sprayed as something passed through her right shoulder, slicing it open and revealing the ropes of muscle underneath. She had survived more than three hundred team matches without a defeat. All that work, gone in one horrible instant. All that hope.

The notification unrolled its bright blue banner cheerily, blissfully unaware of her plight.

✦NAGIKO HAS BEEN ELIMINATED BY WRAITHX✦

You're never going to make it to regionals, Lissa thought in a numb voice that sounded like it was coming from the end of a long hallway. *Never.*

She stared at her body on the ground, splayed limp among its rich red robes. All that finery didn't mean a damn thing when you were dead. And as she thought this to herself, she realised the anger that had driven her to this point had evaporated. The adrenaline was gone, too. A bone-deep exhaustion seeped into its place, cold water filling her up on the inside.

A foreign thought appeared in her mind, so strange it bewildered her.

It's a good thing Quin can't see you like this.

"Let's regroup," Jae-Jin said, and vanished to the lobby.

CHAPTER TWO
LISSA

I CAN'T LOSE like this. I just can't.

Disheartened after the defeat, the team had chatted back and forth in the lobby before agreeing to sign off for the night and meet at PlaySpace tomorrow. Jae-Jin, as usual, had some ideas to bounce off everyone. Lissa liked the guy, but being friends with him was like gaming with an army sergeant sometimes. Everything was about how to get better. How to snipe the other player without taking a hit. How to chain spells to target the enemy at the exact millisecond they were about to fire. How to iron out your every flaw. A robot that never makes mistakes.

She wished she could become that. A person who never felt stupid, never messed up or had feelings that didn't make sense. There were days—not many, but some—where her games felt clean and fast, and her heart jittered with a surge that felt electric. Those times were the most addictive because she never knew when she was going to connect to that weird high. It was like you were in the world's fastest car and it would never run out of gas. But perhaps most beguiling of all was the sense that this was a glimpse of that mindset that Jae-Jin talked endlessly about. It was always fleeting, but she'd experienced it a handful of times. On the good days, she felt as if she might be able to catch up to it.

"You gotta practie," Jae-Jin would say when she tried to explain the feeling. "Play and play and play until your every breath and thought and bead of sweat is the game. You're one and the same. You're unbeatable in that state. That's when you'll know you've got what it takes."

She wanted that. But she was afraid. Because it felt like if she did that, she might lose herself.

Her brother's face appeared in her mind, as it often did since his passing last year, and Lissa closed her eyes hoping to shake it free. As usual, she failed. Instead, the wild gold of his hair filled Lissa's mind, all sunbeams and wheat and long summer days. She missed the smell of that hair, the way that it felt to bury her face in it as a kid when they wrestled on the living room floor. It was comforting and familiar and felt like the safest place in the world.

Now it hurt to think about it, because it was gone, along with the rest of him.

Why did you have to die, Quin?

In her mind, Lissa watched as her brother regarded her with that soft, untranslatable gaze. The murmurs of sibling-language moved softly through his eyes. Hope. Trust.

The ache in Lissa's heart grew stronger.

A knock came at the door, and her brother's image dissolved like a handful of sand.

"Lissa?"

"Come in, Dad."

The door opened. Lissa looked at her father's grin and wondered for perhaps the millionth time how he managed to stay so upbeat. He wore an old grey t-shirt with a messy sketch of trees across the chest and striped pyjama pants. His hair was starting to turn silver at the temples and crow's feet had bloomed at the edges of his eyes. Lissa's mind wandered for a moment. Were they there before Quin died? Or had they begun to appear before, and she hadn't noticed?

He regarded her with an amused expression and took a sip of tea from his favourite mug, a big blue glazed thing that looked as if it had been carved from a single lump of clay. Toast, their chocolate lab, poked her head between his legs, tongue flopping with exuberance.

"You look sadder than a wet rat."

Lissa sighed, looking at her computer screen. She still hadn't left the *Ancestral* lobby. Nagiko, her avatar, alternated from one badass pose to another, brandishing the souped-up daggers Lissa had equipped her with before the match.

"Yeah. We got wiped."

"You don't get beaten much these days."

Despite her dad's kind words, she still felt that flush of shame. She felt as if when she lost, it meant she was falling backward, losing progress. She always had to claw her way forward, even if she only progressed by an inch. Losing meant feeling these emotions, and she was willing to do whatever it took to avoid them.

"Some player I've never seen before sniped the whole team. It sucked."

Nodding, her dad settled into the worn grey armchair

in the corner of the room, tucking his feet under him as if he planned to stay for a while. Toast trotted right behind him like a faithful shadow, circling the floor at his feet a few times before settling into her own spot.

"Maybe they have something to teach you."

Lissa's nose wrinkled as she considered the idea.

"What do you mean?"

A ghost of a smile appeared on his face.

"As I've got older and looked back at my life, I've noticed that the things that seemed the most terrible and hurtful always had something to teach me. 'Course, if I was busy being mad about it, or feeling sorry for myself, I wasn't going to be able to see that. And usually, I was just that. Always too busy worrying about how my world was falling apart to see the bigger picture." He took another sip of his tea, repositioning his hands to better wrap around the mug and gather up its warmth.

Lissa listened quietly.

"Sometimes I needed to get years behind me before I could see that those events changed me. Mostly for the better, too. Adversity is weird like that. We can't control what happens to us in many situations, but we do get to pick the way we react to it."

"So," Lissa said, looking at the ceiling in thought, "being beaten just now has some great lesson to teach me?"

Her dad's green eyes watched her as he drank his tea, steam drifting into his eyelashes. Lissa could have sworn she saw a glint of mischief there, like a cat in pursuit of a particularly plucky bit of prey.

"Probably. What did they do to beat you, for instance?"

"They were... fast. And they cloaked themselves so we couldn't track them."

"What else?"

Lissa replayed the match in her mind. The opponent used a divide and conquer approach, but something about the way it was executed didn't make sense to Lissa just yet. It seemed that what had provoked her most was the silence between kills, the way she'd gotten more upset when she felt she wasn't in control. So, it hadn't been as much about what they did as it had been the way she'd reacted to it.

"They set us up so I was thrown off guard. And I got pissed off."

Her dad nodded sagely.

"Hard to focus when you're mad, isn't it?"

"Yeah."

They sat quietly for a few moments.

"You know," he said, "one thing your mom taught me when we were still married was that getting angry is often a choice."

The mention of her mum brought back the sinking feeling in Lissa's chest. Along with it came a memory. It was long before the divorce. Mum had headed off to work and was informed upon arriving that she'd lost her job. She'd worked with the same practice as a children's therapist since long before Lissa was born. Her mother had come home early that day with no fanfare, as if it was perfectly normal for her to arrive at half past two in the afternoon, and set her bags down on the chair she spent long evenings reading in.

After she told the family what had happened, she'd taken some vegetables out of the fridge to prepare a salad for dinner. Lissa had been twelve, Quin four.

She remembered climbing into a chair at the kitchen island to keep her mum company, watching her face carefully as Quin played with a puzzle on the living room floor. Lissa hadn't understood much about jobs at the time, but she knew that losing one was not a good thing.

Are you upset that you won't have a job anymore, Mum? she asked.

Her mother had looked up and smiled, and Lissa remembered the feeling of being smiled at in that way, like standing in a patch of warm sunlight and feeling it gently soothing your forehead and cheeks.

I'm not, she had replied. *Something better is coming.*

"Lissa?" her dad said. "Still with me?"

"Ah, sorry," she said, shaking her head to clear it. "I was remembering how Mum wasn't mad when she lost her job. Anyone else would have been. But not her."

Her father nodded, and his smile grew wider.

"It's hard not to get angry in life when things don't go your way. But seeing the way your mum reacted when things happened that would have made me angry threw me for a loop. It was like she knew without a doubt that no matter what, things would be fine. It was bewildering sometimes! I'd come across a spot of bad luck and feel like the whole world was against me. Then I'd tell her what had happened, and she'd nod and listen and sometimes she'd smile, like she knew something I didn't. She had some secret that seemed to keep her spirits bright. I hoped that if I hung around long enough, it might rub off on me."

They both laughed. Then her father's face softened, and in it, Lissa saw how much he missed her.

"Anyway, I guess it worked. I find myself not so angry these days." Then he looked up at her screen, where Nagiko continued to show off her fierce stances, her fiery scarf trailing out behind her.

"Let me ask you this," he said, gesturing at the avatar. "Why do you like to play as her the most?"

Lissa turned her attention back to her screen. Nagiko wore a long black tattered skirt and a black hood hemmed with bloody red fabric that hid most of her face. Its length went past her knees. Her black leather boots were flat and laced up and an inky waistcoat bound her trunk with buckles. Her hands were wrapped with leather. In each, she held heavy scimitars with fabric-bound hilts, their tips stained dark.

"Well, she's a badass. I like being a badass."

He laughed. "What does it feel like to be a badass, though?"

Lissa watched Nagiko extend an arm and point, regarding an invisible enemy with her steely gaze: *You're done.*

"Powerful. Like I'm perfect."

Her dad put a warm hand on her shoulder.

"It's fun to play someone like that. But remember, you don't need to be perfect in real life. All you really need to do is take a deep breath and get back up when you get knocked down. Fall down seven times..."

"...get up eight," she finished for him.

"Gotta love a good Buddhist proverb," he said. "You gonna keep playing?"

"No, everyone signed off. We're gonna meet up at PlaySpace tomorrow anyway. Talk it over, try to figure out what happened."

"Good." He planted a kiss on the top of her head. "Jae-Jin still trying to run the show?"

"Always."

He laughed as he made his way to the door, Toast following. "Say hi to Devon for me."

"I will."

Lissa watched them go, then turned back to the screen. Her pointer went towards the icon to shut the game down, but then a little spark fired in her chest. A burst of nerves.

She moused to the player search tab and typed:

WRAITHX

The profile came up fast. The photo was simply a red square. There was no personal info other than the handle, no location. Lissa scrolled down to look at the stats.

More than ten thousand matches? Just over one percent loss ratio?

Lissa had played *Ancestral* with her friends every day since release, yet she hadn't crossed five thousand matches yet. The time she'd put in had helped her to carve her loss ratio down, and as the months had gone by, it'd got progressively lower. But even so, she'd lost plenty while getting the hang of the game. The last time she'd checked, she was at eighteen percent, a number she'd been proud of at the time.

But one-point-three percent? How was that even possible—unless this player hardly ever lost, even when they had just started to play?

Or had they been this good from the beginning?

A green dot with a circle around it showed next to WraithX's username, meaning they were in a match.

Lissa looked at the clock. It was going on midnight. The room was not cold, but gooseflesh rose on her arms. Something in her gut was speaking to her, and even though its language had no words, she understood it perfectly.

She wouldn't be satisfied until she could wield the same kind of power.

CHAPTER THREE
BUBBLE POP!

STANDING OUTSIDE THE door of Bubble Pop! waiting for Ji-Soo to arrive, Lissa could hear the strains of an upbeat K-pop song drifting through the plate-glass exterior. It was their favourite boba spot, and since it was right downstairs from PlaySpace, it gave them both an excellent excuse to visit often.

She glanced up and down the strip mall before turning her attention back to the boba cafe. Everything about the place was a mirror image of Ji-Soo's aesthetic: vivid, musical, and bright. The walls were striped pale pink and mint green and etched with all manner of mismatched teacups. Round, baby blue tables of various sizes dotted the floor, their tops lacquered with sheets of classic manga: *One Piece, Dragon Ball, Urusei Yatsura*.

As Lissa idly watched through the windows, a large group sitting around one of the biggest tables happily nursed on pastel drinks with oversized straws. A girl with violently red hair pulled her friend's sleeve and pointed to one of the illustrations on the table, clearly reliving a memorable moment of the story. The girl minding the store came to the table to check on her customers. Even she looked like she'd stepped right off the streets of Harajuku with her waist-length, deep green hair and flouncy black and white dress, which was patterned with little cat heads. As she made her way back to the counter, she idly twisted a few locks around a finger, then looked up with a grin as she recognised the song playing on the flat-screen TV behind her. She started to shimmy her hips as she made her way behind the counter.

Lissa considered herself more of a goth soul on the inside, but she liked Bubble Pop! anyway. It was so vastly different from everything she was naturally attracted to. Or maybe it was watching Ji-Soo light up every time they went inside to order drinks as relentlessly cute as the place itself.

Her best friend was clearly in her element here. But then again, she was a perfect match for it. Her typical garb was delightfully mismatched and yet somehow stylish. She frequently wore embroidered peasant blouses, brightly coloured stockings, and the loudest Doc Martens she could lay her hands on.

Lissa grinned thinking about it and went back to reading her phone. Ever since the alarm had gone off that morning, she'd been digging through the *Ancestral* forums looking for mention of WraithX. She knew her team wasn't the first to suffer such a defeat at this player's hands. At first, her searches turned up nothing as a lot of players didn't openly discuss usernames—it was considered bad form. But when she sifted through a recent thread of players talking about their worst defeats, someone finally mentioned something that sounded familiar.

➢**SuicideForest2881(1 day ago):** *Dude, I got WIPED once when I was playing in the middle of the night with my friends. It was freaky because of how they did it, too. Fast as hell and the next thing I know the whole team is done. It took less than a minute. Pissed me off because we didn't even get a chance to react. I still don't know how they did it.*

She thumbed her way to the comments.

➢**CloudStrafe(1 day ago):** *OP did your team members go all funny? Like they couldn't hear you on the mic?*

➢**3LicksToTheCenter(1 day ago):** *maybe some1 is hacking the game*

➢**SuicideForest2881(12 hours ago):** *Doubt it. Hackers have better things to do.*

➢**SeokjinsBackTho(1 hour ago):** *What bugs me is how we couldnta responded, like there literally wasn't time*

Lissa frowned at her phone, then typed:

➢*Hey OP was their username WraithX?*

"Lissa? Lissa!"

Lissa looked up to see Ji-Soo sashaying across the parking lot in her direction. She wore a medium-length silver wig that fell in soft curls, and her fiercely pink patent leather boots, white lacy socks, and matching baby-doll dress gave her the air of a punk rock fairy. A plastic necklace adorned with oversized gummy bears swung around her neck. As she got Lissa's attention, she executed a less-than-perfect pirouette, and both girls laughed.

"You look so serious," she said as she got to the sidewalk. "Did someone die?"

"Just my dignity last night," Lissa replied, sighing.

"What, because we lost?"

"*How* we lost. I still don't know what happened. And I can't lose like this. Not if I want to have a chance at the championships when they're announced. And regionals are coming up soon!"

Ji-Soo pressed her lips into a thin line.

"Lissa, you're way too hard on yourself."

"Not that again!"

"Really, you are. You're a great player. Have some boba and chill out."

Lissa sighed in frustration. "Well, that's what we're doing, aren't we?"

"Not yet." Ji-Soo gave her a winsome smile and held the door of Bubble Pop! open, shaking her head from side to side as she recognised the music playing.

"I love this song!

The girls at the big table were gathering up their things to leave. One of them caught sight of Ji-Soo and gazed at her with open awe. Lissa was used to watching Ji-Soo get this kind of reception. When they'd first met three years ago, Lissa was awed by how courageous Ji-Soo's sense of style was. Her look was for no one but herself, and she liked it that way. Anything less wasn't even an option. Plus, she was two years Lissa's senior, which added to her air of magic.

"Molly!" Ji-Soo said to the green-haired girl behind the counter. "I love your nails."

Molly giggled while extending an arm, moving her hand back and forth as if through water. Each pointed fingernail was a deep glittery green with lighter ombré accents at the tips. A tiny silver ring pierced the pinky nail.

"Isn't it fun? You know I can't resist a good green."

"It's perfect on you. Now if only a good green boba would come along," Ji-Soo laughed. "Honeydew counts, I guess."

Lissa watched the TV as the girls chatted. On it, a pulsing beat played as a group of young Asian men dressed in vampiric outfits danced effortlessly around jewel-toned velvet couches. The camera cut to one member's eyes, lined in a smoky glitter.

"This is my best friend Lissa," Ji-Soo was saying. "I don't think you two have met yet! Molly just started here last week. She and I were in the same art class in freshman year."

"Not hard to guess that," Lissa said, smirking at them.

"Ha! I guess you're right. Molly, what flavour should I do today?"

Molly pursed her lips, looking thoughtful.

"You might like... oh, I know. I'll make it a surprise and see if you can guess."

Ji-Soo nodded happily, her pigtails bouncing.

"Grass jelly or tapioca pearls?"

"Pearls, please."

"Sure. And you, Lissa?"

"Taro blended with pearls," Lissa said, unzipping her purse. Ji-Soo slapped her hand away.

"Noooo. My turn. Besides, your birthday is coming soon, and we need to start celebrating that."

"It's two weeks away!"

"So? I celebrate all month for mine. And turning seventeen is a little bit magical."

"If you say so," Lissa said grudgingly, while a hint of quiet pleasure glowed in her chest.

"Let's sit while she makes them."

Lissa nodded, walking to a table for two next to the window. A delightfully plump lucky cat figurine waited for them, waving its paw at the sun. Ji-Soo slung her blue plastic tote bag over the back of the chair and sat, gathering her knees up to her chin and wrapping her arms around them.

"Now!" she said, holding a single finger up in the air. "My best friend needs revenge, and I am the perfect person to help her plot it." She tittered in a perfect imitation of a queen gone mad. "NO ONE MUST CROSS HER!"

Lissa stifled a laugh, rolling her eyes instead. "I don't know about that, Ji. I just... ugh." She rubbed a hand over her eyes.

"Did you sleep much?"

"You know I never do."

Ji-Soo arched an eyebrow. "So. Eyes on the prize: what do we need to do? Learn this person's tricks?"

Lissa's mind went back to the match, bringing shadows of her feelings along with it. The feelings of isolation, being lost. She hadn't even seen the player that killed them all. A coal of anger glowed in the pit of her stomach as she remembered how it felt, to be completely helpless.

"Lissa?" Ji-Soo peered at her.

"Ah, sorry," Lissa said. "Yeah, a player like that will be in regionals, that's for sure."

"Whenever they happen, anyway." Ji-Soo snorted sceptically.

"They will." Lissa gave Ji-Soo a look she hoped was encouraging, but her friend still looked grumpy. "The player base has grown crazy fast. No other game has raked in players quite like this. And if I'm playing like

44

this when regionals happen, there's no way I can beat a player like—"

"Eh-eh!" Ji-Soo wagged a finger in the air in front of Lissa's face, making the same sound one would make to stop a naughty dog in its tracks. Her friend's eyes grew wide. "None of that talk here. We are here to discuss *victory*. I know you want to compete. I do, too. And I think we both will. Don't forget that just one floor up from where we're sitting right now we have a team of people who are in it with us. And you know how good they are."

Lissa couldn't deny that. She nodded. Ji-Soo cocked her head to the side as Lissa slumped across the table from her, and her gaze grew soft.

"Here's the thing, Lissa. Winning... it's not just your skills. It's how you *think* about it. Everything from the thoughts in your head as you walk up to the computer to the split seconds where life or death depends on your next move. If you think you're going to fail... that's a self-fulfilling prophecy."

"But I don't—"

Ji-Soo's eyebrow arched as she interrupted her friend.

"You do. And that's OK. I'm just saying, you have a choice."

Ji-Soo's phone vibrated against the tabletop. As she grabbed it, the charms dangling from it swung, a blur of tiny bunnies and ice cream cones. She read the text, grinned, and turned the phone around so Lissa could read it.

Jae-Jin: *We're waiting on you two. Bring your boba upstairs!*

Lissa laughed. "He's keeping tabs on us."

"That, or bringing our drinks there with us every day makes it kind of obvious where we go first."

"Right." Lissa took a deep breath and stood up, fastening the clasp on her purse. As she stood, she realised Ji-Soo was standing right in front of her, waiting for her to look up.

"What—"

Ji-Soo's tiny hand closed around her wrist.

"Lissa. I believe in you. Don't forget that."

Before Lissa could respond, she was engulfed in a fierce hug. She rested her head atop her friend's, and for just a moment, it all felt OK.

CHAPTER FOUR
THE LITTLE FIGHTER

FOR DEVON CLARKE, PlaySpace was home. Not that he didn't enjoy the home he had. He lived in a cosy apartment only a fifteen-minute walk away, and it was well-equipped with all the things he could ever need, plus a few indulgences: an overstuffed chair half as old as he was, and a much-loved red drum kit he'd inherited from his best friend in college. Charley, the old black stray cat he found yowling near his front door a few years back, now warmed the chair when Devon was away. It was a good life, and he was frequently grateful for it.

Going home was one kind of feeling. Comfort, silence. Going to PlaySpace was another. It felt like being a kid on Christmas morning and waiting for his dad to get his bathrobe on and come settle down by the tree. But the best part was that it felt like that every time he walked up to the doors and fished the keys out of his pocket. It was like opening a present every single time.

Maybe that was because it was a place he had created himself. Or a reminder that he'd had a dream to own a place like this for people like him to go, and he had accomplished it. But most of all, even when there wasn't a single soul in the 'Space, there was still a charge in the air. To Devon, it was a physical remnant of what hundreds of gamers left behind, that thing that pulsed in all their hearts: to connect to their own kind, and to excel, to push, to win.

He was, after all, one of them, even if he didn't compete anymore. When he had started his own journey, there was no PlaySpace, no watering hole to meet others like himself in person. There were dozens of online communities back then. But he was a man who felt his best in the physical presence of other people. In the end, he stuck to playing on his own. He'd had a lot of time on his hands back in those days, so most of his free moments were spent behind his computer screen. That same excitement he felt today in the air at PlaySpace was palpable in his chest each time he logged on, wondering if he could maintain his winning streak just one more day.

His memories wandered. Long, hot summer afternoons, the sound of the living room fan on high. Percy, their basset hound, sighing in his sleep. Dad watching kung fu movies to pass the time. When Devon heard the familiar sounds coming from the television, he'd drift to the living room to join his father, sitting on the floor in front of the old busted easy chair with the hole in the seat where the dog had gnawed it.

The people on the screen seemed like the most powerful humans in the world to Devon, not an ounce of doubt or fear in a single one of them. Devon carefully memorised their names and held them close like magical talismans: Bruce Lee, Jackie Chan, Jet Li, Sammo Hung, Donnie Yen, Michelle Yeoh. These were people who never had to fear walking to school alone, being bullied, coming home crying with skinned knees after being shoved to the ground and called names he wouldn't dare to utter aloud. These people would fight back and win.

When he was fourteen, he discovered *Street Fighter* in the arcade. This, Devon thought, was the closest he could get to learning how to fight. He quickly saw the ways each character used moves that he had seen on his dad's old TV on all those hot summer days. But they weren't exact copies of them. Sometimes they were a bit of what he'd seen before with a bit of something new mixed in, making them all the more fascinating.

Watching the bigger kids play, he also noticed something familiar: swagger. In a way, it was like watching his beloved kung fu masters face off against one another, except these masters wore jeans and t-shirts. This one kid, Elijah, had been his favourite to watch. Not only was he good—he beat just about everyone else he played—but he was Black just like Devon, and no one gave him a hard time for it.

All that, Devon mused. All those little moments. They all added up to the fifteen-year-old that showed up for tournaments, the sixteen-year-old that won them, and the eighteen-year-old that won the title at the International Underworld Championships. They called him "The Little Fighter"—a short, scrawny kid who hammered the odds and then some. Every time he won, he felt more and more like he was leaving those bullies behind, flying high above their heads as they stared up after him. He had never hit back, but he didn't need to. This was better. This was knowing he could beat another master, fair and square.

And then at twenty-eight, he had left it all behind.

"Devon? We're gonna go grab sandwiches, do you want one?"

He came out of his reverie to find Zio grinning from the doorway of the tiny room he called an office, clad in her usual black hoodie and ripped jeans. He blinked a few times, realising he'd come in to do some paperwork and lost himself to the allure of old memories instead.

"Maybe I should just choose one for you?" Her smile grew.

"Ah... yeah. That's a good idea." Devon rubbed his forehead and smiled back at her. "Got to thinkin' about the old days."

"I got you." Zio tapped a finger to her temple, her expression wry. "Order's right up here." She turned to leave, then spared a glance over her shoulder. "You should come out and listen. We met a pretty savage player last night and Jae-Jin's in full strategy mode."

"I will," Devon said, standing up and stretching his arms above his head. "Savage, huh?"

"Yep," Zio replied, taking a glance at her watch. "See you soon."

Devon watched her go, closing the door behind her with care. A glance at his watch showed him he'd been lost in his head for almost an hour. Felt like five minutes. Standing, he made his way across the room, the image of the boy he'd been burning in his chest. It was accompanied by a familiar throb, and he placed his hand over his heart for a moment to steady himself.

50

"I got you, buddy," he murmured, opening the office door.

A few short steps down the hallway and the place that once lived only in his mind sprawled out before him in reality. Pearl-white walls set a dramatic backdrop to crisp red geometric patterns that burst up from the floor and faded as they reached the ceiling. Modern black sofas and chairs, all lived-in by now, nestled into a high-pile carpet a vivid shade of red. Massive 4K TVs hung on the wall at three-foot intervals, their bound cords snaking towards the floor. Devon saw a black backpack he didn't recognise slung next to one of these stations, mentally making a note to greet the owner when they reappeared.

Devon had opened the doors to PlaySpace three and a half years ago, in January. He'd never had a sliver of doubt that it would do well, and he had been right. Not that he was rolling in money—that wasn't exactly how running a gaming hangout worked. But he'd saved all his winnings in his competition days, leaving them untouched in a savings account. And it felt right for him to use them to create a place where people like him could hang out and sharpen their skills, maybe go on to compete themselves one of these days.

Once that got the doors open, he got the idea to host competitions to help pay for the overhead, and his kids were every bit into it as he had hoped. Even better, they also quickly became aware that a place some of them considered a second home—or for a select few, a first—needed their support in order to keep breathing. Devon had seen many a donation roll in via the PlaySpace Venmo, and they gave him a feeling of gratitude he'd rarely experienced before.

The familiar beats of Keiichi Siguyama's 'Buggie Running Beeps 01' pulsed out of the big speakers mounted over the door. Devon grinned. He loved this song and never tired of hearing it come up on the shop's playlist, its insistent thump always tingling in his veins.

As he nodded his head, the front door opened and a person he'd never seen before walked in. Devon caught mild flickers of feminine expressions in the face but sensed his new guest identified as masculine. Their dark hair was cropped short, and they wore a Marvel t-shirt, emblazoned with Captain America, dark blue jeans, and red Converse. A grey canvas backpack covered with enamel pins was slung over one shoulder.

They looked at Devon with shy eyes the colour of Mexican amber.

"Greetings!" Devon said, turning his brilliant smile on them. "Welcome to PlaySpace!"

As usual, his warmth melted even the most nervous of new people. A small smile appeared on the new guest's face, and Devon saw that they felt comforted. It was a gift he had, and while he didn't know where it came from, he was really glad he had it.

"I'm Ray," they said. "I'm, ah, new to the area. Just moved from Rochester."

"Well, you're welcome here, Ray," Devon said. "Let me show you the ropes."

Ray's smile deepened.

"I'd like that."

As they walked through the shop together, Devon could already tell that Ray was going to be a permanent fixture, despite seeming younger than the others. Something about their disposition—gentle yet eager—told him they would mesh perfectly with the gamers he'd seen every day for the last three years. They continued to chat as Devon showed them the gaming stations, the break area, and the hangout rooms in the back. As they walked past one of the conference rooms, Devon got a glimpse of his favourite kids, clustered around a table screen with faces so serious they could have been planning the next world war.

"Yo," Devon said to the group, and they all looked up.

"Dude!" A tall Asian teen with a military-precise haircut looked up at him, his rectangular glasses flashing thanks to the fluorescent lights above. "Where you been? We need your genius."

"You'll get it. But first, meet Ray. They're brand new to the area."

"Hey, Ray. I'm Zio." She put down her sandwich and waved at him. "May I introduce you to… Team Phoenix! That's our team name." She motioned to the end of the table. "Oh, and Devon, your sandwich is over there."

"Thanks," Devon said, grinning at her.

"Jae-Jin," the tall one said, nodding. "You play *Ancestral*?" He gestured at the screen. "We're just puzzling out how we got beaten last night."

Ray cocked their head, putting their bag down on the table and walking over to take a look. "I sure do. What happened?"

As Jae-Jin showed the new recruit the replay of the match on the screen, Lissa and Ji-Soo appeared in the doorway. Devon regarded them with a warm smile.

"Ah, always fashionably late. It must take time to score that boba."

"Shut up, Devon," Ji-Soo replied, giving him a hug. "We need sugar to survive, you know."

"Of course," Devon laughed. "Well, the gang is analysing why you took a beating last night, so you're just in time. Oh, and that's Ray. It's their first time here."

"Another *Ancestral* player?"

"Yep."

Lissa and Ji-Soo both eyed the new kid with interest, then turned back to Devon.

"Sweet," Lissa said. "We can always use more of those. Wonder what class they play."

"Only one way to find out."

Ji-Soo snorted. "True. Do you have time to sit down with us though? I'd like to know what you think after you see the replay."

"For sure," Devon said. "Let me grab a drink and I'll be there in a minute."

Lissa and Ji-Soo pulled up chairs as Ray looked up to see who was joining them.

"Hello! I'm Ji-Soo and this is Lissa." Ji-Soo paused. "May I ask what pronoun you use?"

"Ah!" Ray looked distinctly relieved. "Thanks for asking! It's 'he'."

"Sweet." Ji-Soo grinned. "Finally, Jae-Jin isn't the only dude anymore."

They all laughed, an easy, sweet sound.

"Hey, I never minded," Jae-Jin said, adjusting his glasses.

"Well, we did," Lissa said. "You can get bossy sometimes."

Jae-Jin shrugged.

"So… do you all normally play together?" Ray asked.

Jae-Jin nodded. "We really want to be ready to compete when competitions get announced."

"Whenever that happens." Ji-Soo rolled her eyes. "Feels like waiting forever."

"How long have you all been playing?"

"Everyone here has played since launch," Lissa volunteered, grinning. "What social lives?"

They all laughed, their faces happy and true.

"Cool, me too," Ray said. "What classes? I'm a Mender."

"Brutalist," said Ji-Soo, flexing an imaginary muscle. The others tittered, and Zio assessed her friend's tiny bicep with her fingertips.

"I play Morteist," Jae-Jin said. "Death is my jam."

"Fits you perfectly," Lissa said, taking a long sip of her boba. "Oh, and I'm a Plunderer. Assassination arts make me feel like a badass."

"Which she *is*," Ji-Soo said as Lissa playfully shoved her.

"Shut up."

"I won't," Ji-Soo said matter-of-factly.

"I used to run Morteist, too, but I mostly play Weaver these days," Zio said. "Sex is cool, but have you ever gored a few dozen Onyx?"

They all laughed, the melody of their voices intertwining. Although none of them heard it, there was an imperceptible click in the air. It was the moment they all became friends.

CHAPTER FIVE
BEATING THE UNBEATABLE

BY THE TIME Devon came back with a mug of coffee in hand, the laughter in the room had dissolved into an observant silence, and Jae-Jin had the floor.

"Before we figure out why we were beaten," he said, "we need to figure out how it happened in the first place. We know the enemy is highly experienced. But it doesn't make them impossible to beat. We just need to look closely at what happened to understand what strategy was used."

"The 'Beat Everyone's Butt in Under Thirty Seconds' strategy," Zio muttered.

"Wait," Devon said, making his way to their side of the table. "Before you get any further, I want to watch the match."

Nodding, the group moved aside to make room for him to roll up a chair and sit down. Jae-Jin started the stream from the beginning, explaining as he went.

"There's nothing odd about the first half. We're on the South Ending map, which everyone here has played hundreds of times—we know its advantages and blind spots. We all played our mains last night."

Devon's eyes moved quickly across the screen, following Lissa's avatar as she scouted the area. Red dots bloomed on the mini-map—their enemies. The team's blue dots were spread evenly around the field, covering the weak areas. As Devon watched, the two at southeast and southwest vanished.

"That's where Zio and I were sniped," Jae-Jin noted, pointing. "This is part of a larger strategy. As soon as we were gone, they unleashed a flood. Smart thinking on their part—divide and conquer. Only Lissa and Ji-Soo were left at that point, leaving the graveyard vulnerable. Lissa fortified the weak point here"—he pointed to a narrow passage—"but without the rest of us to thin the flow, Onyx made it through. There were more than ten and they were all Raging. Which means—"

"Two Weavers," Devon said. "Weaver class can only cast Raging on a maximum of five Onyx at a time, so…"

"Right. But we've seen that before, too; just not super often. So even though we weren't ready, the girls reacted fast. The other team did wait to execute until Ji-Soo's Death Flight was drained, so we know they were watching several points before the strike. They were very careful on timing." Jae-Jin pointed to Ji-Soo's Transcendence gauge to illustrate his point. "You'd assume that all this was set up to take us out. But what's fascinating is that they were also prepared in case this didn't work. The Raging Onyx attack should have ended it—it would have for weaker players. Lissa and Ji-Soo reacted with zero time to think. Under the circumstances, they did incredibly well."

Devon nodded, eyes never leaving the screen. Lissa glanced at Ji-Soo to see a flush creeping up her neck.

As she watched, her friend quickly swept her hair over the offending area.

"So, it shook us up, but we survived it. It seems they were expecting that. We thought at this point all we needed to do was kill the last one standing—the Master. We didn't expect him to be cloaked, because we've only seen that once before. We've also never lost in this way, so no one could have anticipated what happened next."

Lissa felt angry all over again as she watched it play out. Jae-Jin's kill, then nothing. All of them trying to secure the map, thrown off by the long silence. And then Zio's death, so lightning quick it disoriented them all. Devon was the one to hit pause this time.

"Was that a one-hit kill?"

"Yeah." Zio's voice was bewildered. "That's never happened to me before. It was so fast I don't even know what I was hit with."

"Did you see them?"

"No, no one appeared near me."

"Which means it wasn't a Brutalist or a Morteist," Ray said. "You would have seen either of their attacks."

"Well, we think." Zio blinked, her green eyes glinting in the light.

They all nodded, looking thoughtful. After a few moments of silence, Jae-Jin hit play again.

"Who noticed that they were cloaked?"

"Me," Lissa piped up. "I saw a brief flash on the map. If I had blinked, I might have missed it. I'm assuming the only reason I saw it was an error on their part. But watch what happens to Jae in this part. On the map."

Devon's brows furrowed as Jae-Jin's dot wavered.

"It looks like something's wrong."

"Exactly," Lissa said. "We thought it was a bug. Which blows my mind, because if they're using some sort of mod to cause a glitch…"

Devon's eyes glittered. "But an immensely powerful one, if that's the case."

"It's messed up," Zio remarked, her tone angry. "An unfair advantage."

Jae-Jin shook his head.

"Remember. They can only do it once. After that, we learn and adapt. If we see this happen again, we know it's no glitch. We'll remember and be ready."

As Lissa watched her own death for the second time, a flash of light unfurled across her brain. She'd seen the weapon she'd been killed by that night, just for a split second, but she'd been so angry she hadn't grasped what it was. As her body fell to the ground, she saw it clearly—the blade embedded in her shoulder looked like a crucifix.

"Crossblade," she blurted. "It's a Plunderer. Just like me."

"Ah!" Devon drummed the table with an open palm. "Makes perfect sense. Thrown weapon, no sign of the enemy."

The screen turned dark, displaying the match results. Both Jae-Jin and Lissa had run undefeated streaks prior to it—his 406, hers 329. Lissa wasn't surprised Jae-Jin hadn't mentioned it. He wasn't the type to talk about his feelings. From months of playing with him she knew he had emotions, but he was a master of keeping them under lock and key. If he was phased by this defeat and the loss of his streak, he showed no sign of it.

"Did anyone research the leader?" He paused

mid-sentence, looking down at the screen again. "...WraithX?"

Lissa was already nodding. "I did."

"OK. What did you learn?"

"I'll show you. Let's go to the front room."

The group gathered their things quietly, filing back into the gaming room. A few regulars lined the wall near the door, all three playing *Ancestral* matches. One, a lanky girl wearing overalls, got taken out and threw her baseball cap on the floor, a trail of curses streaming from her lips.

Lissa headed for the right wall to the line of stations where she and the team typically played and took her usual spot on the sofa. She unzipped a backpack the colour of burnished steel and took out her Orb, clicking the button on the bottom of the sphere-shaped controller to power it on. A small blue light between the thumb pads came to life, blinking as it paired with the TV. A loading bar appeared on the screen as the game synced to the cloud.

After about ten seconds, her hub screen appeared. Nagiko, her avatar, stood front and centre, looking foreboding with her oversized hood and bloody weapons.

"Oooh, I like that coat," Ji-Soo said. "Is that new?"

"Sort of," Lissa replied. "Looted it off a kill a few matches ago."

As she clicked her way through a few screens to her match history, the group watched as she found WraithX's username and clicked it. The profile looked just as barren as it had the night before. Just the red square for a user photo, and no indication of where they could be from. Lissa smoothed her thumb along the front of her Orb to scroll down, showing the part of the screen with WraithX's match stats.

"Ten *thousand*?" Ray wore an expression of shock. "How could they have played that many matches unless... they spent all day, every day in the game?"

"They might." Devon looked troubled as he went on, "This could be a young player, maybe not in school or working. If they're talented enough—and clearly, they are—they may be playing full-time already."

"But there aren't even *Ancestral* championships for them to be sponsored in yet."

"There will be," Devon replied. "You can bet on that. That's what you're all training for, isn't it?"

Everyone fell silent. He was right.

"That's the lowest loss ratio I've ever seen," Jae-Jin said, pointing. "And it doesn't allow for much, if any, early losses. Either this is not this player's only account... or they came into *Ancestral* knowing exactly how to play it perfectly."

"Doubt it," Ji-Soo said. "This is a skilled player for sure, but let's not make them mythical. Most people have alts. Pretty sure Wraith here has a few, too."

"All right," Jae-Jin said with the tone of a teacher silencing a rowdy homeroom class. "So, there are some variables. But what's most important here is not that we lost. We can't judge our value as a team on any one match. What we can do is use each loss as a way to see our weak points, maybe some we weren't even aware of. The only way to get better is to look closely at those once they're unveiled. This player did us a favour. That's why I see them as a teacher, not an enemy."

That's why he's the leader, Lissa thought. *And he's right.*

"What I see is that you're dealing with an unusual hybrid," Devon said, his long fingers steepled in front of his face. "I know that the typical MOBA—that's multiplayer online battle arena, by the way, for those of you who may not know what it actually stands for— operates differently than the fighting game community does. But in the Fighting Game Community, each player has their own unique vibe. Sometimes you feel outplayed because they're faster, or more precise. Those people have put in the practice, and it shows. But then, there are others that feel like they are actually *in* your head. They're guiding your choices and you don't even know it. And before you know it, they've messed you up *and* taken advantage of you."

"Feels bad, man," Ray said, and they all laughed.

"What I'm saying is," Devon continued, "if we want to learn from WraithX, we need to play them again. And again. Which, looking at that match history, they're playing often, so it shouldn't be too hard. Send a challenge, wait for them to accept, and see what happens."

"I did find one thread about them," Lissa piped up. "I think so, anyway." She took out her phone and opened it to the forum she'd been browsing while waiting on Ji-Soo at Bubble Pop!, then offered it to Devon. The others drew close to read the screen over his shoulder.

"Huh," Ray said. "It's not a confirmation, but... it does sound like this is what happened to you guys."

"Maybe," Lissa said. "I have to dig more. But I think Devon is right. We should all keep an eye on this player and challenge them if we can. We can't learn how we're being beaten unless we get beaten some more. And as

far as being good enough to take on championships…
what better way is there than to play people better than
us?"

The others nodded, thoughtful looks on their faces.

"I see it like this," Devon said, gesturing with
his hands as if presenting a grand idea. "This team
just got stronger in several ways. One, you've been
given an opportunity to learn and improve from the
type of player you'll see winning competitions. I've
been in many, as you all know, and I recognise the
temperature of those moves. I've played people this
good, and better. They may wipe the floor with you,
but if you don't waste time feeling sorry for yourself
you can learn exactly what to do to beat them. You
just need a technical, objective approach."

"So, Jae-Jin will be the first to beat them," Zio
blurted. The others giggled while Jae-Jin adjusted his
glasses, but he wore a modest smile.

"Could be. He does have the ability to disconnect
from the emotional side of it—that's a rare quality.
But sometimes the emotion can drive you, too." He
grinned at Lissa. "That's where you come in."

Lissa looked sheepish, even as Ji-Soo clapped her
on the back.

"The other thing," Devon said, "is Ray. None
of you run Weaver, and he does. Every class has
strengths and weaknesses, but if you have one of
each on your team, you have the best possible options
at your disposal. This will also affect how the team
runs. So, I'd say the first thing you need to do is start
playing together and see how you click."

Ray beamed. "Let's go then."

"Wait. One more thing."

All eyes settled on Devon, anxiously awaiting his words.

"You all have what it takes. I just met Ray, but I think he does, too. You all care about the game, not just winning, but *how* you play. That matters. You each have a distinct style, and that matters as well. If you all work together the way I think you will, you have an honest chance at championships. Remember, most of all, if you're going to get there, the way you think matters just as much as the way you play. If not more."

"Were you a pro competitor?" Ray asked.

Devon nodded, one hand going to his locs and twisting them idly. "I was. But that's a long story and I'll save it for another day, when your fingers are worn down to nubs and you've played so hard your eyes don't work anymore. Then this old man will regale you with stories of ye days of olde."

Ji-Soo giggled. "Devon, you're not *that* old."

"Feels like it some days. Anyway. I wanna watch you all play. We doing this today, or what?"

CHAPTER SIX
JI-SOO

A PERSON WANDERING into Ji-Soo's office by accident might have thought they'd stumbled into a waking dream—or a Japanese vintage toy museum. In a way it was just that, as Ji-Soo had collected dollhouses for years, carefully curating a collection that brought her great joy. The black floor-to-ceiling bookcase against the far wall sang with colour: it housed vivid replicas of houses and cottages, each in mint condition. Dolls with lustrous curls and gorgeous, oversized eyes filled with stars lined some of the shelves. Their pristine outfits were one of Ji-Soo's primary sources of fashion inspiration.

The art on the walls echoed a similar sentiment. The classic oil paintings of landscapes one might find leaning forgotten against thrift store walls took on something new thanks to the addition of giant, brightly coloured mechs or skyscraper-sized monsters, both towering over people no larger than ants. A glance at the plastic tarp and hastily closed paint cans below the paintings made it clear who the artist was.

A thick shag rug the colour of a baby's blushing

cheeks covered the floor. Several pairs of Ji-Soo's shoes lay cast to one side: three-inch butter yellow platform sandals, red plaid Doc Martens with canary yellow laces, blue velvet combat boots with silky ribbons. Gotham, Ji-Soo's big black and tan dog, flopped lazily near the shoe mountain, blissfully inhaling the beguiling fragrance of his owner's socks.

Ji-Soo sat at a white desk tucked into one corner. While her collectibles covered every other surface of the room, the desk only held one item: a chrome stand with two massive, curved monitors attached to it via a chunky metal arm. Ji-Soo gazed up at the screen on her left, where an eBay auction for a pair of knee-high, opalescent boots with a two-inch neon pink platform ticked away towards its expiration date. A pink pastel mouse nestled in her left hand. It was atop a mousepad with an illustration of a cartoon-style white llama.

Tapping F5 to refresh the monitor, Ji-Soo nodded to no one in particular. Chasing online auctions was one of her favourite hobbies. In the rare times she wasn't tracking down some impossibly obscure item, she found her time in the world uncomfortably slow. She always preferred to be busy, whether it meant working on becoming a better *Ancestral* player or beating yet another poor bidder who thought they had a chance of winning any auction she had her eye on. Her lightning reaction time as she gamed was partially gleaned from the art of sniping auctions at the very last second, a dirty trick she was particularly proud of.

The timer on the auction showed six minutes to go. She felt a sparkle of anticipation. Only three hundred pairs of these boots had ever been made, and they'd sold out within ten minutes of going on sale. She hadn't been lucky enough to score them that day, so she'd kept an eye out for them on the auction sites ever since. She wore a size five, so finding her size this way required a lot of patience. But about seven months after the boots sold out, she was rewarded with a notification that someone had listed a pair. Now the end was drawing near, and her adrenaline surged. She relished every second of its bright electric jolts.

She moused over to the other monitor. Two windows were open there: the *Ancestral* lobby, where a stack of game invites (mostly from strangers who had eyeballed her stats and wanted her muscle for their party) sat unread. She only played with her local friends these days. When *Ancestral* was smaller, she'd been willing to party with people she didn't know, and had even met some players she liked enough to play with again. It was a friendlier world back then. But it'd gotten weirder as it'd gotten bigger. Much weirder.

The other window was Parse(d). As social media went, it was by far her favourite platform. But since it catered to bloggers of all sorts, she loved to take pictures of her outfits and post them so people would compliment her taste. Not only that, but it was lucrative. After she'd racked up twenty thousand followers, Parse(d) contacted her and offered her an option of monetising her posts. While she still dreamed of being known as an esports competitor, she was happy to do this in the meantime. It paid her rent and made it possible for her to live on her own, something she'd quietly worn as a badge of pride after leaving home when she was seventeen. Plus, it gave her a terrific excuse to buy new wardrobe additions.

Style posts were the furthest thing on her mind at the moment, however. Feeling sheepish, she moused to her history and clicked Jae-Jin's page. When it loaded, she glanced over the last few posts (and there weren't many). After making sure she hadn't missed anything, she clicked his profile picture so it filled most of her screen.

Ji-Soo would have opted to be stoned to death in public rather than anyone find out how often she looked at Jae-Jin's photos this way. Staring at a photo of a boy on her computer was not only pathetic, but in this particular case, hopeless. The fashion blogging world might think she was an amazing person, but she figured even they would think staring at a guy she had no hope of ever dating was sort of sad.

It was ironic. She had never been a shy girl at any time in her life, always comfortable with goofing off with complete strangers she'd met five minutes prior at a party or being the first to grab the mic when she went to karaoke with her friends. But four months ago, when Jae-Jin walked into PlaySpace only two days after moving from New York, she transformed into someone she no longer recognised. It was like stepping into a puddle to discover you'd sunk to the bottom of the earth.

He was handsome, with just the kind of angular jaw and sharp features she found attractive. But it was his presence that affected her most—a quiet, careful thing, like an unsure ghost considering contact with the world of the living. She got the sense of a person carefully shielding the majority of himself, yet choosing to pour all of his energy into one task in order to succeed. That first day he came to PlaySpace he sat down, adjusted his glasses, and took an Orb so well-worn out of his bag the grey plastic had faded to white on the touch pads. They'd all watched him play, rendered speechless by what the new guy could do. His focus was intense. He was also so fast that he cleared the map by himself in under five minutes.

"Wow. We got a gem here!" Devon said that day, clapping Jae-Jin on the back. And when Jae-Jin looked up at him with the barest hint of a smile, Ji-Soo's heart tumbled into a crevice, without a single cry on the way down.

He became a regular in their group as her friends warmed to him. None of them seemed to mind that he was so reserved. As a teammate, he was a dream: extremely disciplined, hyper-focused, and a natural leader. He naturally fell into the role during their matches but handled it with fairness and diplomacy. They joked about his rigid approach, but truthfully, it made it easy for them to follow his lead. They all trusted him when it came to playing *Ancestral* together. He may not have known it, but Ji-Soo's crush allowed her to see something wonderful: that the furtive smile she noticed on that first day had grown to one that reached his eyes. A little fire burst in her heart every time she saw it.

Ji-Soo knew Jae-Jin spent long afternoons in the gaming station furthest from PlaySpace's front door, probably so that he would be left alone. She understood that need and admired his focus and determination. While most of the gamers that hung out in the 'Space took breaks to get cans of soda from the vending machine or chat with Devon about strategy ideas, Ji-Soo noticed that Jae-Jin always stayed rooted in his corner as still as a stone.

Ji-Soo assumed he'd grown up a solitary child. It was the only way she could imagine a person so perfectly at ease in their own company. She grew up surrounded by loud, playful brothers, quick to drag her outside to play hide and seek or shoot hoops until the sun went down. When she was alone, she wasn't sure what to do with herself. Jae-Jin, on the other hand, seemed perfectly happy to be in his own company day after day, hour after hour. She often looked at the back of his head as she passed through the front room, wondering what his interior world was like. Did he have friends? A girlfriend or boyfriend? Did he care about anything other than the game?

Sometimes she wandered over. He always seemed polite, but quickly turned back to what he was doing within a few seconds. He wasn't a chatty person. And yet she wanted to learn from him. So, she sat and watched as he blasted through one battle after another with military precision. Even though few words were exchanged, she secretly enjoyed these times. Sitting near him was enough for her.

He rarely lost a match. But one day, she watched an Onyx horde appear out of nowhere and maul him. He'd just taken down an onslaught and unloaded everything he had. Jae-Jin's play style was never to be left vulnerable until you were the only player left on the field. And it'd seemed like he was primed for victory—right up to the moment where two red dots appeared on the mini-map. They sniped him within seconds.

He sat watching the kill screen in silence. Ji-Soo noticed his fingers, clutching the Orb with such pressure that his knuckles trembled. It was a tiny movement. But she saw it.

"Jae-Jin? Are you OK?"

He didn't turn to her. His eyes never left the screen.

"I was almost three hundred wins in."

Ji-Soo watched his profile while her heart sped up in her chest.

He's actually upset, she thought. *I've never seen this.*

"You can do it again."

He turned and stared her right in the eyes. The look was sharp and distrusting. But in it, she saw a hint of confusion and—just the barest glimmer—hurt.

"I'm not sure why you would say something like that."

Her heart wavered with a burst of nerves. But she took a deep breath and went on.

"Because I'm sure of it."

He had continued to look at her. Never once had he ever looked into her eyes for so long. Then he'd dropped his gaze, unzipped his backpack and stashed his Orb in its holder.

"I have to go."

"Are you coming to the dinner tonight?"

Jae-Jin shook his head as he stood up and slung his backpack onto one shoulder.

"I have to get more practice in. Have fun."

Before she could think of another word to say to him, he was gone. The man could remove himself from a room faster than anyone else she'd ever known. She'd sat in the void his absence left behind, her mind a chaos of thoughts and feelings.

I saw his feelings. I saw—

You pissed him off.

No. You told him what you really thought.

Did he... see how I feel? Is that why he left?

A timer went off with a sharp ping, startling Ji-Soo back into the present day. The memories started to soften as she realised she was about to lose the auction because she'd been lost in thoughts of Jae-Jin. Again.

Patting her cheeks to wake herself, she shifted her attention back to the left monitor and opened a few extra browser windows. The first was the main auction page, while the second was the confirm bid screen. She typed in her maximum bid and left it, then clicked to the first window and pressed F5 to refresh it. The numbers were starting to rise. She wasn't alone in the game to win these, which was not a surprise considering they were so rare.

After getting that set up, Ji-Soo opened ScriptKitty, an app she used for every auction she bid in. This clever little program popped up on her radar about five years ago. Made by a programmer known as littlemeowmeow, it monitored any auction the user wanted to participate in using server time. By doing so, it was able to place a bid at the exact moment necessary in order to win an auction. Best of all, it meowed when it won.

Ji-Soo either sniped auctions manually or using ScriptKitty depending on her mood. Sometimes she felt like it was too easy to let the app do the work. Sure, it ensured success, but it also presented no challenge. Manual sniping was thrilling in a different way. Instead of relying on server time, she just felt out the rhythm of the last few minutes. It gave her a burst of self-satisfaction if she won this way.

Well, I could really use a pick-me-up today.

There was a minute left on the clock. She looked between her options for a few more seconds, then settled on the manual approach. Her finger tapped F5 in a consistent rhythm as the bids went up. No one was bidding big—just a few dollars here and there. The max bid she had in mind was one hundred dollars more than the current price, so she felt she'd probably win this one. But she remembered that there could always be another her somewhere doing the same thing. Or maybe even two or three.

Twenty seconds left. Fifteen. Another tap of her finger and the bid went up by fifty dollars.

Ah, here we go.

Refresh. Another twenty dollars.

Refresh. Ten seconds.

Ji-Soo closed her eyes and concentrated, then clicked the right mouse to let her high bid fly. She tapped F5 one last time and opened her eyes.

CONGRATULATIONS, RETROSHOUJOQUEEN!
YOU ARE THE WINNER OF THIS AUCTION!

A bubble of joy rose in her chest and popped, leaving her feeling high and sparkling. They were going to look so awesome with her short skirts and dresses. She imagined stomping her way up the stairs to PlaySpace feeling every inch the badass she was. Her wardrobe was her favourite hobby outside of gaming. Nothing felt better than reinventing herself over and over every single day.

"Gotta pay," she said to herself in a sing-song voice,

mousing through the checkout screen. She'd done it so many times she hardly needed to read the directions. But her attention drifted to the other monitor for a moment, and it settled back on Jae-Jin's photo, the high she'd felt seconds ago beginning to lose its charge.

He wouldn't notice if she had the coolest outfit in the world.

Ji-Soo tried not to indulge in moody thoughts, 'so when her computer chirped to signal she was getting a video call she felt relieved. Then she clicked the notification and her heart sank just a little bit lower.

Jye-Hi Park calling

Mum.

Ji-Soo loved her mother, but she didn't like her. She found it hard to look at her face, with its deep grooves of worry and disappointment. Every conversation with her was a minefield. It wasn't a matter of what would blow up, but when.

After fighting a brief temptation to ignore the call altogether, Ji-Soo pressed the button to accept it.

"Ah, Ji-Soo. You look thin. Are you eating enough?"

"Yes, Mom."

"Well. Eat more, then. Do you cook for yourself out there?"

"Sure," she said, thinking about the dozen bags of leek and pork dumplings stuffed in her freezer. That was kind of cooking. In a way.

Her mother nodded. The movement was stiff and slow.

"Did you want to talk to me about something?"

"Well. I just wanted to see how you were doing out there."

Even though the words seemed caring, her mother looked pensive. She rarely called Ji-Soo since her daughter had moved to the States. But considering the circumstances that led to Ji-Soo moving away, she was surprised her mother called at all.

"I'm fine. How's everyone else?"

"Fine. Cho and Jin are good. Oh, Jin joined a team here. I forget the name. But he's living with them now, so he's not at home anymore."

Scenes flashed in Ji-Soo's mind in a matter of seconds. Laughing with Cho and Jin as they played games together as kids. The way she always coached Cho. How she felt safe with her brothers. Happy. And then the day her mother told her she couldn't play with them anymore. The closed door of the gaming room she was no longer allowed to go into, a sight that hurt so much it was hard to look at it.

"I see," Ji-Soo said, unable to come up with much else. She watched as her mother looked down at her hands, examining the squared edges of her nails. They were lacquered a garish shade of magenta with a light pink glitter at the tips.

"So, you're getting by out there. The office job is going OK?"

She nodded. Lying to her parents was second nature by now.

"You know you can come home anytime if you need to. It's really a waste to pay rent out there when you could live here for free. Especially if you aren't even studying."

"Mom—"

"Well, we could just use your help here. You know your father and I are getting older."

Ji-Soo stared down at her desk. A part of her started to shut down against a speech she'd heard so many times she could have repeated it word for word.

"And since you're the eldest—"

"Not that again."

"Yes, that again. Don't you know what that means? The restaurant belongs to you already. A business you don't need any education to profit from. All you need to do is come home and take it over." Her mother mimed wiping her brow, a weary man bearing the weight of his toil.

"Mom, you know I left because I didn't want to do that."

"Do you know how selfish that is? Putting what you want before the needs of the family?"

Ji-Soo shook her head in frustration.

"Aren't Cho and Jin bringing in income? Since they're working so hard to become pro gamers?"

Her mother shook her head to indicate the topic was not up for discussion.

"This is not about them."

Ji-Soo peered at her mother's face and realised this wasn't her garden variety of passive aggression. She had been a worried-looking woman ever since Ji-Soo had been a child. But what she saw etched into the lines of her mother's face today was more than worry. It was fear.

"Is everything... OK over there?"

Her mother sat silent for a moment. Her hand went to her mouth. Ji-Soo felt a surge of alarm as she watched, unsure what was happening. Slowly it registered that her mother was trying not to cry. Her throat worked, the crepe-like skin hitching like a fish struggling to breathe on land.

Ji-Soo watched, stunned into silence. The only other time she had ever seen her mother cry was at her aunt's funeral. Ji-Soo had been six years old. Even then, her mother had turned away from her so fast she wasn't even sure if what she'd seen was real or just a passing shadow.

"Mom?"

Jye-Hi shook her head, her hand still clamped tight over her mouth as if letting it go would mean the end of her.

Ji-Soo's heart hammered in her chest. She felt a stab of empathy for her mother. She'd hurt Ji-Soo countless times over, left her feeling as if she was hardly worth anything, and that her dreams didn't matter. But as she watched her struggling on the screen, she wondered what it would be like to swallow a lifetime of emotions and keep them there. To always feel them roiling in your stomach, rising to your throat. To never be able to say what you really meant.

All this mingled in her mind as her mother finally removed her hand to reveal a mouth like a twisted scar, poorly sewn shut.

"Your dad."

"What—"

"I can't talk about it now."

Ji-Soo's anger rose in her stomach, hot and sour, to intermingle with the fear she felt. The sting of tears came, and she steeled herself against it. She didn't want her mother to see her cry. Not even if her father was dying. She loved her, but she also hated her. She felt choked by all of it, unable to breathe.

"If your father calls, you don't say anything."

"What would I say if you won't even tell me?"

"Still. If he calls. Don't tell him."

Fury twisted in her gut as she realised she already knew the answer to the question rising to her lips.

"He would never call. You know that. And why bother to bring this up if you won't even tell me what's wrong?"

Her mother blinked, her face stony. There was a time Ji-Soo would have felt ashamed speaking to her mother this way. But not now. Not anymore.

She paused, tempted to say something cruel, but the urge melted under a wave of sadness. This would never change. Any of this. All she wanted was a straight answer so she could understand the situation.

But that wasn't the way her family worked.

This is why I left. Why I never want to go back.

"I have to go, Mom," she said. "I'll get back to you." She clicked the button to end the call without waiting for a reply.

She covered her face with her hands and sat still for some time. The darkness there was comforting. It felt like blotting out the world. And yet a flurry of thoughts beat at the door to get in, a cacophony of unwelcome knocks. She imagined herself having to pack her bags and go home. Leaving PlaySpace, leaving Lissa, leaving her friends.

Never seeing Jae-Jin again.

She listened to her own inhalations as her emotions whirled round and round. Eventually Gotham came to nuzzle her leg, and she welcomed the comfort. She was going to need it.

When she looked up, Jae-Jin looked back at her.

CHAPTER SEVEN
SPECTRE

LANA HADN'T MOVED in many hours; she had lost track of how many. The room she sat in was small and dark, the only furniture a battered futon on one of its last lives, illuminated by the glow of a massive flat-screen television hanging from the wall. She stared around her room through thick, round glasses with gleaming silver rims. Black hair with shocks of purple, blue and green trailed down her shoulders, cut shorter on one side than the other. Her small body was swaddled in an oversized military green coat lined with worn sherpa, and her legs were tucked underneath her. Black and white tattoos snaked up both shins.

The futon floated in a sea of crushed papers, stacks of books, and uncapped pens leaking ink into the floorboards. Cardboard moving boxes of various sizes lined the walls, some stacked up to the low ceiling. One of the larger ones had been clawed into and now overflowed with an endless mountain of black clothing. An enormous cat with reddish-orange fur snoozed contentedly atop these, occasionally emitting a small snore.

A medium-sized box that looked well travelled lay open next to the futon. In the shadows, its tangles could be mistaken for the probing arms of an unfamiliar creature crawling the bottom of the sea. A closer look revealed dozens of *Ancestral* Orbs in states of near death. The buttons on some lay at strange angles. Several were cracked open, spilling their digital guts into a cardboard grave.

Lana held fast to the Orb in her lap, a tiny planet to hold close. It was painted matte black. She stroked the thumb buttons idly as she watched the screen, waiting. Patience was one of her strongest suits, and she embraced it now as she looked at her match screen to see who the next challenge would be. At this time of night, local players were not as active, but the American players were just waking up. These were the ones she relied on to sharpen her teeth.

When the wait was long, she returned to her stats screen to count her kills. Tonight, as usual, she maintained an undefeated streak. She'd played sixty-four rounds since she sat down, most of them over in less than ten minutes. While it had been a rush at one time to beat people that fast, lately she didn't feel anything. It was getting old, maybe. Victory was one kind of high, but true challenge was another. And there had been a severe shortage of the latter these days.

She felt a warm body brush against the edge of her thigh and looked down to find a small, desperate face staring up at her.

"Perseus," she said, her tone shaped by love. "What do you want, boy?"

The huge cat headbutted her shin fiercely. There was no clock in the room, but one wasn't needed as her roommate was happy to remind her it was dinnertime.

An ache bloomed along her right side as she got up from the chair. Like her other injuries, she paid it no mind whatsoever. Living with pain had been her everyday life for so long that she had no memory of what it was like without it. Some would be angry or miserable living this way. She saw it as neither; only the reality of her life, and one she had little say in.

The kitchen counters were also piled with boxes, these smaller than the ones in the living room. She moved one aside to retrieve a bag of cat food and scooped some out to fill Perseus's bowl. His sing-song meows certainly weren't her language, but no translator was necessary to understand them. She petted his big head as he started to crunch his way through the food. Little chewed bits flew here and there. Even though his mouth was full, he started to purr.

Lana made her way through the piles of junk back to the television to find a blinking invite awaiting her, a tiny American flag icon next to it. She settled into her chair and picked her Orb up off the floor. As she thumbed the right pad to wake it from sleep, it twitched once in her hands and grew warm, giving off a nearly indiscernible hum. It was amazing the things you grew attuned to hearing when your life was lived in silence. The tiny whistle of Perseus's breathing when he dreamed, the awakening of a fall morning, her own breath, mortal and fragile: these were the melodies of her life.

Her opponent had chosen Xi'Shannah Market, a colourful map densely packed with tight passageways crammed with vendor stalls. There were entrances to its respective graveyards on the northwest and southeast ends, but small passageways could be found along the edges that also led to them. It was a challenging map, and one that she enjoyed for that very reason. Plus, she always enjoyed the carnival of colour, perfectly accompanied by the joyful cacophony of rabab, oud, and kamenjah.

She thumbed the left button to confirm and waited. Those long, sacred seconds before she dropped into the game were precious to her. They crackled with life and promise, but there was also peace there. It was the only respite she had.

✦MATCH BEGIN✦

As usual, the map started in a narrow, cobblestone-lined hallway. Flags, purses, hammered trays, and teapots were hung from floor to ceiling in vendor stalls so closely crammed the goods spilled haphazardly into neighbouring spaces. Behind her, an alcove led to a short path to the graves. It was one of three entrances, making the task of keeping the enemy out of it particularly trying. But as she'd long learned to master the simpler levels, these more complex maps were her preference by far.

Lana stood still as she assessed the map. Masses of Onyx awaited her, to be expected. Swimming in the sea of them was one player dot glowing in the southwest corner.

One? They're alone?

She was taken aback. She rarely ran into challengers willing to play her solo, much less play solo at all. Rather than reduce the number of Onyx as some might do to even out the chances for a single player, *Ancestral* doubled them. Which explained why the map was swarming. Those creatures were going to have to go before either of them had a decent shot at each other.

Either this one hadn't checked their stat screen beforehand, or had and didn't care about the consequences. She was tempted to check them herself, but pushed away the itch. It would have been easy to assume her challenger was a fool. But in her time playing she knew one thing for certain: assumptions of any kind were dangerous. Still, her interest was piqued.

She spotted two Onyx moving slowly along the map's eastern wall, trying to make their way to her by taking the long way around. These side-creepers aimed to take advantage of players that only focused on what was right in front of them. She snaked down an alley, switching between rows as she went to make her passage appear erratic in case her opponent was watching. As she drew to the edge of a stall draped heavy with leather bags of countless shades of ochre, her eyes flicked to the map again.

She turned on her cloaking ability with a button tap, pairing it with Fade, a spell that allowed her to teleport up to twenty feet in a perfect instant. She only had a moment to register the Onyx's presence as her claws reached out and crushed their torsos, jerking them as they crumpled to the ground. Her tentacles caressed the bodies as she moved over them to make her way up the eastern wall past a stall of old cages manned by a snake charmer. He tossed a cobra at her as she passed. She ducked in perfect timing, used to the game's little touches.

A pack of Onyx spilled into her path from an alcove to the right, knocking some tin teapots to the ground as they trundled along. She bashed the one closest to the front with a claw as the others grunted in surprise. The health circles of two others caught fire. Within a few moments, the rest followed suit.

There was a time when Lana considered Raging Onyx to be a threat. Today was not that day. She continued to bash the beasts, ducking their swipes when it was necessary. One's head squelched between one of her claws like an overripe grape. She was about to chop through the rest of them with light attacks when she noticed five more taking up the rear. They weren't Raging yet, but they would be soon.

Might as well, she thought.

She triggered a Transcendence with a pop of her finger. The writhing mass of feelers dancing beneath her waist glowed with an emerald light and exploded out in every direction, reaching for the throats of the eight Onyx that were still alive. They coiled around once, then twice as the beasts gagged. Saliva rippled from their mouths in rivulets. They were uglier than ever.

The sky darkened as she held her prey. As the Transcendence entered its final stage, a circular symbol cut into the air above their heads in a vivid purple, depicting a star with several other lines drawn around it ending in tiny circles. Lana watched as the lines lit up from left to right. When they finally connected, all her tentacles clenched simultaneously. Death all around her, all at the same instant. It might have been terribly skewed and unfair, but it was also pretty fun.

Leaving the bodies behind her, she crept into a

narrow passage between two merchant stalls. Each was lined with huge sacks overflowing with legumes, potatoes, and grains. Behind these stood an old wooden bookcase lined with glass jars of many sizes, all filled with spices. Bare light bulbs dangled overhead. The proprietors were nowhere to be found.

Her opponent's dot wasn't too far away. A few more Onyx stood between them, and she moved in their direction, intending to take them out to clear her path to her objective. They came into view, and she reared back with a claw. But as it hit the first of them, she noticed the other player had broken away and was darting towards a different entrance to the graveyard. Trying to take the win while she was occupied.

Lana activated cloaking again, pairing it with Fade. She vanished from the Onyx's sight and reappeared a few paces from the graveyard entrance to see a Brutalist charging towards it at full speed. She strafed to intercept its path and bashed it in the face with one of her claws, feeling a glow of satisfaction as it bounced off her invisible form and hit the dirt. She was going to strangle it. This would be fun.

The Brutalist rolled to the right as it pulled its hand scythes from the sheaths on its legs.

An impressive recovery, Lana thought. *But it won't last long.*

Her opponent looked around to find the thing that had hit them. There was nothing—at least, nothing that she saw. Cloaking was the dirtiest trick in *Ancestral*'s playbook as far as Lana was concerned, but it was also available to her thanks to a simple mod, so she saw no reason not to use it. Still, that feeling gnawed at her once again: regular players just didn't pose any threat anymore. The high of a real challenge was missing.

If she'd been in a different kind of mood, she might have drawn it out. Instead, she bore down on the Brutalist and clamped its neck in one of her giant claws. As the player struggled to free itself, Spectre—her avatar—drew the lifeforce from her victim's parted lips. It passed from one to the other in a golden stream of light. Her claws dropped the body as the familiar congratulations scrolled across the screen.

If I'm going to keep going, she thought, *I need a real challenge.*

CHAPTER EIGHT
THE MAN IN A RED CAP

THE GLASS CANNON was in a part of town Lissa never visited. She knew the gaming bar was a great place to hang out and hone her skills when it came to competitive play. Despite that, something kept her from making it a habit. She loved the idea of a place created just for people like her—awkward types with imperfect social skills—and knowing most of the inhabitants spoke her language. But actually speaking that language with strangers was another story altogether. She was still not so sure the world contained many people worth trusting.

She eased her Honda between two white cars and switched off the ignition, glancing around to make sure she had everything she needed. A black leather laptop bag made to look like a giant tome of spells occupied the seat next to her. She peered inside at her Orb in its purple velvet drawstring, nestled atop her phone and wallet, and took a deep breath. Nervous flutters spread through her chest like tiny bolts of lightning.

Crossing the parking lot, she took a moment to

admire the bar's front doors. They were twice as tall as her and made of a burnished gunmetal. Blackened rivets lined the edges, and the handles were pipes mounted on round metal plates. She paused, breathed in deeply through her nostrils as Devon had taught her—it steadies the spirit, he always said—then pushed open the door.

The decor had changed since her last visit, which was long before *Ancestral* even existed. The wall behind the bar depicted the entire first level of *Super Mario Bros*, one she'd memorised as a child with a Nintendo controller nearly glued to her chubby fingers. In front of it, several girls with brightly dyed hair colours and tattoos were busy making drinks for their customers. One with hair the faded blue of a robin's egg glanced in her direction, her gaze ringed with sooty eyeliner.

A song from a chiptune band she liked pumped through the bar's sound system, filling the long room with an appealing cheer. To her left, an area for tabletop gamers was sparsely populated by a few residents. Six guys were carefully adjusting their playmats and shuffling their decks for a game of Magic. A cute couple in retro-inspired outfits sat a few tables behind the Magic players. The girl, whose vibrant red hair was pulled into a high ponytail, laughed happily as her date patted a stack of board games on the table in front of them. Lissa grinned. They were cute.

Off to her right, circular tables were set up like battle stations, ringed with flat-screen monitors. Some players sat in chairs before them, Orbs in hand. Others milled about the room, talking to others or looking uncomfortable. A few teenagers were clustered around an intense-looking blonde guy wearing a red baseball cap as he played, watching his screen with rapt attention.

Lissa made her way to the host station as a cocktail of scents drifted through her senses, some less pleasant than others—she wondered why deodorant was a foreign concept to some people who loved video games.

Behind the station, a man with tortured-looking platinum hair scribbled something on a clipboard. An oversized bomber jacket hung loose on his small frame, covering his hands up to the knuckles.

"Uh, excuse me. Where do I sign up for the tournament?"

He looked up through messy bangs. His expression identified her as an intruder in his private quarters.

"Here. Wait a sec." He scanned the clipboard again, then looked across the room. "I gotta find the guy with the card thingy. Here." He thrust a clipboard in her direction. "I'll be back. Oh, there's a pen there." He gestured to a pen cup on the counter before vanishing into a back room.

Lissa flipped back a few pages to find an empty spot to write her name and contact info, noticing as she went that much of the handwriting was borderline unreadable. She printed her name and placed the clipboard back on the counter, returning the pen to its cup. Bomber Jacket had not come back yet, so she glanced around the room instead. None of the faces here had ever come to PlaySpace—that she would have remembered. In a way she had hoped she might see someone she knew, maybe to strike up conversation with them. But on the other hand, it might have been easier to know no one, to just focus on the game, the win.

"You on here?" Bomber Jacket had returned, peering at the sign-up sheet.

"Yeah, I need to pay," Lissa said, fumbling in her messenger bag for her wallet. Once she found it, she fished it out and handed over her card.

"Sweet," he said, sticking it into a white plastic device. "It'll email you a receipt. Go to"—he paused, waiting for the transaction to finish and show him the info he needed—"ah, thirty-two. Third table from the door, left side."

A firework of nerves bloomed in her chest as she made her way over. As usual, it was mostly men in the room. This was something Lissa had seen many times before and had no choice but to get used to. Even so, at moments like this she always felt as if she'd barged into the gentlemen's smoking room with her cleavage showing.

Many of the chairs were occupied, but two at the table she'd been assigned still stood empty. Breathing slowly through her nostrils to steady her nerves again, she took her Orb and stand out of the bag and placed it on the table before her. The people near her spot barely registered her arrival, most of them deep in practice runs. A skinny, nervous-looking Black guy on her right, wearing rectangular glasses with thick lenses and a blue striped shirt, sat clutching a modded-out red Orb with stickers all over it, staring at his monitor with a pained expression. She glanced at it. He was in the net, about to choose what branch to take next.

A feeling like a ping went off in her heart.

Talk to him.

Her inner compass rarely steered her wrong.

"It's hard to choose, right?" she said, gesturing at the screen.

He looked up at her with a mixture of relief and gratitude, and she felt a needle-prick of empathy when she saw the face of a person who clearly needed someone to talk to. Her hunch had been right.

"Impossible," he said, pushing his glasses up his nose and sighing. "The skills start to get so much stronger, and I feel like if I choose one route..."

"FOMO," Lissa said, snorting.

"Yes!" the guy said, shaking his hands in the air in frustration and laughing. "This damn game. What do you play?"

"Plunderer. You?"

"Weaver. I love nature so I couldn't resist. All those big bad earth spells. It's just too tempting for a guy who would happily sit in a forest all day long." The guy glanced around for a moment. "Is this your first tourney?"

Lissa shook her head. "No, why do you ask?"

"Well. First off, you're a girl and I hardly ever see girls at these things. So, it's nice to see these stinky dudes don't chase you all away." He laughed. "Also, you're friendly. It's just my second, and... well, people just haven't been that friendly at these."

He reminds me of Quin.

Lissa's heart jumped as her brother's face materialised in her mind. It wasn't the way he looked but... something. Something about him felt familiar. The way he smiled.

As she thought of it, a grin bloomed on her face.

She extended a hand to her seat mate and watched his face light up in reply.

"I'm Lissa."

"Lucas. Nice to meet you. Seriously, you're the first friend I've ever made at a tourney. Maybe that's why all the dudes are afraid of girls that game. You're so much more down to earth than they are. Meanwhile they're all caught up in who they're gonna beat. Like a bunch of puffed-up peacocks."

Lissa laughed.

"Seriously! Look at them. So worried some other dude is going to wipe the floor with them." He lowered his voice. "I mean, did you see that group clustered around that dude with the red cap? You'd think they were planning a world war, not doing an *Ancestral* run."

Lissa glanced back in their direction. Red Cap had clearly won a match, judging by his expression. Several of the guys were trying to talk to him, but he didn't seem to be acknowledging them. There was something about his face that Lissa didn't like. Something strange.

She turned back to her new friend.

"I like your style, Lucas."

"Man! Thank you!" He stuck a hand into a black messenger bag with a few sewn-on patches. She had a moment to notice several—a neon D20, a pride flag, a stylised Yoda from *Star Wars*—before he came up with a bag of trail mix, offering it to her. "I was starting to lose hope that there were any decent people in this scene."

"Well, you know esports. Like you said, it's all competition."

"Do you consider yourself a competitive gamer?"

Lissa noodled the question around in her brain for a minute.

"I am but... not in the same way? Like, I am. No doubt. I want to be one of the first women to win a regional *Ancestral* championship."

"Whoa!" Lucas gazed at his friend with a newfound awe.

"But I guess to me it's not about who I'm better than," Lissa said as she powered on her monitor. "The only person I really compete with is myself, if that makes sense. Beating my own scores, my own records."

"You could teach all these dudes a thing or two, then." He grinned at her.

"Have you ever been to PlaySpace?"

"PlaySpace? What's that? I just moved here."

"Really? From where?"

"New Orleans. I grew up there, but my dad got a new job a few months ago, right after I turned sixteen. So, here we are."

"PlaySpace is a gaming cafe. It's over by Johnson Creek where the park with the big statues is. The owner is even an ex-competitor! I'm there just about every day. My friends and I have been hoping to compete as a team when *Ancestral* regionals get announced."

"A gaming *cafe*?" Lucas exclaimed. "We don't have those where I come from. That sounds awesome. Do you work there?"

"Oh, no." Lissa thought back over what she'd just said. "I guess I just sounded that way. PlaySpace is like my home away from home. I feel like it's a part of me."

Lucas smiled, reflecting the warmth in her face back at her.

"I'll definitely check it out. If it's that meaningful to you, it must be a great place."

"For sure," Lissa replied, coming out of her little reverie. "So, what about your Brutalist? Where you gonna take it?"

Moving his mouse to wake up the screen, Lucas clicked away from the net to show her his character. It was a level thirty-six and starting to gain some moderately strong attacks. While she'd only played Brutalist a little in the beginning when she was deciding what class she wanted to play, she knew it well from playing with Ji-Soo.

"Well, it's an offensive powerhouse which is why I picked it. I always like to tank. I love how strong it feels to play this character. But I also know focusing on just brute strength can prove to be a weakness later. Some of these new moves offer buffs and I'm not sure if I should lean towards those or keep building attack power."

"I'd say it depends on your goals," Lissa said. "Do you enjoy soloing with random teams, or do you want to play with people you know?"

"I used to play with my friends back home, but after I moved, I stopped seeing them online as much," Lucas said, disappointment showing in his face. "So, I far prefer to play with people I know, but I don't know anyone here yet."

"You know me."

Lucas's face brightened.

"I do."

"So," Lissa said, "how you choose your build depends on what role you want to play in your team. Let's say you and I played together. I run Plunderer, so I can take health from the enemy, but my class has low HP compared to yours. If you run a high damage build, you might be able to keep Onyx clear of me, but if they get past you to me, I don't have the best defences."

Lucas nodded, looking thoughtful.

"But if I balanced my current attacks with some buffs…"

"You could fortify the rest of the party. If we had a Mender, it might not be as big of a deal because their healing powers could balance it out. But as I'm sure you know, sometimes it's hard to find one."

"Right—I've been thinking about building one of those, too."

"That's smart. It's good to have a few builds to choose from, although don't listen to me. I clearly didn't follow that route."

"Plunderer is the coolest-looking class, though."

"You think?" Lissa looked at her monitor, where Nagiko stood at the ready, gleaming daggers with hilts wrapped in dangling strips of red fabric in each hand.

"To me, yeah. But I wanted more muscle."

Both laughed as a voice boomed across the room.

"Challengers, we will start in five minutes. Please join the lobby with your team of choice."

"You're on my team," Lissa whispered to her new friend. "My teammates are joining, so I promise no one sucks."

"But what if I suck?" Lucas said, looking anxious again. "It sounds like you guys are well versed. I haven't played competitively much yet—"

"But do you play for fun? Or do you want to go to championships?"

The young man's brow darkened as his gaze went to the floor. Perfectly understanding his struggle, Lissa waited as he gnawed on the idea. After a few moments, he looked up at her and gave an emphatic nod.

"Yes. I want to go. Especially if I can fight on a good team."

"Then this is how you learn to do it. You might be less experienced than us or make mistakes, but it's the only way to get better. So, it's OK to fail."

"I like that."

As the two of them made their way to the game lobby, Lissa picked up her Orb and offered it in Lucas's direction.

"Friend me and I'll add you to the team now."

Lucas obliged, holding his Orb close to hers. There was also something about it that looked a little different, although she couldn't quite figure out what it was. Both controllers blinked blue, searching for a connection. After a few seconds, the blue gave way to a steady purple glow.

"Your Orb looks tricked out," Lissa said. "I'd love to know what you did to it. I haven't started doing stuff like that with mine yet, although I know I should learn."

"I'll teach you!" Lucas said in a bright voice. "It's easy and fun. And overclocking them makes your attacks *way* faster."

As they both put on their headsets, Lissa heard Jae-Jin's voice.

"—so then I add some stuff from the farmer's market, you know. Dried shiitake mushrooms are the best, you gotta have those, and—"

"Since when do you cook?" Lissa said, and the other voices on the line burst into laughter.

"Hey," Jae-Jin said. "I'm not cooking, just adding some things to ramen. Makes it better."

"So that's why you couldn't come today. Had to stay home and make your top ramen fancy."

"You're the worst," Jae-Jin said in his dry way. "You know I have chores today."

"I brought a new friend I met here," Lissa added. "His name is Lucas, he's a Weaver, and he's somewhat new to tourneys. So, I thought we could show him the ropes."

"For sure," Jae-Jin replied. "Welcome, Lucas. Let us know if you have any questions."

"Thanks, I will."

"I'm here, too," Ray piped up. "Hey Lissa! Welcome Lucas! Sorry I couldn't be there in person today, I overslept. Again."

"Ray is our Mender," Lissa explained. "We're so lucky to have one. The healing spells are great, of course, but Thirst of the Leech makes that class so much fun to play."

"Oh, man," Lucas said. "Isn't that the one where the bugs surge up out of that black river and suck the enemy to death?"

"Yessss," Ray said, and the relish in his voice made everyone laugh. "Oh oh, here we go."

As the level loaded, the group found themselves in the Temples of the Elder Gods, a dense, overgrown forest dominated by the ruins of ancient Xi'sho houses of worship. These foreboding stone sanctuaries towered above their heads and were densely covered with intricate designs from bottom to top. Faceless gods writhed in bas-relief on the side of each entrance, their heads piled high with ornaments. Their blank stares left a chill in the air.

Huge oak trees with thick trunks loomed on all sides, their massive roots bursting from the dirt below. The foliage above their heads was too dense to let in much light, but the little there was played along the crumbling walls of the old structures looming before them.

"Let's split up. Two at a time," Jae-Jin said. "Ray and I will go to Wu'sho Temple. Lissa, you and Lucas go to Qi'sho."

Jae-Jin and Ray vanished into one of the temples on their left. Lissa moved towards the hefty columns that framed the entrance of Qi'sho Temple. She'd walked through this alcove many times before, and yet, it always put her on edge to be in an enclosed space with nowhere to run. She checked over her shoulder to see if Lucas was following. He was—and close enough to be her shadow.

A mess of fallen bricks blocked the Qi'sho Temple entrance, their surfaces mottled green with moss and rot. Lissa sprang from one to the other, careful not to let her feet linger for too long. Too much weight and these could collapse at any moment. She approached what was left of the doorway, her eyes flicking to the mini-map to keep an eye on her teammates.

"Good so far," Jae-Jin said. "They may be in the other temples—"

"Here!" Ray said. "One's in here."

"Vine 'em." Pleasure was already prickling in Jae-Jin's voice. "I'm checking the second level."

Lucas hopped onto the ledge of the first level of the

Qi'sho Temple, Lissa close at his heels. They moved into a dark stone room, the ceiling over their heads partially crumbled away. Swinging her lantern, Lissa checked the room's dark corners and found them empty. They inched towards the open space above their heads as a notification appeared, perfectly timed with a hoot of triumph from Ray.

✦XXKILLER278XX HAS BEEN
ELIMINATED BY DYNAMIX✦

"Nice, Ray!" Lissa said. "First blood!"

"Nothing like choking a man to death with a vine," Ray said, and Lucas chuckled.

"Otherwise, we look clean—let's move to Ba'sho and San'sho. Careful when you exit. People love to wait there to snipe."

The parties moved towards the entrances of their respective temples. As Lissa neared the doorway, a skull came flying and nearly grazed her face, shattering against the wall behind her.

"Careful," Lissa said, strafing to the left. "At least one Morteist out there."

"I got something for that," Lucas said, firing off Scythe Slash through the opening. It didn't connect on the way out, but the blades cut through some meat as they flew back to his hands.

✦BICHWHATEVA HAS BEEN
ELIMINATED BY IMPACT✦

"Lucassss!" Lissa cheered. "Sweet!"

"Don't go out yet," Jae-Jin warned. "They might rush us."

A guttural bellow sounded outside, and Lissa's skin prickled with discomfort. As another returned the call in the hopes of finding its kin, Jae-Jin tossed a tracker through the doorway. It lit up the mini-map, briefly showing the positions of the enemies on the field for three seconds.

"They're in San'sho!" Ray said. "Three of them, anyway."

The party darted in the direction of the temple, which was situated further away from the others. A tunnel of tightly twisted branches led to its entrance. As they ran up towards it, Jae-Jin threw a handful of skulls into the dark. The party watched as the death heads swirled to form a massive spectre, easily the size of a bear. Its jaw unhinged and it howled a gust of agony into the tunnel.

✦YAHYAH898 HAS BEEN
ELIMINATED BY JAEBOMB✦

Lucas cheered. "Didn't even get a chance to come out."

"Leer of Mortality—satisfying every time," Lissa chuckled.

"Don't get cocky, guys. We still have more to do," Jae-Jin said.

The four darted through the tunnel, avoiding the bodies as they made their way to the other side. The entrance to the San'sho Temple stood some thirty paces away. It was clutched tight in the roots of a primeval tree, its tentacles white with age. Bricks it had pushed out of place as it took hold were scattered around the entrance. The bodies of a few downed Xi'sho lay nearby as well. Lissa noticed that one's head had been flattened so completely that its features had drowned in misplaced flesh.

"Something's been here," Lucas said. "Maybe still inside."

"Not inside," Jae-Jin said. As they watched the scene, an Onyx emerged from an alcove in the tree's roots, gnawing on a human leg. It tried to grind its way through a strip of tendon, found it too difficult, and spat it on the ground with a grunt of disappointment.

"Wait—" Jae-Jin started, but before he could get another word out Lucas darted forward to attack with surprising speed. The beast's howl of rage rent the air as it dragged a battle-axe that had survived many a war through the dirt and up into the air. Lucas took advantage of the weapon's slow ascent and went for the creature's exposed belly with his scythes, yelling with excitement.

"How ya like that, buddy?"

The other three dashed into the fray to assist. Ray's Mender extended its bony arms as a spray of rotting swamp water plumed forward and shot into the Onyx's mouth. It staggered, choking on the soup of decay. An excruciating howl came from the nook in the roots. The party turned to find several more snarling Onyx emerging. Saliva streamed down their chins.

Lissa swung her lantern in a quick attack, stunning all three and chipping away at their health. She kept an eye on her power circle, waiting to stack up the combos she needed to cast a Transcendence. The Onyx she had been hacking away at crumpled to the ground, rotten breath trailing warm from between its teeth.

"Whoa," Lissa said as she watched the body of the Onyx she'd just killed submerge under a black wave.

Another fell and splashed beside it, quickly sinking into the swamp below. As it churned it formed a circle around the party, significantly reducing their damage taken. She looked up to see Jae-Jin's battle-axe decapitating the last two Onyx in a single mighty swing, leaving a trail of dark energy behind. It was Final Exit, his most powerful Transcendence, and he had timed it well.

"Good," Jae-Jin said, calm as a man playing a long game of chess. "We're down to the leader. Let's get inside."

"Seems like an easy match so far," Lucas said.

"Never speak too soon," Lissa murmured, her eyes scanning through the dim light and over the mossy walls. As the silence grew, her mind flashed back to the match with WraithX. A nervous shock spiked in her chest.

What if it happens again?

"They've moved on, I think," Ray said, moving fast around the perimeter of the temple. "Track again, Jae?"

"I only had one, unfortunately. Anyone else have one?"

"Nope."

"I don't, sorry."

"All right then," Jae-Jin said. "Let's get back out and do this the old-fashioned way."

"Jiu'sho Temple?" Lissa suggested.

"Sure."

They emerged to find three Raging Onyx lumbering down the tunnel, closing in fast. Jae-Jin's voice was steady and alert as he called out to the team.

"Ray! Tundra Magic!"

"On it, boss," Ray replied as his Mender moved into a squat and sank its fingers into the dirt. The ground trembled beneath them as a deep rumble emanated from the centre of the earth. With a lightning crack, fissures split under his hands and surged across the ground before them. One of the Onyx paused for a millisecond too long and tumbled down one of the steadily widening crevices. The other two jumped out of its growing path, nimble as hyenas. Before Ray could stand, one of these leapt to his side with horrible speed and gored his shoulder with its teeth.

"*Damn* it! There goes my no-hit bonus," Ray grumbled as Lissa cast Steal Essence, draining the Onyx nearest her and topping Ray's HP back up with its energy.

"Thanks."

"I got you."

"Death Flight coming," Lucas said, breathless. "A few more seconds."

"I'll hold them off," said Jae-Jin, as he hurled handful after handful of skulls in the Onyx's faces, blinding them momentarily. They snarled in annoyance, swinging without sight, the terrible squeaking of their knees rending the foetid air. One landed a few blows on Jae-Jin, shattering the combo he'd been building up and knocking him flat. A swing from Lissa's lantern was the only thing that kept them from leaping onto his prone body.

"Now, Lucas! If you can!"

Lucas's avatar had already bowed its head. Its wings lashed the air as they reached towards the sky, metal gleaming in the soft light of the grove. A second before they moved, the last standing Xi'sho emerged from the mouth of the tunnel, guns blazing. An Equalist.

"Now that's timing," Lissa said as Lucas's wings made their great sweep forward, blowing their opponents back several feet. Before they could regain their footing, the wings had made their transformation to swords. As he executed the sword swing, the two final Onyx were sliced top from bottom, their torsos falling gracelessly to the ground. The Equalist had rolled away in the meantime, perfectly avoiding one of the most powerful Transcendence moves the team had at its disposal.

"Ugh," Lissa said as their opponent vanished into the tunnel. Jae-Jin dashed, already in pursuit. The others trailed behind, ducking left and right to avoid the bullets flying through the air.

"If we can corner him, Souls of the Pack is ready," Ray said, his voice excited. "That should finish it."

Jae-Jin didn't reply, his axe bobbing on his back as he darted ahead. Lissa knew how he could be in the endgame. As good a leader as he was, he also tuned everything else out when he was focused on the final target. This was the point at which they had to know each other's moves so well that they could work together without words.

"There!" Lucas yelled. "The clearing!"

Lissa spotted a flash of the Equalist's red boots as it dashed through the field where they'd started the match. She put on a burst of speed to reach it faster. As she closed in, Lucas's avatar descended from above, wings fully spread to glide down at just the right speed. Lissa had a moment to marvel at how fast he was before he landed atop the Equalist, tackling them to the ground.

"Yes! Nice!" Jae-Jin yelled into the mic. Lissa giggled. He did have his uncharacteristic moments, even though they were few and far between.

Shots blasted erratically as the enemy tried to break the hold, but they were drowned out by the sound of thundering hooves that signalled the start of Ray's Transcendence.

"Yeah, Ray, stomp 'em!" Lucas said. "Go, go!"

The thunder grew louder. As the earth thrummed beneath their feet, a dozen animals poured forth from between the trees. Moose led the pack with their great antlers thrust forward. Wolves twice as big as dogs darted between their legs, snarling. Wild boar brought up the rear with their heads bobbing wildly, teeth splaying from their mouths like a wild burst of weeds.

Lucas jumped out of the way as the stampede drew close. The Equalist was not so lucky. The animals drove forward with mighty cries as their hooves trampled his body over and over, squelching what little life was left. Its guns clanked to the ground, cold and useless.

✦THEMINDKILLAH HAS BEEN
ELIMINATED BY DYNAMIX✦

"Yes! Yesssss!" Lucas yelled, pumping a fist in the air. Lissa high-fived him, high on the energy of the win as Ray hooted into the mic. Jae-Jin, as usual, waited for the cries to subside before speaking.

"We did well," he said when the noise died down. "Did you shake your opponent's hand?"

Lissa looked at the space across from her for the first time since the match started.

"There's no one there. They must have left right after the win."

"Ah, well," Ray said. "Well, I gotta hop off, I have a class to get to tonight. See you all tomorrow at the 'Space. Great game!"

"Same for me, I need to finish making lunch," Jae-Jin said. "Text me if you need a team, Lissa."

"Sounds good."

Lissa and Lucas removed their headsets just as Bomber Jacket was making his way to their side of the table. He stared at Lissa for a few seconds too long before he spoke.

"You two made it to the next round. Come back next week and you'll play against the other winners from today."

"Cool," Lucas said, looking like a kid on Christmas morning. Lissa watched his face for a moment, a little glow of happiness blooming in her chest. It was a great thing, she thought, to see a person shine so bright.

The sound of a chair scraping the floor cut through the murmurs of post-game chatter. Lissa looked to her left to see the guy in the red cap had stood up and was staring at her from across the room with something like a glare. She felt instantly uncomfortable.

"Want to get burgers, Lissa? My treat."

Grateful to be spirited back into the conversation, she turned back to her new teammate.

"I'd love that."

CHAPTER NINE
MASTERMIND

LOGAN WILLIAMS WAS not a quitter. If anything, he considered himself the kind of man to get the job done. It was for this reason that he was still awake while the rest of the boys slept, passed out on sofas and tables and just about anything other than their own beds. You could party hard with the rest of 'em, smashing glasses and hollering big words all night long—and he did, because he had every intention of living his life to the fullest—but you couldn't just bow out when you had work to do.

That was not how champions behaved.

He had never been much of a sleeper anyway. He'd kept his mother up all hours, she'd told him, long after babies were supposed to grow past their bedtime-hating stage. It wasn't that he rebelled against her when it was time to go to bed, with her kind, tired face and her weak smile. He'd never done that. His childhood bed had been a cosy place with its cloud-soft covers and should have lulled any normal kid to some gossamer dreamworld in a handful of minutes.

But as soon as he laid his head on the pillow, it was

as if the thing was infused with all the world's energy crammed into a soft rectangle. Within seconds he was so awake that sleep felt impossible. He'd groped for it the way one does for the details of a dream as it falls apart in the waking mind. And that's how it'd been for the last twenty years. This was why he often said sleep was for the weak.

And so now he was propped up in a busted, threadbare couch chair, an unremarkable shade of taupe, which was pushed a couple of feet away from the living room wall. He glanced up at the blue and white banner in the entryway that faced the front door of the frat house. A green-skinned creature leered back at him, the glass contraption on its head protecting a pink, pulsing brain. Between its claws, it held a partially shredded banner with words that looked as if they'd been scratched in with a dull knife: Team Mastermind.

The gaming tables—nothing more than a couple of dinky plastic event numbers with folding metal legs—were on the opposite side of the room, but they were littered with crushed Rager cans—the company that sponsored them—and empty red plastic cups that Logan had no intention of picking up. That was too much work, and it wasn't his mess anyway. He made a point of drawing people away from that area during parties, but they seemed to make a beeline for it no matter what he did. It was annoying. But they always wanted to know about the setup. The line-up of mounted monitors and Orb rests made it clear that it was more than just gaming for fun.

Logan knew there were a few other *Ancestral* players in the frat when he moved in. At the time it hadn't been on his mind to try to form a team. He'd only been a few months into playing the game himself, although he'd entertained a few four a.m. fantasies of hoisting a gleaming gold cup above his head while faceless fans cheered from behind the glare of the lights. It wasn't so much a dream as a thing he knew he deserved, along with every other bounty life could bestow. As far as he was concerned, he was just on this trip to get what was coming to him.

His Orb cast a screen on the wall where he was playing a solo match in the San'sho Lands of Prayer, his personal favourite map. The shifting sands of the desert terrain made it easy to hide. Also, choking Onyx to death with a fistful of sand was something he loved to do, indicated by the fact that he'd been doing so for the last four hours.

To his left, he'd propped his laptop open on their old coffee table to stream the match. It was early as hell, but some people were watching. Lately, he'd noticed more people from overseas popping up when he played at this hour.

As the kill screen came up and he won the match a sliver of light peeked through the blinds of the window over the kitchen sink, positioned perfectly as a sniper's shot into his right eye.

"Jesus Christ," he said, putting the Orb down and heading across the room to close them tighter. The microwave clock told him it was twenty to eight in the morning. He rubbed his eyes and picked up the coffee pot, which smelled stale. No one had emptied it since Friday; it was now Sunday morning. The sink was piled high with unrinsed dishes and cups, but he was able to rearrange them enough to get a clear shot at cleaning out the pot and refilling it with fresh water, careful to steer clear of one bowl with an unidentifiable dried substance in it. He took the pot back to the stand and turned it on. The burbles of the machine warming up was a nice sound. Liquid energy would be here soon.

A familiar groan came from the other side of the living room. Logan knew its melody well: finding yourself alive with a throbbing headache and every limb of your body heavier than Stonehenge. He padded across the kitchen and into the living room in his bare feet, careful to step over the beer bottles and their spilled contents. An old grey velvet ottoman his roomies had fished off the street months ago was shoved into the corner across from the gaming tables. A slender man with messy, longish hair was curled into the foetal position atop it, his hands covering his face in the classic gesture of a dude with a bangin' hangover.

Logan crouched next to him, waiting to see if his presence would be noticed.

"Bro? You OK?"

The index finger and middle finger parted to show one bloodshot eye. The man mumbled something indistinguishable into his palms.

"Can't hear ya, dude."

The eye blinked slowly as its owner processed this information. The palms parted at the bottom to let the mouth emerge.

"Bathroom."

"You need help?"

The man nodded from behind his palms. Logan placed an arm around his shoulders and pulled him up to a sitting position. With his hands still clamped over his face, he looked very much like a child trapped in a twenty-two-year-old body.

"Tyler... you gotta see to walk, man."

Tyler's shoulders drooped. His hands came down slowly. The guy had no trouble with the ladies normally—he was tall and had a real charmer of a smile—but Logan would bet his last dollar his fan club would be nowhere to be seen if they got a look at him now. He hadn't shaved for days, and his lips were badly chapped. The dark circles under his eyes added fuel to the fire.

"Come on," Logan said as he looped an arm around his friend's waist. It felt insubstantial. It dawned on Logan that Tyler hadn't just dropped weight playing basketball in the afternoons with his jock friends (not that he'd done that in months anyway). He could feel the guy's ribs.

Standing slowly, he guided Tyler to the bathroom down the hall, pausing a few times along the way. He'd barely closed the door when he heard the toilet seat hit the tank and the sound of retching. He rubbed his eyes again as the roasted fragrance of coffee wafted his way.

After pouring himself a cup he made his way back to the chair, figuring Tyler would either fall asleep on the toilet or crawl out of the bathroom when he was ready. He liked the guy and liked playing with him, but he was also well aware of his faults. His inability to stay sober was one of them. And now that *Ancestral* regionals were about to be announced—or so the Rager rep had told him, anyway—they were going to have a chat.

Footsteps shuffled down the stairs. Jared appeared wearing a bathrobe and an oversized white t-shirt with unidentifiable stains near the collar. It mostly disguised his growing gut. It was impossible to tell if he was wearing underwear or not, although Logan thanked whatever higher power of the universe that chose to save him from seeing his friend's junk.

"You still up?"

"Never slept."

Jared looked at the closed bathroom door. "Tyler in there?"

"Yep."

"Man." Taking notice of the coffee, he ambled over to the counter to pour himself a cup, then came and sat down next to Logan on a lone red barstool near the chair. "You talk to him?"

"Today." Logan nodded. "As soon as he comes back to reality."

"Didn't he hook up with some chick last night?"

Logan snorted as he woke his Orb from sleep.

"I dunno, man."

Jared frowned.

"It's annoying sometimes that the most lazy-ass member of this team gets the most attention."

Logan reached out and clapped his friend on the shoulder.

"That, my dude, is chick logic. That's why I live by my motto: Bros first. Besides, we'll have our pick of 'em once we win this regionals title."

Jared grimaced, shaking his head.

"How we gonna do that with him though? He's such a good player when he's on it, but he's been a mess lately. We've been able to do it till now somehow but we gotta keep that top spot."

Logan sat down and began powering through a solo match, not looking up from the screen as he spoke.

"Then we kick him out. I don't care how good he is."

"I thought he was one of your best friends."

"Not when he's playing like crap, he's not." On the screen, Logan's Mender pulled an opponent close as a tangle of seaweed wrapped around its throat. The swamp goddess leaned forward and exhaled, a plume of filthy water flowing from her mouth into his. The kill banner unfurled a few seconds later.

✦BICHPLZ HAS BEEN ELIMINATED BY WRAITHX✦

The bathroom door creaked open. Both men looked up to see Tyler holding fast to the doorknob with a few wet spots on the front of his t-shirt. He looked more alert than he had when Logan had found him on the ottoman.

"Screw tequila, man," he croaked.

"You gotta get it together, bro," Jared said. "We gotta practise today."

Tyler peered at the microwave clock.

"It's eight a.m. on a Sunday. There's plenty of time." He groaned, holding his head. "I need aspirin." He headed through the kitchen and started pawing through the cabinets in search of a painkiller.

"Well, I'm up since the sound of you barfing was too loud to sleep though. So I may as well go get my Orb. Gonna shower real quick, but I'll be back."

Jared made his way upstairs, taking his coffee with him. Logan continued to play as Tyler dry-swallowed three aspirin, then came back over, looking at him.

"You're pissed at me, aren't you?"

"Not pissed," Logan said, still looking at his game. "I just need you to get it together or Team Mastermind's gonna be Team Nobody real soon."

"We're still at the top of the leaderboards."

"And what if we had to defend that right here, right now?" Logan said, still focused on the screen. "Look at you. You couldn't play."

"Why are you giving me grief, man? You were right there partying with me last night."

"But I'm training this morning and you aren't. That's the difference. Do you think we're always gonna be at the top? Because I can tell you, we're just big fish in a small pool right now. Click over to the national leaderboards sometime. The last time I looked we were down in the eight hundreds. We have a long way to go."

Tyler made his way over to the stool Jared had occupied a few minutes before. His face was sour.

"I don't want this the same way you guys do. I thought I did. But not anymore."

Logan finished off his last opponent with a brutal quickness, then turned to look at Tyler.

"When were you planning on telling me this?"

"I just did."

"Well, I don't care if you want it or not."

Tyler narrowed his eyes. He looked confused and exhausted.

"We can't afford to lose you. You're too crucial to the team. But I'm telling you now that if you don't get it together and play the way I know you can, we're gonna have problems. I'm not losing no matter how many bottles you throw in the way."

"I just told you I'm not into it anymore."

"You have to be. We can't replace you right now. Besides, your wild nights are courtesy of them right now." He nodded in the direction of a stack of Rager boxes next to their gaming tables. "You think we can afford to party like this without a sponsorship? We can barely keep this place afloat. If it wasn't for Chad's rich parents dishing out the rent, we wouldn't even have this dorm."

Tyler ran a hand through his dirty hair, looking around the room in frustration.

"So, you're telling me I can't quit."

"Yep."

"You can't tell me what to do."

"Yes, I can."

"You're a dick," Tyler said, standing up with such force that the stool toppled to the ground behind him. Both men ignored it. "I'm not your slave, you can't just make up rules and expect me to obey them."

Logan looked at his friend sharply.

"I just did, and you bet your ass you'll obey them. Get it together. If you don't, I'll make your life hell. You think about that next time you're eyeing some chick you want to drink the night away with."

"Screw you." Tyler headed for the stairs, wobbling as he went.

Logan turned his attention back to the screen. He flicked his way through menus to the stats board, setting the filter to his region. He did this dozens of times a day, sometimes on his phone when he was away from the game. It gave him a brief moment of relief every time he saw their name on the top of the US leader board. The gap between them and the number two team was wide enough that he didn't worry too much about them stealing their slot. But what he did worry about—and he had shared this fear with no one else—was being eclipsed by some motley crew that would shoot up the ranks out of nowhere. He'd be the chump then. The guy who had worked so hard for so long, only to lose it all to some nobodies.

He'd seen it before. To a certain degree, that's how Mastermind had done it, although he'd credit it to hard work over talent. That, and the six of them clicked perfectly when they played together. They'd gotten along, too. At least, until this Tyler business got in the way.

When he'd moved into the house seven months ago things had been different. It was still a messy frat occupied by a bunch of clueless boys trying to figure out their lives, and he was one of them, so that was OK, but when it came to the game, they were all on the same page. They got to their classes and maintained their grades, but what they really wanted to do was form a winning team.

It was Chad who suggested the tables setup. They'd all pitched in and managed to score two of them from a sorority having a yard sale. Logan had helped Chad carry them in and set them up, and they'd 'borrowed' a few folding chairs from the storage room at the meeting hall. It was far from a glamorous setup, but it worked. And sometimes when they all sat and played together, Logan would imagine how it might be when the tables were much nicer, and their monitors grew from dinky hand-me-downs to massive screens and their trashed dorm was nothing more than a rags to riches memory.

His imagination had wandered far and wide: living in a high-rise in a swanky penthouse, having a gaming pad so slick other players would burn with jealousy at the sight of it. Their team logo plastered all over the walls, not on some cheap flag all of them had pooled their pennies to have printed. A lounge area with leather massage chairs and a huge 4K TV and a shelf for all their trophies.

Longing for it was one thing. Logan didn't wish for it the way a kid dreams of a thing he wants to have, but doesn't actually believe he'll get. Instead, he saw it as an inevitable reality. One that he and his boys were destined for and entitled to... as long as Tyler got his act together.

That was why he wasn't overly surprised when the email from Rager came. In fact, they were late as far as he was concerned. Mastermind had been on the top of the leaderboards for weeks by the time it popped into his inbox. The offer was about what he'd expect at their level, with a fun twist: Rager was an alcoholic energy drink, and they wanted to send cases of it over. They also wanted to know if Mastermind planned to participate once regionals were announced, and if so, could Rager pay their entry fees?

Damn skippy they can, Logan had thought. He was only mildly disappointed they hadn't offered flights and a hotel, too. But lucky for them, Seattle was a three-hour drive, and cramming six dudes into one hotel room was a trick he'd pulled before. Besides, Rager was just a stepping stone and he knew it. They were small fry—very small fry—on the world scale. But getting a small company meant larger ones would eventually notice. And when they won regionals, they'd have their pick of the bunch.

It was after they'd accepted the offer that they went from weekend parties to weekday parties. Three-times-a week parties. Every night parties. There was always alcohol in the fridge rather than just what they could afford. And no matter how much of it they drank, Rager sent more. The company was delighted to see its product on camera when Mastermind streamed their matches.

Mostly the guys handled themselves well, which was what Logan had expected. After playing with them for six months he felt he had a pretty good handle on them, but Tyler had been the wild card. Despite all of them being good and working well together Tyler was on another level. Some kind of freakin' prodigy. He never lost a match that Logan knew of. He was fast, crazy fast. It was as if he had a map of how the match would go in his head before it started, and he knew what direction to head in at all times. He'd have been a good leader if he thought to call any of this out, but he wasn't much of a talker unless a woman was in front of him. In the game he worked silent and quick, vanishing on the regular to clean up the map here and there. The dude was a ninja.

He'd never seemed like the responsible type out in the real world, but he was so damn good at *Ancestral* it didn't matter. The others covered for him in the house without talking about it: doing dishes he left behind, turning away girls looking for him when he was already 'entertaining'. All of them knew that he was the heart of the team, even if he didn't seem to know it himself. And more than once each of them had the thought that when they had a chance to finally compete on a stage, that Tyler would be the one to get them there.

And now it was like this.

Logan realised he was gnawing on his bottom lip as he tasted the metallic pang of blood. It was a nasty habit, one he'd had since he was a kid. He only did it when he was stressed, and as he thought about all this, he realised that was very much the case. He was also afraid, although he would go to his grave with clenched teeth before he would admit it. Because if Tyler left, he took his magic with him—the world would see that Mastermind had really just been one great guy with a bunch of mediocre guys around him sopping up the spotlight. They'd lose their sponsorship and their followers and people would make fun of them. That was what would happen.

Jared reappeared at the bottom of the stairs with barely towel-dried hair. He looked much more awake—the shower had clearly done him a favour— and had his coffee cup in hand. His previous attire had been traded for a pair of grey athletic shorts and a massive Run DMC shirt. His Orb dangled from its strap on his left wrist.

"All right," he said as he made his way over to where Logan sat. "Lemme refill this cup and it's on."

After topping off the mug, he headed over to the gaming tables.

"You wanna set up over here, man?"

Logan looked in his direction.

"Yeah. I don't know why I settled over here in the first place."

"Actually, wait."

Logan watched as Jared wandered back to the

kitchen, opened the cabinet under the sink and took out a garbage bag. He came to the table and shook the bag out to open it up.

"Can you hold this?"

Logan stood and put his Orb down in the chair, then walked over to take the bag from his friend. Jared extended one arm across the length of the table and used it to sweep the empty cans in the direction of the bag. They clinked as they made their way inside.

"That's better. I just can't play in a mound of garbage. Here, I'll take that."

He made his way to the back door, and Logan heard the sound of him stuffing the bag into one of the garbage cans outside. The sound of a dog barking a few doors down drifted through the air before he came back in and shut the door. Then he returned to the table and parked himself at the chair closest to the end. Logan followed suit, taking the chair across from him.

"Where you wanna start?"

"Your pick, man," Logan said. A wave of exhaustion had rushed over him out of nowhere. He shook his head to clear it away as he reached over to power on the monitor.

"I'll do it 'random'."

His character screen loaded. He stared at his Mender with bleary eyes. There had never really been any hesitation on his part when it came to picking who to play. This beauty, with her ink black hair and joyless face, was the only option as far as he was concerned, despite the formidable powers the others wielded. Something about her had just called to him from the very beginning.

"Should we stream?"

Logan looked in the direction of his laptop.

"I was before you got up, with the mic off. I'll just move it over here."

Jared nodded, watching him amble across the room and carry his MacBook to where they were set up. He paused to check if Tyler was around before asking Logan.

"Did you say anything?"

"You bet I did."

"How'd he take it?"

"Not well."

A long silence unrolled between them before Jared spoke again.

"I'm worried, man."

Logan fished a cheap-looking vape out of a pocket, eyeballing it before taking a drag. Finally, he responded.

"I don't think he's going anywhere."

"Why not?"

"Because if he does, I'll straight-up kill him. Now let's play."

CHAPTER TEN
A SPECIAL
ANNOUNCEMENT

LISSA WANDERED THE space between the world of sleep and waking, comforted by the primordial fog where the real world faded. This place was comfort. Solace. Everything blurred at the edges. Sometimes waking, leaving this place, felt like the last thing on earth she wanted to do.

Thoughts entered, sharp as needles, quick like the stabbing of a tattoo artist's tool. Repeated pinpricks, each more nervous and insistent than the last.

I have to learn to mod my Orb or...

But Lucas said he'd teach you.

But I should have learned on my own by now.

I'm lazy.

I'm going to disappoint my friends.

I'm not good enough for a real tournament.

The kill screen rolled across the back of Lissa's eyelids, a leering marquee.

✦MONONOAWARE HAS BEEN
ELIMINATED BY WRAITHX✦

Lissa's heart rate ticked up as she tried to wish the thoughts away, already knowing they always won.

Defeated, she opened her eyes. The ceiling fan whirled lazily above her as exhaustion held her head fast to the pillow. She hated waking up this way. But it happened almost every morning. Some were worse than others. Sometimes, on some rare, blessed occasions, the voice went silent for a day or two. She didn't understand why, but she was happy to take whatever reprieve she could get.

She thought of the voice inside her as a tiny chattering monkey with bulging red eyes and a frozen grin. She imagined holding it in the cup of her palm as it flapped its arms in a horrible dance set to a rhythm only it could hear. In her fantasy, sometimes she balled her hand into a fist to crush it to death and silence it forever. But if she uncurled her fingers, it would be mysteriously unharmed, this wretched thing that was never born and would never die.

Sighing, her head rolled to one side of the pillow. Her phone lay there, its notification light blinking green: one-two-three-four-five-six-seven-eight.

Eight messages?

The image of the monkey dissolved into sand as Lissa shifted closer to consciousness, grasping the phone off the nightstand and flipping open the case. Her lock screen was a wall of notifications from Parse(d), the social media site's group chat app she and her friends used. Above that, she had a direct text from Ji-Soo, every word in capital letters:

LISSA! REGIONALS!

Lissa sat up in bed, her bleariness cut cleanly away. For a moment everything felt perfectly frozen in time: the soft cotton of her nightshirt gentle on her skin.

The brightness of the sun seeping through the linen curtains. Toast laying across the end of the bed, her delicate snores wafting in the silence.

Before she knew it, the moment had passed, and her thumbs were flying across the screen to open the chat and read what she'd missed. Everyone was typing at the same time, and Lissa scrolled up quickly to try to catch up on the log.

> **Jae-Jin (8:06 am):** *It's regionals time.*

> **Zio (8:42 am):** *WHAT.*

> **Jae-Jin (8:42 am):** *Check your email.*

> **Zio (8:42 am):** *@Lissa! @Ray! @Ji-Soo! WAKE UP*

> **Jae-Jin (8:43 am):** *You know they sleep later than we do.*

> **Zio (8:43 am):** *I know but this is big! I'm gonna call them!*

> **Jae-Jin (8:44 am):** *Why? They'll see it when they get up anyway.*

> **Zio (8:44 am):** *Because I'm EXCITED. Aren't you?*

> **Jae-Jin (8:45 am):** *Of course I am.*

> **Jae-Jin (8:45 am):** *but I'm not gonna blow up everyone's phone over it, not everyone gets up early. We all knew this was coming.*

> **Ray (8:49 am):** *WHOA GUYS*

> **Zio (8:49 am):** *AHHHHSLKJAHLAKJSHA*

> **Ray (8:50 am):** *I'm so glad you called, best news to wake up to ever!*

> **Zio (8:50 am):** *@Jae-Jin SEE I WAS RIGHT*

> **Jae-Jin (8:52 am):** *brb coffee*

> **Zio (8:53 am):** *argh trying to get Ji-Soo to pick up but she's not answering*

> **Zio (8:53 am):** *I NEED EVERYONE HERE TO SHARE MY JOY*

> **Jae-Jin (8:59 am):** *We need to firm up some things*

now that this is really happening.

➤**Jae-Jin (8:59 am):** *and we need to solidify the Team Phoenix brand if we have any hope of getting sponsored.*

➤**Ji-Soo (9:07 am):** *I'm here*

➤**Ray (9:07 am):** *Ji-Soo regionals is happening! In Seattle!*

➤**Ji-Soo (9:08 am):** *finally. I'm texting Lissa. Best bday gift ever*

➤**Zio (9:08 am):** *I think she's been more excited for this than any of us. She works so hard*

Lissa frowned at this last comment as she started to type.

➤**Lissa (9:22 am):** *REGIONALS!!111!*

➤**Ji-Soo (9:22 am):** *YASSSSSSSSS*

➤**Ray (9:23 am):** *Lissa omg I am so excited, couldn't wait for you to get here. Can you believe it?*

➤**Jae-Jin (9:23 am):** *It only took them a year.*

➤**Zio (9:24 am):** *you really are a glass half empty kinda guy, aren't you?*

➤**Jae-Jin (9:24 am):** *Low expectations means less disappointment.*

➤**Lissa (9:25 am):** *So it's in August. We have two months to train*

➤**Ray (9:25 am):** *Haven't you guys been training for a while now anyway?*

➤**Jae-Jin (9:26 am):** *Sorta. It's different when you actually have the goal in your sights.*

➤**Jae-Jin (9:26 am):** *But... we really gotta pull it together now. Because to qualify we have to be in the top five ranking on the regional leaderboards.*

➤**Jae-Jin (9:26 am):** *I have some ideas though. Need to talk to Devon. I think he'll be able to help us prepare for this better than anyone else.*

➤**Zio (9:26 am):** *agreed*

➤**Lissa (9:27 am):** *I was planning on going over to play today anyway so that works out well. But I may go sooner since I have nothing else planned today*

➤**Ji-Soo (9:27 am):** *Me either. No time like the present!*

➤**Ray (9:28 am):** *I have some chores to do but I plan to be there by about 3*

➤**Jae-Jin (9:28 am):** *I'm going to play a few more matches here and then pack up and head over.*

➤**Lissa (9:28 am):** *A few more?*

➤**Jae-Jin (9:29 am):** *I get up at 6 and play for a few hours every morning.*

➤**Zio (9:30 am):** *You missed your calling in the military*

➤**Zio (9:30 am):** *lol*

➤**Jae-Jin (9:31 am):** *If we want to be good enough for regionals, you'll be doing it with me soon enough.*

➤**Ji-Soo: (9:33 am):** *Yeah.*

Lissa nodded to herself. Jae-Jin might be single-minded, but he was also easily the best player among them thanks to his laser focus and consistency. They all played with the desire to get better. But his approach had a different quality to it. To Lissa, it seemed as if he was fearless. If any of the same demons that inhabited her head were in his, he had perfected the art of hiding them. She flicked to her email app to look at the announcement herself, quickly noticing that her friends had left a few of the details out in their excitement. The most important one—the date for applications—she found buried at the bottom of the message below the lists of sponsors and prizes. July 1, 2030. Next month. She flicked a finger down her phone screen to open the calendar and count how many days were left between now and then.

Only thirteen days.

Her brain started to churn as the purr of her thoughts gained traction.

You need to mod your Orb if you're gonna have a chance at this thing. So, text Lucas. And add him to the group chat while you're at it. But first get to PlaySpace. Talk to the team. We need jerseys. You need to practise. You need to set the alarm for six a.m. tomorrow and start whipping your butt into shape.

Her anxiety rattled. When challenges came along her path, she often felt simultaneously overwhelmed and terrified. It was enough to shut anyone down and, in fact, had immobilised her in the past more than once. She had no idea these were panic attacks until she talked to Ji-Soo about them one day and watched her friend's face darken with concern. That was when she learned it wasn't normal to feel these things. She knew she should tell her dad, but she didn't feel ready to just yet. He had enough to deal with on his own.

She did have one defence when the feelings got intense—the breathing Devon had taught her. And as the trembling energy of overwhelm raced up her throat, she closed her eyes and envisioned his face in her mind, the kind eyes, the comforting smile.

Through your nose first... one, two, three...

Lissa breathed. A sense of calm flickered as she counted the inhales. And as she allowed herself to sit in the middle of all this new information, a clear thought settled into her mind that didn't need to shout to be heard.

Jae-Jin is right. Devon has been through all this before. He'll know exactly what to do. So, one thing at a time.

Lissa opened her eyes, threw off the covers and headed for the bathroom. Before she could even think about becoming the first *Ancestral* regional champions, she needed to take a shower.

LISSA WAS RUNNING a round brush through the ends of her hair when she heard a knock at her bedroom door. She expected her dad to peep his head in, but instead Ji-Soo appeared with a confident grin. She wore a slate blue wig that faded into a soft seafoam green at the tips, a brightly striped sweater, and olive cargo pants. The cuffs were tucked into a pair of pink and purple Doc Martens with the silhouette of a sculpture on the sides. Surely she'd chosen an equally loud bag to go with her ensemble, but it was nowhere to be seen.

"So, if I know you—and we both know I do—I know that you're a wreck right now," Ji-Soo said, raising an eyebrow in Lissa's direction. "But on the plus side, your hair looks great."

"I'm actually not," Lissa said, shutting off the dryer and setting it on its stand. "How's that for insane? I feel OK."

"That *is* insane. Almost as crazy as the idea of Jae-Jin noticing I'm alive."

"His loss if you ask me," Lissa quipped, adding a touch of lip gloss and a few swipes of black mascara. "But I guess everyone's love life aspirations have to be back-burnered if we have a chance in hell at this thing."

Ji-Soo sighed.

"Lissa. I've known you your whole life and I'm not going to try and change you now. But for just this one time… do you think you could consider that we can and *will* make it?"

"I don't know that for a fact."

"OK, fine. Neither do I. But I do know the way we think affects things. Look at Jae-Jin. Do you think he's sitting around thinking that our chances are slim?"

Lissa had been putting away things on the bathroom counter, but now she stopped and looked at her friend, whose face had gone from sunny to overcast.

"He's not. I can tell you that. He's looking at the end goal. And I think we should think about what we can learn from him—and from Devon."

"That's the first thing on my mind," Lissa said. "Getting to PlaySpace and talking to Devon. Because yeah, one part of me wants to just play and play and play till my fingers bleed. But that's not going to make me a great player."

Ji-Soo was nodding. A flicker of sadness appeared in her eyes, hesitated, then decided to stay. She made her way to Lissa's carefully made bed and sat on the edge, facing the bathroom door.

"Can I talk to you about something?"

Lissa looked at her friend, then came to sit down next to her. Ji-Soo looked at her shoes, tapping her boots against one another.

"So, my mom called a few days ago."

A peeved expression appeared on Lissa's face.

"Is she still trying to get you to go home and take over the restaurant?"

Ji-Soo's shoulders drooped as she spoke.

"I mean, yeah. But it was different this time. I think something's wrong with my dad."

"You *think*?"

Ji-Soo looked up at her friend. Her face looked both sad and humiliated.

"I know I've told you before that my family is weird. We don't just... say things outright. No one does. But my mom said something that made it sound like something was wrong with my dad. She looked upset. But then I asked what it was, and she told me she couldn't talk about it right then."

"That is bullshit."

"You're telling me. And the messed-up part is, she could be using this as a trump card to get me to go home. You know she's all about the guilt." Ji-Soo laughed unhappily. "That's my family for you."

They sat in the quiet for a few passing seconds. Then Ji-Soo spoke up again.

"She almost cried on the call."

"Your *mom*?"

"Yeah."

Lissa shook her head. "You've always told me she was a total ice queen."

"She is. It's why I was so freaked by it. Most of the time it's the same old story: you're abandoning the family, you're wasting your life, we're ashamed of you. I know how to deal with all that. But this is something different. And worst of all, I don't know what it is."

Lissa watched Ji-Soo's face. Her eyes looked glossy and afraid. She reached over and wrapped an arm around her.

"I can't believe this is happening when regionals are finally here," Ji-Soo said after a minute or so. "I can't miss that. I just can't."

Lissa nodded, then laid her head on Ji-Soo's

shoulder. The other girl did the same. They sat silently for a while.

"You know," Lissa said, "I'm going to support whatever you decide to do. Even if it means we have to go to regionals without you. I know things have always been tumultuous with your family. But if something is wrong with your dad and you choose not to go back, will you be OK with it?"

"I don't know," Ji-Soo replied, her voice hoarse. "He's never been nice to me. Neither of them have. I think I'll cry when he's gone, but I'll also be relieved."

"Are you worried how it would affect your mom?"

Ji-Soo thought on this before replying, nodding her head as she did.

"More my brothers. They worship my dad." She paused. "Mom told me Cho is living with an esports team now."

"Oh, man. Salt in the wound."

Ji-Soo sighed. "Under the circumstances I don't really care. They're boys, they get treated with all the privileges boys get in pro gaming. I love my brothers. I miss them. But we've grown apart since I moved away. Honestly, I hope Cho succeeds though. I want him to be happy."

Lissa hugged Ji-Soo once more, then stood up. Her hands went into the pockets of her jeans.

"You know you don't have to decide today."

Ji-Soo nodded. "You're right. I will soon. But not right now."

Lissa's phone vibrated, rattling against her nightstand. She picked it up to peer at her notifications.

"It's Lucas. He's going to meet us at PlaySpace and show us how to mod our Orbs."

Ji-Soo perked up, her familiar grin reappearing.

"He sounds like the coolest."

"He really is. You'll see soon. Do you feel OK to go, after what we just talked about?"

Ji-Soo nodded.

"You support me more than my own family ever could, Lissa. Thank you for that."

Lissa smiled and hugged Ji-Soo tight.

"Now," Ji-Soo said when the two parted. "Boba?"

CHAPTER ELEVEN
MODDING THE ORB

THE FIRST THING Lissa saw when she opened the door to PlaySpace was a hunched figure sitting on the grey sofa in the entryway. A worn green ball cap with fabric fraying around the brim covered his face. An oversized white hoodie and similarly baggy jeans swallowed what looked like a thin frame. He spun a red Orb through his fingers as it appeared to hover, never touching his palms.

As the bell on the door jingled, Lucas looked up and broke into an endearing smile, like a kid on the playground who's proud to show off a missing tooth. Lissa felt goofy as she grinned back. Something about him made her feel brighter, like even if she made a big fat mistake in the middle of a match and humiliated herself, he'd be next to her all the while, grinning in his crooked way.

Before she knew it, he was standing up and giving her a bear hug, and she squeezed back as if they'd known each other for ages.

"Friend," he said, striking a pose that would have looked right at home in a *Dragon Ball Z* smackdown.

"You ready to bring your Orb to the *next* level?"

"Only if it's over nine THOUSAND!" she growled, and the two dissolved into happy giggles.

"This must be Lucas," Ji-Soo said as she trailed in, ending a phone call and tossing the device into a purse shaped like a milk carton.

"Yeah. Lucas, this is Ji-Soo, my best friend."

Lucas stuck out his hand to shake, turning his big smile on Ji-Soo. His eyes took her in as she gripped his hand, and grew a little wider.

"You're... *really* cool," Lucas said, and Ji-Soo giggled.

"I hear you are, too. I wanna hear more about this whole modding Orbs thing."

Lucas nodded emphatically. "Yeah! I'm happy to show you."

"Man, what's going on in here?"

Devon ambled into the lounge with an energy drink in one hand and an apple in the other. Lissa noticed he'd added some tiny beads to the locs nearest his face that looked like little skulls. She detected a sparkle of amusement in his eyes.

"Devon! This is Lucas. We met at the tourney last weekend."

"Sweet! You excited for regionals?"

Lucas's eyes grew wide.

"I was born for this, my dude. And this—"

He twirled his Orb in one hand and spun it like a basketball, grinning.

"—is my weapon of choice."

A hearty laugh bubbled out of Devon.

"You, I like. How is it that the best people always find their way to us, Lissa?"

"Well, I found him."

"You sure did. Lucas, can I see your Orb for a minute?"

"Surely." He handed it over without missing a beat. The three of them watched as Devon examined the device, making an effort to handle it with care. After checking out the buttons, he spun it upside down to look at the panel on the bottom, which held the internal components within. His brows pushed together as recognition crept onto his face.

"Did you... solder the panel in a new position?"

Lucas bobbed his head. "Yep. And I also rewired a few of the connectors. It's a good device, but it could be better. This one is now, anyway. Those extra couple of seconds I get out of it can mean winning matches I'd have had no chance at otherwise."

Lissa peered at her friend.

"Lucas... how did you learn to do this?"

"Oh, my dad. He repairs computers for work, and he's also built them all his life, so I got to watch him do it growing up. He helped me build my first when I was nine. Wasn't very good, but... it turned on?"

Devon laughed again, in that way he did when he was enjoying himself. The sound of it made Lissa a little happier about the stray she'd brought home.

"Your dad sounds like a cool dude," Devon said.

"He can be!" Lucas nodded before getting back on point. "Anyway, the Orb is just an independent system. A little computer, you might say. So, like everything else of that nature, it can be modified if you know the basic components. I did have to break a few to figure out what I did, but now I have plenty of spare parts on hand in case I want to build one from scratch one day."

"From scratch," Lissa repeated, nodding slowly. Lucas caught the look on her face and turned a warm smile in her direction.

"Don't sweat it, I'm not gonna make you remember all this stuff. You can watch if you wanna learn, but if it's too much for you, no big deal. I bet there's a lot of things you're great at that I would totally mangle."

"Just between you and me," Devon said, sitting down on the sofa, "Lissa is the most gifted *Ancestral* player I've ever seen."

"*Thank* you," Ji-Soo piped up in agreement as Lucas nodded next to her.

"Trust me, I noticed!"

"Guys," Lissa said in a pained tone, looking down at her boots.

"All right, fine. I know you hate it when I tell the truth," Devon said, giving Lucas a secretive glance. "Don't let me keep you two if you're gonna start crackin' Orbs. We have a few new people coming by today, so I gotta get ready to show them the ropes anyway."

"Speaking of the ropes," Lucas said, "how does this place work, anyway? Do you buy a membership?"

Devon nodded. "First visit is free. After that, people can sign up for pass packs or for monthly memberships. The latter is cheaper, of course. There's a VIP membership option open to you after a year. Which, of course, she has." He gestured in Lissa's direction with a pointed finger and a wink.

"Gotcha. Well, you should probably give me a rate sheet then, because I have a feeling I'll be hanging around."

Devon chuckled. "I'll find one for you before you

leave. Lissa, you wanna show him around this time, since you two have already hit it off?"

He grinned and wandered away before she could answer. She looked at Lucas and found him watching Devon with the expression of a man newly in love.

"If you think he's cool now, wait till you hear about his competitive gaming days."

"Really?"

"Yeah. They called him The Little Fighter."

Lucas shook his head. "Man, I feel like I stumbled on the jackpot. I have no idea how long it would have taken me to find this place. And everyone's so nice."

"Speaking of, let's see who else is here. You've played with some of them already, so you've kind of met a few of them. But let me show you the rest of the 'Space, first."

"I'm gonna run to the bathroom," Ji-Soo said. "Catch up with y'all in a minute."

They murmured their assent as she walked away. As they made their way to the gaming stations, Lucas gave a little yelp of glee.

"These carpets are the coolest!" he said, pointing at the floor. Before she knew it, he had slipped off his shoes and was rubbing his socked feet on the rug's pile. Lissa half expected him to get on the ground and roll around in it.

"You're kind of like a puppy," she said, laughing at his blissful expression.

"I get that a lot. So... you know all these people?" He glanced to his right, where a few guys in hoodies and jeans were setting up a match on the monitor in front of them.

"I know a lot of them, but as *Ancestral*'s gotten

bigger, more and more new people keep showing up. Which I'm glad for, since I know it helps PlaySpace thrive. But there's a part of me that misses when it was just us."

"Us?"

"Ah, me and my team. Which, now that you've seen this area, we should probably introduce you to."

"Cool. I'm ready." Lucas stood up, and Lissa noticed that there wasn't a glimmer of nervousness on his face. She had a brief flash of envy as she wondered what life without social anxiety was like.

"OK. This way."

When they got to the door of their unofficial training room, Jae-Jin was the only person there. He was bent over one of the table monitors. As usual, he looked extremely focused on what was surely a replay. A pen and a scratch pad sat to the left. As they watched, he muttered something to himself and paused the replay to scribble on the paper.

"Hate to interrupt your tactical research, but I want you to meet someone."

Jae-Jin looked up. For a millisecond, Lissa saw what it was that her best friend liked so much about him. His features were very attractive in an angular sort of way despite his eternally pensive expression. But as soon as he started talking, he went back to being regular old Jae-Jin, a guy who took everything way too seriously but was kind of lovable because of it.

"Hello," he said with no change of expression whatsoever.

"Do you remember a few days ago when we played the tourney I went to? With my new friend Lucas?"

"This must be him," Jae-Jin said, rising from his

chair and making his way over to them. He stuck out a hand, which Lucas shook.

"You had some clever moves, man."

"So did you," Jae-Jin replied, much to Lissa's surprise. "First time here, yeah?"

"Yeah. I had no idea it was here. Wish I had known sooner. I usually play alone at home."

"Do you mostly run Weaver?"

Lucas looked thoughtful. "Well, I had intended to just play one class first. But I got curious, so I did a little levelling with Morteist. Such a fun character."

"That's my main."

"Yeah, I remember! I just love the spells. So now I practise that one sometimes, too. I figure it makes sense to have more than one strong option on hand. That way you can adjust to play with more teams."

"He thinks like a strategist," Jae-Jin said, giving Lissa a clinical look. "This is good. We need more of that around here."

"Lucas, show him your Orb."

Lucas swung his backpack around to the front and unzipped the large pocket. He fished the Orb out of a medium-sized drawstring bag and presented it with both hands. Cocking his head to one side, Jae-Jin drew closer to the contraption.

"Is it modded?"

Lucas bobbed his head again. Without a word, he flipped the device over to show the panel on the bottom.

"Is there something different about it? I have to admit, I am not tech-savvy at all."

"Ah, nothing wrong with that. Let's sit down and I'll show you as best I can with this one. I think Lissa's going to let me mod hers next, so when we do that, you can see exactly how I do it."

The three made their way back to the table, and Lissa and Jae-Jin each settled next to Lucas to watch. He laid his drawstring bag on the table and flipped his Orb on its top. Nestling it against his right hand, he pointed at the panel on the bottom.

"So, I was telling Devon in the other room that an Orb is just a tiny, fairly simplistic computer. The same way you can overclock a computer by altering the CPU's clock rate, you can alter this puppy. Do you know anything about overclocking?"

"Not a thing," Lissa said. "No one on this team is much into tech. In fact, one of the reasons so many people are attracted to *Ancestral* is because it doesn't require a computer to play. Just the Orb."

"Right," Lucas said. "Well, there's some complexity to it, so I'll try to give the TL;DR version. So overclocking sounds like a thing nerds do to their computers in the dark, and while that's sometimes the truth, it's nowhere near as technical as it sounds. Every CPU has a clock rate, which tells the computer what speed to run at. Moderate overclocking means tweaking the clock rate a few speed grades higher than the specs. This is not dangerous at all when you know what you're doing. With me so far?"

Both nodded. Lucas nodded with pleasure as he went on.

"Awesome. So, you get the real results when you move into more than a few speed grades. You can also overclock your memory and graphics cards on a computer. Boom!" He shook both hands in front of his face in an explosive motion. "The key to doing this well is to perfectly balance the way all these systems play with one another. I had to break a few Orbs to figure that out. But I am pretty sure that some players at the top of the leaderboards are working with clocked Orbs. And I figured since I want to hit it, too, it was worth it to lose a few to figure this out."

"So could mine break if you do this?" Lissa asked.

"Highly unlikely now that I've sorted through the issues on my own models. But I can't one hundred percent guarantee it would be safe. Ninety-nine percent, sure."

"He can do mine, if you don't feel comfortable, Lissa," Jae-Jin said. "I want max performance, and this is something I could never do myself. Worst case, I buy a new one."

Lissa glanced at her lap. Her hands rested on her bag, and she could feel the Orb within. It was cool to imagine it becoming more powerful than it was now. But she also wondered if she might feel like she was cheating by doing it this way.

"So," she said as she looked back up at her friends, "will this give us an unfair advantage?"

Lucas shook his head with emphasis.

"An advantage, yes. Unfair, no, not in my mind. This is more like changing your old running shoes for brand new ones. You can still do all the things you like to do. They'll just feel cleaner and better. Like the day you took your Orb out of the box."

Jae-Jin nodded, his expression thoughtful.

"OK," Lissa said. "I'll do it."

"Yay!" Lucas held a hand up in her direction. She reached up to return the high five, feeling cheesy and happy at the same time.

"How long does it take?" Jae-Jin asked.

"Maybe an hour or so. Do you two want to watch?"

"Heyo," said a voice from the door, and the three looked up. Ray and Zio stood there, both holding fast food bags that smelled of oil and fried deliciousness. Zio was stuffing a few fries into her mouth when she caught sight of Lucas.

"Well, hello, new face," she said after swallowing her food. "Are you by any chance Lissa's tourney friend?"

Lucas looked up with a grin.

"That's me. I'm Lucas. And your hair is awesome."

"Thanks!" Zio said, a delighted sparkle in her voice as she tucked her purple locks behind her ear. She made her way to his side of the table, plopping herself in the empty chair at his side. "So nice to meet you! Ray told me you were a beast in the game the other day. I figured we'd see you around here eventually. Do you want some fries?"

"I'd love them, but I'm about to break open Lissa's Orb so I probably shouldn't have greasy hands."

"Break it open?" Ray said, sounding bewildered.

"Well, overclock it. I've done my own and Lissa was interested in having hers done, too, since she wants to compete in regionals." Lucas moved his own Orb to the left and rustled in his backpack, taking out a smaller zippered bag and his phone. He tapped the screen to bring it to life and opened a folder named CLOCK'D. A bright orange icon called Timetuner was first in this folder, which he opened as the group watched.

"Timetuner," Zio said in a hushed tone. "I love it."

"I just told Lissa and Jae-Jin, but if you want to

watch it takes about an hour. I can try to explain as I go if anyone is interested."

Zio and Ray drew closer.

"I'll take that as a yes," Lucas said, laughing. "OK, so it all starts by connecting the Orb to an overclocking app via Bluetooth. It monitors the process and gives me access to the system's clocks. But one thing I discovered is that even though you can overclock it without opening it, it hurts the Orb's ability to do other things. By removing the panel and reversing its placement, I'm able to give the wires room to breathe and slightly reposition the components. This allows me to alter the clock to the speeds I want. Lissa, may I see your Orb?"

The rest watched as Lissa unzipped her bag and handed the Orb over. Lucas took it and unfurled a piece of thick black felt before laying it down. Holding it in place, he removed a small plastic stand from his own zipper pouch and placed it underneath, giving the device a firm place to rest.

"First, let's get this connected to my phone..."

Lucas swiped his phone to bring its screen to life and tapped through Timetuner. Then he turned the Orb upside down and depressed a button right below the panel. It flashed blue, confirming the connection.

"OK," he said. "Now we open it so we can make room for the system to breathe once I modify it."

The friends watched intently as Lucas took a plastic glove from his pouch and put it on. He unscrewed the panel and reached inside, turning his fingers with the tiniest of movements.

"Did you ever build models?" Jae-Jin asked.

"I haven't, but always wondered if I might like it."

147

"My dad and I did when I was smaller." Jae-Jin took his phone out of his pocket. "Wonder if I have pictures. Anyway, you need a steady hand and to be slow and careful with your movements or you'll ruin the model. Watching you just now reminded me of that."

"Building models seems like a very Jae-Jin thing," Zio said, peering at him over her cat-eye glasses.

"All right, that's done," Lucas said. "Now, we play with the clock." He tapped the app again and rotated the phone sideways. When he moved his hand, the group could see a black screen with two electric blue circles on the display. Both were encircled by numbers. Sliders for the core clock and the memory clock of the system nestled between. As they watched, Lucas started to move the slider for the core clock one tick at a time.

"Can you hurt the Orb like this?" Ray asked.

"Sure, if you don't know what you're doing. Before you get a feel for a system it's a matter of trial and error. But I'm comfortable with this generation of Orb now. When it gets updated, I might be back at square one again." A white bar appeared around the left circle as Lucas spoke, slowly making its way around the perimeter.

"I wonder," Zio said, "if high-ranking players are working with overclocked Orbs?"

"Almost certain they are," Lucas replied. "Before I modded mine I struggled to get a one hundred streak on solo. Now I can coast to three hundred easily."

No one said a word, but the awe was palpable in the room. Lissa noticed Ji-Soo had returned and pulled up a chair to watch.

"I feel like Devon should be here to see this," Zio said. "I'll be right back."

"He's showing new people around," Lissa called after her friend.

"Just gonna check!" Zio yelled from down the hall.

Lucas chewed his bottom lip as he worked, fully absorbed in the task at hand. After making a few tweaks, he replaced the panel and screwed it back into place.

"No soldering?" Lissa asked, still watching his every move.

"I've been working on a new approach in the hope I won't need to do it anymore. The sacrifice is that it's not as fast, but it's still going to be much faster than what you're used to. If you want to go more, you can tell me and I can take it further."

She nodded, a big grin spreading across her face. She couldn't wait to try it out.

AFTER LUCAS WAS done and handed Lissa's newly tweaked Orb back to her, putting his things away, the team bantered back and forth about all the things they would need to do before regionals.

"I'm excited but overwhelmed, honestly," Ji-Soo said.

Jae-Jin twirled a pen through his fingers, one at a time.

"We need to think like a team before anything else."

Lissa frowned at Jae-Jin.

"We already think like a team."

"On a different level. Sure, we play together. But developing your team, representing your team...

that's major league stuff. If we're gonna play out there, we need to evolve."

"How many of you are on the team?" Lucas asked.

"Well, that's the next question. We all play together regularly. But how many of us want to do this for real? I know we've all said so at one time or another. But now we really have to decide."

"I've wanted this since I was a kid." Zio twirled her necklace around a finger as she spoke. "But you all know this by now. I am one hundred percent in."

"I figured it's a given I'm in," Jae-Jin said. "Lissa? You too?"

Lissa opened her mouth to reply. Fear twisted in her stomach, leaving waves in its wake. Of course she wanted to. It was all she'd wanted for months. But now it was here and she was terrified.

"...I'm scared to death. But I'm also more excited than I've ever been. I wanna run down the street singing at the top of my lungs and then go hide in my bed."

Everyone chuckled, nodding in agreement. She noticed even Jae-Jin had given a barely perceptible nod.

"So, yeah. I might be freaked out about how it's gonna go, but I plan to try and do my best."

Still twirling his pen, Jae-Jin looked in Lucas's direction.

"So, Lucas," Lissa said, "what about you?"

Lissa watched as a gamut of emotions flitted across her new friend's face. Excitement, nerves, hope.

"Truthfully... I was hoping for more time to get better before regionals happened. I knew they would come, just not when. But I don't think I could know they were happening in the same city I live in and just sit them out."

"Says the guy whose Orb is probably faster than all of ours combined," Jae-Jin remarked in a dry voice. "But you need a team of six to enter regionals. So, we need one more person to enter as a formal team."

Lucas stared at Jae-Jin for a moment.

"Are you... saying what I think you're saying?" He looked like a man newly informed he'd won the lottery, teetering on the verge of a state of delighted shock.

Jae-Jin returned his stare. Then his lips curved into a rare smile.

"Welcome to Team Phoenix."

Lucas pushed back his chair, stood up, and threw both arms in the air, hands outstretched as he hooted aloud and the rest of the room laughed at his exuberance.

"YESSSSSS!"

AFTER LUCAS CAME back down to earth, the group decided to move into the lounge to watch Lissa play with her new toy. They found Ray and Devon standing in the middle of the room, chatting and laughing.

As the group drew near, Devon turned to them with a sunny smile.

"The party appears!"

"Ah, you're done already?" Ray looked embarrassed. "I was hoping for Devon to come watch Lucas work, but we got distracted..."

Devon clapped a giant hand onto Ray's shoulder.

"No stress. Just guy talk." He turned his attention

to Lissa. "All done? About to try it out?"

Lissa nodded. "Yep. Have time to come watch?"

"I do," he said. "Let's go to Jae-Jin's favourite spot."

Most of the monitors in the lounge were occupied, but Jae-Jin's corner stood empty. This tended to be the case when he wasn't using it. Other people who came to the 'Space on the regular seemed to get the message—no one other than Jae-Jin really set up there. While he wasn't the type to intimidate others on purpose, his personality did the job for him sometimes.

"Can't believe I'm stealing your chair," Lissa remarked as she settled in, tucking her legs under her and taking out her Orb.

"I'll allow it," Jae-Jin replied, triggering amused laughter from the others.

Lissa pressed the power button to bring her Orb to life as Devon reached up to turn on her monitor. She logged in with her thumbprints by pressing them onto the device's two top touch panels. The group watched as her lobby screen loaded, showing her stats off to the left side.

"329's your solo record? Damn. That's good."

Lissa looked up at Ray as he ogled her numbers with great interest.

"I've been chipping away at it," Lissa said. "I try not to play solo when I'm tired or worn out from team matches. Only when I feel really good and confident. It's not going as fast as I'd like, but every step counts. As long as I keep the streak, that's all that matters."

"I like that." Ray nodded, a thoughtful look on his face. "Hey. Hang on a sec."

The others looked up at him as he spoke. He tapped a finger against his lips, thinking.

"Should you play with one of us, instead of solo? That way there's less danger of losing your streak. You'll have support, just in case playing this way throws off your regular timing."

Devon pursed his lips. "That's a good idea. Or at least, it seems like one. Lucas?"

"Yeah, it can't hurt. Things do have a new rhythm once you're clocked."

Lissa nodded. "OK. Who?"

"I'll do it," Jae-Jin said, pulling a chair over from the empty station on the left.

"But you need a screen."

Jae-Jin said nothing as he positioned the chair directly in front of the wall. Then he sat down and got his Orb out, placing it in his lap. As the group watched, he powered it on and flicked a switch on the bottom of the system. A pleasant tone emitted from the device as it cast a single beam of blue light forward. The spot of colour shimmered as if finding its place in the air, then opened up into a digital screen. The *Ancestral* log-in page appeared on it.

"I don't use this function much since it drains the battery fast," Jae-Jin explained, "but this way you can all watch both games. Lissa, I'll invite you now."

He set the perimeters for the match and sent the message. As the game loaded, the screens flipped through concept art for several of the game's maps. In one, a Weaver stood at the edge of a pit of fire spitting sparks into the air before him. Another looked out across a lush forest as an airship made its way across the skyline, sailing fast towards the sinking sun.

The match opened up on a map known as The Hell Pits. A massive cavern carved of black rock yawned above their heads. From its ceiling hung strange protuberances that looked like the gigantic spines of animals, some of their ribs still intact. These alien structures also lined the walls. Light came in from somewhere above too far away to see. Behind them, a massive arch with wrought iron gates chained shut marked the entrance to the map's graveyard. This map had a great advantage: before the Onyx could invade the burial grounds, they had to gnaw the chains off—which took some time.

A few feet away stood rock outcroppings with glowing red runes carved into them. The ground beneath their feet was shot through with threads of lava, burning fierce and fast. As they adjusted to their surroundings, the deep, plaintive cry of a horn filled the room. Jae-Jin was the first to react, running off to the right at the sound of it.

"I'll cover this side," he said to Lissa, already in leader mode. "You check the left."

Lissa's eyes flicked up to the mini-map as she darted off. Four red dots and a swarm of blue. Plenty of Onyx to pick off, but she wasn't so worried about them for the moment. Having double her numbers to deal with was her primary concern, so the sooner they could take them out, the better. Two of them were in the northern part of the map. She strafed to the left to check the side, noticing immediately that her movements felt quicker.

"Lissa? You feelin' it yet?"

She nodded in response to Lucas's question, then realised he was likely looking at the screen, not at her.

"Yeah, it's different. Good."

As she passed a rocky outcrop the colour of tar, two skulls whizzed inches from her face and hit the wall to her left, exploding on impact. She blocked it with the wide end of one of her daggers. A Morteist was near. A glance at the mini-map told her it was on the other side of a pit of bubbling lava a few feet away. Volcanic rock of varying sizes encrusted its borders. Shiny black creatures smaller than bats tittered as they splashed in the muck like ducks in a lake.

"Got eyes on one at northwest," Lissa said. "Closing in now."

"I'm coming."

Crouching, Lissa hid behind the largest of the rocks and waited. It was early in the match, so neither of their special attacks were charged just yet. This was going to be blade to blade for now. A Morteist could seem impossible to beat because of its huge axe, but it also had a gaping weakness: speed. The weapon it wielded was so heavy that a player running the character had to have a pitch-perfect grasp of its timing in order to deal damage and not leave itself vulnerable.

"Come on, friend," Lissa said, her voice musical. "Come and get it."

The Morteist lumbered out from behind a rock a foot away and swung. The moment Lissa registered the attack she could tell the person playing didn't know how to handle the character. She darted into the wide-open space of its midsection and slashed with both daggers. The top of the torso and the bottom slid in opposite directions as they parted, hitting the ground with a sickening *thwop*.

✦M4NGIMAL HAS BEEN ELIMINATED BY NAGIKO✦

"Down to three," Lissa said as she swiped potions off what was left of the body. Jae-Jin bounded up to her, checking out the corpse.

"One of my own. Too bad. Guess they didn't know how to heft that axe."

"They rarely do. But I feel faster, too."

"Cool. Let's go take it out on those guys."

Lissa followed his lead as he let a handful of the skulls from his belt fly in the direction of the Onyx horde moving fast in their direction. One clamped onto the face of the beast closest to the front. It began to howl and wave its arms wildly as the skull gnawed the flesh off its face. It struck the creature behind it with its flailing and shoved it into the others, knocking them down as neatly as a bowling ball would a set of pins.

One Onyx's health circle burst into fire.

"Sail the Styx?" Jae-Jin said as he wound up for another axe slash, doing his best to cut them down before the rest of them went Raging. One Raging Onyx was not a huge deal. A gang of them, however, was another matter—especially with only two of them, and three enemy players still on the map.

"Close," Lissa said as she blasted the group with spinning attacks to build up the strength to cast her Transcendence. The Raging Onyx was pushing itself to its feet, despite Jae-Jin's axe strikes. As it rose to its full height, its hideous eyes glowered, and Lissa's Transcendence meter reached its peak.

"Now!" she cried.

The scene before them was swallowed by a mighty

black plume. Then a boat cut through the inky blackness, manned by a single figure of unnatural height. The head of a massive vulture curved up from the bow. Its neck was cloaked in oily feathers and gave way to a face covered in thin red flesh. The eyes that stared out of its face were still as stone.

The six Onyx they were fighting just a moment before were all crammed into the boat. As the ferryman rowed his way downstream, hands started to reach up through the water towards the vessel's passengers as a low moan emanated from the dark lake. First there were three, then a dozen, then more and more arms crammed between like some horrible sea kelp. They pulled the Onyx one by one off the ferryman's boat as they howled and thrashed. In the space of just a few seconds, all of them had been pulled underwater.

The plume of darkness evaporated, leaving Jae-Jin and Lissa on the field. The Onyx were gone.

"I have days where I wonder if I should have been a Plunderer," Jae-Jin said. "When it comes to death attacks, it really does give my class a run for its money."

"Let's go see what that guy down south is doing," Lissa said, eyeballing the mini-map. "We've pushed back the ones near the graveyard, but we still have to pick those off."

She bounded off in that direction, passing a tower of charred rock with spikes protruding from its spire. Both human and animal bones littered the base. As troubling as the sights of this map were, Lissa had seen them so many times she hardly noticed them anymore; they were no more shocking than a tree or a bush. But as she passed the tower and continued south, she drew close to the area that creeped her out every time, no matter how many times she played.

The structure looked like a crudely fashioned one, its walls perhaps made of rock or mud or both. But where the roof should have been, there was a human head. Half of one, anyway: its mouth wasn't visible, but its nose and cheeks seemed to morph out of the walls. It had massive ears, a hairless scalp, and one terrible staring eye that lolled in its socket. It followed her now, just as it did any time a player ran past it.

"I hate that thing," she muttered, more to herself than Jae-Jin.

"There's someone in there," he said, making a hard left and running into the cavernous opening at the bottom of the head-rock.

"Of course there is," Lissa muttered, following her friend. She ignored the unpleasant tug in her gut as she drew close, bones crunching under her feet. Training her eyes not to look up, she passed through the opening into blackness. The lantern at her waist came to life and illuminated the room just in time for her to watch Jae-Jin's axe slice a Brutalist's right arm clean off the shoulder.

✦UNICORNGRRRL HAS BEEN
ELIMINATED BY JAEBOMB✦

"Bye, girl," Lissa said, earning a chuckle from Jae-Jin. He leapt over his kill and dashed outside.

"Horde coming from the south. This might be all of them."

As she came out into the light, she saw exactly what he meant. A swarm of Onyx poured towards them from three different directions. Lissa thought a dozen, maybe a few more. Jae-Jin was already hurling his skulls at them. She was about to dash in to join him when she saw a familiar figure emerge from the swarm to the left.

"The Weaver, Jae-Jin! Be careful! It's in the middle of the—"

As she spoke, their opponent unfurled vines from its fingertips. They wrapped around Jae-Jin's neck and arms with frightening speed, encircling them over and over as they grew tighter. He struggled to swing his axe to get free. Lissa darted toward his captor, intending to slash the vines, but the Weaver shot another set with its other arm. They bound her arms in a millisecond. Her daggers were useless. Her heart thudded in her chest as she realised they could lose the match in the next minute.

Soul Drain was her only option. She cast it on the Weaver, hoping against hope that it could get at least one of them free. The Onyx surrounding them were only a few paces away. Their vacant faces rattled with an empty joy, eager to gnaw the flesh off their bones. But they were distracted by the Weaver's cry as it fell backwards. The vine that had held Jae-Jin had dissolved, as Soul Drain had taken the power it needed to sustain it.

Her partner slashed the shambling Onyx back as his axe whistled through the air. As he did, fog settled over the hellish field—the beginning of Final Exit, his Transcendence. Jae-Jin bowed his head and grasped his weapon with both hands as it glowed a fierce red. His body began to twirl, the axe picking up speed as the centrifugal force grew stronger. Onyx body parts flew in the air: an arm, a head, a torso. He careened into the Weaver, and one of its mighty antlers cracked and fell from its head as it stumbled. For a brief moment, Lissa felt a pang of sadness at the sight of it, even though it was still her opponent. There was something about seeing the mighty fall.

Lissa thought they were almost in the clear. Final Exit had wiped them all out, and now they were down to only one opponent. She turned to Jae-Jin to see his avatar falling to the ground. A cloud of fat, writhing leeches clung to his skin, his health circle dwindling at an alarming rate.

"Jae-Jin!"

"Move! It's a Mender!"

She strafed to her right, conflicted. On one hand, a Mender posed a major threat: its Thirst of the Leech Transcendence siphoned her opponents' energy away, leaving them useless while its health and magic gauges rose to full power. She didn't want to abandon Jae-Jin, but she'd need to be quick or it would turn on her and take the match. She gulped down a potion to boost her health and dashed behind an outcropping of rock. Her mind buzzed like a hive of angry bees.

You have to take it out before it can cast that again. Or you're done for.

As she racked her brain for a solution, a notification popped up on the screen.

✦JAEBOMB HAS BEEN ELIMINATED BY CANTALOUPEBRO✦

"Use your speed, Lissa," Jae-Jin said, sounding placid for a man who'd just been viciously killed. "You have the advantage now."

"You can do it!" Lucas cried from behind her chair.

"Yesssss!"

"Finish it!"

Lissa's lips curved into a smile as her friends cheered her on. She was just a little bit shy of having enough essence to cast her second Transcendence, The God's Theft. As long as she could stay clear of the Weaver long enough to build her meter, she still had a chance to take the match. Or Jae-Jin would respawn by then. Either way, it was time for a little game of hide and seek. She watched the Weaver's dot move on the mini-map. It hesitated for a few beats, then started heading towards her.

Lissa took off running in the direction she'd come from, back past the head-cave with its one ghastly eyeball and the bubbling lakes of fire with their gibbering creatures. Her heartbeat quickened as she watched her essence gauge, willing it to fill. One unbearable second ticked by after another as the Weaver gained on her. Lissa heard the sound of a tusk hurtling through the air towards her and rolled out of the way with less than a second to spare. It was giving chase to try to trap her before its own Transcendences were ready. But she was a thread away from casting her own. It was going to be a matter of who could execute first.

Her finger hovered over the button as the Weaver bore down on her, trying to shoot seaweed down her throat. It missed its mark by less than an inch as it glazed her face with sea slime. She slashed it with a dagger and sent slices of it flying as her Transcendence gauge hit its max.

Now.

Her Plunderer threw its arms wide as they morphed,

quickly growing to twice their size. They shot forward and wrapped around the Weaver at the exact moment it cast Soul of Decay, its own Transcendence. But Lissa was faster. Her opponent's life drained away as the embrace drew it forth. It was on the verge of death when she let it go and it dropped on the ground, a barely functioning sack of flesh. Her knives went into the chest and cut a ragged slit that poured blood.

Jae-Jin respawned just in time to see Lissa reach into the Weaver's wound and yank out its still-beating heart. She grinned in real life as she crushed it like a ripe tomato.

⚜XXMEANNCLEANXX HAS BEEN
ELIMINATED BY NAGIKO⚜

"Brutal," Jae-Jin said as The Hell Pits faded into the post-match summary screen. "I think you were faster, too."

"I was—especially right after you went down. I think I might not have been able to pull it off before Lucas fixed my Orb up." She turned in her chair, smiling at her friends, who were nodding and looking generally impressed. Lucas caught her eye, made a fist, and pulled his arm down in a gesture of victory: *Yes!*

"It's a significant difference," Devon said, stroking his chin. "That I can tell, and it's been a while since I played. The first thing we should probably do—if Lucas wants to, that is—is mod up the rest of the team," Devon said. "Then we can start training in earnest. Four months may not sound like much, but it's plenty of time." He flashed a dazzling smile at the group. "Plus, you've got me."

The group hooted and cheered.

"I feel so loved," Devon said, putting his hands over his heart. "You may not love me for long after what I'm about to put you through, though. But if you trust me to get you where you want to go, this phoenix is gonna *fly*."

PART TWO
JULY

CHAPTER TWELVE
PLAYER TWO

As SHE LAID awake while the clock on her bedside table inched its way towards four in the morning, Lissa thought (as she often did when sleep eluded her) about the days before her brother died.

If someone had told her when she was a kid that her favourite activity when she got older would be watching Quin sleep, she'd have laughed in their faces. But she had learned that the world is strange and unkind, and sometimes it digs into the darkest corners of our imagination, takes what it finds there and makes it real. Just to see how we might cope with it.

That was how she found herself at fourteen years old, standing in a hospital room with plain, painfully white walls, watching the slow rise and fall of a little boy's chest as if it was the most fascinating sight in the world. Before he'd gotten sick, breathing was a thing she'd taken for granted as the rest of her life flew by. But after she watched her brother nearly choke to death in front of her eyes, that had changed.

When she listened to him sleeping back then, and it was a good day, she heard the surf. The soft white noise of the waves moving back and forth in their reliable patterns. A song no human could understand, but they were all drawn to anyway. The tide could change and usher in chaos at any moment. But that day there had been peace and silence in the rhythm of her brother's breathing, and it soothed a soul long ragged and torn.

She remembered glancing at the door as a few nurses walked by outside. She remembered feeling alert, despite barely sleeping three hours before they'd come to the hospital. It was Quin's third time in a month. She remembered watching her father physically steer her mother out of the hospital room to make her go home to sleep after close to forty-eight hours there without as much as a nap. Both of them were exhausted, and even though Lissa knew her brother was safe in the hands of his doctors, she also felt it was her turn to watch over him.

What she'd done that day was pull a chair close to her brother's bedside, take his hand in hers, and talk to him about her memories of all the games they'd played together over the years. Since she was the older sister, he was always her player two—and an enthusiastic one at that. Those long days spent in front of the television immersed in fantastic worlds with her eager, sweet brother by her side were some of her happiest experiences.

Even though he was asleep, Lissa believed Quin could hear her. And so she'd sat close and watched her brother's dear, tired face and allowed herself to remember a bittersweet time when he was healthy and whole and no terminal illness lived and breathed in his tiny lungs. When he'd clapped his hands in excitement as she powered on the console and handed him the controller. His already-reddish cheeks had glowed with delight.

"Remember when we decided we were going to get every single achievement we could in *Invasion of the Planet*, Quin?" she'd said in a quiet voice as she stroked his hand. A smile warmed her face as the memory found its colour, filling in the details that were hazy only a moment before.

"We played it over and over every day after school like it was our job. Defending earth from an alien invasion was the coolest, especially blowing up the huge robots that the UFOs dropped. You loved going after those. I had to yell at you to wait for me. Remember?"

No response. Lissa's eyes wandered over her brother's beautiful golden eyelashes, long on his cheeks. His characteristic blush had long since faded. Her heart lurched, desperate to unload all the what-ifs and buts she carried around in a too-heavy sack, but she breathed deep and pushed it down again. Not now.

"We finished and we got New Game+. And that's when we found out that we could get those new guns. Crazy guns. There was some rocket launcher you could blow up a city block with. What was it called? The Leveller? The Devastator? Something like that. We were hundreds of hours in before we finally got it. We were so excited, we ran around the house screaming. Mom thought we'd gone nuts."

He stirred in his sleep and smiled. Remember? a ghostly memory whispered to her.

He heard me, she thought back. *I know it.*

This little inner whisper pulled her back to the present. Lissa turned in her bed to rest on her left side, tucking one hand under her pillow and drawing the other close to her chest. The memories were moving forward, picking up speed. Her gut quavered. She'd been on this ride many times before and it was not a good time, but she kept getting back on anyway. Her therapist had advised her to "focus on the good memories." Good advice, but also hard to do when after a certain point they were so deeply intertwined with the bad.

There she was again, frozen in shock as the nurses rushed into the room when Quin's heart stopped. Sobbing against her mother's chest after the defibs bounced her brother's body violently against the hospital bed and he took his first shaky, painful-sounding breath after over a minute of nothing. Bringing him home again, the relief in his weak smile, only to bring him back again a few days later when he started to lose his appetite. Bringing him tiny bits of food prepared by hand in hopes that he might eat a few bites, or the right thing might make him remember what it was like to be hungry, even for just a few moments. Something was better than nothing.

The ride sped up again, careening into the day the defibs could no longer work their magic and the little boy she had spent her childhood shooting robots and excavating treasure with died on the hospital bed in front of her. No more player two. Not now, not ever.

Then Mum had left, too. And she and dad were alone.

In some ways it felt like a long time ago. But on nights like this, when the grief glowed in her chest like a hot piece of coal and kept her awake, it still felt like yesterday. There was a time when she felt like she could never play a game again. Not without him. A few weeks after his death, she'd put away all the consoles and controllers in a cardboard box, folded it shut and carried it up to the attic. Because looking at the bright plastic reminded her of a lifetime with her brother, and in this horrible new reality, he no longer existed.

As the years went by, she missed games. Not only had she loved playing with Quin, but she loved playing. Her dad, who grew up playing games on his computer, always came to see what they were playing, pulling up a chair to watch sometimes as they explored another shrine or chatted it up with the residents of a new town.

From time to time she'd see an ad for a game that looked interesting to her. Sometimes on a website or at the beginning of a video. Every time she considered trying something new, the idea was followed by a flush of guilt. Like she was leaving Quin alone in a dark place he couldn't escape from as she went off to have fun, closing the door as he cried.

While all those other games tempted her, seeing *Ancestral* for the first time had been completely different. She remembered seeing a trailer a few weeks before the game dropped. Watching Onyx teem into a graveyard and dig up its dead with their bare hands as the villagers screamed and wept. Each of the heroes appearing one by one and blasting the creatures back with their powerful weapons and spells. The last to appear was the Plunderer. Its shredded black robes twisted around its gaunt frame as it whirled into the graveyard, slashing two Onyx out of its way with a mighty swing. Then it had cast Sail the Styx, and Lissa had watched, astonished, as the ferryman came and claimed what was left of the enemy.

If the other games she'd been drawn to beckoned to her knowingly, this one reached out to clasp her wrist, its touch warming parts of her that had been cold for a long time.

Playing *Ancestral* looked like a blast, no doubt. But it also struck a chord deep inside her that it was a game about protecting the souls of dead family members. And when Ji-Soo announced that she intended to play and asked if Lissa would join her, she'd lain awake just like she was right now and thought: *Maybe. Maybe I will.*

Sometimes she liked to imagine Quin as a young man. He'd be ten now if he was still here. It was so easy to see him in her mind's eye, Orb in hand, happily figuring out the this- and-that of *Ancestral*'s world. He would have adored it. Lissa knew this for a fact, and it was with her every time she played. Crazy enough, she felt there was some shred of her brother with her she could sense sometimes, and she felt it most strongly of all when she was in the game. In those moments, she could feel him flickering like a tiny fire.

She'd never breathed a word of this to anyone.

Reaching out from under the covers, Lissa took the phone off the charger and slid a finger across the screen to the voice recorder. The screen opened to reveal a log of past recordings of varying lengths. Bringing the phone close to her face as if to make a call, she tapped the record button.

"Well, I'm up," she whispered. "Haven't left you one of these in a while. The regional tournament I've been hoping for is finally coming. I'm excited and scared all at the same time." She sighed. "I wish you were here. I know I say it all the time, but you'd love *Ancestral* so much. It's so fun. I think you'd be a Brutalist, as much as you always loved climbing trees and playing in the garden. You get to control nature and use it to your advantage. And you even get to shoot vines from your fingers! It's so cool."

Lissa paused, thinking of the last few days.

"I made a new friend, too. I don't know him too well, but I really like him so far. His name is Lucas and we met at a tourney I went to not long ago. There's something about him that reminds me of you."

Lucas's face rose in her mind. The toothy grin—his front teeth were longer than the rest. His warm brown eyes and skin. The rectangular wire-frame glasses that made him look just a little bit geekier. Lissa looked at this in her mind's eye and once again felt an unexplainable sense of peace. There was something special about him, all right.

"Sometimes... people like him make me feel like everything is going to be OK. And that's a big deal. Because for so long after you left, I felt like it would never be OK again. How could it be when you weren't here? The world felt wrong, off-kilter. At first, I was sad, but then all of a sudden one day I was furious that life did this to you. Why not some horrible person, a murderer, a thief?"

The anger she'd felt then flashed brief in her heart, a reminder that it wasn't all gone just yet.

"But maybe some part of you still exists, in other

good people. That's kind of how Lucas makes me feel. Like I can see a little sliver of who you were in who he is. If that even makes any sense. Anyway, I miss you and I wish you were here. I'd love you to meet my friends and be on my team. I have no idea how I'm going to win this thing, but I'm going to try as hard as I can."

Laying in the dark, Lissa felt a tiny burst of hope.

"Cheer for me, Quin," she murmured. "I'm going back to sleep."

CHAPTER THIRTEEN
KNOW THY ENEMY

As THE MEMBERS of Team Phoenix cut a meandering path to PlaySpace's door on a sunny Saturday morning, Devon threw it open and splayed himself in front of it. He wore a dark blue cape over his striped t-shirt and blue jeans and a proud smile.

"Friends!" he said warmly.

"Devon," Ji-Soo said, looking the man up and down with a critical expression. "What's with the cape?"

"Today is a momentous day!" Devon had clearly chosen to gloss over Ji-Soo's question. "The first step towards your regionals victory, yes! You're all registered, it's all official. We have so much to discuss."

Ray giggled. "I'm ready to learn all the big secrets."

PlaySpace was nearly empty save for a couple of young kids straddled up to the TV nearest the door. Lissa had seen them a few times before, but had yet to learn their names. She guessed that they couldn't have been more than ten years old. From time to time, Devon allowed parents to use the 'Space as an after-school activity spot if the kids were well-behaved and willing to help with some chores to keep the place clean. Lissa didn't know for sure, but she had a feeling he didn't charge them, which just made her like him all the more.

"Conference room! This-a-way!"

"He sure is chipper," Jae-Jin remarked from behind them. Lissa sensed Ji-Soo's barely perceptible tremble as she realised how close he was to them. It made her smile. She knew her friend well. Also, if these two didn't end up together, then Jae-Jin was a damn fool.

Lucas was the first into the conference room, and they all heard him gasp.

"Devon! Oh my gosh, you did this?"

The long table in the centre of the room had been outfitted with three enormous double-sided monitors. Each had an Orb charging station set up in front of it. Between the monitors were little blue plastic baskets crammed tight with bottles of water, bags of mixed nuts, and beef jerky. On the far wall facing the door, a big white flag hung with a crimson silhouette of a phoenix raising its wings to the heavens inside a circle.

They looked up to find Devon in the corner near the door with his arms crossed, his infectious grin holding fast as he watched the others take in the sight of his handiwork.

"You like it?"

Zio was standing behind one of the chairs and taking out her Orb to set on the charger. Even as she did so, she continued to look around her with an expression of awe.

"It's amazing. I can't believe you set all this up for us. Even the phoenix!"

"Oh, you just reminded me, there's one more thing. Hold on." Devon dashed out of the room, his cape flapping behind him, and quickly returned with a cardboard box in hand, its flaps folded in. He walked to the head of the table near the monitor Jae-Jin so often used to rewatch old matches. The rest of the group stood up, peering in Devon's direction as he placed the box on the table and started to unfold its flaps. But then he stopped, both hands still resting on the edge of the box, and turned his attention to the six faces watching his every move.

"Today is such a special day. Being on a team is an honour. A team as good as the six of you are, even more so. Those really don't come along every day. And watching you all, it seems to me that you found each other just the way you were supposed to."

Jae-Jin's face broke into a rare smile. Devon was the only one to see it.

"I've said many times before that I believe in all of you, and now we get to put the magic I see in what you all have together to the test. You've had a name for a while. But when it comes to the esports world, there's one crucial thing that makes you feel like a team."

He reached into the box and held up a shirt. The thin white fabric glimmered pearlescent as light danced across its surface. The collar and arms were edged with brilliant red. On the front right, a phoenix cut across the fabric in the same crisp colour, its wing reaching towards the left shoulder. Devon turned the jersey to show that the bird's other wing extended across the shoulder blades. In the middle of this wing was Lissa's gamertag in white letters with gold edges: Nagiko.

Jae-Jin took a few long strides to the front of the room and engulfed Devon in a hug. If the room had already been speechless when they saw the jerseys, they were doubly so now. Devon patted his back soundly, chuckling.

"Thank you," Jae-Jin said, looking awed as he stepped back. "Thank you."

"Wow," Zio breathed as her ability to speak returned. "Devon, I LOVE THEM!"

"They are beyond cool. I can't believe we get to wear those!" Ji-Soo came to give Devon a hug and peer into the box. "Did you design them yourself?"

"Yep. Fun fact: after I decided to quit competitive, but before I built PlaySpace, I taught myself graphic design. Took a ton of online courses and found I had a flair for it. Doing freelance came in handy when I needed money. Anyway, I considered showing you all the design first to see if you liked it, but I was so attached to the idea of unveiling it like this that I decided to take a gamble. I figured if you hated them, well, we could always go on to plan B."

"Who could hate this?" Lissa said as she held up the jersey, then held it against Ray, who was smiling so hard his eyes had all but vanished into his cheeks. "Like, I don't think I've ever said this about any jersey I've ever seen, but it's beautiful. I can't believe this will represent us."

"The monitors are new, too." Jae-Jin looked up from the one he was examining. "Did you buy these just for us?"

Devon nodded.

"I've wanted to outfit this room for a long time and have it be a team training space. I hoped to have multiple ones at one time, so I've tucked cash away here and there for years in hopes of building them. The 'Space is making more now that more people are playing *Ancestral*, too, especially with regionals officially coming." He nodded his head in the direction of the front room.

"Anyway, as much as people play here, I've never really seen a team click together the way you guys have. Sometimes you get two or three people trying. This is why I say being on a team is an honour. Especially a team that works as hard as you guys do. That means you truly all share a goal."

He took the remote off the table and turned on the widescreen TV mounted on the far wall, then took out his phone to connect the two.

"So, speaking of a goal," Devon said as he waited for the TV's Bluetooth to recognise his device, "I did a few things since we last spoke. Other than redecorating."

The group laughed. Lissa grabbed a bottle of water from the basket nearest her and uncapped it, taking a long sip as a black screen with a list of numbered names appeared behind Devon.

"There are some good sites that keep tabs on *Ancestral*'s rankings other than just the official in-game leaderboards. I'm sure you all probably know of them already. After looking through the legit ones I found Shardtracker to be the best in terms of consistency and accuracy of information." Devon looked in Jae-Jin's direction. "Is this your favourite, too?"

"It is," Jae-Jin replied.

"Not surprised. So, let me share some of what I

discovered in my travels." Using his phone to scroll and click, Devon chose a few filters to show them a new list.

"First, this is a regionals competition, which means we are one of eight regions competing. As I'm sure you all know, winning this competition would mean moving on to compete against the seven other winning teams in nationals. I've been through all these rounds before, and even though I'm sure a lot has changed about it since my days, it wasn't so long ago that it rules my experience inaccurate. In fact, I think we'll find a lot of things about these competitions fairly unchanged."

"Wait a sec," Lucas said. "Are there videos of when you used to compete?"

"Oh, yes. Many. Jae-Jin has watched them all. He can show you how to go through them if you'd like."

Lucas nodded, his eyes starry at the thought.

Moving on, Devon pointed to the list on the screen. Each name was accompanied by the logo of an American flag.

"So, this is the regional ranking for the northwest United States. This is solo ranking—I'll get to team ranking in a minute. One thing I wanted to point out is that several of you are fairly high up here, which I'm sure each of you respectively knows. But what you may not know is what a good position this puts us in to drive you higher on the rankings between now and the event." Devon scrolled down. "Here's Jae-Jin at sixteen, our highest-ranking player in this room. Lissa's only a few behind him at nineteen. Then Ji-Soo is here at thirty-four. Three team members in the top fifty is a great start to where we want to go."

He scrolled back up and clicked another tab.

"These are the team rankings. This is where we need work. But the good news here is that if your solo rankings are that high, all we need to do is mobilise. Build the Team Phoenix name as you learn to play, think, and breathe as a team. Three months may not seem like much. But the scene also changes constantly. New people rise to the top all the time. And this time, those people are going to be the people in this room.

"So, let's think further ahead. Because that's what champions do best, in all honesty. They win because they're three steps out from where the rest of us are."

He clicked a few more times and a new list unfurled. This one was dotted with flags from all around the world: Japan, Korea, France, Germany, Canada, Italy. A flick of Devon's thumb took them to the top of the list. He shook his phone in the direction of the names there.

"Get to know these names. These are the best *Ancestral* players in the world right now, and you have to think about how to beat them. You'll only have to defeat a small selection of them in this regional to take the cup. But as I said before, things change fast in this world. So that could change, too."

Suddenly, Lissa stood up from her chair. Her face tightened as she approached where Devon stood, looking at the top of the list.

"Lissa? Everything OK?"

As she read and reread the gamertag in the first slot, the sensation of freezing cold water bathed her neck and shoulders, dripping down her spine. The room sat silent behind her.

WRAITHX

"Guys," she said without turning around. "This… this is who we fought the night we lost our team streak. The match where the opponent cloaked and took out me, Jae-Jin, Zio, and Ji-Soo within a few seconds."

Devon looked at the name, blinking as if in disbelief.

"*That's* the player? Seriously?"

Lissa nodded slowly.

"You randomly matched with the world's top *Ancestral* player?!" Lucas said from behind them. "What are the odds?"

"Well, they weren't number one that night, because I looked on the leaderboards and didn't see them. But they must have climbed it fast," Jae-Jin sighed. "They wiped the floor with us that night. I've rewatched that match a lot. Haven't been able to figure out what strategy we could have used to win. This explains why."

The room nodded, most of them lost in thought.

"Hang on," Lucas said. "That covers things we don't need to worry about for now. But what about the top tier regional teams on here? What do you know about them?"

"Wait," Lissa said. "What team is WraithX on?"

"Mastermind," Jae-Jin replied. "I looked them up a little while ago. They're sponsored. By Rager. Not a huge company. But still."

"You'll need to learn them inside and out if you want to find a way to beat them," Devon said. "Find their matches and start watching them."

Lucas nodded, looking determined.

"I'll look into them and report back," Jae-Jin said. "You should all do the same. Oh, and one other thing.

When regionals got announced I mentioned that I get up and play early before my day starts. I know most of you aren't early risers, but if anyone wants to join, now would be a good time. Think about it and let me know."

Even Zio, who was typically quick to tease Jae-Jin, quietly nodded. She was known as the night owl of the group, even more so than Ji-Soo. And a few minutes later as Lissa watched her best friend walk to the other side of the table and exchange in a few hushed words with Jae-Jin, she marvelled at how much the world around her could change in a single day.

Devon tapped his forehead with a finger. "The kid's bright. So, as your officially unofficial coach, that's where I'd recommend you begin. Saddle up, play some matches, and feel out how you work together best. Since Ray and Lucas are newer, you need to sort out how they fit into the puzzle. But from what I've heard, that seems to be coming pretty naturally." He put the remote down as he made his way to the door, then turned around when he got there, hand on the knob. "I'll be out front if you need anything. Good luck and rise strong." He winked and closed the door behind him.

The room burst into excited chatter as they fished their Orbs out of their backpacks and dove into the snacks Devon had left for them. Jae-Jin stood, waving his hands to get their attention.

This is the beginning, Lissa thought. *Of everything.*

CHAPTER FOURTEEN
LEADERS

As Ji-Soo jerked awake to the insistent blare of her phone's alarm and reached for it to shut it off, she saw a bleary, half-formed image in her mind of the people tasked with making phone alarms, hunched over their computers in an effort to manufacture the most horrible sound possible. She felt a brief flash of hate for them. Why couldn't they make something that could get a person out of bed without bringing them to the cliff's edge of a heart attack?

She checked her phone and groaned. Quarter to six. And a text notification from her mother. She swiped it away without reading it.

Even though she'd known she would have to get to bed earlier if she was going to make a habit out of rising at this hour, shaking off her night owl tendencies wasn't exactly a walk in the park. Normally, ten p.m. was the start of her favourite of the day's hours. People turned out their lights. The world got quieter. Sometimes she even wandered out for walks and relished the silence that hung in the streets—this beautiful, rare sound that was so hard to connect to, but so soothing to be with when it could be found.

She also streamed at night. This was her primary way of making money since she'd come to the States, along with what she made being a Parse(d) influencer. She often imagined her parents finding out about this hobby, losing their temper, and disowning her on the spot. Which, of course, they probably would. Despite their horrified faces hanging in her mind's eye, she still logged on every night. She had rent to pay. And without her parents hanging over her shoulder, making a living doing something she loved was actually an option.

It was astounding to her that she could hang out in her bedroom playing games and be with other people doing the same thing at the same time. Even wilder was the idea that people tuned in from all over the world to watch her play games and talk to her or subscribe to her channel. Creeps had wandered in and out from time to time, but that was what the ban button was for.

Sometimes her little community talked about the game, or their lives, or even their problems. One of the things she loved the most was watching a person share an insecurity or a fear in there and another offer support to them. It was unreal that within the culture of one of the harshest places a person could go, people like this also existed and reached out to strangers. She'd loved streaming from the beginning, but after seeing that aspect of the culture, it became a part of her. An essential part.

So even though the magic hour had come last night, as it always did, she didn't give herself over to its charms. Her usual habits beat on the window of her mind and screamed for her attention. Rather than give in to them, she put on her pyjamas and brushed and flossed her teeth. Gotham wandered into the bathroom and sat watching her with a sweet, bewildered face that Ji-Soo roughly translated to *you're in the wrong room, Mom.*

At half past ten she'd gotten into bed, ignoring the itch to check her phone. The dog looked at her for a few moments before hopping in next to her. He turned left, then right, then left again as he found the perfect nesting spot he was looking for, exhaling a sigh of doggy relief. Ji-Soo watched him, feeling a small glow of gratitude. She was glad he had joined her. Maybe listening to him sleep would help her to sleep, too.

Unfortunately, it had not gone that way. She willed herself not to check the clock, but she knew from the quality of the darkness outside her window that she'd been awake for a long time. Her brain buzzed with fragments of half-formed ideas and hopes. Every time it reminded her what she was waking up early to do, a trembling rose of excitement blossomed, then another, and another.

Jae-Jin. I'm going to play with Jae-Jin.

Now that time was here. Her excitement was shot through with thick bursts of exhaustion, but she threw back the covers and headed to the bathroom. At least she didn't have to worry about putting together an outfit or doing her makeup. They would just be using voice chat today, so she could play in her pyjamas with her unwashed hair piled in a bun atop her head.

You can learn from him, she thought as she scrubbed fluoride across her teeth. *You're good, but not good like that. We have to be our best to have a chance to win. So, I need to get better to help the team.*

When she finished her routine, Gotham followed her to the kitchen as she put coffee on. She took down a big, handmade blue mug with a purple rim and glanced at the kitchen clock. It told her she had just enough time to pour a cup and get back to her desk. She was about to head back that way when Gotham let out a small whine.

"Oh, sweetie," Ji-Soo said, realising she'd forgotten in her excitement to feed the poor dog and let him out to go to the bathroom. "I'm sorry. You must be malnourished."

The big animal snuffled happily as she scooped out some dry food and placed it in his big silver bowl, then plunged his face into it with enthusiasm. Ji-Soo nodded to herself and headed towards the office with her steaming mug in hand, making a mental note to come back and check on him in a few minutes.

She'd left her Orb on its charger overnight on her desk. The blue glow signified it was fully juiced, and she took it off and thumbed the system on. Both monitors turned on as she sat down—motion-controlled tech really was every bit as handy as she'd always dreamed it might be—and she reached for a silvery capsule next to her mouse. Popping it open, she took out her earbuds and put them in, listening for the tone they made when they powered on.

"Ji-Soo?" Jae-Jin said in a whisper.

She twitched. She hadn't expected him to be there the moment she put them in, as if he'd been waiting there all along for her to appear. But one look at the system clock—six a.m.—reminded her of why. Jae-

Jin was famously timely, and today was no exception.

She'd also never heard him say her name before, much less whisper it. She shook her head to snap herself out of the weird tingling it triggered from the back of her neck to her wrists.

"I'm here," she managed in a tone of voice she hoped came off as normal.

There was a pause before he spoke again.

"Are you the only one in your house?"

"Yep. I live alone."

"Ah, OK." Ji-Soo noticed he was still careful to whisper, despite this information.

"I'm guessing you don't?"

"Ah, yeah. I've never told you? I live with my parents."

"You're not really the sharing type, Jae-Jin."

"Ah. Yeah." She heard paper shifting on his end. Had she made him uncomfortable? It wasn't like his reserved manner was a secret. He took jokes about it in stride at the 'Space. But sometimes Ji-Soo wondered what he was thinking when he gave a faint smile in reply.

"So... let's talk about a few things before we get started."

Did he... make notes for this?

"So... we've played together in a group before, but I have no one-on-one experience with you. So I'm glad we're doing this because it can help me better understand how you play."

She knew there was nothing remotely romantic about his words. But goosebumps were rising on her arms anyway. She rubbed them up and down, grateful that he couldn't see her.

"I went back and watched a few matches we've been in together. The biggest weakness I can see so far is that you're impulsive. You don't seem to think ahead to what will happen after a big encounter, only how to get through what's right in front of you."

Ji-Soo said nothing. Her heart sank in her chest like a damaged sea vessel.

"The reason you aren't as disadvantaged by that as other players might be is because you have incredibly fast reaction time. And you're inventive." The sound of the rustling papers came again. This time, it was clear to Ji-Soo that he was turning pages. She also heard him scribbling something down with a pencil, its scratchy noise unmistakable. "I noticed in several of the replays that you employed solutions that were unusual. You also had very little time to think about them, which also works in your favour."

"OK. So, what do you think I need to work on most?"

"Well." The papers shuffled. "I think you can play to your natural strengths by learning to think a few ticks ahead. You've never had any formal training in strategy, right?"

"Only tips from Devon here and there."

"Well, he's good, so that clearly helped you along the way." He paused. "Can you hang on just a second?"

"Sure."

The sound on the other end went muffled, as if he was holding a phone against his chest. She was able to make out a woman's voice. While she couldn't hear the words, she recognised their cadence. If it was his mum—and she assumed it was—his family spoke

Korean at home. Ji-Soo had never heard Jae-Jin speak a word of it before this.

The mic returned to normal, and Ji-Soo heard the sound of a door being shut with care.

"Sorry about that."

"No worries."

"So, you always play Brutalist. What is it that appeals to you so much about this build?"

Ji-Soo's eyes wandered back to the game. She was on the *Ancestral* start screen, so she clicked the logo to log in and watched her character load. Sh0uj0, her main, stood proudly in her striking suit of matte black armour with her wings outstretched. Known as 'The Light God' (or goddess, in this case), this hybrid of a paladin and a warrior captured the essence of courage and power. She was a tank but also lithe, able to hit hard and fly fast. Her crystalline eyes and smooth white hair also appealed to Ji-Soo, who found her own mousy features to be average and boring.

"Well... she's the most well-balanced of the options. Like a tank but not as slow. So, I get the best of both worlds. She's basically a paladin, but way cooler than any other one I've played."

"And where do you see her on our team?"

"The front lines," Ji-Soo replied without hesitation. "She can take more abuse than any other character. The others can cast and heal while she holds the horde back."

"Agreed. And I am the second strongest. My thought is that the way we ought to structure this team is with you and I as the leaders. A good commander is essential to a team's success. If we can learn to work together in a way where we are thinking two steps ahead together, we can provide adequate protection and keep us all alive."

This is more than one-to-one practise, Ji-Soo thought. *He wants us to be partners.*

Partners.

Her ability to pay attention wavered as she realised this might be the closest she ever got to him. And if it was, it was better than nothing. Which is what she had been to him before this conversation began.

Ji-Soo realised she'd tuned out as his voice seeped back into her consciousness like a volume knob gently turning back up.

"...what do you think?"

"I'm sorry, the coffee stopped working for a minute there. Could you repeat that?"

"I said that this will require you to tweak your play style somewhat and it may be difficult to adjust to. Do you think you can do that?"

Soft images flashed through her mind: Winning a regional trophy. Holding Jae-Jin's hand triumphantly in the air. Him looking down at her—smiling, even!— as the audience clapped for their victory.

"I won't know until I try. And I'm willing to try."

IT WASN'T UNTIL a few matches later, as well as after a break to let the dog out, that Ji-Soo began to wonder if she'd realised what she'd signed up for. She'd played with Jae-Jin on a team many times before, but she quickly learned that having his razor focus trained on her was a very different experience. Their friends joked about his military approach, and he always seemed to take it in stride. But now she was his grunt, and he seemed to be relishing every minute of it.

"No, no, no!" he cried as she triggered Death Flight on a mass of Onyx bearing down on them.

"What's wrong with using a Transcendence on a horde?" she said as her mighty wings swept back to execute the attack.

"Nothing as long as you know *when* to use it. See how there are four opponents on the map?"

"I do, but they're way up north."

"That doesn't mean they'll be there for long. You can't panic when a horde rushes your way. Just think of Onyx as what they are—filler. Yeah, we need to keep them out of the graveyards, or we lose the match. But the game is built to make you waste your big spells on them so you won't be ready when the other players come for you. After your attack wipes this group out, just stay put for a second. Watch what happens."

As usual, the Transcendence ended with a pile of Onyx bodies on the ground. They were in a clearing in the Qi'sho Observatory map, which was dotted with towering pine trees under an azure sky that seemed to go on forever. It was pretty, but also offered lots of places to hide. Ji-Soo felt nervous as she realised it would be a perfect time for a player to snipe her from a secret spot behind an ancient trunk.

They both watched the map. The four dots that were clustered a moment before spread out and headed towards them. Five seconds ticked by as they approached. When the dots drew close two Menders appeared, their forms draped in seaweed and pond scum. Ji-Soo turned just in time to see a Weaver emerge from the trees behind her.

"And here comes the fourth," Jae-Jin said as a

Plunderer made its way in from the east. "Now, watch."

One of the Menders darted towards them first. Jae-Jin fired off a handful of skulls, dealing damage to both the approaching enemy and the one behind it. The Weaver came for Ji-Soo a second later and she rolled out of its way with milliseconds to spare. A massive tusk split the dirt next to her face, the impact rattling her teeth. She looked up to see Jae-Jin's axe splitting the Nature God from head to belly. The two sides peeled apart limply as the body tottered on its furred legs. A moment later it was crumpled on the ground.

✦SHATTERURBONES HAS BEEN
ELIMINATED BY JAEBOMB✦

Ji-Soo was about to get up when a black flash passed through her field of vision. She slashed with her crossblades, quick to move, but the enemy was quicker. The Mender that Jae-Jin had fired at earlier was still coming. A voluminous twist of seaweed the colour of oil was winding around her leg, tightening its grip like a murderous cobra. She continued to try to cut it away, but her blades fell short, slashing through the air in desperation.

"Jae—"

Before she could finish his name, all the skulls he'd thrown earlier in the fight rose from the ground. Ji-Soo watched her health steadily drain as they arranged themselves into a fearful visage that towered over the field like some horrible god. She pounded the button to use one potion after another to keep from dying as Jae-Jin's Transcendence reached its peak. The skull's jaw dropped open as it unleashed an unearthly howl, this spirit from another world who luckily was willing to serve them for a few precious moments. Clouds of dark smoke poured forth from its jaws. Their opponents forgot themselves as they writhed, choked, and clapped their hands over their ears. Ji-Soo grinned. If any spell was really fun to watch, it was Leer of Mortality.

The smoke cleared to reveal a beautiful sight (in the world of *Ancestral*, at least): not a single creature left alive.

✦ARASHIINTHEBUSHES HAS BEEN
ELIMINATED BY JAEBOMB✦

✦PATTOYOURCATTO_BRO HAS BEEN
ELIMINATED BY JAEBOMB✦

✦MZ_BADASS_99 HAS BEEN
ELIMINATED BY JAEBOMB✦

"And that's the match," Jae-Jin murmured as their kills faded out, replaced by the match stats screen. "So, what did you learn in this battle?"

"Onyx are a distraction, not my top priority."

"OK. What else?"

"Using my Transcendence on them left me vulnerable to my real-life opponents."

"Right. I had mine ready, so we were able to win. If I made the same mistake you did, we'd both be dead right now."

Ji-Soo felt a flush of shame, but said nothing.

"This is what I mean by learning to think two steps ahead. Learning this is good for two reasons: one, because now you won't do it anymore when you know a better way, and two, you can take advantage of it when your enemy does it, which happens often in the lower leagues. But you can be sure that when we play regionals, we won't get those kinds of cheap chances. Think of learning to play like this as forming a ring of protection around the team."

Ji-Soo heard a woman's voice from the other line. This time the Korean came across clearly: *Can you come help now?*

"I've gotta sign off and get some chores done. This went well. Same time tomorrow?"

Ji-Soo's mind flashed with a hundred different thoughts.

When will I find time to stream?

He wants to do this every day?

I'm never sleeping again.

We might really have a shot at regionals this way.

She said none of these things.

"Sure."

"OK. Talk to you then."

CHAPTER FIFTEEN
A TINY CONNECTION

As THE TOWERING red paifang that marked the entrance to the Temple Street night market swam into view, Lana thought (and not for the first time) that the famous tourist destination would make an excellent *Ancestral* map.

The last of the day's light faded as she closed the distance to the gate. It reached four stories into the sky with its noble red columns, each carved with Chinese characters the locals called zhuyin. A green and white bar with traditional illustrations of blooming trees and wild animals spanned the columns at the top, and above these stood two dark green roofs with curling corners in the classic paifang style. A small plaque in the middle with lacquered gold writing declared to the world in both Chinese and English that this was the famous Temple Street.

On any given day it was crammed with gawking tourists snapping photos and standing stock still in the middle of foot traffic as if they were the only people on earth. Typically, this would have been annoying to her. She hated nothing more than people completely unaware of common courtesy. But they spent the most time ogling the cheap t-shirts and knock-off Gucci purses, which were the parts of the market she had no reason to visit anyway.

The cacophony here sang to her. She also adored its smells: the pungency of freshly caught sea life, the savoury tingle of roasted pigeon, the earthiness of Chinese herbs. Fortune tellers beckoned in gullible travellers only a few feet away from opera singers resplendent in their fine silks and elaborate headpieces.

Lana adored this place. From time to time she would leave her Orb silent on its charger and try to forget *Ancestral* for a while in favour of trekking to the market on foot. It was a long walk, but she enjoyed these quiet stretches, talking to no one as she cut through the city with its dense herds of mask-wearing cattle. She was a stranger in a strange land. But all the better for it.

The thing that had driven her out of the apartment today was the need to think. That, and an overwhelming craving for soup dumplings that she could not satisfy with what was currently available in her freezer. The food she stockpiled was fine most of the time: frozen soups ready to microwave, bags of shumai, fish balls to add to piping hot broth. But some days there was nothing that calmed her more than to sit in a coffeehouse with the fragrant steam from a cup of tea warming her face and feel alive in the world. A twinge in her heart told her it was exactly what she needed on this humid evening. But first, food.

The market was tightly nestled between two walls made of impossibly tall residential buildings in various depressing shades of grey. Over the top of this alley festive red flags hung on long strings. There was no city in the world—and she'd been to many—that loved red more than China. It was their fire, their luck, their happiness. She'd spent less than a year here but was charmed by the culture in a way she never had been elsewhere. There was an industrial spirit infused into everything, a determination to endure that she found infinitely admirable.

Also, the night here was ten times livelier than the daytime. She loved that.

She nudged her way through the crowd to move in the direction of her favourite food stall. After navigating around a poky family with three kids screaming in Mandarin and a woman wearing a huge green transparent visor hauling what looked like a dozen plastic bags, she finally made it to her destination. The woman behind the counter, who'd served her two dozen times before, showed no sign of recognition whatsoever.

"What you want?"

"Xiao long bao," Lana replied, reaching into her hip bag for her stash of yuan. She waited until the woman held out her hand to give her the payment, knowing she would snatch it away as she always did. She was not disappointed. A minute later she was handed a round wooden steamer atop a metal plate.

"Return when finish!"

"Mm goi." Lana didn't bother to look up to see if she'd been acknowledged. Instead, she held the steamer close as she walked to the nearby eating area. Round wooden tables with royal blue metal legs stood in a cluster, mostly packed with people hunched over steaming bowls. She spied one red stool that was unoccupied and made a beeline in its direction.

Three other people sat at the table with enormous bowls of noodles, leaning over and sniffing the steam curling into their faces. An older man with salt and pepper hair was halfway through a platter of wok-fried seafood. His hand was clamped around a beer so cold beads of condensation clung to the bottle. None of them looked up as Lana pulled out the stool, sat down, and fished a portable chrome soup spoon out of a clear plastic case in her bag.

She took the top off her steamer to reveal ten perfectly shaped soup dumplings. She blew on them to cool them, trying to summon the patience to wait for the right moment despite her hunger. Finally, she eased one onto her spoon with a pair of wooden chopsticks, careful to position it just right so the broth inside would spill perfectly into the spoon so as to not waste a single drop.

The comforting spill of the savoury flavour on her tongue lulled her back into her thoughts despite the loud chatter of the people around her.

The night before, she played until she felt burned out. Hopeless. The desire for a challenge had gotten worse, and the more she sought one out, the more convinced she was that it wasn't there to find. She'd tried filtering matches in hopes of setting some up with other high-level players. The problem was, there weren't enough. Perhaps enough to make a team or two, but none did the wise thing and played together to combine their strengths. Instead, they seemed to use their impressive power to crush every fight with regular players they came into contact with. Which, she had to admit, she'd done, too, at one point in time. But a system she'd thought could have been brilliant was quickly becoming a flaw due to a bottleneck: there simply weren't enough people playing at this level. If there were, it would be a blast. But it wasn't.

Not wanting to face the nervous twitches that had become an unwelcome companion these days, she'd logged into her favourite *Ancestral* forum instead. At first, she'd come there to find that sometimes people talked about being defeated by her. She'd once read these accounts with relish, deeply amused to see their frustration. But after months of it, they'd become commonplace. Boring, even. Not only did she stop caring if she beat people or not, she lost all the pleasure she once got out of reading about it.

What she did enjoy was the feeling of lurking behind the scenes, watching others without contact. And since enough people had talked about meeting her in-game, she wanted a way to avoid recognition. One day, she opened her laptop and logged out of her old account, following the steps to make a new one with a throwaway username.

When she felt restless and unsatisfied, she went to the forum and read the threads. As she'd scanned one discussion about players looking to max their levels, an interesting username among the comments caught her attention.

MONONOAWARE

The phrase referred to one of Lana's favourite concepts learned from her days in Japan. There was no good word in English for it, so it was hard to explain to Americans, but the essence was to have an awareness of the impermanence of life. It was a beautiful, bittersweet feeling, and one she knew all too well since she'd been a young adult. As a person who had spent so much of her life alone, she had all the time in the world to feel life passing and to wonder if it was all the more exquisite because she couldn't hold onto it.

She'd clicked the profile and opened an instant message before she had time to think about what she was doing.

>**hellodearone:** >*i love your username. are you from japan?*

A message to a stranger, one she had no reason to send and to someone who had no reason to reply. And yet ten minutes later, one came.

>**MonoNoAware:** *I'm not. But I fell in love with that concept the moment I learned it :)*
>**hellodearone:** *i did too. just never thought I'd see it on an ancestral forum*
>**MonoNoAware:** *Are you from Japan?*
>**hellodearone:** *no. i learned about it when I was there though*
>**MonoNoAware:** *Oh wow. I've always dreamt of going there. Was it wonderful?*
>**hellodearone:** *yes. i still miss it. i plan to go back someday, when i can*
>**MonoNoAware:** *You're so lucky you've gotten to travel! I've never left the US yet. Hope one day I can for an Ancestral tournament... it's a crazy dream, but I'd love to go to one in China or South Korea one day.*
>**hellodearone:** *how long have you played?*
>**MonoNoAware:** *Since launch. You?*

➢**hellodearone:** *same*

➢**MonoNoAware:** *Are you going to do regionals where you live?*

➢**hellodearone:** *i'm more of a lone wolf. don't play with teams much*

➢**hellodearone:** *do you have a team already?*

➢**MonoNoAware:** *I do and we are starting to train for our regional. I hope we can get good enough to have a chance to compete.*

Lana stared at the screen for a while, unable to decide what she should say next. Her heart felt like a plucked string shaking off its reverberations. Why was she nervous talking to this stranger? And excited?

➢**hellodearone:** *you make me wonder if I'm missing out*

➢**MonoNoAware:** *Oh, well... I don't mean to make you think that. For me though, it's the most exciting thing that can happen for the community.*

➢**hellodearone:** *hmmm.*

➢**MonoNoAware:** *What class do you play?*

➢**hellodearone:** *the moment i saw the plunderer i knew it was what i had to be.*

➢**MonoNoAware:** *Me too!! That character is so solid. We should share tips!*

Lana stared at the words on her phone screen for a few moments before typing her reply.

➢**hellodearone:** *ah i'm not that good yet.*

➢**MonoNoAware:** *No hurry! I'm always happy to make new Ancestral friends so if I learn new things, I'll be sure to share.*

She looked at the screen again, her fingers hovering over the keyboard.

➢**hellodearone:** *do you play a lot?*

➤**MonoNoAware:** *Yeah, every day. Getting ready for regionals will probably mean I have to play more often than that. But I think it'll be fun. I want to become a better player.*

Me too, Lana thought. *But I don't know how anymore.*

➤**MonoNoAware:** *Well, it's getting late here so I have to get to bed, but thanks for messaging me! If you want to add me as an Ancestral friend, my username is Nagiko. TTYL!*

Lana sat staring at the last message for a long time. The room felt colder than it had just a minute before, and she pulled her hoodie closer. At her core, a cauldron of emotion bubbled, a strange brew of ingredients she didn't recognise. How long had it been since she'd spoken to another player? Two months? Three?

How long had it been since she'd spoken more than a few words to anyone?

Uncomfortable, she finished the last of her soup dumplings in a few quick bites and wiped her spoon off with a napkin, replaced the top of the bamboo steamer, and stood up. At the same moment, the crowd parted as a grubby-looking kid ran through, clipping her arm hard when he passed by. Her fingers instinctively tightened around the tray just in time to keep the steamer from sliding off and hitting the ground. A harried-looking woman ran after the kid at full speed, her housedress flapping in the breeze as she yelled at the child in a hoarse voice to "stop causing trouble!"

That's Hong Kong. Never a dull moment.

Relieved that she wouldn't have to try to explain what might have happened to the food stall worker in her shabby Cantonese, she carefully made her way back through the crowd and placed her items in an already-overflowing rubber dishpan on a metal stand off to the side of the stall. It looked as if it hadn't been cleared out all day. Flies buzzed around dried food crusted on some of the plates. She glanced back over at the stall to see the woman who had served her before slapping food onto plates with a grim expression on her face. She appeared to be the only one working.

It was a lonely place. She'd known that the second she stepped off the plane for the first time. Flying over the city, she looked down on a towering metropolis surrounded by lush forests. There was plenty of room, but people insisted on packing themselves like sardines into the city, choosing to live in homes no bigger than coffins just to be near other people they never spoke to.

Lana wove past waves of people as she headed out of the market. Her heart felt light and strange in her chest. She wanted her favourite coffeehouse, her cup of tea, her quiet corner table where she could lay out her journal and notes and lose herself for a few hours.

She also didn't want to be alone anymore.

CHAPTER SIXTEEN
REPLICANTS

"Is THIS THE place?"

Ji-Soo peered through the windshield at the neon sign on the front of the restaurant. An elegant pink script spelled out the word *Replicants* next to a massive bowl of glowing noodles. A few were being lifted out of the soup by a pair of violently blue chopsticks.

"Yep. This is it."

Lissa guided her car into one of the compact spots and turned off the ignition. Ji-Soo reached into the backseat and fished out a tall patent leather tote bag in an intense shade of bright green. Her friend eyed it as it came into view.

"Did you... match your bag to the restaurant's aesthetic?"

"Well, it is cyberpunk inspired," Ji-Soo said as she tossed her hair—today a long mint bob with blunt bangs—over her shoulder. "How could I not dress for the occasion?"

"Don't you always?" Lissa said as she grabbed her own bag, opened the door and got out of the car.

Lucas and Devon were waiting outside, checking their phones. They waved as soon as they saw the girls approaching. Lissa noticed Devon was rocking a new hairstyle, his dreads piled high atop his head and wrapped to resemble a pompadour. He was also sporting a few blonde locks that hadn't been there a few days ago.

"Right on time!"

"Look at that cool hair," Lissa said, motioning towards Devon's head.

"You like it? I just got it done." Devon struck a pose, turning to the side to show off his profile. "I feel so light though. It's weird not to feel hair swinging all around my head."

"Now I feel boring," Lissa lamented, patting her dark brown hair.

Ji-Soo frowned in her friend's direction and slapped Lissa's leg with her bag.

"As if!"

"I can't believe you two haven't been here before," Lucas said through a happy smile. "I found it my first week and I was addicted instantly. This has gotta be the best ramen in the city."

"It's further north than I usually go but I'm always up for an adventure." Lissa smiled back at him. Lucas could have suggested a much crazier prospect and she'd have gone along with it. She had made up her mind that he was one of the good guys.

"Who else are we waiting on?"

"Just Ray and Zio, but I'll text them," Devon said as he pulled his phone out of his back pocket. "Let's go in and get settled."

The dark, narrow restaurant was modelled to

perfection after a side alley lifted right out of a bustling, overcrowded metropolis. Neon signs of all shapes and sizes hung from the walls and ceiling, blinking their empty promises. A huge rectangular white sign with red and blue Chinese characters stretched across the entirety of the right side of the restaurant. To their left, transplanted bus stops with loud pink advertisements on the sides promised extremely low phone service rates. As they drew closer, they saw that the benches within had been removed and replaced with little bars where guests now sat, sucking noodles from their bowls with great relish.

"This place is wild," Devon said as he took it all in. Lucas turned around to find the rest of his party in a similar predicament, looking around themselves in awe.

"Believe it or not, the food is better than the atmosphere. Our table is over here."

He led them to a roomy corner spot. Jae-Jin sat at the far end of a booth upholstered in shiny white tufted fabric. His face was illuminated in the darkness by his phone screen as he read something with great interest.

"Have you ever come out to eat with us before?" Lissa said as she slid in next to him. "Pretty sure this is basically a miracle. The apocalypse must be upon us."

He didn't look up from his screen as he spoke.

"This is a business meeting. You'll see what I mean in a second."

Lissa rolled her eyes, turning back to the table. Each setting was adorned with a single white cloth napkin and a pair of lacquered red chopsticks the colour of a ripe tomato, laying atop a tiny ceramic rest.

"This might have been better in front of a screen, but I wanted us to have fun," Devon said as he wriggled into the booth. "Plus, Lucas talked up the food so much I figured we might as well chow down while we talk about how to take this competition by the balls."

Ray walked up to the table just in time to hear the end of Devon's sentence. He snorted as he sat down.

"I've been here for five seconds and Devon's already talking about balls."

Devon shrugged as he turned on his most charming smile.

"Why mince words? We can't live forever, folks."

A tall, slender woman with waist-length royal blue hair appeared seemingly out of nowhere at the head of the table. She wore a plastic raincoat with an opalescent gleam over a tightly fitted patent leather tank dress the colour of steel. Her multi-coloured eyelashes were so long they brushed against her brow bones. Lissa tried not to stare, but just before she averted her eyes, she noticed that the falsies were encrusted with tiny flowers.

"Welcome to Replicants, friends. Can I get you all something to drink?"

She nodded politely after taking their orders and turned to leave, her coat squeaking as she walked. Ji-Soo peered over the table at the boots the waitress wore.

"Those are missing from my collection... but not for long."

Lissa snorted. "Your boot museum is waiting to be erected."

"I'm here!" Zio cried as she ran up to the table. She wore ripped jeans and a t-shirt that said *Straight*

White Men Ruin Everything in bold black type. Devon took one look at it and burst out laughing.

"That shirt is amazing, Zio."

"Thank you! Sorry I'm late. This place is a trip!"

"Come in, come in," Devon said, scooting over. "You're just in time."

"OK," Jae-Jin said, putting down his phone. "Let's get down to business." He nodded to thank the waitress as she placed a glass of water with a lemon wedge in front of him. "So, since we last got together, Lucas and I have both been researching the competition. As those of you who watch the leaderboards know already, Mastermind has been rising through the ranks the last few months. The same ones I thought we might have to go up against in the long run."

"Mastermind," Ji-Soo said. "With the WraithX dude."

"Right." He picked his phone up and turned it to face the table. Six guys wearing black and red jerseys with their arms folded looked back at them from the screen. The one closest to the front was blonde and wore a red baseball cap backwards. One eyebrow was cocked to match the smirk on his face.

Lissa's mouth dropped open as recognition dawned on her. That look he'd given her after they'd won that day at the Glass Cannon.

"Lucas," Lissa said. "That's... that's..."

"Who?"

"Remember the guy at the tourney with the red cap? The day you and I met."

"Oh, yeah," Lucas said, nodding. "I do now. He had a little cluster of fanboys around him."

"That's how it starts, usually," Jae-Jin said. "Players gain fans in person or via streaming. People see a name climbing the leaderboards and want to watch to see how they win. Next thing you know, you have fans. As far as I can tell, they've never formally competed as a team before. I dug around to try to find out if any of them have esports experience before *Ancestral*, but I couldn't find any. So as good as they are, they're also a first-time team, just like us."

"People on the forums say they're jerks," Zio piped up.

"That guy in the front sure looks like one."

"I've read that on the forums, too." Ray made a face as if he'd smelled something bad. "And that they don't play fair."

Jae-Jin nodded.

"That's what I heard, too. So I searched to see if they've streamed any of their matches, and sure enough, there's some... funny business in some of them. Also, they have their own channel, which is something we might want to think about for our team in the long run."

"I could set that up for us, easy," Ji-Soo said, "since I stream myself."

Jae-Jin nodded and held up a finger to indicate that he had more to say.

"That would be great, Ji-Soo. But let me fill in the picture here. As far as I can tell, their greatest asset is their teamthink. They goof around a lot when they play. But they can afford to because despite that, they run a tight ship. What's really interesting to me is that the leader doesn't call the shots the way we do when we play, for instance. From time to time he might call out one command or other. But they seem to operate as if they have one brain, which is common to see in championship teams around the world."

The group nodded in silence. Zio sipped her drink, a bright purple concoction with a tall metal straw.

"Do they live together or something?" Lissa asked.

"Hard to tell. I looked through their social media accounts and there are pictures of them playing in the same room. But it could be one of their houses just as easily as it could be a gaming house. Either way they play like a team that practises daily."

He paused.

"And they have a sponsorship already."

Ray coughed on a mouthful of Coke. "What?"

"Scouts watch the leaderboards. And they used to come to tourneys to look for talent. But if you think about it, it makes more sense to find it before that rather than throw your hat in the ring at a major competition where other sponsors will be doing the same thing. My guess is that they found these guys via their streams and decided to take a chance on them. Tried to get in on the game early."

"Who's the sponsor?"

"Rager, remember? That newish energy drink company," Jae-Jin said. "You must have zoned out the first time I mentioned it."

"Maybe." Ray looked relieved. "So not, like, a huge company."

"No." Jae-Jin paused to take a sip of water. "And the sponsor situation has become so shifty out there that it's hard to know if they're legit or not. Either way, Mastermind has already attracted attention.

They have a presence. And that's something we need if we want a chance to succeed."

"That can change fast," Devon said as the blue-haired waitress returned to the table, tablet in hand.

"Are we ready here?"

The waitress tapped out their orders with a hypnotising quickness, fingers flying over the screen. Once she turned and headed back into the shadows with her coat making its squeak-squeak-squeak sound, Devon turned his attention back to the table.

"I always say things have changed since my time. But only in certain ways. Some things about competition really stay the same no matter what. Trust me when I say if you start climbing those leaderboards as Team Phoenix, you'll get noticed quick. Coming out of nowhere is a solid advantage. Works great for ninjas."

The table laughed. The joke even earned a rare smile from Jae-Jin.

"So don't focus on what they have that we don't. Back up and focus on what we *do* have: a team that has terrific skills, communicates well, and actually likes one another. Don't underestimate that last part. There's a lot of magic in that."

"You have a great attitude, Devon," Ji-Soo said.

"Thank you! It matters more than you think," he replied. "Not just in this, but in life, all around you. Bring your best attitude to the game and you'll be unstoppable." He laughed to himself. "It worked for me. I mean, trust me, there was no reason a scrawny Black kid who was constantly picked on had any hope of winning anything, much less a championship. I was told I would fail just about every day of my life back then."

The table fell silent. None of them had ever heard this part of Devon's story before. After a few seconds ticked by, Lissa spoke up.

"What made you decide those people were wrong?"

Devon looked thoughtful as he nursed the question.

"I never decided. I knew they were wrong. Don't ask me how, but I did. I grew up watching a lot of martial arts movies with my dad. All my heroes kicked ass and took names no matter what the situation or how insane the odds. They were minorities, too, like me, and they never let it stop them. So, I think what I learned from them was how important it is to endure. Always."

As if to punctuate his sentence, the waitress reappeared with a huge black tray in hand. Four blue and white bowls roughly the size of her head sat atop it, each of them gushing steam.

"Tonkatsu Black?"

"Me," Devon and Ji-Soo said at the same time. Devon passed a bowl to her first, careful not to let it spill as he nudged it along. After another trip back and forth to retrieve the rest of their food, all seven of them were ready to eat.

"It smells amazing!" Ji-Soo exclaimed as she tucked her napkin into her lap.

"It is," Lucas said. "Let's dig in!"

The conversation at the table fell silent as everyone feasted, the sign of a meal well-enjoyed. Jae-Jin was the first to speak up after making his way through half the bowl.

"Maybe I am missing out on these dinners."

"Jae-Jin!" Lissa put her chopsticks down. "Did you really just say that?"

"I did. Commit it to memory forever."

"We always want you here, you know," Ji-Soo said, staring into her ramen broth.

He looked in her direction, saying nothing, but Lissa sensed the language of his body next to her. Tension, but also something else. Just a flicker.

"I'll keep that in mind."

"It's the power of the ramen," Lucas said as he nibbled a piece of bok choy from between his chopsticks. "It's miraculous."

"You aren't wrong. I'll be back for this." Devon picked up his bowl to sip from it.

"Maybe this should be our victory dinner," Zio offered. "When we win regionals, we come back and order anything we want."

The waitress returned to check on them, refilling glasses and trading banter. She took away a few empty bowls and promised to return with a dessert menu, praising the merits of a summer special called anmitsu.

"So, this is my suggestion," Jae-Jin said. "Let's add team practice at PlaySpace daily. Same time every day. If we need to tweak it because of anyone's schedule we can. But I like the idea that it's consistent. Also, I think that it would be to our advantage to have two leaders calling the shots in case one of us is downed. I've asked Ji-Soo to partner with me on that, and it's been going well, so we'll practise that formula from here on out."

As he spoke Ji-Soo reached for Lissa's hand under the table and squeezed it tight. Lissa squeezed back, proud of her friend.

"Ah, that's brilliant," Devon said. "Good thinking.

And Ji-Soo's the perfect pick, too."

"What time works for everyone? I know it's summer break but some of us may have stuff to do." Jae-Jin picked up his phone, tapping to open the calendar. "I should be open by noon every day."

"I could do any time after one," Ray said. "I have chores in the morning but that would give me enough time to get over to the 'Space."

Lissa nodded. "I can do noon, too."

Devon looked in Ji-Soo's direction. Her eyebrows were furrowed as if she was doing equations in her head.

"Looks like hard work over there."

Ji-Soo blinked twice, laughing as she realised what Devon had said.

"I went into the zone. Yeah, I'll be there at noon."

"I have to talk to my boss," Zio said. "I typically work night shifts but every once in a while they call me and ask me to pull a double. If I can make sure that I'm in the clear for those then I can do noon, too."

"But when will you sleep?"

"Until 11:30," Zio said, winking. "Remember I live less than ten minutes from PlaySpace."

"I'll have the coffee on then," Devon said, laughing. "Your commitment is admirable."

"I usually help my parents out in the morning, but I am pretty sure I can get my chores done before noon," Lucas said. "Worst case I'll be a little late. But I'll do what I can."

Jae-Jin looked at each of them as he nodded.

"All right. Sounds like we have a plan, team."

CHAPTER SEVENTEEN
DON'T GET COCKY

"I DON'T WANT to brag, but I think we're on a streak," Ray said.

"Ray!" Zio said from her seat across from him, her face hidden by her monitor. "You know it jinxes our luck the minute you say that aloud."

"OK, but can't I be proud for a minute? We have yet to lose a match today."

Ji-Soo stood up to look at her friend. She sipped a bubble tea the colour of faded lavender with a pile of boba at the bottom. Round oversized glasses with electric blue rims framed her dark eyes, and her hair was pulled up into a messy bun. She looked at Ray and gave a decisive nod.

"Good point. Also, we might want to break for lunch. We've been playing for hours."

Jae-Jin pushed his chair back from the table, sighing like a man who has endured much and knows more is on the way.

"I'm not hungry myself. But Ray's right, we've made good progress. I'm pleased with how it's going so far. We've come a long way in just a few weeks."

"OK, OK," Zio said. "You guys have a point. I just want our lucky streak to keep going!"

"Faster Orbs, faster games," Lucas said, wearing his trademark grin. "But there's a lot more to it than just luck. I can feel us really clicking together as we play more and get the rhythm of each other's play styles. We're killing it."

"Whoa, the leaderboards!" Ji-Soo was looking at her laptop, which she'd had open next to her since early that morning. "Did anyone else look before now?" She turned the computer and held it so her friends could see. The *Ancestral* leaderboards, filtered by region, showed that Team Phoenix's rank had increased by four spots since they'd sat down to play that afternoon. It was hard to believe that a few weeks ago they'd ranked in the three hundreds. Today their score was in the low two hundreds—and with luck, they'd break into the top one hundred soon enough.

"What about 'em?" Devon said as he walked into the room with an oversized red coffee mug in hand. He wore a red hoodie over a black t-shirt with a silhouette of Bruce Lee in one of his signature poses. His dreads were piled high on his head and tied in place with a colourful strip of fabric.

"Look!" Ray said, pointing. "Ji-Soo, click into our profile."

The Team Phoenix page looked handsome after a bit of love from Ji-Soo, who had taken the time to connect all their profiles, upload a banner Devon had worked his graphic design magic on, and fill in some info about who they were and where they hailed from. But by far the most exciting thing on the page was the arrow next to their team name, which indicated they'd come on in leaps and bounds over the last few weeks. Their streaming profile was also gaining a steady flow of new followers as well.

"I hate to disappoint you, but I'm not surprised," Devon said, smiling broadly. "I've known from the beginning that once you all put your heads together you were going to kill it."

"At this rate we should have no problem taking on Mastermind," Lucas said, all bravado. "We'll be right up there next to them in no time."

Devon nodded, his face thoughtful. Then he reached for one of the empty chairs and rolled it to the side of the room, plopping down and spilling a few drops of coffee on the sleeve of his hoodie in the process.

"Glad you said that because it reminds me of something," he said. "Jae-Jin, have you been sharing Mastermind's matches with the team?"

"Ji-Soo and I have been going over them after our morning sessions. But no, we haven't done an all-hands yet. I wanted to watch them more so I could continue to learn about what they do in the field to keep their high rank. Because I know they can't always play the same way, or they wouldn't be where they are."

Devon snapped his fingers. "Exactly. You're a sharp one."

"That said, maybe it's time," Ji-Soo piped up. "At the very least we can share what we do know so everyone else sees what we see. That also lets us figure out if we can steal any of the moves from their playbook and adopt them for ourselves."

Devon laughed in his warm way.

"Some days I think you folks hardly need me. But

what Lucas said actually reminded me of something I wanted to talk to you all about. Was I interrupting anything?"

"Nah," Lissa said. "We were thinking about eating but hadn't gotten very far."

"This won't take long." He paused. "So, in my competitive days, I always figured my biggest challenge was going to be the other team. And I was wrong about that. Which is a mistake I don't wanna see you make if I can help it."

"But if the main objective isn't the other team, then what is it?" Jae-Jin adjusted his glasses as he spoke, looking genuinely interested.

"You. Or in my case, me."

Everyone in the room fell silent, waiting for Devon to continue.

"I didn't have a coach in the fighting game community. That wasn't really a thing back then. What you did was learn from other players. You watched hundreds upon hundreds of matches to see what they did that worked and what didn't. Then you tried it all out for yourself, stumbling the whole way and making God knows how many foolish mistakes. It's easy to stay focused when you're like that. Trying with all your might to claw your way out of the heap."

He paused to take a sip of his coffee.

"I had no one to tell me that the real danger comes when you start to get good. Good enough that people notice your scores, talking about you, watching your matches to figure out your strategies. Because the desperation that comes with being a nobody starts to slip away. And something comes to take its place, so quietly you could miss it if you don't know what to look for—which I didn't. I just kept riding that wave of excitement, getting doused left and right by adoration and attention and all the things I craved but never got before I became a competitive gamer. I couldn't get enough of it."

Ray cocked his head to one side

"So it's bad to enjoy the limelight?"

"Enjoying it isn't the problem. *Relying* on it is. That, and this little monster that grows in the back of your head that keeps whispering to you that you're the best. You're unbeatable. You're invincible. It's always hungry so you constantly have to feed it, always clawing at you and begging for more, more, more. And if you look right at it, what you see is that it's terrifying that at any moment you could lose all this and go back to being a nobody."

He paused.

"Anyway. My point is this—congratulate yourselves and be proud of what you achieve. You work hard and you deserve your victories. But also remember that pride grows like a wild animal inside you. No matter how well you train a tiger, it's still wild. If you get too relaxed, too sure you've got a handle on things, all it takes is one wrong move before you get eaten."

Ji-Soo's eyes widened.

"If you can find a way to stay close to that gift that desperation gives you—to work as hard as you can, knowing every moment counts—while taking your wins in stride, knowing at any time you *can* lose it all, you'll be better equipped than I ever was."

Each member of the team nodded except Jae-Jin, who sat still as a stone as Devon told his tale.

"There's one more thing. Just like you, the other teams you face are vulnerable to the same things. If you know these pitfalls in yourself, it opens the door to a great advantage: recognising when your opponent is weak because of them."

"Ahh," said Zio. "I like that."

"So, let's take Mastermind as an example. What do we know about them?"

"Tight teamthink."

"Solid players," Ray volunteered.

"Sponsored."

"They seem full of themselves."

Devon clapped his hands together, pointing at Ji-Soo.

"That. That last one. You know what that means?"

"The little monster is alive and well," Jae-Jin said with a smirk.

"Right! And if you know that, then you know...?"

"Even though they're on top, they're afraid to lose that," Lissa said, feeling awed and excited.

"Correct. And if they're afraid, they have a weakness. So, watch for it. Exploit it. You might only see it for a millisecond on the field, but you're fast enough to catch it. All of you are."

An audible rumble came from Devon's midsection. He clapped a hand to it as the others laughed.

"I guess my stomach has had enough of my long-winded speeches." He stood up. "Did this help?"

"Yeah," Ray said. "It's a lot to think about. But I like it. You're awesome, Devon."

"So are you." He grinned. "I'm gonna go microwave a burrito. If you think all this over and have questions, come ask me."

The room was silent after he left as the team mulled over his words. Lucas idly spun his chair in a circle as he turned his Orb over in his hands.

"I wanna play them," Zio blurted out. "We should send an invite."

"Mastermind?"

"Yeah."

"I don't think we're ready to do that yet," Jae-Jin said. "The impulse is understandable. But we want to go in with a chance to actually beat them. I don't think we're there. Moving in a good direction fast, yes. But you have to remember that first match will leave a powerful impression." He looked at Ji-Soo. "Actually, Ji-Soo and I have talked about this, and she has some great insight."

Whoa, Lissa thought. *Did Jae-Jin just... compliment her?*

"Since they hold the top spot in the region, like Lissa said, it's likely they are worried about keeping it that way. The best impression we can make is a slow and steady one. By creeping up the leaderboards, we not only boost our own standing, but they'll see us as more of a threat over time. That's the position we want them in when we finally play them. If they're afraid now, they'll be even more so when they go into a match with a team that they think could take their ranking away from them."

Jae-Jin nodded.

"She's right. I want to play them—and crush them—just as much as you do. But let's do it right."

Zio adjusted her glasses.

"I have an idea. Instead of going for lunch, why don't we just order pizza so we can keep our flow going?"

"That's a good idea!" Ray picked up his phone. "I think I have a discount code, too."

Jae-Jin shrugged. "Works for me. I'm still not hungry."

The others bantered back and forth about toppings of choice as Lissa sat silent, her head bowed. She flicked the right stick of her Orb with her thumb once, twice, three times.

"Lissa? Are you gonna weigh in on this?"

By the time she looked up, all eyes in the room were on her. She looked up to see a familiar expression on Ji-Soo's face. That special best friend knowledge, that something was wrong.

"Are you guys ever afraid that we can't do it?"

No one spoke. Lissa's words hung in the air. Ray, who had been in the process of ordering the pizzas through his phone, placed it down on the table to look across the room at her.

"I am."

Every person in the room looked in Jae-Jin's direction with varying expressions of disbelief. Lissa was perhaps the most shocked of them all, struggling to string words together as she spoke.

"But you—you're—"

"I know the only way to defeat that fear is to work every day of my life on getting better. So that's why I get up early every morning. That's why I play a minimum of four hours every day. And why I watch past matches to figure out where we went wrong, or other teams' matches to learn from their victories. I do all that because it feels better to take action than it does to sit in the 'what if' of being afraid."

The room remained silent. Lissa glanced at Ji-Soo

and noticed that she didn't look surprised at all. The look on her face was hard to identify.

"He's right," Lucas said. "Being scared is normal. But it's what you do with it that matters. If you use it as fuel to push forward..."

Jae-Jin gave a single nod.

"But if fear can destroy the other team, won't it make us weak, too?" Zio said.

"Only if we let it. If there's one thing I know for sure—and this is what Devon just said, more or less—so much of esports is a mind game," Jae-Jin said. "Of course, the training matters, the effort matters, but Mastermind are really into messing with their opponents. It's in their name, even. And I don't think we should go that route."

"It's not in this group to do that," Ji-Soo said. "Firstly, no one here sucks."

The room laughed.

"If we have any role to play, it's gonna be the good guys," Ray volunteered. "We're Daniel and they're the Cobra Kai."

"Who's Mr. Miyagi, then?" Zio asked, chuckling.

"Devon, obviously."

"Yeah, he's got a lot of wisdom to share," Lissa said. "We're lucky to have him. And I agree with Ji-Soo. Even if the win depended on it, I don't think Team Phoenix would ever approach the game in the way a team like Mastermind would. That's not who we are."

Jae-Jin glanced at his watch.

"We should get back in soon. I'm going to go outside and stretch my legs. Ji-Soo, come with me."

Lissa watched with wide eyes as her friend followed

Jae-Jin out of the room. Ray saw the look on her face and laughed.

"It's cute, isn't it?"

Lissa blinked in disbelief, taking a sip of water from her bottle.

"I wonder if they're dating yet."

Lissa coughed mid-sip, a spray of water misting across her lap. Ray came around the table and patted her back. Lissa cleared her throat a few times, then pulled a paper napkin from her bag and wiped up her mess. She glanced at Ray, then around the room. Zio had already settled back at her monitor and replaced her headset. Lucas was standing in the doorway making a phone call. Neither even seemed to notice the conversation.

When she did reply, she dropped her voice to a whisper just to be safe.

"I can't believe someone else finally noticed she likes him."

Ray's face broke into a wide smile and he started to laugh.

"What?"

"Oh, Lissa. Everyone's noticed."

"Seriously?"

"Well, except Jae-Jin, that is. He seems clueless. Maybe."

Lissa shook her head.

"I just hope he doesn't lead her on without realising it."

Ray glanced in the direction of the door that Jae-Jin and Ji-Soo had walked through a few minutes ago.

"I don't know. I think something good is happening. And I like it." Ray's eyes sparkled with mischief. "A little romance is fun."

"Well, it'll be fun to watch it happen if you're right."

"For sure. Do you like anybody?"

Lissa shrugged. "Not really. But I wouldn't have time to hang out with them even if I did. My whole life is practice right now."

Ji-Soo and Jae-Jin reappeared, each holding a bottle of water. Lissa noticed the ghost of a smile on Jae-Jin's face as he made his way back to his seat. Lucas wrapped up his call and stuffed his phone into his bag, grinning as he did so.

"Talking to your girlfriend, Lucas?" Zio raised her eyebrows in his direction.

"Heck, no. My dad just called. Wanted to know how our practice is going. He's funny." Looking around, he settled back into his chair. "We ready?"

"Maybe we can climb a few more spots today," Zio offered.

"No maybe about it," Ji-Soo said with confidence. "I've got all day."

"All right, phoenixes," Jae-Jin said as he created their next match. "Let's rise."

CHAPTER EIGHTEEN
A FRIEND IN THE DARK

"ANDDDDDD JAEBOMB SCORES another for Team Phoenix! Insane! They're always sharp on the field, but this match is just above and beyond!"

Lissa peered at the screen as the announcer's voice blared from outside her headset. Her team was nowhere to be seen through the trees, which hung heavy with moss and rot. She was in the Jiu'sho Swamps with filthy water pooling over the toes of her boots. A spike of fear pierced her chest as she looked at the mini-map. It was swarming with enemy dots, but not a single blue one. Her teammates were nowhere to be seen.

"Dynamix has been an absolute beast tonight. And it looks like he's gearing up for a third Transcendence. It's been a close call for Phantom more than once this evening—"

Lissa looked to her right. Jae-Jin, Ray, Ji-Soo and Lucas sat in the chairs next to her wearing their jerseys and headsets. All four were deeply focused on their screens. She watched as Jae-Jin called out a command and watched his lips move. No sound came out.

"...here comes Dynamix with Soup of Decay! This could be devastating if Puppet doesn't have a defence in mind, because the others are too far down the map to get to him in time—oooh! That was painful!"

Lissa reached out and shook Jae-Jin's arm. He didn't respond. She looked down at her own hand. Could he even see her? Was she real?

"Nagiko isn't responding to JaeBomb's commands. Is something wrong?"

Lissa turned in her chair to look at the shoutcasters. A man wearing an electric blue sportscoat and a woman with violently red hair pulled into a high ponytail leaned close to their mics, their faces animated.

"Onyx pouring in from the west—JaeBomb coming up to head them off. But Dynamix and ImPact have their hands full already! Can he handle this by himself? And is Nagiko off the grid?"

"I don't know, Becky, but one thing's for sure. Phantom is on the razor's edge, and at any moment they could take the lead..."

Lissa turned back to her monitor in time to catch a brief glimpse of movement between the trees. She watched as Onyx emerged, first two, then four, eight. More than she could ever take on by herself even if her Transcendence was charged—and it wasn't. In a few moments she'd be overwhelmed.

"Jae-Jin! I need help!"

She looked at him. Nothing. It was as if she was invisible. Helpless, she watched as the kill banner flashed across her screen.

"Whoa! Aaaaand Phantom has taken down ImPact. We could see the tables turning here—"

"Yes, John, that was huge! Phantom now has the

advantage, thanks to Nikki Cross. She's a terrific example of how to play Weaver class to perfection and her response time is incredible."

Panic. Lissa felt as if a vice was tightening around her throat. The team was losing, and no one could hear her cries for help. She hammered the attack button as Onyx poured into her space, snarling.

"Jae-Jin! Ray! Zio! ANYONE?"

"This match has changed hands so fast! That's all it takes, just one move—"

"John, look! Look at Quin Walker!"

Quin... Walker?

"There's no one to block him and he's headed for the graveyard at full speed! If Team Phoenix can't stop him, they're about to lose the match—*and* the championship!"

"Phantom is jockeying for the top spot, and they could get it tonight, John! In a few seconds we'll have a winner here, and I could see them taking it!"

Lissa felt a wave of nausea wash over her, bringing a terrible disorientation with it. A click came in her headset and the voice of her dead brother spoke through the line.

"You're done, Lissa. Done."

She jerked awake, her skin clammy with cold sweat.

SHE LAY IN the dark for what seemed like a long time. Her heart was hammering when she woke from the dream, beating its rhythm into her throat. She breathed through her nose slowly as she willed it to slow down.

She grasped for her phone in the dark and came upon its familiar shape pushed to the far side of the nightstand. Half-awake, she swiped her way to the app she wanted and opened it, then hit the plus button to start a new recording.

She opened her mouth to speak and found words suddenly impossible. Tears crested in the corners of her eyes. Her fingers curled around the phone as if to crush it to pieces.

"You died and left me here," she said, her words wavering. "And I leave you these stupid messages hoping you'll hear them, maybe, but there's nothing."

Silence. She felt a wave of despair roll over her. How pathetic was she, crying alone in her bed in the middle of the night, leaving a message for someone who would never hear it? She knew it was just another nightmare—one of many—but she felt as hurt as if Quin had really threatened her. She tried to shake off the remnants of the dream and instead felt anger rising up her throat. She clapped a hand over her mouth just in time to muffle a loud sob.

Her alarm grew, pulling her further into consciousness, as grief rose in her like a steadily building wave. It was immense, overwhelming. As it came down, she feared she might drown in it. She wrapped her arms around herself as it crashed onto her and wracked her body, shaking its barriers.

He was gone. And after all these years, she kept trying to find some way to not accept it.

She touched the stop button as a terrible weight settled over her chest. Scrolling down with a finger swipe, she looked at months of voice messages and felt ashamed. Foolish.

She was about to click off the phone screen when a notification appeared.

➤**hellodearone:** (4:32 am) *are you awake?*

Lissa blinked at the message. She wasn't sure where her new friend was texting from, but either they were in a different country, or they had a solid case of insomnia.

Just like me.

➤**MonoNoAware (4:33 am):** *Yes. Had a bad dream.*

➤**hellodearone (4:33 am):** *i hope i didn't disturb you*

➤**MonoNoAware (4:34 am):** *Not at all. I was just lying here.*

➤**hellodearone (4:36 am):** *i have bad dreams too. more often than i'd like.*

➤**MonoNoAware (4:37 am):** *I wish I knew how to make them stop.*

➤**hellodearone (4:39 am):** *me too*

Lissa stared at the screen as the seconds ticked by. Part of her was tempted to just talk about her dreams, talk about Quin, pour all her confusion and pain into the glowing rectangle in her hands and hope she could give it away for good. Her friend had bad dreams, too. Maybe they'd understand.

But she hesitated. She didn't want to chase this new person away.

➤**MonoNoAware (4:40 am):** *Why are you up?*

➤**hellodearone (4:41 am):** *ah, it's daytime here. just taking a break from the game for a while.*

➤**MonoNoAware (4:41 am):** *Where do you live, if you don't mind me asking?*

➤**hellodearone (4:42 am):** *i've been in hong kong for a while now*

➤**MonoNoAware (4:43 am):** *Oh wow. Cool.*

➤**hellodearone (4:44 am):** *how's training for your regionals going?*

➤**MonoNoAware (4:45 am):** *Pretty good, I think. I just don't know how we can beat the guys that are at the top.*

➤**hellodearone (4:45 am):** *what's your region?*

➤**MonoNoAware (4:46 am):** *Western US.*

➤**hellodearone (4:46 am):** *do you mean team mastermind?*

➤**MonoNoAware (4:47 am):** *Yeah.*

➤**hellodearone (4:47 am):** *give me a second.*

The minutes wandered by as Lissa waited for another message. Her eyes drifted to the shadows on her bedroom wall, cast by the branches of the tree outside. Long, strange shapes. She traced them with her gaze, disjointed images running through the haze in her half-awake brain. The practice room at PlaySpace. Ji-Soo's necklace with the gummi bears. Quin laughing. Her dad, peeking through her bedroom door to say hello.

➤**hellodearone (4:56 am):** *i can tell you how to beat those guys.*

Reading the text pulled her a few ticks towards consciousness. She sat up in bed as she typed her reply.

➤**MonoNoAware (4:56 am):** *Seriously?*

➤**hellodearone (4:57 am):** *they're running more on steam than they are full power. i'd need time to sift through more matches but i've seen them play before. they aren't championship material. what's your team called?*

➤**MonoNoAware (4:57 am):** *Team Phoenix. But we're way down on the leaderboards compared to Mastermind.*

➤**hellodearone (4:58 am):** *you guys live up to your name. big leader board jumps the past three weeks.*

➤**MonoNoAware (4:58 am):** *We're trying.*

➤**hellodearone (4:59 am):** *do you stream your team matches?*

➤**MonoNoAware (5:00 am):** *We have for a little while, but we're finally getting more serious about it. Do you want me to link you to the channel?*

➤**hellodearone (5:00 am):** *yes. that would help.*

➤**MonoNoAware (5:01 am):** *Give me a second and I'll get the link.*

Lissa thumbed between screens and opened the streaming app. Once she had the link, she dropped it in the chat, feeling a tickle of nerves as she did so. She knew she was a good player. And yet, she was worried what her new friend might think.

➤**MonoNoAware (5:02 am):** *You said you weren't very good at Ancestral but... I don't think that's true. you seem like you have really good insight about strategy.*

➤**hellodearone (5:04 am):** *i just really like to watch matches. i'm better at watching them than playing them, i think*

➤**MonoNoAware (5:05 am):** *Do you stream, too?*

➤**hellodearone (5:05 am):** *no. people watching me makes me nervous*

➤**MonoNoAware (5:06 am):** *LOL*

➤**hellodearone (5:06 am):** *what? what'd i say?*

➤**MonoNoAware (5:07 am):** *Well, it's just that esports is a weird hobby to choose if you don't like people watching you.*

➤**hellodearone (5:07 am):** *you're right.*

➤**hellodearone (5:08 am):** *i actually feel pretty stuck with the game right now.*

➤**MonoNoAware (5:09 am):** *How come?*

➤**hellodearone (5:09 am):** *well i don't play with people. only solo.*

➤**MonoNoAware (5:10 am):** *But there's a solo mode, there's nothing wrong with that.*

➤**hellodearone (5:10 am):** *i'll never make it to a competition as a solo player though. you read the regionals fine print, i'm sure. there is no one on one.*

➤**MonoNoAware (5:11 am):** *That's true. But didn't you say you didn't want to compete?*

➤**hellodearone (5:14 am):** *i think i'm just too afraid to*

➤**MonoNoAware (5:14 am):** *Afraid you'll be beaten? I mean, I'm afraid of that, too. I think everyone who competes has to be afraid of that. But it's also a thrill, it's a push, a way to challenge yourself.*

There was no reply for a while. Eventually Lissa lay back down, still watching the screen, feeling her exhaustion in every limb. She'd been on the verge of drifting back to sleep when she felt the phone vibrate in her hand.

➤**hellodearone (5:26 am):** *maybe i should try.*

Bleary-eyed, Lissa typed a quick reply before fading away completely.

➤**MonoNoAware (5:26 am):** *We'll talk more soon. I gotta go back to sleep. And thanks for looking at Mastermind and at our stuff. I'd really like to hear more about what you think.*

➤**hellodearone (5:27 am):** *you will.*

CHAPTER NINETEEN
DRIVING FORWARD

JI-SOO HEARD THE call of a strange bird as she ducked behind the village elder's hut, leaving a pronounced silence in its wake. Its song bothered her to no end. As many times as she'd played on the Xi'sho Village map she'd never once laid eyes on it, only heard its plaintive voice from some faraway place, singing of a terrible sadness in a language she could never understand.

"Three headed down your way, Sh0uj0."

"I got it."

Ji-Soo glanced to her right. Huts stretched out in front of her at uneven intervals in various states of disarray. A wooden hobby horse and a ring toss toy, both roughly carved, lay forgotten nearby. A clothesline with several worn-looking shirts and a threadbare bedsheet stood by the hut closest to her, and it was this she dashed to next as she made her way north to meet her enemies.

As she drew close to the border of the village, she caught sight of them: two Onyx, accompanied by a Turned player, emerging through the trees that separated her and the edge of the forest. She laid low, waiting for them to stumble into her line of sight, but also aware one glance at the map would give her position away.

The terrible squeal of Onyx knees drew closer as they barrelled right up to the clothesline. Ji-Soo watched as their dirt-encrusted boots drew into view. She had a moment to notice unusual greenish spatters on the toes before she aimed at their shadows and threw her weapons in a gap between the bedsheet and the shirt hanging next to it.

A splash of blood hit the sheet as her crossblades made contact, followed by a bewildered grunt. For the hundredth time, Ji-Soo thought the Onyx AI was dogged but not particularly smart. As she contemplated this, an Onyx body slumped against the sheet and fell into her lap.

"One down," she said as she backflipped to throw off the corpse and change her position. The other Onyx must have dodged her shot and fled, as she saw a red dot on the map heading back towards the forest. Fine. She could take care of that later.

"Let's get that Plunderer off the map," said Jae-Jin, sounding steely as always. "I'm heading down."

"Yep."

Ji-Soo's eyes flicked to the graveyard at the edge of the village as she did dozens of times during every match. No dots near it yet, but they would be soon enough. Going straight for the graveyard when the match started was a fool's errand, anyway. No good player would do something so predictable. Then again, there was no promise these were good players.

The Onyx that escaped her daggers was circling her

now, a hut's distance away. Jae-Jin's dot showed he was on the way, but in the meantime, she thought she could clear this one out. *That,* her mind whispered to her, *and Jae-Jin will be impressed with me, too.* She was hardly cognisant of this internal murmur as she trekked between the village well and a half-burned hut to seek out her prey.

"Group on my tail," Jae-Jin said just as she spotted the lone Onyx. "Be ready when I get there."

"Yep," Ji-Soo said, firing another crossblade. The creature grunted as it ducked at the last second, the weapon whizzing past its cheek. She knew not to use any of her heavy attacks—or her Transcendence meter—on a single enemy or Jae-Jin would give her a speech. But at this point it was more than that. From what she'd learned in the weeks they'd played these daily matches, her view of the game's strategy had changed. Before, she'd rushed in with too much power. She'd played as if a time bomb was ticking beneath her, and she had to kill everyone before it went off. But as hundreds of matches ticked by, she saw it wasn't the best approach. It made you lethal, but vulnerable.

She advanced closer and the Onyx did the same, saliva dripping through its fangs and onto its misshapen fists. She chucked a few more blades and watched as the beast dodged left and right.

Pain in the ass.

Uttering a battle cry, the Onyx swung a stone axe half the size of its body in her direction, engraved with crooked runes she was unable to read. It made a *whoomph* sound as it travelled towards her face. She rolled to one side with a few seconds to spare. As her opponent stumbled to gain control of its weapon after missing, she ended her roll in a crouched position and unfurled a single wing, blades gleaming. They sliced neatly through the creature's knees in a spray of blood. Its body hung in the air a moment, as if confused to discover it had lost these crucial pieces, then collapsed to the ground with all the grace of a potato.

"Just in time," Jae-Jin said as he drew behind her. "What happened to your Turned?"

"Dunno," Ji-Soo said, standing up. "He'll be back soon enough."

A few ticks of silence elapsed. If she had been asked, Ji-Soo would have said she could feel Jae-Jin frowning at her during it.

They looked up at the same time to see a Turned player round the corner around the village elder's hut. It wore long dark robes from the waist down and a matching hood with long pieces that wrapped around its neck. Its bare chest was caked with dirt and sweat. Huge, rusted scimitars with intricate carvings on the blade were clenched in each hand.

Ji-Soo rolled to the left twice, sure that those blades would be hurtling through the air where her head had been a millisecond before. When she came up, she saw Jae-Jin was also rising from a dodge, tossing skulls at the intruder's hooded face. It moved its head left and right with terrible quickness, a jerky, unnatural motion that made Ji-Soo's stomach turn. She hadn't seen that move before. Maybe it was new, or above her character's level? She made a mental note to check the player's stats out after the match to find out.

Ji-Soo heard the sound of the Plunderer casting Soul Drain, an unpleasant sound like a toothless creature sucking liquid through a straw. She looked at her Transcendence bar to find it had been drained by fifty percent. Now she couldn't cast Death Flight as soon as she'd planned. She leapt backwards to get out of the Plunderer's direct line of sight, using her wings to gain extra height. As she looked down from her vantage point above the huts, she saw Jae-Jin using his axe as a shield against the Plunderer's scimitars, which were flying at him with dizzying speed.

"He drained me. Keep him busy—we don't want Sail the Styx."

"I've got you."

Ji-Soo's Transcendence bar was refilling, but with painful slowness. The Plunderer had yet to look up as its focus was trained on Jae-Jin. It was at that moment that Ji-Soo figured out where the other Turned had gone. She caught sight of it darting at high speed between the huts behind Jae-Jin, coming straight for his back. It was closing the distance too fast.

"No!" she yelled, dropping down into the space between him and the Turned. It was another Brutalist like her, its eyes wild. It leered at her as it unleashed one of its wings in her direction. She rolled out of the way at the last possible second and heard a cry of fury behind her.

"Jae-Jin! Cast—"

"I am," Jae-Jin said, extending his open palms to the air. A spiral of skulls poured from them and spun into the air to take their final form. The massive skull took shape in the air, its empty gaze chilling. As its jaw unhinged and its wretched scream rent the air, they both watched as the Turned on each side of them crumpled helplessly to the ground. Ji-Soo noted with amusement that one stray Onyx had turned the corner behind the Plunderer just in time for the skull to open its mouth. Its expression twisted into comical bewilderment a split second before its body was ground to dust; the face of a beast who has seen the end of the world and doesn't know how to process it.

✦ARIZER HAS BEEN ELIMINATED BY JAEBOMB✦

✦DOMINATOR HAS BEEN ELIMINATED BY SHOUJO✦

Ji-Soo sighed with satisfaction as she leaned back in her desk chair.

"Even you have to admit that was good."

Jae-Jin laughed under his breath. Ji-Soo felt a girlish burst of delight at the sound of it.

"It was. But it's been good for a while, really." She heard him take a sip of something she guessed to be coffee. "At first, I was disappointed that none of the others wanted to do these morning runs with us. But it's made you and me a tighter team in the end. And when we play with them, the commands from you and I flow together perfectly. I feel positive about our odds."

Ji-Soo giggled.

"What?"

"You still sound so clinical sometimes."

"Well, I am. My dad is that way, so that's probably where I get it from."

"Did you grow up here?"

"Yeah. My mom and dad are both from Busan though. His company offered him a job in the US the year before I was born, so we've lived here ever since. Twenty years."

"I noticed you speak Korean to them."

"Ah, yeah." Jae-Jin sounded embarrassed. "My

mom's English isn't great. My dad's is OK but he prefers Korean at home. It's weird to me that they moved here, because they've never seemed like they wanted to be here."

"Mine either."

"Your family's from Korea, too?"

"They're still there, in Daegu. I live here by myself."

"You moved alone?"

"Yeah."

"Would have thought you'd have wanted to stay considering the esports scene there."

Ji-Soo paused, trying to decide how much of her life to share.

"I have two brothers there who are both competitive players. I used to play with them growing up, but my parents wouldn't allow me to play after a certain age. So, it would have been impossible for me to pursue a gaming career there." She sighed. "Besides, the American scene keeps growing, and I thought here I might get less flak for..."

"Being a woman."

"Right."

There was a lull in the conversation. Ji-Soo was about to break it by suggesting another match when Jae-Jin finally spoke again.

"My parents don't approve of my playing either."

"Really?"

"That's why I get up when it's still dark. The best time for me to play at home is when they're still sleeping. Plus, I do chores for them in the morning, so I wouldn't have time to play then anyway. And they don't ask where I go in the afternoons so coming to PlaySpace is not a problem."

"Doesn't your mom see you playing when she comes in your room?"

"That's what alt-tab is for," Jae-Jin said, in a voice so dry that they both dissolved into laughter afterwards.

"Our families sound a lot alike," Ji-Soo said when she regained her composure. "I'm kind of surprised, but kinda... not."

"I've never told anyone about my life with them," Jae-Jin said. "Not anyone on our team. I try not to talk about my family in general. We're there to play, not to have a therapy session."

"But they like you and would want to be your friend for more than just that, I think."

"I dunno. My dad always says I can't trust anyone." Ji-Soo was taken aback. "Really?"

"I've heard that since I was a little kid. Don't trust people. That and how you have to have a respectable job so you can take care of your family."

"Oh, man. My parents own a restaurant back in Daegu. And guess who they want to take it over when they're ready to retire?"

"You, of course."

"Yep. So not only am I declining that option, but I moved to America to have a life of my own. If there was an award in my family for selfishness, I won it."

"Still though, that's brave," Jae-Jin said, his voice dropping into an even lower whisper. "If I could move away from my family... I would. But I'd feel horrible about it. Leaving them to fend for themselves."

"But isn't that what we're all supposed to learn to do? Take care of ourselves?"

The line was silent for so long that Ji-Soo thought the connection had been lost. That, or she'd gone too far.

"Jae-Jin?"

"I'm here."

She waited a moment before she spoke again, unsure where to go from here.

"Anyway, did you want to—"

"You're right."

Her eyes widened and a flick of nerves passed through her. It wasn't at all like him to admit such a thing. But then again, nothing about this conversation was like him, and she didn't know what to make of it.

After a pause, he went on.

"I know what I really want to do is play professionally. And if we do well at regionals, I can't keep this a secret from them anymore. I'm going to have to tell them."

His voice shook as he finished the sentence. Ji-Soo heard a nervous sigh on the other end of the line.

"If I can do it, Jae-Jin... I'm pretty sure you can, too."

"Maybe so," he said with an uneasy laugh.

Ji-Soo's phone vibrated on the desk next to her. She picked it up to find a glowing Parse(d) notification on the screen.

"Hang on," she said, unlocking the screen. "Someone's texting."

"Me too," Jae-Jin said. "I think it's the chat."

➢**Lucas (7:06 am):** *Is anyone up? The leaderboards have refreshed!*

➢**Ji-Soo (7:06 am):** *Wow, Lucas. I didn't think you got up so early.*

➢**Lucas (7:07 am):** *JI-SOO!*

➢**Lucas (7:07 am):** *Please go see!*

➢**Jae-Jin (7:08 am):** *How can that be right? We were*

in the seventies last night when we stopped playing.

➤**Ji-Soo (7:09 am):** *Must have been a glitch and it didn't refresh until now.*

➤**Lucas (7:09 am):** *45th! We broke 50!*

➤**Jae-Jin (7:09 am):** *Excellent.*

➤**Lucas (7:10 am):** *We gotta tell the others. This is huge.*

➤**Ji-Soo (7:10 am):** *They're not awake yet. They'll see the chat when they wake up*

➤**Lucas (7:11 am):** *I know but... aaaaagh.*

➤**Jae-Jin (7:11 am):** *You could be practising with us if you're up at this hour, you know.*

➤**Lucas (7:12 am):** *Oh, I haven't gone to sleep yet. I'm about to but I just thought I'd randomly check and I found this.*

➤**Ji-Soo (7:13 am):** *Wait, did you say you haven't gone to sleep YET?*

➤**Lucas (7:13 am):** *I'm a night owl so I do most of my practice runs then and sleep for a few hours when the sun comes up.*

➤**Ji-Soo (7:14 am):** *Well. Wow.*

➤**Jae-Jin (7:15 am):** *I don't want to rain on your parade, Lucas, but we still have a lot to do.*

➤**Lucas (7:15 am):** *Oh, I know.*

➤**Ji-Soo (7:16 am):** *This is amazing. I'm so excited!! I can't wait for everyone else to get up and find out*

➤**Lucas (7:17 am):** *Speaking of, I better get to sleep myself. See you guys this afternoon for practice!*

A few moments of silence passed before Ji-soo spoke up.

"Will you be happy until we're number one?"

"Nope," Jae-Jin said. "But that's the perfectionist in me. Nothing's ever good enough until you're at the top, you know?"

"Spoken like a true Korean," Ji-Soo said, and they both laughed again.

"I have to head out for the usual, but I'll see you this afternoon at the 'Space."

"Ah, yes," Ji-Soo said, smiling into her microphone. "So, I'm guessing you don't want me to let on that you're not actually a robot?"

"That would be good," he said, sounding more like his old self.

"But now I know the truth."

"Well. It's OK if you know. Bye."

Ji-Soo sat still in her chair long after the call had ended, her heart light with excitement and hope and hundreds of emotions in between.

CHAPTER TWENTY
THE CHALLENGE

"Hey," Jae-Jin said. "We have an invite."

The practice room was silent. Jae-Jin looked around at his friends to find them all lost in their screens, wandering far from reality. Lissa was the only one not wearing her headphones, but she didn't respond.

"Guys?"

"It can wait for a second," Lissa said, putting her head down on her folded arms. "I've played so many matches my brain hurts."

"It's from Mastermind."

Ray stood up from behind his monitor with wide eyes. His mouth slowly dropped open.

"Say what?"

"Yeah. They want to play us."

Ray was shaking Zio and Ji-Soo out of their headsets, repeating the news.

"Is it time?" Zio asked, a mischievous smile spreading across her face.

Jae-Jin contemplated her question as his eyes fell to his lap, turning his Orb in his hands. When he looked up, the other five watched his every move like hungry dogs.

"Ji-Soo, what do you think? I'm not the only leader here."

She smiled, a blush rising to her cheeks.

"I think we can do it."

"I think the same." Jae-Jin stood up. "But let's take a break before we accept. We've been in here for—" He stopped to look at his watch.

"Seven hours," Lucas supplied, fishing an energy bar out of his backpack. "I got here first, and it was around eleven. Devon and I chatted for a while. But even with that I think we were all playing by noon."

"This is a big deal though!" Ray exclaimed as he waved his hands in the air like an excited bird. "They're challenging us! That means they noticed us!"

"I mean, I would hope so." Lissa propped her head on one hand and woke her laptop with the other, bringing a screen with the *Ancestral* leaderboards on it to life. "We've been in the top twenty for over a week now. With luck, we could break into the top ten soon."

"No such thing as luck," Jae-Jin said. "Practice, skill, and determination. That's got us this far." He unscrewed the cap of a plastic water bottle and took a long sip.

"See, I disagree." Lucas grinned, tapping a finger to his temple. "I think all those things are the foundation. But I think luck plays a role, too. It's like having magic on your side."

"Could be." Jae-Jin shrugged in his direction as he made his way out of the room.

"I'm gonna tell Devon. See if he can sit in." Ray,

still animated, clapped his hands and headed in the direction Jae-Jin had gone a moment before.

Ji-Soo looked at Lissa sitting in her chair. Her friend appeared dazed and tired. As she caught Ji-Soo's eyes, she blinked and shook her head as if to clear it.

"Should we walk? Get another tea?"

"I don't think sugar will help right now. But... fresh air is a good idea. Maybe just to stop and clear my mind."

Ji-Soo nodded, slinging a shiny bag the exact shade of a pink neon sign across her chest. It matched her Doc Martens perfectly.

"I'm ready when you are."

Lissa nodded, flicking her status to 'away' before setting her Orb into its stand. She unzipped her backpack and fished out her phone, tucking it into her back pocket, then stood and nodded.

"Let's go."

The girls emerged into the main room to find it much busier than when they'd first arrived. Every monitor in the room was on, each with a match going. All the sofas and chairs were taken. Some people sat on the floor, while others stood behind the sofas cheering their friends on or ranting when they were taken out. A chorus of groans came from the station near the front door as the Weaver on screen went down at the hands of a Plunderer. A tall, skinny guy wearing a backwards baseball cap and a Supreme t-shirt got up from in front of the monitor, threw his Orb in the chair in frustration, and stalked out the front door.

"Dramatic," Ray murmured to himself. "But when did the 'Space get this busy?"

"Seriously. I guess we've been too lost in our own world to notice."

Devon moved between groups, checking in to see if they were doing well, picking up empty cans and snack bags as he went. A cluster of girls yelled and high-fived one another from the far corner where Jae-Jin once used to play regularly. One jumped up and down in excitement as Devon approached them, her long, blonde pigtails flying behind her. She grabbed his arm and pointed at the screen as she squealed with delight.

"Wow," Lissa said as they made their way to Ray, who was standing near the front counter. "It's wild in here."

"It sure is. I'm waiting for Devon to talk to him about the Mastermind match. But I don't think he can step away with all this."

"I've never seen it quite like this in here before," Lissa said, nodding at the room. "Just like us, I guess. Hoping to win a few rounds at regionals."

"Level sixty!" a woman with short-cropped hair yelled from the back of the room.

Voices around the room cried out in reply.

"Wha—?"

"In your game now?"

Now most of the heads in the room had turned. The few not in-game drifted in her direction to watch what was going on. She was standing in the Sea of Trees, one of the game's most creative maps. It was a wide, rolling ocean with no visible borders (although an industrious player could find them if they ventured far enough in one direction). Hundreds of tree species swayed in the water on all sides, from the weeping willow to the delicate birch. Players were forced to scale them and jump from limb to limb to avoid drowning in the depths below.

Ray, Lissa, and Ji-Soo had all turned to watch as a crowd gathered around the player. She was scaling a sturdy-looking baobab tree when Devon ambled up to them, his arms full.

"What's up, little birds?"

"Just feeling sorry for that girl," Ray said, turning away from the match. "She's gonna get hosed. Oh—let me help you."

He stepped behind the front counter, emerging with a white garbage bag in hand. Once Devon had dumped his stuff inside, Ray set the bag aside behind the desk.

"Thank you, good sir. So, what's goin' on?"

"Mastermind wants to play us."

Devon clapped his hands together with the look of a boy who's been told he can eat ice cream for every meal.

"Is that so! And when will this face-off happen?"

"Well, whenever we accept and they're online, I guess. We wanted you to come watch, but..." Lissa gestured at the room.

"Tell you what." Devon glanced around at the crowded play-stations. "Are you all taking a break?"

"Yeah, we haven't since we got here."

"Wow. Yeah, you need one. Remember, your play quality will degrade if you don't stand up once in a while! And remember to eat!"

"Yes, Dad," Ray said, giggling.

"It's hard." Lissa's eyes dropped down to her worn-out Converse. "Especially since we're running out of time. Only a few weeks."

Devon clapped a hand on her shoulder, and she

looked up to find him gazing intently into her eyes.

"Lissa, do I need to go fetch you some boba?"

"Oh, God no," she said, brushing his hand away as the others snorted.

"It might help you take yourself less seriously!" Ji-Soo said, doubling over in a laughing fit. Lissa frowned in her direction.

"Me too serious? What about when you and your *boyfriend* give the commands?" she said, crossing her arms and waiting for Ji-Soo to blush. To her surprise, she did not.

"Ooooh." Ray raised an eyebrow. "These are fighting words."

Devon waved a hand in the middle of the face-off. "I don't care who fetches Lissa's next drink, but I do care if you wait for me to play the match. It'd be good for me to see them in action, so I can watch what they do. It's a Monday, so the doors close in a little less than an hour. If you can waste some time until then I can join you in the war room."

"Deal," Ji-Soo said. "But do you need any help in here?"

"Ahh, I got it," he said, shooing them away. "Go outside. Breathe. Look at something that's not a screen for a while." And with that he was off across the room again to help a scrawny kid waving his Orb in the air, its error light blinking fast.

Ray held the front door open for them, and the three spilled out onto the walkway outside. The traffic hour had already passed, and the surrounding neighbourhood had softened into early evening silence. Bubble Pop! still had its lights and music on, but it was empty except for the girl working at the counter, reading her phone and sipping a tall plastic tumbler of what looked like iced tea. A woman walking two Siberian huskies on bright red leashes was visible across the way near the park, but she was the only person on the street to be seen.

"I wonder where Jae-Jin went," Ray said, looking over the balcony.

"Probably his car," Ji-Soo remarked. "He goes to sit in there sometimes to clear his head out, he says."

The other two slowly turned in her direction as Ji-Soo gazed out over the parking lot, her expression soft. They both watched her for a few moments before Lissa spoke up.

"Please tell me that fool has finally figured out what a catch you are."

"Ah," Ji-Soo said, waving a hand in front of her face. "It's not like that."

"Are you *sure*?" Ray asked. "Because for a guy who hardly makes facial expressions, telling you about his car meditation habits seems like serious intimacy to me."

"Yeah, and he asked you to take a walk with him the other day." Lissa's expression was smug. "That moment had some *big* romance energy. Something is up. Even if you two don't know it yet."

"I just don't want to think that! What if I'm wrong, you know?"

Ray stretched his arms overhead and yawned, revealing a sliver of belly from beneath his Green Lantern shirt before noticing and tucking it back into place.

"Not wrong. I don't think so, anyway."

Ji-Soo was silent. One hand played in her hair,

twisting strands around her fingertips. She glanced to her left and right, then down below. Jae-Jin's black Honda sat across the lot with the dome light on.

"I really like him," she said quietly.

Lissa looked at her friend's small face, the purse of her lips, the pastel blue collar at her neck. Ji-Soo, the spunkiest person she'd ever known, the person who was rarely if ever afraid.

"Hasn't it been that way for a long time though?" Ray asked.

"It's different. It's a lot more than it was before we were leading the team together. Now we have a partnership. And he's starting to tell me things…"

"Like?" Ray paused. "Sorry—that's nosy. I just realised how I sounded."

"It's OK," Ji-Soo said. "I'm just scared I'm imagining it all. Worst of all, I feel distracted all the time. And I'm worried it's affecting how well I play."

Lissa shook her head with emphasis.

"It hasn't. I've played an insane amount of matches today alone, and you were rock solid in all of them."

Jae-Jin's car door opened, and the dome light went out.

"He's coming back," Ray said. "We better wrap it up or scatter. I think I might actually run into Bubble Pop! before they close. Do you two want anything?"

Lissa shook her head.

"Sugar isn't enough to carry me right now. I need an illegal dose of caffeine, straight to the bloodstream. Which reminds me, Devon probably still has the coffee pot going in there."

"I'll see you two in a few then." Ray jogged down the stairs, taking some two at a time. He and Jae-Jin murmured greetings as they passed one another.

Lissa reached out and took Ji-Soo's hand, giving it a brief squeeze before letting go.

"It'll be all right," she whispered, and then Jae-Jin appeared at the top of the stairs. He caught sight of them and nodded, making his way over. Lissa was once again amazed. This was not something Jae-Jin would have done a few months ago.

"Hey, guys. Ready to get back to it?"

"Well, we told Devon and he wants to sit in on the match."

Jae-Jin glanced over his shoulder at PlaySpace's front door. Through the glass they could all see a few pockets of kids shouting. Devon stood behind one of them, cheering them on.

"He doesn't exactly look free at the moment."

"He's not but he asked us to wait." Lissa stole a look at her watch. "He has to close in forty-five minutes anyway."

"I don't know how it got so late," Ji-Soo said, rubbing a hand over her eyes. "Time is all blurring together lately."

"Hm. Well, I guess I'll practise solo till then. Unless you want to do runs with me?" Jae-Jin turned to look at Ji-Soo. Lissa forced herself to swallow the smile that she felt watching the two of them.

"OK, but I gotta eat something first. Let me see if Devon's got anything left in his stash."

She headed for the door as Jae-Jin fell into line behind her. He turned around right before going inside.

"See you soon, Lissa?"

"Yeah. I'll be there."

259

Her hand was in her pocket reaching for her phone before the door swung shut. She tapped open the app she used for the *Ancestral* forums to find the chat thread she wanted.

➤**MonoNoAware (7:22 pm):** *They challenged us.*

The dot next to her friend's username glowed green. Lissa hadn't told a soul—mostly because she didn't understand what, exactly, she was feeling in the first place—but lately she had been thinking about hellodearone a lot. It was strange. She had so little to go on to think about them at all. She didn't even know which gender they were. But something about the chats they'd had stuck with her long after they ended.

She'd also talked to them a lot more than she'd talked to Quin lately. And she had to admit it felt a lot better to talk to someone who talked back.

➤**hellodearone (7:28 pm):** *Mastermind???*
➤**MonoNoAware (7:28 pm):** *Yeah. Just a little while ago.*
➤**hellodearone (7:29 pm):** *that's amazing!! yes yes yes! did you play them yet?*
➤**MonoNoAware (7:30 pm):** *We're about to shortly. I wanted to ask, did you ever have time to check out their matches? If you have tips, I could use them, lol.*
➤**hellodearone (7:30 pm):** *you bet i did. but what i found out on the forums is even better. two major things. one, they tend to play erratic. people playing them say it's even more so lately, so you can use that to your advantage if you can get a handle on it. it throws a lot of their opponents off so it often ends up in their favour. but just expect the unexpected with them all the way.*

➤**MonoNoAware (7:32 pm):** *OK. Can do.*

➤**hellodearone (7:32 pm):** *the other thing is juicier, but it could be a rumour. a few people are saying that their star player is super off lately. still making his kills but just barely. whatever's going on, he used to be super tight but something is making him sloppy.*

➤**MonoNoAware (7:33 pm):** *You mean Tyler Peterson? ChaosRing?*

➤**hellodearone (7:33 pm):** *ah yeah. that's the name.*

➤**MonoNoAware (7:34 pm):** *Just realised how early it is there. Sorry if I woke you.*

➤**hellodearone (7:34 pm):** *i don't do much sleeping, remember.*

Lissa stared at her screen, her skin tingling as she considered what she was about to say next.

➤**MonoNoAware (7:35 pm):** *Do you have a real name?*

Minutes ticked by, each stretching to unnatural length. Had she offended them? Would they stop talking? Her nerves jangled as she imagined the latter, going back to being curled in her bed around her phone whispering messages to her dead brother she hoped no one would hear.

➤**hellodearone (7:42 pm):** *Lana.*

➤**MonoNoAware (7:42 pm):** *That's a pretty name. I'm Lissa.*

➤**hellodearone (7:44 pm):** *that's a pretty name too :)*

➤**hellodearone (7:45 pm):** *i have to try to sleep a little soon. but will you let me know how it goes? i'll be sending good vibes your way.*

➤**MonoNoAware (7:45 pm):** *Yes. Thank you so much, too. I owe you.*

➤**hellodearone (7:46 pm):** *not at all. good night, lissa.*

The green dot next to her username turned into a little yellow moon. Lissa scrolled back up, rereading the chat a few times over. The tingle in her skin grew louder than ever. An electric bump went through her system as her eyes scanned over the last line again.

I have a crush on a strange girl from the internet.

A bubble of excitement rose through her belly and up her throat as she thought the words. She felt silly, as if she wanted to dance and jump and act like a fool, to yell to the whole world: I like someone! And maybe, just maybe, they like me, too!

She did none of this, although she imagined it all.

Your friends will think you're a complete nut job, that's for sure. Especially Ji-Soo.

Lissa felt a flicker of shame burn in her as she realised she was going to keep Lana a secret from her best friend. Because as much as she wanted to tell her, another part of her realised how crazy it all was. Liking someone she'd never even seen before. Just because they chatted a few times. And so what, if it seemed like Lana was supportive and kind and friendly? It was the internet. People could look like anything they want.

There's no need to say anything to anyone. She's just a friend. That's all.

She recognised the lie she was trying to tell herself the moment it entered her mind. But because it was easier than trying to deal with the truth, she decided to roll with it anyway.

Her reverie was interrupted by loud chatter coming from PlaySpace's front door. She realised that all the players from earlier were pouring out with backpacks and Orbs in hand. Meaning it was closing time, or about to be, anyway.

As she watched the last of them move along Devon appeared at the rear, saying his goodbyes to the whole gang.

"—great matches, everyone! We'll be back tomorrow at noon, see you then! And remember our late nights are Friday and Saturday, OK?"

The stragglers waved, promising to return bright and early. As they drifted away, Devon turned his attention to Lissa.

"Ready to beat Mastermind to a pulp?" he said, offering her a broad smile as he held the door open. She returned it, feeling simultaneously nervous and grateful.

"Absolutely."

CHAPTER TWENTY-ONE
THE MATCH

"ALL RIGHT, GUYS," Devon said after they'd all filed into the back room and settled into their respective seats. "I have some cleaning to do, but it can wait."

"We can help you after," Ray offered. "It's the least we could do, really."

Devon brought his hands under his chin and fluttered his eyelashes, affecting the air of a delighted schoolgirl. Despite the tension in the room, they all laughed at his silliness.

"I am the luckiest to have such delightful people in my establishment. But seriously. Let's talk about this before you suit up and sign in. How are you all feeling? Do you feel ready?"

"I'm ready," Zio said, pounding one fist into her open palm. "We're gonna steamroll 'em."

Jae-Jin nodded in her direction.

"I feel prepared."

"I do, too," Ray said as he and Lucas high-fived one another. "I think we can do it."

"For sure," Lucas quipped, doing a funky little dance. "We got this."

Devon looked in Ji-Soo and Lissa's direction. Ji-Soo looked thoughtful with her elbows on her chair and her fingertips steepled in front of her.

"Ji-Soo? You look like you've got something to say."

She looked at him with a slow nod.

"I think it's great everyone is hyped and feels ready. But I'm also thinking about the advice you gave us, Devon. We've gotten good. I look at our trip up the leaderboards and I think, man, we have to be awesome to have done that. Exceptional, even. But I don't want ego to lead us."

"Do you think that's a problem now?" Lucas asked.

Ji-Soo's eyes travelled from person to person as she considered his question.

"Not yet."

"I think you guys are safer than you think," Devon piped up. "Trust me, I see you all every day. I see you play. Keep doing what you're doing. And remember, no matter how good any player is, they're always on the edge of a fall. Even you. Play with that in the forefront of your mind, and it keeps the little monster at bay. Always."

"That's so stressful to think about." Ray frowned. "But you're right, it's a fact. How did you learn to manage that?"

"I never did. That's one of the reasons I walked away. I didn't truly learn that lesson until I had years to reflect back on it, to think about how I could have done it differently. And the thing I looked back on the most was how I was never in the moment. I was always looking back, wondering if I'd trained enough, or looking forward thinking about the next thing, the next kill, the next challenge."

"But how do you stay in the moment?" Ji-Soo asked. Devon flashed a smile at her.

"That, my friend, is something monks have been trying to figure out for thousands of years. Everyone says meditate, so that's what I do. Try it out sometime. You never know what you might find in the silence, you know?"

They were all nodding when a familiar ping came from Lissa's laptop. She moved to check the notification.

"They sent a second invite."

Devon gave a hearty laugh as he clapped his hands, rubbing them together excitedly.

"They're antsy. All the better for you. Anyone got an extra headset I can use?"

"I do," Lucas said, grabbing his backpack. "Just earbuds, but it's better than nothing."

He handed a black capsule to Devon, who popped it open and inserted the contents into his ears, adjusting them to find the perfect fit.

"All right, guys," Jae-Jin said. "Are we ready?"

"No offence, dude, but you're doing it wrong." Lucas grinned in his direction.

"Huh?"

Lucas struck a superhero pose: fists at his waist, legs splayed, head to one side. Then he threw his hands up, cupped them to his mouth and yelled, "ARE WE READY?"

"YAH!" Ray yelled back, hooting.

"Ah, I see." Jae-Jin adjusted his glasses. "The pre-match yelling. Never really got that."

Lucas gestured to the room to stand up.

"Actually, let's do this. Everyone put their hands in."

Ray and Jae-Jin came around the table to join the others in a loose circle. One by one, they each placed their hands out, one atop the next.

"Devon, yours goes on top," Zio said.

"Ah, I like this," he said as he placed his last. "Leaders? Do you have something to say before you set sail on this voyage?"

Ji-Soo and Jae-Jin exchanged a brief look. Lissa glanced in their direction, swearing she saw the ghost of a smile on his lips.

"All right, Phoenixes... what are we gonna do?" Ji-Soo said in a strong voice.

"Rise!" Ray yelled without hesitation.

"That's right! Again: what are we gonna do?"

"Rise!"

Her eyes drifted to Jae-Jin.

"You have to do it, too, you know."

He sighed. "Fine. One more time."

"What are we gonna do?"

"Rise!" the team cried, louder than ever thanks to Jae-Jin's shout.

"That's what I'm talkin' about!" Devon cheered, nodding his head to a silent beat. "Let's go!"

The group took their seats, powering on their Orbs. As the game came back to life, they stood on an island surrounded by the ocean, its waters moving to and fro as if a storm was on the way. Below their feet stood a cobblestone path leading to an enormous edifice with massive oak doors easily three times the height of a man. It was built on a rock foundation that elevated it several hundred feet off the ground. A roughly hewn staircase presented a path for travellers to climb to the door. It had the air of a temple, a sacred place where people might come to pray or beg for the mercy of some god they desperately hoped might hear them.

The walls of the structure glowed with light. Its windows reached from floor to ceiling and came to a point at the top, stained in vibrant shades of blue, green, and yellow. Each depicted a series of scenes with one common theme: the sacred Shards stored in the mouths of past Xi'sho ancestors. The rounded ceiling was also tiled in a brilliant shade of blue that glimmered in the bright afternoon and came to a sharp spire of gold, where the light of the day danced and sang.

"The Shard Sanctum," Ji-Soo said. "Check the perimeter first, I see enemies there. Ray and Zio right, Lucas and Lissa left. We'll cover you."

The teams took off down their respective pathways, while Ji-Soo and Jae-Jin kept an eye on the mini-map as they held their ground near the bottom of the staircase. A cluster of red dots milled around the centre of the sanctum as they watched.

"There's no way they're just sitting there waiting for us."

"Unless it's a tactic. But if so, it's not one I've seen before."

"Onyx," Lucas said. "Four here by the trees."

"Call if you need us."

"Nah. We got it." He brandished his crossblades and ran at his enemies as they caught sight of him and started to snarl. As he drew close to where they stood, Lissa sailed over his head and landed behind the creatures, taking up the rear. She aimed for the vulnerable space at the back of the knees with precision. The Onyx howled as the tip of her scimitar penetrated its flesh. With a flick of her wrist to the left and right, she finished the cut and watched with relish as the body tumbled to the ground next to the one Lucas had killed just a moment before.

"Plunderer and Brutalist is such a good team," Lucas said as he unleashed Wings of Fury on the remaining two Onyx. One leapt out of the way as his mighty metal wings whooshed through the air. The other was caught by the attack, neatly split in half mid-chest. Lissa leapt over the bodies to take off after the one remaining Onyx, which was hightailing it in the direction of the sanctum stairs.

"Straggler comin' your way," Lucas said.

Jae-Jin responded with a handful of flying skulls, teeth chattering as they sailed through the air. They slammed into the fleeing creature as it staggered from the impact and groaned with rage. Jae-Jin took advantage of the moment by winding up his axe and slinging it at the prone beast as it struggled to find its footing. As Jae-Jin connected, they all heard the heavy sound of blade splitting meat. The Onyx looked down at the hatchet embedded in its side for a few moments in a stupor before it crumpled to the ground under its weight.

"Clear on this side," Zio said.

"Great. Let's go up."

"What's up with the cluster?" Ray asked as they headed up the stairs.

"I think we're about to find out."

As the team drew close to the towering doors and threw them open, the gaggle of enemy dots spread out, radiating to the edges of the room.

"That's dirty," Lucas said, his frown audible in his voice.

Yeah," Ji-Soo said. "They're not messing around. I'll go first. Stay close."

The room that towered over them was built to inspire awe. Below their feet, the entryway was hand-carved to resemble a round Celtic maze. Paths looped back and forth aside one another on their journey to the centre. The labyrinth shone with bits of coloured sunlight, filtered through the stained-glass windows. The effect was beguiling, suggesting a mysterious sanctuary of magic.

Imposing stone columns stood around them on all sides and continued across the room, giving way to a highly detailed vaulted ceiling. Lissa glanced up at it, thinking for the first time that it resembled the ribcage of some vast beast's skeleton.

A line of five stone pillars stood in the middle of the room, each containing a replica of the Shard of each Xi'sho race mounted in the centre. Each was wide enough for several people to stand and worship at their bases. Or to perfectly hide a group of enemies behind them.

"Two behind the San'sho pillar," Jae-Jin said. "Go slow."

As they moved towards the first of the monoliths, a handful of ivory tusks shot through the air just inches from the group's left.

"Weaver."

"Yep. Ray, watch that one while we keep forward."

"Right."

Nothing else came from the darkness as they crept

around the side of the Wu'sho pillar. The red dots around the edges of the room were perfectly still on the map, which unnerved Lissa as she watched them. A part of her had been afraid of surprises ever since the day they'd all died in that one strange match. Before that, she'd known what to expect, even in the worst fights. But now she knew things could happen that she couldn't even imagine.

"There should be two enemies here, but there's nothing."

"Cloaked?"

"Watch out!" Ray yelled as a sound came from above. The party looked up just in time to see two Plunderers hurtling down from their hiding place in the rafters, shrieking like they'd gone mad. Both brandished their scimitars. They collided with Ray and Zio at the same time, pushing both to the ground.

"Fall back!"

"But they—"

"Fall BACK!" Jae-Jin repeated, his voice rising as he swung his axe. It whizzed past one of the Plunderers as it leapt off Zio to get out of the way. The other ducked close, pinning Ray closer to the ground. Lissa watched in amazement as Ray wrapped both arms around the Plunderer in a fierce embrace. They looked less like two combatants than an odd couple caught up in some strange moment of romantic fervour.

Blackened, rotting seaweed sprouted from Ray's fingertips, flying fast to its destination. It wrapped itself around the Plunderer's eyes first, then wove its way up its nose and finally into its mouth. The beast convulsed as it started to choke.

"Ray! Roll!"

Releasing his arms, Ray was already moving as Jae-Jin's axe came down, decapitating the bound Plunderer in one fell strike. Its arms still flailed in the hopes of finding purchase, desperate for something to cling to, but found none.

✦JAGUAR HAS BEEN ELIMINATED BY JAEBOMB✦

Ray, Zio, and Jae-Jin dashed for the entryway just in time to see Lucas slicing down a few shambling Onyx with a single unfurled wing. The others stood nearby, weapons at the ready.

"My stealth bonus is gonna be high today," Lucas remarked, mostly to himself, as he shook the Onyx bodies free of his wing before drawing it back to his body. Ray glanced behind them.

"The Plunderer that was on Zio is nowhere to be seen. Also, they're clustering at the back of the sanctum now. What the hell is this strategy?"

"Cat and mouse is what it is," Devon said, speaking up for the first time. "They're baiting you to see who'll run out of patience first in the hope they can gank you again."

"I'm the queen of patience." Ji-Soo sounded confident. "But I also don't think we have to wait it out the way they want us to."

"Souls of the Pack will work," Zio said. "It'll run through all their hiding spots. But my Transcendence bar has a way to go before I can cast it."

"Let's see if there are more Onyx for you to farm to get it filled up." Jae-Jin dashed down the steps. "Follow me."

The team followed, Ray at the back and keeping an eye out for a few wandering red dots somewhere below their position. As they came around the right side of the sanctum they were greeted by an unwelcome sight: five Onyx with glowing red eyes.

"Perfect," Jae-Jin said. "Do what you know, folks."

"Woo-hoo!" Lucas leapt into the air, using his wings to glide over the tops of the Onyx's heads. They snarled in his direction and swiped their claws in the air. Ray dropped to a crawl as they ogled the sky, distracted by Lucas's flight.

"They might be Raging, but they sure aren't smart," he said as his fingertips spread wide, palms open. A black cloud rose from them and descended on the Onyx, who began to shriek as leeches emerged and latched to their bodies. One stumbled out of the cloud with a fat black creature clinging to its lower lip, howling with dismay as the reptilian body grew fatter and fatter.

"I do love me some Thirst of the Leech," Lissa giggled.

"Good move, Ray!" Ji-Soo said. "Now if Zio's meter is ready—"

As she spoke, the Onyx tore the leech from its lip. A spray of blood accompanied it in a perfect fan, spattering Zio and Ray. Both turned to react but couldn't match the creature's speed. In one swift movement it pierced Zio's throat with all four claws.

"Shit!" Lissa cried.

✦ZIO2GO HAS BEEN ELIMINATED BY ONYX✦

"That SUCKS!" Zio cried into the microphone in frustration as the rest of the team descended on her killer. "Ugh!"

"It's OK, Zio," Ji-Soo said when she got her wits about her. "It happens."

"But from an NPC? And in this fight of all fights? Dammit!"

"Now you'll have to take a stealth approach." Devon spoke quietly. "None of the rest of you have a Transcendence that can smoke them out, right?"

"We don't."

"All right. You're far from out of the game. They're still huddled in there waiting for you. What's plan B?"

"Most agile members go in as a decoy," Jae-Jin said. "That's going to be Lucas and Ji-Soo. If they draw fire, but can then fly out of attack distance, that will prepare them both for their Transcendences. As they escape one of us comes in with a heavy attack—Lissa would be great with Dark Rush or Soul Drain here. Then our Brutalists come down and bam, two Transcendences in a row."

"Yeaahhhh!" Lucas cried. "Let's do it!"

"All right. Up again." Ji-Soo's voice rang with determination.

They headed back to the door, watching the mini-map. Ray spoke up.

"If they hadn't taken out Zio, wouldn't they be sitting ducks in there?"

"Strategy after," Devon reminded him. "Stay in the moment."

"Copy."

As they walked through the doorway again, they were greeted with what looked like an empty room. The enemy dots stood in groups of two behind the pillars. Still waiting.

"On my mark," Ji-Soo said. "Ready, Lucas?"

"Born ready."

"Three, two, one... go."

The two progressed into the room with care, past the wooden labyrinth carved into the floor, past the first pillar. Ji-Soo cut left, while Lucas came right, both holding their crossblades at the ready.

"Now!" Jae-Jin yelled.

Their enemies poured forth from behind the pillars like some terrible biblical flood: two Plunderers, one Morteist, and a Mender. The other two members of the team were nowhere to be seen. One of the Plunderers cast Soul Drain a split second too late as Ji-Soo and Lucas both ascended in near-perfect timing, bodies carried towards the ceiling by their magnificent wings.

"They see you!" Ji-Soo said as the arc of her flight carried her backwards towards the door. "Be care—"

She was cut off by the roar of Dark Rush as Lissa twirled in the air, releasing a dozen spectres of smoke that flew at their enemies. The attack hit the Morteist and the Mender squarely in the chest. Both their statuses ringed yellow, showing they were now suffering from confusion, which would buy the team a few precious seconds.

"Ray!" Ji-Soo cried. Within seconds, seaweed slithered around their opponents' throats. They struggled to pull it off but to no avail. Ji-Soo took the opportunity to slice them both through with Wings of Fury, hooting with pleasure as their kill notifications hit the screen.

✦_JOKER_ HAS BEEN ELIMINATED BY SHOUJO✦

✦SABERZ HAS BEEN ELIMINATED BY SHOUJO✦

"Double kill!"

"Take that, Mastermind!"

Ji-Soo smiled to herself at the sound of her teammates' cheers. But it promptly faded off her face as the next notification popped up.

✦DYNAMIX HAS BEEN
ELIMINATED BY CHAOSRING✦

"No!" Ray yelled, his voice hoarse with frustration.

"Ray? What happened?"

"Ganked. I'm sorry, guys."

"Brutalists?" Jae-Jin sounded uncharacteristically tense. "We need you now! It's four on four!"

"Lucas! Trigger now!"

"OK!"

His wings cut through the air as he descended to the ground. The Plunderers closed in, nearly on top of him the moment his feet made contact with the floor. Lissa watched with her heart thumping in fear.

If they cast a Transcendence before he does, it's over.

She let out a shaky exhale as the familiar slowing of their surroundings began. Lucas's avatar struck a pose of reverence as his chin drew close to his chest and his hands came together in prayer. His mighty wings rose. Unknowingly, Lissa held her breath, watching as the Plunderers lost their balance in the powerful wind of his wings sweeping forward. She felt a stab of crazy hope as the feathers separated into swords and Lucas reached up to take hold of them. Was it fast enough? Transcendences couldn't be intercepted—but sometimes they could be survived. Would Mastermind survive this one?

✦JAGUAR HAS BEEN ELIMINATED BY IMPACT✦
✦CHAOSRING HAS BEEN ELIMINATED BY IMPACT✦

"That was the hotshot," Jae-Jin said. "ChaosRing. Nice work, Lucas."

"Thanks, boss!" Lucas said, breathless. "Narrowing it down here."

"What about WraithX?" Lissa heard the fear in her own voice and instantly regretted speaking.

"Yep, just the leader is left," Jae-Jin said. "He dashed out. Around the back of the building now."

"Why would he go out there when Onyx are still spawning?"

"To throw a few barrels in our way, I'd guess," Ji-Soo said.

Lana's advice rose in Lissa's mind: *They tend to play erratic.*

"We should expect the unexpected," Lissa said. "Be defensive."

"I'm ready for 'em." Lucas's glee was crystal clear in his voice. "Let's go, let's finish it!"

"Lucas," Devon said with the tone of a teacher trying to be patient with an erratic child. "Wait. Remember. Slow is fast."

"Lissa is right. Let's proceed with caution," Jae-Jin said as he moved towards the door. "Let's go."

As they descended the staircase again, they watched as the single enemy dot moved counter-clockwise, then clockwise in a half-circle around the back of the building. It seemed to be avoiding moving towards their position. As this dance went on a new cluster of enemy dots bloomed, closer to their opponent than them.

"Take the other direction. He'll trigger Raging on those Onyx for sure," Ji-Soo said.

"Copy that."

They headed northwest, closing the distance step by step as the sanctuary cast its shadow over their passage. They saw the Onyx first. Five of them had taken notice of the sound of their approach and waited with claws bared. The one nearest the front gave a battle cry and thrust its chest forward, spreading its arms and outstretching its fingers. When its head rolled forward on its neck again, its eyes glowered at them, angry and red.

"At least we called that one," Ji-Soo muttered as she darted towards them. The Onyx nearest to her ducked as she slashed at it with both blades. It shoved its body weight into hers, throwing her to the ground. Ji-Soo was quick to try to cast Wings of Fury but as her wings extended flat against the ground, two other Onyx moved atop them, holding them in place. She was trapped.

"Help!"

"Hold tight, Ji-Soo!" Lissa rushed to her, her robes flying as she pulled back both arms to ready her scimitars, panic pulsing in her throat. They couldn't afford to lose now. Especially down to four against one with Mastermind. There was no way they could take this. No way.

✦JAEBOMB HAS BEEN ELIMINATED BY WRAITHX✦

✦IMPACT HAS BEEN ELIMINATED BY WRAITHX✦

"No!" Lissa yelled as her temper bloomed, struggling against the urge to turn and see what had happened.

Focus. Get Ji-Soo out.

Lissa knew the leader was behind her now where her friends had been alive a moment ago. Her teammates rarely fell to Onyx these days. Which meant she had milliseconds before he came for her. She hammered the button for Dark Rush to push the Onyx off Ji-Soo's wings, then swung her arms. Her scimitars cut through Onyx flesh and their howls rent the air.

Why isn't Devon saying anything? We're about to die!

"If you have advice, the time is now," she said into the mic, breathing hard. Ji-Soo rolled away and leapt to her feet.

"Lissa—"

"Be careful! The leader's—"

She had no time for the rest. The screen slowed as WraithX moved into view. He was a tall, gangly Weaver draped in moss and rotting weeds. His avatar's hair burned with green fire as it clutched its staff close to its pendulous breasts. Its cracked, stained fingernails were so long they curled at the ends of its twisted fingers. Lissa had a moment to look into its eyes and see a creature with a soul so empty that it frightened her before it raised the staff into the air with both hands.

A vile soup poured forth from the jewel embedded in the staff and drenched Lissa. She looked down to find the armour on her arms rotting before her eyes. As the metal fell away the liquid met her flesh and began to gnaw its way through that, too. She stared blankly as the flesh gave way to muscle and then to bone. Depression was settling over her, a dense cloak that lay heavy on her back and shoulders.

✦NAGIKO HAS BEEN ELIMINATED BY WRAITHX✦

✦SHOUJO HAS BEEN ELIMINATED BY WRAITHX✦

The silence in the room was broken by the sound of a direct message notification from Lissa's laptop. It had been sent to the Team Phoenix stream account. She placed her Orb in her lap and turned to check the message.

>**WraithX (8:39 pm):** *GG, Phoenixes. Shame you never had a chance. But you tried.*

"What does it say?" Zio asked.

Lissa shook her head, unable to say a word. As the others recognised her paralysis, they got up one by one and came to stand near her. Devon leaned over her shoulder to read the message. As they stood in the quiet, he placed a warm hand on her shoulder.

"This isn't over yet. Now everyone pack up and get out of here. We'll discuss it tomorrow."

PART THREE
AUGUST

CHAPTER TWENTY-TWO
SORE WINNERS

"YOU THINK THEY'RE really a problem?"

Logan sat cross-legged in the busted armchair, hair tousled and feet bare, chewing on a straw he'd fished out of a McDonald's cup left over from lunch. He wore nothing but a pair of navy running shorts with a white stripe up the side. His once taut abdominal muscles were starting to soften from months in front of a screen, but still looked admirable. Jared stole a glance at them every now and then, wondering what it would be like to have so little fat on your body.

"I think they could be," Logan shrugged.

Jared frowned, then took a slug from the can of Rager he clutched in one meaty fist. He wore his trademark ratty bathrobe with its frayed tie and holes along the seams. Logan stared at him and wondered—not for the first time—if he realised that most hobos were better dressed than he was.

"Where are the others?"

"Hell if I know. I never know where Tyler is these days. Chad is probably"—Logan paused to glance at his watch before going on—"doing whatever it is he does after classes."

"Just seems like we should all be talking about this," Jared said.

Logan gave him a sharp look.

"You think I'm not gonna tell them, too?"

Jared visibly recoiled as the familiar Logan Williams temper appeared. Every guy in the house had seen it at least once, and none of them ever wanted to see it again. He changed his tone to that of a teacher comforting an unruly child.

"Of course you are, man, that's not what I meant. All right, so you think lil' Team Pee-nix is a threat. Tell me why."

Logan glowered.

"Why don't you tell *me* what you think went wrong during that match?"

"Uh." Jared looked uneasy. "Well, we won, so—"

"Think bigger, dumbass."

"They killed five of us?"

"Bingo. What else?"

Jared's eyes wandered around the room.

"They... took out Tyler early."

Logan waved his hand in the air with a peeved expression.

"Not exactly a surprise in the current situation. I'll talk to him again, obviously..."

Jared's face grew uneasy.

"I really don't know, man. I mean, we still won. At the end of the day that's what matters to me. Keeping our streak."

Logan looked at the floor like an exasperated father who has patiently tried to explain something to a small child unable to parse his meaning. He took a slow, deep breath before he looked up and continued.

"When a match is *that close*, that matters. You should know this. We won by a hair, and that's because I managed to pull it off by myself. None of you could help because you were already lying dead on the ground. *That* is a problem. Get it?"

The worried expression on Jared's face told Logan he was getting somewhere.

"If you want to keep the streak," he continued, "you need to know how you got there to begin with."

"We've worked well together from the beginning, though," Jared said. "You know we were always good. A lot better before Tyler fell off the wagon, but I don't think it was his fault this time."

Logan shook his head, making a sound of disapproval.

"I disagree. Because if he was performing the way we know he can, I never would have ended up on the back of the map using Onyx as a shield to try and survive. Old Tyler would have wiped the floor with those losers long before that ever could have happened."

Jared paced back and forth. He tried to take a sip from the Rager can, saw it was empty, and pitched it at the overflowing garbage bin at the edge of the kitchen. It hit the rim with a clank and tumbled to the ground. A few drops dribbled out onto the floor as he went to pick it up and deposit it where it belonged.

"So, what do we do?"

"Rethink our strategy," Logan said.

"But it worked for every other team we've ever played on that map—"

"Did they look like every other team?"

"No, but—"

Logan shook his head, got up, and walked to the fridge to swing it open. It was the bachelor's dream: solidly stocked with Rager, alongside a few stray bottles of ketchup and mustard. There was not a scrap of food to be seen. He grabbed a can and popped the tab. Jared watched him nervously as he took a long sip. There were no empty cans around him, meaning this was his first drink of the day. So this conversation was coming from a completely sober state of mind, which Jared knew to be the most dangerous of all Logan's moods.

Logan ambled back over to his seat, but instead of taking it, he faced Jared and put a hand on his shoulder. Jared twitched under his touch.

"If they pull something like that at regionals and we can't respond fast enough, then we lose everything. Our sponsorship, our followers, our liquor supply. Everyone will want to know about the hotshot new team that leapt up the leader board and took out Mastermind. We'll be old news. Is that how you want to be remembered? 'They used to be good, but not anymore'?"

Jared shook his head. His eyes were frightened.

"Where did we screw up?"

Logan settled back into the chair and took another sip from the can. Jared felt a tremble of relief that the eye contact between them had been broken. There was something hard in those eyes, something icy. He didn't know how to describe it, but he knew he didn't like looking at them.

"Well, the luring trick didn't work with them. Most teams get impatient and then sloppy in response to that. They didn't, which means they're good strategists, so we have to consider other approaches. I haven't watched the replay yet, but I plan to shortly. Start to see if I can find their weak points and figure out how we can use them to our advantage."

Jared nodded. He hated strategising, preferring to be told what to do. But he knew better than to mention this now.

The front door opened, and both looked up to see Chad walking in, his forest green backpack slung over one shoulder. He wore a frayed white baseball cap, jeans, and a yellow polo shirt with red details at the collar. He popped an earbud out of one ear.

"Yo," he said, cocking his head. "What's going on?"

"Talking about last night," Jared volunteered.

"What about it?"

Jared stared at Chad, motioning silently with his eyes and hoping the message was received loud and clear: *He's pissed.*

"I can't believe I have to explain this a second time." Chad slung his bag onto a nearby table.

"It was close. But isn't it nice to have that challenge, for a change? I enjoyed it personally. It was a rush to feel that we had to fight for it. It's been a while since I felt that."

Logan sat stony in his chair without a word. Chad wasn't afraid of him, and he knew it. He sifted through his options as he decided how to respond.

"I'm not a thrill-seeker. I want to know we'll win." Chad shrugged.

"Each to his own. That's no fun to me. But at any rate, is that the issue? What, are you worried we'll face them at regionals?"

"You can bet on it."

"He thinks we have to change up our strategy." Jared stole a glance at Logan before he went on.

A few moments of silence wandered by.

"I'm gonna call a house meeting," Logan said. "We only have a few weeks left before we compete. We need a solution to this ASAP."

"Tonight?"

"The sooner the better."

Chad nodded, collecting his things from the table and hefting his bag onto one shoulder.

"I have a few school things to do but I'll be here for the evening. Just tell me when. Is Tyler here?"

Jared shrugged.

Chad flicked his gaze in Logan's direction.

"You know, when this is over, you really should kick him from the team. I like the guy, but on a competitive level he's dragging us down big time." He paused. "Sorry, I know he's your bro."

"Not anymore, he's not," Logan said as he crossed his arms and let out a sigh. His body language told an incomprehensible story. A bell pealed outside to signal that six o' clock had rolled around.

"All right, I'm heading up," Chad said as he made his way towards the stairs. "Let me know when."

"Yep."

A few words of conversation trailed down as he crossed paths with someone on the second floor. The sound of footsteps came on the stairs and Tyler appeared, looking more well-rested than he had in some time. He was clean-shaven and his hair was styled, and he wore a crisp plaid button-down over a white t-shirt and fitted jeans. He grinned genuinely at his roommates.

"Well, look who it is," Logan drawled. "Going on a date, pretty boy?"

"Yeah, in fact. You remember Hannah from the party a few weeks ago? Dark brown hair with purple in it?"

"Not really," Logan said. "I can't keep track of all the girls you bring in here. Not without a spreadsheet."

Tyler cocked an eyebrow.

"Jealous much?"

Logan was out of his chair in an instant. He paid no attention to Jared as he shrank into a corner of the room, mumbling something like *don't hurt him, man, he's not, I don't think you should.* What he did pay attention to was Tyler's eyes as he shoved him into the wall next to the staircase. That cocky glint went out of them and for just a sliver of a second before the anger showed up, there was fear. Terror, even.

A smirk blossomed on Logan's face. It was great to see this spoiled brat lose his sparkle. Because it was his fault that they were on the verge of losing, and he didn't seem to care about that one bit. But Logan was happy—ecstatic, even—to drive the point home.

Gotta teach you a lesson.

"You have the nerve to come down here all polished up for a date when it's your fault that we're losing everything we've worked so hard for?" he screamed in Tyler's face.

"Whoa, man, what the—" Tyler spluttered, trying to push Logan off him. Jared spoke up again from the background, one tick louder this time.

"Logan, man… go easy on him—"

"Shut up!" Logan roared over one shoulder before turning back to his friend. The fury in his chest was bright as he looked into Tyler's eyes, remembering. He was the first person he'd ever seriously played *Ancestral* with. The person he'd hit one high score after another with. The person he thought would be next to him the day they won their first trophy as they screamed and cheered beneath the warmth of the stage lights.

"You're... crazy," Tyler said, his voice cracking. He'd looked so polished a few minutes before. But now he just looked sad and thin and tired.

"Am I? Or am I just doing what no one else here has the balls to do?"

Tyler lifted his head to meet Logan's eyes.

"No one else here is enough of a dick to scream in my face. Only you."

"Whatever. Let's get to the point. Regionals are close. We need you to play right. So, I'm gonna need you to make me a promise."

Tyler's eyes flicked over Logan's shoulder to Jared, who had taken a few steps forward. He wouldn't help. This much Tyler knew. He was too afraid of Logan to stand up to him. So, he was on his own.

"I'm already gonna play regionals, man."

"I need you to play it *well*. Wherever the old you went, I need you to reach in there and bring him back."

"Maybe you should dry out for a little bit, man," Jared offered from the background. "We've been a little worried, you know?"

Tyler looked at the two men as if they were stupid.

"And chill on the girls," Logan said. "It can wait till this is over."

Tyler snorted. "You're not my goddamn dad, you know."

Logan stared at him for a few moments in silence. The next sound in the room was the painful snap of an open hand hitting skin with an intense impact. Tyler moaned, both hands going to his face, and he hunched over.

"Let's see how your date likes your new face," Logan said, chuckling. "Bet she'll love that."

Tyler rose to standing again, his left hand still pressed to the spot where Logan's palm made contact. The rest of his face was bright red.

"I'm done here!" he yelled. "And I hope your precious Mastermind *crumbles*! The only reason you're doing this is because you guys are crap without me."

He fled towards the stairs. Logan watched him with relish as he disappeared, hearing the murmurs of someone speaking to him up there. Chad, probably.

"You shouldn't have done that," Jared said, his voice low.

"Oh, I absolutely should have. And sooner, too." Logan walked into the kitchen and turned on the faucet to wash his hands.

Jared said nothing. Memories of himself as a kid flashed in his mind. Trying to avoid the bullies at school, hiding behind the bookcases in the art room as they ambled by. Working hard to keep the peace while his mum and dad yelled at each other. Sneaking snacks up to his room and stashing them in his nightstand like some weird squirrel.

He shuddered, shaking his head to clear the memory away.

"I'm gonna settle in for practice if you wanna join me," Logan said as he dried his hands with a dishtowel, then paused when Jared did not reply.

"Bro?"

"Ah, yeah," Jared said, barely glancing in his direction. "I just gotta shower first. But I'll join you in a little bit."

"Suit yourself."

CHAPTER
TWENTY-THREE
ARE YOU THERE?

LISSA LAY IN bed staring at the ceiling, resisting the urge to pick up the phone and leave her brother yet another message he would never hear.

The light outside glowed against the blinds on her window. Little birds sang in the trees outside, as they did every morning. She remembered a time when she found their songs beautiful. Now she associated them with lying awake in the early hours of the morning, exhausted, whispering into her phone as she curled her body around it. Their song was the score of her struggle, and despite their joy, she couldn't help but hate them a little for it.

Her chest felt heavy, a glass case holding a cumbersome artefact. She wrapped her arms around herself hoping for some tiny bit of comfort. At times like this she thought about waking up her dad, climbing into bed with him. She wasn't little anymore, she knew, but hoped he might receive her anyway, in that way he always did when she was a little girl and she would hold up her arms for him and he would scoop her up from the floor into a warm, wonderful hug.

She couldn't bring herself to do it even though she wanted to. She knew he had his own burden to fumble through. Carrying hers as well would be too much.

She reached for her phone to look for the time: 6:12 a.m. She also had notifications. She swiped them with a finger to find one from Lana.

➤**hellodearone (5:46 am):** *what happened last night? did you win?*

A stone sank through her stomach, warm with shame. Would Lana think less of her because they had lost?

➤**MonoNoAware (6:14 am):** *No.*
➤**hellodearone (6:14 am):** *did you stream it?*
➤**MonoNoAware (6:15 am):** *Yeah. But I feel embarrassed for you to watch.*
➤**hellodearone (6:15 am):** *i won't watch it unless you want me to. but if you do want me to, i think i can help.*

Lissa looked at the words for a long time. They were considerate. They reminded her of her father.

➤**MonoNoAware (6:18 am):** *OK.*
➤**hellodearone (6:18 am):** *let me pull up the channel. give me a little bit.*
➤**MonoNoAware (6:19 am):** *Sure.*

She twitched with surprise at the sound of her door creaking and looked up to find Toast's nose poking through the crack. She gave a little whine that said *hello, I'm here, look at me.*

"Come up here, baby," Lissa said, patting the bed next to her. The dog didn't hesitate. A few seconds later she was settling down in the pool of blankets near Lissa's legs. Her warmth felt welcoming. Lissa laid a hand on the dog's head and was rewarded with a contented canine sigh. Toast had been sleeping with her dad more often these days, but it was nice to know she remembered to come check on her, too. Lissa smiled in the dark.

In these quiet moments, her thoughts turned to regionals. Their badges had come in the mail a few days ago. She remembered turning the bright piece of plastic with her name on it over and over in her hand as little fireworks burst in her chest. Lissa Walker: Team Phoenix was printed on the little sticker at the bottom. Of course, she'd known for a while they were going—their applications had been approved early, which was a great relief for everyone—but seeing it, holding it in her hand, was different. It made it real. Her phone buzzed on her bedside table.

➤**hellodearone (6:31 am):** *do you realise how close you came to beating them?*

Lissa blinked at her phone as her brain parsed what the message said.
Did we?

➤**MonoNoAware (6:32 am):** *I hadn't thought of it that way. I guess I was just thinking of win or lose, and I know we lost.*

➤**hellodearone (6:33 am):** *well, that's one way of looking at it, but it's not the only one. as i see it, you reacted quickly to their shifting tactics, had terrific teamthink and communication, and were by far the superior team in the match even though you lost at the end.*

➤**MonoNoAware (6:34 am):** *But...*

➤**hellodearone (6:34 am):** *but?*

➤**MonoNoAware (6:35 am):** *What did we do wrong, then?*

➤**hellodearone (6:36 am):** *i think the player that defeated you seemed exceptionally fierce. you each went for a different approach but what i see is that your team lost its rhythm. Each addressed that player separately in the end even though you came at them together. if you had come at them as one mind, a body with all parts moving in harmony, i think you could have won.*

Ah, Lissa thought. *She's right.*

➤**hellodearone (6:37 am):** *were you nervous at this point in the match?*

➤**MonoNoAware (6:37 am):** *I was. And then when he killed Ji-Soo—Sh0uj0, the Brutalist on the ground near the end—I got angry.*

➤**hellodearone (6:38 am):** *Is Ji-Soo your friend in real life?*

➤**MonoNoAware (6:38 am):** *Yeah. My best friend.*

➤**hellodearone (6:39 am):** *that's the key.*

➤**MonoNoAware (6:39 am):** *What do you mean?*

➤**hellodearone (6:40 am):** *you reacted as if he was hurting her in real life. but he's not. what happens in the game isn't real. if you believe that, you can stay neutral during a match. you won't be shaken by emotions, and they can't cloud your judgement.*

Jae-Jin's stoic expression appeared in Lissa's mind, how he so often seemed emotionless when they played.

➤**hellodearone (6:42 am):** *lissa?*

➤**MonoNoAware (6:42 am):** *I'm sorry. My mind wandered for a minute. One of my team members, he's really... emotionless? Or it seems that way, anyway. We poke fun at him for it. But now I am* *realizing that it's probably part of what helps him play so well.*

➤**hellodearone (6:43 am):** *what's his username?*

➤**MonoNoAware (6:43 am):** *JaeBomb.*

➤**hellodearone (6:45 am):** *ah yes. I noticed him. his style is so clean, so quick. is he the leader of your team?*

➤**MonoNoAware (6:45 am):** *One of two.*

➤**hellodearone (6:46 am):** *two leaders in case one falls, yes? that's very smart.*

➤**hellodearone (6:47 am):** *so, will you try to play them again before regionals?*

➤**MonoNoAware (6:47 am):** *I don't know. I honestly hadn't thought that far yet. We'll meet later today for practice and I'm sure we'll discuss it then.*

➤**hellodearone (6:48 am)** *i wouldn't play them again before that if i was you.*

➤**MonoNoAware (6:48 am):** *Why?*

➤**hellodearone (6:49 am):** *because as of right now they think they've conquered you. let them think that when you meet them again. and then come at them as hard as you can.*

➤**hellodearone: (7:00 am):** *you have what it takes to win.*

➤**MonoNoAware (7:03 am):** *Really?*

➤**hellodearone (7:03 am):** *absolutely.*

Lissa felt tears sting her eyes. She felt overwhelmed and grateful for this strange voice somewhere on the other side of the world.

➤**MonoNoAware (7:04 am):** *Thank you.*

➤**hellodearone (7:05 am):** *i'll be cheering for you. so when do you have to meet up for practice?*

➤**MonoNoAware (7:05 am):** *Noon.*

➤**hellodearone (7:06 am):** *maybe you should get*

some more sleep before then.

➤**MonoNoAware (7:06 am):** *Yeah.*

➤**MonoNoAware (7:07 am):** *Lana? Can we... play together sometime?*

➤**hellodearone (7:10 am):** *ah, i dunno. i feel embarrassed about it. like i told you, i'm not that good.*

➤**MonoNoAware (7:11 am):** *I don't see how that can be possible when you have such good insight about the game.*

➤**hellodearone (7:15 am):** *well. let me think about it, ok?*

➤**MonoNoAware (7:15 am):** *OK.*

WHEN LISSA OPENED the door of Ji-Soo's silver Mini Cooper to hop into the passenger seat, her friend looked across at her with a cocked eyebrow.

"All right, I'm ready to hear about how hopeless our chances are," she said, flipping pink wavy hair over one shoulder. She looked like a punk rock mermaid in a silvery blue dress the colour of a fish's scales with a black leather jacket on top. "Lay it on me."

Lissa looked down at her lap, thinking about the conversation with Lana.

"I think we can beat them."

Ji-Soo reached over and touched Lissa's face.

"Who are you? What did you do with my bestie?"

"Stop-p-p." Lissa brushed her hand away, giggling.

"I'm just saying, who's this positive Polly in my car? I don't know her."

"I think I know what some of the mistakes we made are and how we can correct them."

Ji-Soo nodded as she steered the car onto the

highway, reaching to turn down the K-pop blaring from her speakers.

"All right. I'm listening."

"So last night I went home thinking we'd lost. But the more I thought about it, the more I realised we were closer to winning than we were to losing. We took down almost the whole team. For an elite team, that's hard to do. So, I figured whatever mistake we made, we probably made in the end when we fought WraithX. And one thing I realised is that I got really angry when he took you out. So much so that it clouded my judgement."

"You've always been like that," Ji-Soo said.

"But what if that's also my handicap?"

"Well—"

"We've learned a lot from Devon these last few months that's taken us from good to great. I thought about his main lessons: stay in the moment. Always be aware you can lose anytime. But one he hasn't taught us—mainly because I don't think he knows what a problem this is for me—is not to treat our avatars as if they were the people playing them."

Ji-Soo pursed her lips.

"You sound like Jae-Jin."

"Has he talked to you about this?"

"In different words, but yeah. The way he approaches games has more to do with his upbringing, I think. But he does always stress to me that staying neutral is key in a match."

Lissa nodded as her eyes wandered.

"I wish I'd realised it sooner. I just didn't fully grasp how angry I got sometimes."

Ji-Soo pulled the car up in front of Bubble Pop! and

turned off the ignition, sliding her key out and placing it in her purse. She turned to her friend.

"Lissa, can I ask you a question?"

"Sure."

"Are you angry about Quin?"

A few images of her brother flashed through her mind: eating pancakes together that dad had made for Sunday breakfast. Playing with Toast in the backyard. Staying up late to finish just one more level together. His sweet laugh. His white, perfectly even teeth.

She opened her mouth to reply and started to cry instead. Ji-Soo leaned across her seat to put an arm around her. The car was quiet for a while as Lissa's chest hitched up and down, the grief climbing its way up her throat.

"I'm so angry," she moaned when she was able to speak. "I wanted to spend so much more time with him, Ji. And watch him grow up. I want him to come watch us play and win and cheer from the sidelines, and I want to hug him and show him our trophy and watch his eyes go wide with excitement. But I can't. I can't."

Ji-Soo's embrace tightened as Lissa continued to cry it out, big gluts of sorrow, sharp stabs of regret and fury. She waited through it all as her friend trembled in her arms. And when Lissa was done and she went limp and exhausted, Ji-Soo reached into her purse, took out a cherry blossom handkerchief, and used it to dry her friend's cheeks.

"You OK?"

"Yeah. I just... needed to get it out, I think. I don't feel right crying to my dad, you know? He has enough to deal with."

"It was his loss, too, Lissa," Ji-Soo said in a soft voice. "Maybe he's just as lonely as you are about it."

"Yeah, you're probably right." Lissa's eyes went to the handkerchief in Ji-Soo's hands. "Sorry about drenching your pretty hankie."

Ji-Soo grinned. "That's what it's for. So, I'm going to go in and get us drinks while you take a minute. You want the usual?"

"OK."

"You got it."

The car door closed behind her, sealing the car into a blessed silence Lissa was instantly grateful for. Her head felt heavy and slow. And yet, some part of her felt lighter. Clean. Something she'd carried around for a long time finally let go, sand falling through her fingers.

Her eyes wandered up to the cafe, where she could see Ji-Soo at the counter inside, chatting with the guy working behind the counter. He presented her with a tall plastic cup filled with something pink. A neon blue straw jutted out of the top. The barista laughed, miming the dance that played in the music video on the screen above their heads. Ji-Soo followed suit as her face broke into a sunny smile.

Watching her friend, Lissa realised that she really didn't need to hold onto her pain like some filthy secret. She'd always felt like the burden was so heavy that it was unfair to ask for help. Her mind wandered to her long hours awake in the darkness of the mornings, whispering into her phone's recorder. She'd told Quin how hard it was, how much she hurt, how hopeless she felt. But it never really took away any of the pain. In fact, it burned brighter, because all along she'd known he really wasn't there, and that part was the hardest to swallow.

She'd carried her agony to the dead. But it was much, much better off with the living.

Ji-Soo knocked on the car door, startling Lissa out of her thoughts. She reached over to release the door handle and help Ji-Soo with her cargo.

"New guy in there," Ji-Soo reported as she handed Lissa a frosty cup. "Kelvin. Super sweet. Seemed a little flirty, even."

"Well, who wouldn't flirt with you?" Lissa retorted. "Look at you."

"I suppose you're right," Ji-Soo said with the air of an English princess, fluffing her hair and fluttering her eyelashes. Both girls burst into laughter.

"You OK?"

Lissa nodded.

"Yeah. I just realised... I need to talk to you more."

"Why don't you?"

"It's just... so big. And I don't want to burden you, or anyone, with it."

Ji-Soo reached over and placed a hand on Lissa's shoulder.

"When something hurts that much, you're not supposed to shoulder it alone. You're supposed to ask for help. I'm glad I could be here for you. I mean that."

Lissa nodded.

"Thank you."

Ji-Soo put her boba in the cupholder and clapped her hands like a witch merrily preparing to concoct a mysterious brew.

"Now, since you have so much good insight about

the match last night, I think we should go up and share it with the team. You know Jae-Jin is already up there preparing his master class on the topic." She looked at her friend. "If you're ready, that is."

Lissa flipped down the sun visor and popped open the vanity mirror to examine her face.

"I've looked better, but I'm not sure there's much I can do about it right now."

"Ah! Hang on."

Ji-Soo reached into the backseat and came up with a purple makeup bag covered with bright prints of hand-drawn cats and dogs. She unzipped it and dug through the contents with a finger before fishing out a bottle of eye drops, which she handed to Lissa.

"That should help."

"Sweet." Lissa cocked her head back to squeeze a few drops into each eye. When she handed the bottle back the moisture coursed down her cheeks. Ji-Soo noticed it and dabbed her with her handkerchief again.

"You still look like you're crying, but at least your eyes aren't red anymore." She cleaned away the last of the moisture as a smile appeared on her face. "There we go. Ready?"

Lissa smiled back at her. A shiver went through her, a tingle of hope dancing on her skin.

"Ready."

CHAPTER TWENTY-FOUR
ONE MORE WEEK

DEVON WAS PERCHED on the back of the couch in the entryway of PlaySpace, typing away on his phone, when Lissa and Ji-Soo opened the door. He looked up and chucked his phone into the cushions as if it was the least important thing in the world. Then he spread his hands and lifted them into the air like a Broadway performer about to deliver his big solo.

"The lethal ladies have arrived!" he sang.

"Is this a new thing?" Ji-Soo said, laughing. "It's the first I've heard of it."

"Yes. I made it up. Just now." He leapt to his feet. "I assume you'd like to review last night's match today?"

"Lissa thinks she knows what went wrong already. Actually, her insight is terrific, so we were planning on sharing that."

"Oh, good! I'd like to hear it. They're all in there already, so you should go on back. I just gotta use the restroom and then I'll join you."

He shuffled off in a little dance, humming to himself.

"I swear I've never known a person in a better mood

than that guy," Lissa said as they made their way to the practice room.

"For real. I wonder what his secret is."

They found the rest of the team planted in front of their monitors, already playing practice runs. Ray looked up and acknowledged them with a wave.

"Hi, guys."

Jae-Jin looked up at the sound of his voice.

"Oh good, you're here. Ji-Soo, can we talk for a few minutes before we talk to the group about last night?"

Ji-Soo smiled like a sly fox. "Actually, it's Lissa you want to talk to. She's got more figured out than I do."

"Is that so? Let's sit together for a minute, then." He motioned to the far end of the table, where the monitor was that he used to review their matches. They took their chairs as he pressed the power button. The screen came to life, showing the playback of the match paused at the very beginning.

"So, I've reviewed it a few times this morning and I have some thoughts. But Lissa, why don't you go first?"

"Sure." She touched the screen with a fingertip to push the timestamp forward to their first time entering the sanctuary. "I think we did everything right up to this point. I discussed this with a friend of mine who gave me some great insight. Mastermind had a tight strategy, but we were able to circumvent it. They expected us to all rush in and we didn't, instead countering with our own strategy, which allowed us to successfully take several of its key members out. We also had to come up with that strategy on the fly— great teamthink on our part."

Jae-Jin nodded, eyes on the screen as Lissa pushed the video forward a little more. They watched as the party left, came back, and left again, this time to pursue the team's last living player around the back of the sanctuary. As Ji-Soo fell to the ground, Lissa tapped the screen again to pause it.

"This is where we go wrong. Or, more specifically, where I go wrong. When the Onyx pinned Ji-Soo to the ground here, I lost my temper, so I lost my teamthink. I think that resonated through the rest of us, throwing everyone else off. In that state, it was easy for WraithX to take the rest of us out." She pressed the play button and allowed the rest of the match to play out. It wasn't any easier to watch their defeat than it had been to experience it the night before, but at least she understood the reasons for it now.

Jae-Jin watched to the end without a word. Then he pushed his chair back from the table, stretching his legs out. His face was thoughtful.

"How would you progress from here?"

"By removing the emotional component from the match and understanding that my avatar is not me. Just a vehicle for me when I play."

Jae-Jin flashed a smile so bright it startled them both.

"Finally, someone who understands me."

The girls looked at each other and burst out laughing. Jae-Jin laughed with them, drawing the attention of the others in the room.

"Hey," Lucas said. "Whatever's making Jae-Jin laugh like that, I want in on it because it's gotta be pretty special."

"Soon, we promise." Ji-Soo flashed a thumbs up in his direction.

"Seriously, though. I've never tried to explain this to the room because I wasn't sure if anyone else got it. Even Devon has never talked about it, although he's come at it sideways with the ego thing, mentioning the little monster, all that. People play fantasy games to become someone else, so to try to explain that they're actually not that character, no matter how powerful they may feel..."

Ji-Soo was nodding. He turned to look at her.

"You get this, too?"

"Yeah. I mean, I love playing Sh0uj0. But I like being me, too."

"Man." Jae-Jin cocked his head in disbelief. "And all this time I thought I was the weirdo."

"Oh, you're definitely still a weirdo," Ji-Soo said with a grin. Jae-Jin glowered at her, pointing a finger towards her face.

"I'll come for you later," he threatened.

"Counting on it."

"Should we review with the rest of the team?" Lissa asked. "Now that we have a clear picture of what happened?"

"I'm not sure it's necessary at this point," Jae-Jin replied. "I don't think this is an issue anyone else is having. They all seem pretty objective."

Lissa's eyes went to her lap. She looked like she was wrestling with something. The other two waited for her to sort it out.

"Was I... always the stumbling point?"

Ji-Soo shook her head with emphasis, while Jae-Jin cocked his to one side.

"I don't think so," Jae-Jin said. "Your skills are so excellent that they typically overshadow the Achilles' heel, in my opinion. But since it's Mastermind—who are far, far better than anyone else we've played—we've got them all built up in our heads as the thing standing between us and a victory. I can see how that would sway the balance. I even have moments where I have to grit my teeth, you know."

Lissa nodded as she thought it all over.

"Even with that holdover, we really did almost beat them. Knowing what you know now, I think we absolutely can. Why don't we try a few practice matches with your new thoughts in mind and see how we do?"

"Sounds good." Lissa and Ji-Soo stood, nodding in agreement before they made their way to their separate stations. Lucas looked up as Lissa sat down next to him, offering her the pack of gum that lay near his left hand.

"Want some?"

"Sure." She took a stick and peeled off the silver paper.

"Everything good?"

She looked at him warmly, aware of the care behind the words.

"It is. Thank you for asking."

"Let's kick some butt then."

THEY HAD ALMOST finished their first match when Devon entered the room. He held a tall steel tumbler of what was undoubtedly coffee. He nabbed a stray chair and settled in, waiting for them to finish.

"Is it just me or did we get... tighter?" Lucas said into his mic as the last kill screen popped up. "I mean, that was *fast*."

"Well, regionals are a week away. And we have

played more than we've eaten or slept lately." Ray laughed as he said this. "I have, anyway."

Devon stood up with a wry expression.

"Ray just set up the perfect transition for me. I want to talk to you all about next week." He paused to take a sip from his giant cup. "I know you've all been pulling long hours. And while I won't force you, I'd like to invite you to consider stepping it up even further in the last few days we have."

"What do you suggest?" Jae-Jin asked.

"Playing more. I know some of you have classes and jobs and there may be a limit to how much you can do. But I encourage you to think about the game as if it was your primary job for the next week. Grow closer, as close as you possibly can. Breathe the game, because you want it to be that natural when you're playing it under the spotlights."

He let them absorb the idea before pressing on.

"This is what I always did before big matches. It won me success every time. So, I think it'll work for you, if you're all willing to do it."

"I am." Lissa spoke almost immediately, her voice confident.

"Ji-Soo and I play every morning, then take a break before coming here," Jae-Jin said. "So should we—"

"No, don't stop that. That's great." Devon paced around the room, nodding his head to the beat of an invisible song. "You two being the leaders, it builds just the rapport you need. And I've seen it in action. It's definitely a success."

"I can do it," Ray said. "Stay later, that is."

"I need to shuffle a few things around, but I can, too," Zio volunteered.

Devon's eyes went to Lucas, who had yet to speak. He shrugged, a big smile lighting up his face.

"I would move in if I could. Can I?"

The group dissolved into laughter.

"For the next week, yes. And there's a sofa in my office and in the main room. There's also room for sleeping bags. So, if you play too late and get too tired to drive home, that option is there. I do recommend eating more than potato chips and bubble tea though. Think about treating your body the way an athlete would."

Jae-Jin nodded. "I still work out every morning after the practice matches. Makes my mind feel sharp and clear."

Devon tapped his temple with a fingertip.

"Smart thinking, there. So, another thing I want to do this week is sit with each of you while you play. You're obviously doing really well, but also, even the best player has weaknesses. If I can watch you play multiple matches, I can see them, and if I can see them, I can point them out and offer ways to isolate and eliminate them. So expect to see me at your side sometime over the next seven days. And please don't take it personally—I just want to make sure you walk into that competition as prepared as you can be."

"Speaking of," Jae-Jin said, "Ji-Soo, Lissa, and I discussed our match with Mastermind last night. We know where we went wrong there. We think going forward with that information can make it possible for us to beat them, should we face them at regionals."

"What went wrong?" Lucas asked.

"Me," Lissa said, turning in her chair to face the group. "I got angry when Ji-Soo was attacked and lost my cool. But I know how to avoid doing it in the future now."

Devon clapped, and the others turned to look at him.

"Bravo. A player who can admit their mistakes is a strong player indeed." He glanced at his watch. "So, it's a little after eleven a.m. now. Oh, which reminds me. I need to introduce you all to someone. I'll be right back."

Through the open door they listened as he unlocked the entrance and let someone in. Devon said a few things to the guest, and a woman's voice replied. They shared a laugh. A moment later, he was escorting her into the room.

A petite woman with a shock of curly red hair that hung to her mid-back appeared. It was tucked back on both sides, exposing ears lined with gleaming silver jewellery. She wore a deep white V-neck, cuffed jeans, purple Converse, and a slightly crooked smile.

"Meet Chloe, everyone," Devon said. "Since things have been picking up around here, I thought it was time to hire someone and, you know, take a day off every once in a while."

"Whoa, sweet!" Lucas hopped out of his chair, extending a hand. "So nice to meet you, Chloe!"

The rest got up to follow suit, each taking time to shake Chloe's hand and ask her questions.

"How'd you two meet?"

"Do you play, too?"

"So much to answer," she said, grinning. "Devon and I used to compete together, back in the day."

"Whoa, that's amazing!" Zio plopped her head on one hand as if she was ready to hear a long story. "I'd love to hear about it if you ever want to share."

"Sure—as long as Devon doesn't mind me airing out some of his embarrassing moments."

"I have no fear," he said, striking a pose as Chloe giggled. "These folks already know what a fool I can be."

"But you don't play anymore either, Chloe?"

"It was never quite the right fit for me in the long run," she explained. "I'm more of a board gamer now. I like the slower pace."

"Even so, hang around here a few weeks and you might be playing with them," Devon said, nodding at the team. "They're persuasive like that. So, Chloe will basically be the new me while I focus on helping you guys. I'll be training her this morning, but after that I'll be in to work one-on-one with each of you. Sound good?"

They nodded, calling out to Chloe as Devon led her down the hall.

"Good luck, Chloe!"

"Welcome! Glad you're here!"

"Those two are the cutest," Ray whispered after they were out of earshot. "Devon doesn't have a girlfriend, right?"

Lissa glanced in the direction they had gone in.

"Not that I know of."

A devilish smile spread across Ray's face.

"Oh man, are you already playing matchmaker over there?"

"I mean, she's adorable. And they have history!"

Ji-Soo rolled her eyes.

"She just got here, Ray. Let her breathe."

"Bah! Fine. Let a guy have some fun. Glad she's

here at any rate. Devon could use a break. Has he ever had anyone else work here?"

"Never," Lissa said. "We always just helped him out when he needed it. That was long before PlaySpace was popular though. Most days it was just us and him and the place didn't make much money. We were all worried it could close at any time. I'm so glad that's not a concern anymore."

"As much as I'd love to listen to you two sit here and forecast Devon's romantic prospects," Jae-Jin said in a dry voice, "we should probably get back to the game."

CHAPTER TWENTY-FIVE
LANA'S SECRET

LISSA WAS BRUSHING her teeth in the bathroom, Toast flopped out on the white pile bath rug nearly on top of her toes, when her phone vibrated against the counter. The dog looked up at the sound, decided it was unimportant, and returned to her lazy sprawl.

After rinsing her mouth, Lissa picked up the phone and found a message from Lana waiting for her.

> **hellodearone (10:55 pm):** *i think i know how you can beat them.*
> **MonoNoAware (10:55 pm):** *What? Really?*
> **hellodearone (10:56 pm):** *yeah. ive been watching their matches for a few hours.*
> **hellodearone (10:56 pm):** *their leader uses mods in almost every one.*
> **MonoNoAware (10:57 pm):** *Cloaking?*
> **hellodearone (10:57 pm):** *that and a few others. but it's not legal to use those in competition. i think he'll be wide open without them.*
> **hellodearone (10:58 pm):** *either that, or he'll try to find a way to cheese it somehow.*

Lissa nodded at the screen, reflecting on all she knew about Logan's play style. It made sense.

> **hellodearone (10:59 pm):** *so i think the key is to play it conservative. don't rush in. don't let him provoke you. that way if he does something weird, you'll have space to react to it.*
> **hellodearone (11:00 pm):** *and go in knowing he's going to cheat. because he will.*
> **MonoNoAware (11:00 pm):** *Yeah.*
> **MonoNoAware (11:00 pm):** *Thanks for this, Lana.*

A few minutes ticked by as Lissa waited for a reply that didn't come. Toast wandered in and looked up at her expectantly.

"Come on, girl," Lissa said to the dog. "You don't have to ask."

As if she understood perfectly, Toast jumped onto the bed and curled up next to Lissa's leg, sighing as if putting down a heavy load. Lissa stroked her head gently.

When the phone vibrated again, Lissa realised she had begun to doze. But what she read yanked her back into the waking world.

> **hellodearone (11:06 pm):** *there's something about me i want to tell you. but i'm also worried you might think differently of me.*
> **MonoNoAware (11:06 pm):** *I would never.*
> **hellodearone (11:07 pm):** *ok. can you get up and go to your computer?*
> **MonoNoAware (11:07 pm):** *Sure. One sec.*
> **hellodearone (11:08 pm):** *start up the game. you have a friend request.*
> **MonoNoAware (11:08 pm):** *From you?*
> **hellodearone (11:08 pm):** *yes.*

>**MonoNoAware (11:09 pm):** *I'm so excited! I've wanted to be able to play together forever, but I knew you stopped for a while. I figured I'd ask if you ever decided to start again.*

Lissa clicked the blinking envelope symbol on her screen to open the invitation. It was from a user called Spectre—and now she knew Lana's username. A vague sense of recognition stirred, some key turning in a familiar lock.

Haven't I seen that username before? The forums, maybe?

She moused to click the username and Lana's profile loaded. As she took in what she saw there, ice suddenly shot down her spine, reaching around to dig its fingers deep into her belly.

>**hellodearone (11:10 pm):** *did you get it?*

It was the most accomplished player profile Lissa had ever seen, dwarfing the accomplishments of her own and her entire team. Lana's match count exceeded fifteen thousand matches. And her regional ranking was twelve—which had probably slipped if she really had stopped playing like she said she had. Twelve!

Why did she lie?

>**hellodearone (11:11 pm):** *lissa? please say something.*

Feeling as stiff as if she'd slept for three days, Lissa forced her fingers to type out a response on her phone keyboard.

>**MonoNoAware (11:11 pm):** *I don't know what to say right now.*

>**MonoNoAware (11:13 pm):** *You're, like... a pro player. Like, if you were in my region, you'd wipe the floor with me.*

>**hellodearone (11:13 pm):** *i know but*

>**MonoNoAware (11:13 pm):** *You told me multiple times you weren't good at this game.*

>**MonoNoAware (11:14 pm):** *But now it makes sense why you were able to give such good advice about strategy, I guess.*

>**hellodearone (11:15 pm):** *i lied. and I know how it sounds.*

>**hellodearone (11:16 pm):** *but lately i've known, more and more, that i wanted to come clean with you. because even though we're across the world from one another, i care about you.*

Lissa's heart leapt reading the words. But another part of her still felt betrayed. She watched as the typing symbol ticked next to Lana's username.

>**hellodearone (11:18 pm):** *i played so much at one time and it got... out of control fast. it was a crutch that helped me get through a lot of things i haven't told you about yet. by the time i realised how far ahead I was, i was afraid i could never make friends in the community because of it. that people would only see me as a threat. that's why i always played alone.*

>**hellodearone (11:20 pm):** *are you angry?*

>**MonoNoAware (11:20 pm):** *I don't know.*

>**hellodearone (11:21 pm):** *this is why i was so afraid to tell you.*

Lissa stared at her phone, unsure what to say. Lana was right. Not because there was anything bad about the fact she was such an advanced player, something

Lissa still wanted very much to grow strong enough to become. But the fact she'd lied about it for months made Lissa uneasy.

➢**MonoNoAware (11:22 pm):** *I'm not mad, but I need time to process it.*

➢**hellodearone (11:22 pm):** *i understand.*

➢**hellodearone (11:23 pm):** *i just really hope this isn't the last time i talk to you.*

➢**MonoNoAware (11:25 pm):** *I don't know. But I do need to sleep.*

She put the phone on her bedside table face down, clicking the ringer button to silent. She could feel her heart in her chest, vibrating with something indescribable. And yet sleep also clawed at her, as wide awake as her mind felt.

As her consciousness slipped away, one more thought murmured forth from the last of her waking ones.

You may have to fight her someday.

CHAPTER TWENTY-SIX
ONE MORE DAY

LISSA SAT AT her desk with her phone in her hand staring at the ceiling, ignoring the *Ancestral* lobby screen open before her on the desktop. Toast snored softly from the pool of blankets at the foot of the bed, growling in her sleep every once in a while as she chased some phantom foe only she could see.

Tomorrow.

The early morning insomnia had become so common by now she'd grown used to it, an acquaintance she didn't like to see but had no choice but to tolerate. What she wasn't used to was it paying her a visit before she slept. And yet here it was at the headboard, stroking her forehead with its thin, distasteful fingers.

The last few days should have made falling asleep fast a given. Instead, she'd gotten less than half of the rest she was used to getting the last five nights, and what she'd managed was thin and unfulfilling. The conversation with Lana hung over her as well, making things feel that much harder.

Practice had stretched into the early hours of the morning as Devon joined them in the war room after closing PlaySpace's doors each night. He'd spent hours focusing on each of them as they played match after match, taking time to point out places where their strategy could be tighter or their approach more efficient.

Although the nights were late for him, too, he never complained, which spurred on the rest of them even more. Devon was more than a decade older than anyone on the team. Yet he was pushing through these long nights as if it was nothing (though he always had his coffee in tow). Watching him told Lissa that he cared about their win as much as they did. It constantly reminded her of how lucky they were to have him as a coach.

They'd all worked hard over these last months—their leader board progress was a testament to that—but it was only in this final week that they pushed themselves to their limits. Eating still happened, because if they didn't do it Devon would arrive and peel them out of their seats, but sleeping enough was another matter. Both Zio and Lucas had dozed off at their stations at one point, Zio while sitting up with her Orb in hand. Ray brought a sleeping bag and spent two nights in a row on the sofa in Devon's office, only leaving once a day to go home for a shower. Lissa and Ji-Soo traded their bubble tea habit for coffee.

The hours and days blurred together as they pushed forward. And somewhere in that strange fog of determination and fatigue they all sensed some powerful thing that they were moving closer to. No one would have been able to describe it if asked, but they were all drawn to it. Jae-Jin privately thought of it as their goal, while Lissa thought of it as a treasure that would appear to them if they kept advancing on it. It appeared in each of their imaginations in one way or another, signifying its importance.

Lissa's attention wandered back to the present, and she moved to the bed. She felt a weight in her limbs the moment she laid down, as if each was sinking deep into the mattress below her, soon to thump to the floor. Beneath her exhaustion an electrical current jangled. If her consciousness started to fade, this energy would jolt and dance and shock her back to awareness, spinning scenes in her mind of what she imagined regionals would be like over and over again. She'd watched videos of other championships online, trying to prepare for it. She hoped perhaps she might read something crucial from the competitors' faces or sense it from their matches. But no matter how many she watched, she still felt anxious.

She glanced at her phone, open to her last chat with Lana. It had been several days since they talked. An unidentifiable surge of feeling rose in her chest as she realised that despite all the confusion she was feeling after what Lana had shown her, she missed her. She felt embarrassed by her own emotions as she typed a few words, erased them, typed a few more, paused, then erased those, too.

As she tried to decide what she could possibly say to put her feelings into words, a notification popped up at the top of her screen from the group chat, saving her from having to come up with a decent answer.

➤**Lucas (11:09 pm):** *Who else can't sleep?*

Lissa smirked at the message, opening up Parse(d) with a swipe of her finger.

> **Lissa (11:09 pm):** *Me.*
> **Ji-Soo (11:10 pm):** *Also me. And I'm so exhausted. This is so annoying!*
> **Lucas (11:10 pm):** *Jitters, I guess.*
> **Ji-Soo (11:11 pm):** *The others must be knocked out. Lucky them.*
> **Jae-Jin (11:12 pm):** *No, I'm here.*
> **Ji-Soo (11:12 pm):** *Oh man. And I know how early you got up, because I got up at the same time.*
> **Jae-Jin (11:13 pm):** *Yeah.*
> **Lucas (11:15 pm):** *Do you guys think we can win?*
> **Ji-Soo (11:15 pm):** *I really do.*
> **Lissa (11:15 pm):** *Yeah. I think we have a good chance.*
> **Jae-Jin (11:16 pm):** *It's hard to know.*
> **Lucas (11:16 pm):** *What makes you say that?*
> **Jae-Jin (11:16 pm):** *Missing data. We can't predict who we'll be up against when we make it to the final round. We have no way of knowing if we'll end up against Mastermind or not.*
> **Jae-Jin (11:16 pm):** *But I am sure of one thing. We are going in as prepared as we can be.*

A knock came at Lissa's door. Toast looked up from grooming her paw with great interest.

"Yes?"

The door creaked open to reveal her father. He looked tired despite his smile. He wore his favourite striped pyjamas and his eyeglasses were slightly crooked. The dog whimpered as she caught sight of him and he walked towards her, reaching out his hand to pet her on the head. She closed her eyes in bliss as her tongue flopped out of the side of her mouth.

"She's sleeping in here with you a lot more now. She does the same with me when I'm not sleeping well."

Lissa felt a flash of guilt as she realised her secret had been found out. She glanced at the dog as it happily nuzzled into her father's hand.

"I'm sorry I didn't tell you. I just didn't want you to worry."

"Well. Dads always worry, but I'm not so worried about you. More that I wanted to stop in and let you know I'm here if you need anything. And also to tell you that I'm looking forward to watching you play tomorrow."

Lissa's eyes went wide.

"You're coming?"

He nodded.

"But it's a three-hour drive, Dad!"

"It's not that far. I'd offer you a ride, but I figured you'd be caravanning up with your friends. Good team building before the big showdown and all that." He paused. "I wish your brother was here to see this."

Her emotional meltdown in Ji-Soo's car a few days prior replayed in her mind, what she'd said when Lissa's father had come up in conversation.

It was his loss, too.

Lissa sat up in bed and reached for her father's free hand. He looked down at his daughter's fingers intertwined with his, a soft look on his face.

"It's hard, isn't it, Dad?"

He sat still for a moment before nodding. Tears welled in the corners of his eyes, and he stopped petting the dog for a moment to wipe them away. He looked ten years older in the darkness of the bedroom. But even though she could see his sorrow more clearly than ever before, she felt better. Because it was better than the elephant in the room that they never talked about.

"It is. And for you, too, I'm sure. But I'm also sure you and I can make it through this together. And if there's anything I can do to support you, just ask and I'll be there."

Lissa scooted towards the end of the bed and reached out to hug him.

"Do you think you can sleep? Want a cup of tea or anything?" he asked as he petted her hair.

"You know... that sounds really nice."

He squeezed her one more time, then stood up. "I'll go put the kettle on then. Come on, Toast."

The dog leapt to the floor, happy to accompany her master on his journey to the kitchen. Lissa smiled at the sight of the wagging tail. As her father closed her bedroom door behind them, she remembered the chat and picked the phone back up, scrolling through what she'd missed.

> **Ji-Soo (11:18 pm):** *I'd feel sad if we lost, but I also know I'd feel good about the way I played. I'm proud of how I play now.*
> **Lucas (11:19 pm):** *You should be. It's great.*
> **Ji-Soo (11:20 pm):** *:)*
> **Lucas (11:20 pm):** *It's going to be so exciting. I'm hyped! And yet somehow I have to sleep to get ready! Ugh.*
> **Ji-Soo (11:21 pm):** *Staring at our screens won't help though. I need to get off this thing. And set my alarm.*
> **Lucas (11:22 pm):** *Jae-Jin, even you have to be excited, right?*
> **Lucas (11:24 pm):** *Jae-Jin?*
> **Lucas (11:25 pm):** *Helllloooooo?*
> **Ji-Soo (11:25 pm):** *Bet he fell asleep with the phone in his hand. Wish that would happen to me.*

But I'm going to force myself to put it down now. See you all in the morning!

➤**Lucas (11:25 pm):** *Sleep well!*

➤**Lucas (11:26 pm):** *What about you, Lissa?*

➤**Lucas (11:29 pm):** *Did I lose you, too?*

➤**Lissa (11:34 pm):** *Sorry! My dad came in. But yeah, I'm going to try to sleep, too. I need it.*

➤**Lucas (11:34 pm):** *OK. Good luck. And also, thanks.*

➤**Lissa (11:34 pm):** *For what?*

➤**Lucas (11:35 pm):** *Bringing me into all this. I feel like I found home.*

Lissa felt a flash of something familiar. What it had been like to have a little brother to look after, to watch out for someone younger than her. That flush of pleasure when he smiled or laughed, and she saw the glimmer of joy in his face. Usually, that would have made her sad, made her think of days with Quin when he was still alive. But at the moment it felt all right. Good, even.

➤**Lissa (11:36 pm):** *I'm so glad. <3*

She closed the app before he could respond, wanting to hold onto the feeling, and plugged the phone into its charger. It was quiet in the hall outside. She figured her father was still hovering over the stove waiting for the water to boil. She imagined Toast down there as well, warming her usual spot on the kitchen rug, snuffling contentedly as her tail beat a soft rhythm on the tightly woven sisal beneath her.

Maybe everything is all right this second, she thought as her breaths started to slow. *Dad's here and Toast's here and soon I'll be with my team. And we're going to do the thing I've always dreamed of.*

For the first time, the thought of the tournament didn't frighten her. Instead, the lights of the arena glowed in her mind, rich shades of purple and blue and dark green. The room pulsed with music she felt thumping in her throat. In her mind's eye she saw her friends: Ji-Soo, Jae-Jin, Ray, Zio, and Lucas, handsomely dressed in their jerseys, looking proud as they made their way to a long black and silver table with plush gaming chairs upholstered in a royal blue. The kind of chairs that pro players sat in. The crowd roared around them as they danced to the high energy of the beat, many waving signs and inflatable toys in the air as they yelled and sang.

As the last of her consciousness slipped away, she imagined Quin in the first row, clapping and screaming for her with all his might, his sweet face bright with excitement. She was waving at him when her father opened the door with the tea tray in hand with a steaming red pot and two matching cups. Toast trailed in by his side and came to the bedside to give it a sniff, then turned to her master to find out what she should do next.

Moving slowly, Lissa's father placed the tray on the dresser as he watched her face carefully for any sign of movement. The room was silent except for the ticking of the wall clock in the hallway, marching by each second unfazed by anyone's hopes or worries. Time simply marched by, as it always did.

When he was sure his daughter was deep in dreams, he stepped close to her, kissed her forehead, and padded out of the room.

CHAPTER TWENTY-SEVEN
REGIONALS: OPENING CEREMONY

THE FIRST THOUGHT Lissa had when she stepped into the arena with her team by her side was that they had not opened the doors of a building, but stumbled onto the passage to another world.

At the centre of the massive dome stood a glowing, capsule-shaped stage lined with neon pink lights. Tall columns of light in the backdrop pulsed to the insistent beat of an EDM song interwoven with a string orchestra. Behind the stage, a vast screen that matched the shape of the stage extended halfway around the arena. It showed *Ancestral*'s characters striking poses with bravado, showing off their attacks and defences. As they watched, the Brutalist strode out with hair and cape flying high and strong in the wind. She brandished both crossblades in front of her face with a snarl before sweeping her arms up and back, unveiling her wings at the same time in perfect sync.

"Whoa," Lissa murmured. "I knew I was a badass, but not *THAT* badass."

The seats that curved around the arena went up

four levels and were crammed with masses of cheering fans. Lissa looked around in awe. Some were dressed casually in baseball caps and t-shirts, while others wore face paint and waved handmade signs and inflatable cheering toys in the air. Her mouth dropped as she saw a Weaver cosplayer so picture-perfect he could have stepped off the screen of the game. She marvelled at his antlers, which looked as if they were made out of real wood, and tugged Ji-Soo's jersey to point him out.

"Wow," Ji-Soo said as she caught sight of the costumed fan. "I mean, WOW."

"Are we really here, guys?" Ray asked as the song faded and the strains of a new one began. The melody of a flute was soon joined by a full orchestra complete with a choir. An electric guitar screamed as the chorus began.

"It sure seems that way," Jae-Jin replied as he surveyed the scene.

"Devon?" Lissa said. "Are you OK?"

They'd been so busy staring in awe at the scene before them that none of them had noticed Devon standing behind them, arms crossed and eyes closed. Fans wove around him to dash to their seats. He opened his eyes as he heard Lissa say his name and took a deep breath.

"Drinking it all in," he said. "This is the energy I remember. There's nowhere else in the world that's quite like this—not that I've experienced, anyway."

"Do you miss it?" Zio asked.

"Of course. But I also think I took the right path. After all, here I am in it again after all these years. And it feels terrific. Doesn't it?"

"Yes!" Lucas cried, shaking his fists with fervour. "We made it! We're here!"

"And speaking of that, we need to get to our seats," Jae-Jin said. "Opening ceremony starts in twenty minutes."

They all nodded as they got their bearings. Ray fished out the competitors' guide they were given when they checked in an hour before, to find their seats were roped off on the far-left side of the arena, close to the stage. They headed back out to the building's open walkways to find the appropriate section as hundreds of people streamed past them, chattering and shouting back and forth. Many wore black t-shirts with the *Ancestral* logo, which were for sale at booths around the perimeter of the arena.

"It's crazy to see *Ancestral* like this," Lissa said as they wove their way through the crowd.

"In a big place, you mean?" Ji-Soo replied from behind her.

"Yeah, like... I've been staring at this world on a screen for so long. And now it's everywhere, it's surreal."

"This way," Devon said, pointing to a staircase with a sign that said SECTION B. "Follow me."

They jogged down the stairs to find rows of roped-off seats, some already occupied by other teams. Some stared at them openly as they made their way to their section. They found their seats in the third row, each labelled with a sheet of laminated paper that read Team Phoenix in the same bold red print the *Ancestral* logo was written in.

"Oh my god, SO cool!" Zio squealed, whipping out her phone. "I gotta get a picture of this.

And then we all have to sit down and take a selfie."
She took the pictures and then motioned for her
friends to sit down.

"I hate selfies," Jae-Jin grumbled.

"Hide behind me, then," Ji-Soo said, giving him a
poke in the arm. "You can pretend like you weren't
even here."

Zio waited for them all to file in, shifting her
weight from one foot to the other.

"OK, leave the last seat for me! That way I can get
the best angle."

When they were all seated, Zio held the phone up
at arm's length, adjusting her arms to make sure
everyone was in the shot.

"On three, say Team Phoenix, OK? One... two...
three..."

"Team Phoenix!" the group cried as she captured
the moment.

"Yes! I know I'll cherish this one," she said as she
checked the screen. "It's great! I'll share it in the chat."

"Cool," Devon said. "Does anyone know who's
performing in the opening ceremony?"

Jae-Jin fished a programme out of his back pocket.

"It doesn't say. All this is crazy though. I would expect
this level of fanfare at an international championship,
but..." Jae-Jin paused to look around the arena again.

"A big bankroll went into this, that's for sure."

"I'm super excited just to see *Ancestral*-themed
anything." Lucas was grinning from to ear to ear. "Oh,
snap. Look. The row over from us."

All heads turned to see five guys settling into seats in
the front row one section over. Their jerseys were red
and black. The backs showed a fierce-looking creature

with green skin that wore a helmet made of metal and clear glass. A brain pulsed inside. The creature clutched a banner in its claws with the words MASTERMIND carved into it.

"That's them," Lucas whispered. "Mastermind." As he spoke the blonde guy on the end of the row looked around. He had a handsome profile with a strong jaw and hard blue eyes.

"Logan Williams. The guy that took us out."

Zio's eyes narrowed.

"Gonna have to kick his ass today."

"With an audience of thousands." Ji-Soo grinned mischievously as the house lights blinked three times. "Oh, oh, here we go!"

The music faded as the lights dimmed, giving the arena a fuchsia glow. A bald Black man walked out onto the stage. He wore a striking three piece suit the colour of dark jade. He flashed a dazzling white smile at the audience as he spoke into the mic in his right hand. His rich, velvety voice boomed from the massive speakers that flanked the stage.

"Omari," Jae-Jin said. "The creator of the game."

"Hello, *Ancestral* family! Finally, after waiting for so long, we are all here together. I am your host, Omari Badu, and welcome to the very first Northwestern Regional Championship! How are you feeling tonight?"

The crowd roared, shaking its light-sticks in the air. Ji-Soo squeezed Lissa's hand in excitement, exchanging a gleeful look as she yelled along with them.

"We are so glad you're here with us, because we have a lot to show you. But before we get to that, I want to thank each and every one of you for playing *Ancestral* and making it what it is today. Without your time and passion, we could not be having this event right now."

The crowd screamed and clapped intensely.

"This is just the beginning," Omari said, nodding like a man proudly carrying the weight of great secrets. "If only you all could see what's in store for you next year. Something bigger than we've ever done before, that will make the characters you put so much time into massively powerful. An evolution, if you will. How does that sound, family?"

The cheers were so loud Ji-Soo clapped her hands over her ears. Omari smiled broadly at the cameras.

"But for now, let's focus on what we came here for. The best of the best. Those of you who've shone so bright you've shown us all what we could be in *Ancestral*'s world. And I'm ready to see it live, in real time. Starting... now!"

The towering screens came to life with a flash of fire, lighting the spectators' faces with a reddish glow. They watched in awe as the game's avatars leapt through the flames with weapons in hand, showing off their best moves. The Mender scowled as she cast her cloud of leeches, the Weaver sank his clawed fingers into the trembling soil, and the Morteist stood alongside a leering skull as big as his body. The Brutalist appeared, sweeping her gleaming wings forward with grace as she cast Death Flight.

"We've cast these spells so many times, but they've never looked so COOL!" Ray squealed, clapping his hands. "I love it!"

An all-male team in forest green jerseys appeared onscreen, accompanied by a flourish of fiery sparks. The crowd screamed at the sight of them as the sparks danced to the left and unveiled another group of players. Four men and two women stared at the crowd with fierce expressions. They wore black jerseys with a tornado over the right breast.

"Team Rebellion and Tempest." Jae-Jin watched the images as he spoke. "Both very good teams."

The sparks swirled long across the screen and moved to the right. An all-female team in royal purple jerseys with white markings appeared. The leader wore her dark hair in a long braid and looked out at the crowd with striking green eyes.

"Wow. She's beautiful," Lucas murmured. "Is that—"

"Fallen Angel. The very first all-female pro team in *Ancestral's* history. I've been watching them with great interest since they started playing competitively." Jae-Jin pushed his glasses up with a finger. "Hawkeye, the leader, is very good."

"Will we fight them today?"

"Maybe."

Fallen Angel's images faded as another team appeared in a flourish of light blue glimmers. Two blonde girls that looked barely high school age flanked four boys in the middle. Unlike the ones before them, they were smiling.

"They look so young," Lissa whispered.

"They are." Jae-Jin pushed his glasses up his nose. "That's GDA. But they're good, too."

Another team appeared off to the left, this made up of a mix of men and women wearing canary yellow jerseys. The two men standing near the front were both large with imposing faces.

"Who are they?" Ray whispered.

"SharD," Ji-Soo said as they both watched the screen. "They're behind us on the leaderboard so I'm not too worried about them. But we'll see, I guess."

SharD vanished into an explosion of yellow sparks, giving way to sparkling black as the next team appeared clad in black jerseys with small silver symbols in the middle of their chests. They were all male and Black, with strong, memorable faces. The one in the middle was especially tall.

"Team Sleight!" Lucas was grinning gleefully. "I've watched a ton of their matches. The tall guy, Rogue, is a streamer too."

As Sleight began to fade, a plume of fire blossomed in their place, unveiling an image that struck them all into a moment of stupefied silence: their own faces, Ji-Soo and Jae-Jin standing at the fore. Both gazed at the crowd with stern, powerful expressions. Lissa was still in awe at how badass they all looked as the crowd cried out, their volume startling her. She looked around in disbelief as a chill ran down her arms.

"That's for us," Lissa said as her heartbeat tripled. Devon clapped a hand on her shoulder.

"It is. And you—all of you—worked for it. So be proud right now, no matter what the outcome may be. You deserve it."

The final team lit up on the huge screen: Mastermind, headed by Logan. He had the look of a king who would strike down anyone who got in his way without a second thought.

"He looks... cruel," Zio said, her face troubled.

Jae-Jin nodded in agreement. "The others I am not really that worried about. They're good players, but from what I know Tyler Peterson is still on shaky ground. We could have been up against a major threat if it wasn't for that. But Williams is the wild card. We've already seen what he can do when he's cornered."

"And we know how to handle it," Ji-Soo said as she slung an arm around Lissa's shoulders. "He'll need to change up the game."

"He will," Jae-Jin said, glancing across the row at Team Mastermind again. "You can count on that."

The sharp sounds of sticks hitting drum skins took their attention. Two men and two women mounted each of the four staircases leading up to the stage as drones soared through the air above them, capturing their every step. The performers were clad in stunning gold and red ensembles with cloaks and draped hoods that partially covered their faces. Each wore a huge ceremonial drum strapped to their bodies. They beat them as they marched towards the top. Lissa clapped a hand to her chest, feeling as if each thump was resonating through her heart.

The four drummers were followed by four women wearing the same costumes. Each held a staff roughly twice their own size. They swerved around the drummers and ran to the centre of the stage, huddling together and facing one another as if to hide from the massive crowd. Then all four turned around, extended their rods outwards, and began to twirl them, slow at first and then progressively faster. The team gasped as the ends of each burst into flame and the women stepped out, falling into a sinuous dance.

"This is... whoa," Ray whispered.

"They've come a long way since my days," Devon said. "Crazy."

As the women leapt and danced in the corners of the stage and the drummers beat a furious rhythm, four more men appeared at the top of the staircases. Each of them held red and gold flags that towered above their heads and rippled in the air. The *Ancestral* logo was emblazoned on each one.

"I thought those were usually the team's flags," Zio said. "Aren't they supposed to be?"

"Sure, after the teams earn the right to fly one," Ji-Soo replied. "As of right now there are strong contenders, but no champions. We've only got our leaderboard rankings to show our promise, same as everyone else. Which was third place when I checked it this morning before we left. I hoped we'd be in second, but Fallen Angel still has it."

Lucas tapped a finger to his lips as he considered this information.

"It'd be fun to fight them anyway."

Ji-Soo looked at him. "Fun? Why do you think that?"

Lucas shrugged.

"Everyone can teach you something. But also, they had to go far to get here, just like us. So, they've got grit. And all-female teams are still not the norm."

"They will be one day," Lissa said, her tone firm.

"No doubt. But for now, they're still making history."

On the stage, the performers lined up to take a bow. The announcer's voice resounded through the arena.

"Let's give a big thank you to our talented performers! And now I'd like to introduce your shoutcasters for the evening—they're the ones you really have to impress."

The giant screen showed a long booth with three people seated behind it. On the far left, a blonde woman with her hair swept up into a pompadour wore a white suit and a dark blue in-ear mic with a tiny attachment curving down the side of her face. Silver spikes pierced her ears. She flashed a dazzling smile at the camera and winked. The sign in front of her read Greta Solles.

"That opening ceremony was absolutely fantastic—such energy! Wouldn't you agree, Oliver?"

The camera panned right to frame her seatmate, clad in a brown vest over a striped button-down and finished with a navy-blue tie. He blinked at her through Buddy Holly-inspired glasses, took a breath, and started talking with a distinct cadence.

"You know, Greta, I expected something great, but that exceeded my expectations. Those dancers! And the fireplay! How did they even light those?"

"I don't know, Oliver, but one thing's for sure: if that's how the night starts, we are in for something great. What did you think, Briar?"

The shot shifted to the person on the far right of the table. It was impossible to tell their gender; their look was perfectly poised between masculine and feminine. Either way, they were beautiful with their pale skin and cropped hair the colour of merlot. A floral tattoo crept up the side of their neck from beneath a black fitted jacket with angled shoulders. The same earpiece and mic Greta wore was nestled in their right ear.

"I think it's a great way to show off the power of the game that's captured the attention of the world in less than a year. And with tonight's contenders, I think our audience will soon get to see just what it is that makes *Ancestral* what it is."

"Yes!" Greta leaned in as if she was about to drop a juicy secret. "And our teams are in a unique situation in the esports world. Because *Ancestral* does its qualifiers differently than most other competitive games. For those who don't know, rather than participating in preliminary competitions to be chosen to play here tonight, our six teams had to claw their way to the top of their regional leaderboards—no easy feat when you consider that *Ancestral*'s player base is fourteen million strong."

Oliver made polite applause as Briar took the mic.

"An absolutely insane number—that's two million more than *WarGods*, just to put some perspective on that, and it's been out for many years. So, we really have to consider that the players we're going to see tonight are on the cusp of becoming the biggest stars in esports."

"At a glance it looks like Team Mastermind is our big contender tonight. They've held the top slot on the leaderboards for months and are the only team tonight that's already sponsored—and special thanks to Rager for also being one of our sponsors tonight as well!" Oliver motioned towards the banner behind him, which showed the logos of more than a dozen companies. "I'm sure some of these folks are also here tonight looking for talent as well, so for those of you playing, remember that!"

"Speaking of players, we're about fifteen minutes away from the start of the first match. Here's how it works tonight: there will be three rounds, starting with our eight teams. After the first round, we'll be down to four. And of course, by round three, it'll be our final two. The team that wins that round will be our new regional champions, as well as win our first-ever cash prize of $500,000!"

"When we win that, it's going to PlaySpace," Zio whispered, pinching Devon's arm. He grinned at her.

"I like this 'when we win' attitude."

The screen returned to Omari, who looked every bit a proud papa, watching his child grow big and strong.

"We will begin the first match in fifteen minutes," he announced. "This is it, folks, and we cannot wait! So, if you want to get your popcorn, the time is now..."

Devon pulled out his phone to look at a text message, then turned to the team.

"It's time, guys. We need to meet up in the green room in five."

"Who are we fighting?"

"Fallen Angel."

"Yesss!" Lucas clenched a victory fist. "That's what I was hoping for."

"I'm nervous," Ray said. "Let's go before I glue myself to this chair."

Devon laughed. "I won't let that happen. Follow me."

CHAPTER
TWENTY-EIGHT
REGIONALS: MATCH ONE

LISSA HAD BEEN through a lot of unusual moments in her life, but none of them held a candle to the moment she stepped onto the event stage and felt the cheers of the audience thrumming the floor under her feet. The announcers' voices blurred into indiscernible syllables. She felt frozen, as if time had stopped and she was rooted to the spot where she stood. Then she felt Ji-Soo's arm curve around her. As if a switch had been thrown, time began to flow again.

"One step at a time," Ji-Soo whispered in her ear.

In the time it took them to make their way to the green room, the stage had been cleared and set up for the competing teams. Six booths were placed in a long line at equidistant intervals. Each was lit up in a different colour: red, orange, yellow, green, blue, and purple. A petite staff member with pinkish hair dressed in a red *Ancestral* t-shirt guided them in the direction of the red booth, gesturing for them to take their seats. Her name tag said *Charlie*.

"The crowd," Ray said in a shaky voice.

Jae-Jin settled into a cushy leather chair with bright

blue detailing. He kept his eyes trained on the monitor in front of him as if it were the only item in the room. Each of their Orbs had been fully charged and set on the stands in front of each monitor, and bottles of *Ancestral*-branded water were placed off to their right. Lissa looked up towards the side of the stage they'd come in on. Devon stood just behind a group of event employees with a huge smile on his face. In fact, she realised he'd never stopped smiling since the moment they'd walked into the arena.

"Guys," she said. "Look at Devon. Over there."

He waved as they all looked up, then held both his fists in front of him in a gesture of victory.

"Fallen Angel is here."

The sound of Jae-Jin's voice drew their attention to the booth next to them. Several members of the female team were taking their seats. Hawkeye stood last behind her teammates as she waited for them to get settled. She glanced up and caught Jae-Jin's eyes, and the two exchanged a steely look.

"Ooohh," Lucas said. "So tense! I love it!"

"She will be a strong competitor," Jae-Jin said quietly. "Stay on your toes. Remember, Mastermind is far from our only enemy. There's still a chance we may end up fighting one of these other teams if we make it to the final bracket."

"When, not if," Ray said.

"That's us!" Lucas put on a black headset with the *Ancestral* logo on the cups, adjusting the position of the mic.

"Matches will begin in five minutes," the announcer boomed. "Please go to your lobbies now."

They went silent as they focused on getting logged

in. The shoutcasters prattled on in the background, their voices fading away as each team member put on their headset. Lissa experienced a moment of relief as the big plastic earphones sealed the cacophony away. Here it was silent except for the familiar noises of the game that she'd lived and breathed since launch day. It was terrifying and exhilarating to be in this arena, in this place she had dreamed she might make it to one day. But if she closed her eyes for a moment, she could just be here in the place she felt comfortable: the world of the Xi'sho.

"How's the sound?" Ji-Soo's voice came through the headphones crisp and clear.

"Great. Can everyone else speak, please?"

"Here."

"Yo!" Lucas, chipper as always.

"I'm here."

"Zio?"

The team glanced in her direction to find her fiddling with her headset plug. She popped it into place, noticed she was being watched, and scrambled to get the headphones on.

"Sorry, sorry! I was just checking the connections."

"All good. I can hear you now." Jae-Jin sounded as even-keeled as ever.

"Aren't you nervous?" Lissa asked, her curiosity getting the better of her.

"No."

"Lucky," Ray remarked. "Wish I had those nerves of steel."

"Like I said before, we did our utmost to get here. I feel confident in that. All we can do is play."

The headsets made a brief crackling noise before a

voice spoke on the line.

"Teams: sixty seconds."

Lissa looked down at the Orb in her hands. The paint on the buttons was a different colour now, a thin silver with threads of white starting to show behind it. There had been some mild wear a few months ago, but over the last few weeks she'd really worn it down. She hadn't noticed until now. She stroked her fingers slowly over the faded spots, thinking about all the hours she'd spent to make it to this very moment.

The lobby screen vanished to black. Her breath caught in her throat as she waited to see the map come into view. The screen had barely begun to load when she recognised the slopes of sand dunes in backdrop: the San'sho Lands of Prayer.

"Good luck, teams," the voice said in their headsets. "Begin."

They stood in the midst of a desert. Brilliant white sand stretched out in every direction to touch the edge of the horizon. The only structure in this vast landscape was an enormous building covered with ornate carvings, even whiter than the sands a few hundred paces ahead of them. Its twisting spires reached up towards the sun as if desperate to find some way to make contact. These were tipped with circular symbols made of metal with a line through the lower half. Another short line divided the upper half to the centre. This was the universal symbol of the Xi'sho people, and this church was one of the places they all made a pilgrimage to once in their lifetimes to ask for the favour of the gods.

Jae-Jin sprinted forward first, and the others followed suit as he made his way to the entrance. A few Onyx milled about nearby. They had yet to notice their opponents.

"This map to start with?" Zio said. "I mean, go hard or go home, but still—"

"We'll need to be very careful," Jae-Jin said, cutting her off. "Some parts with close quarters will make it hard for Ji-Soo and Lucas to execute Transcendences because of their wingspans. We need the quickest attackers first. Lissa, Ray, take the lead when we get inside. I'll take these two out first."

Jae-Jin sprinted forward towards the Onyx as his robes trailed behind him in the wind. He held his axe close to his torso as he ran at his enemies, who took notice of him as he approached and howled, their faces contorting to rage. Lissa watched them approaching and caught something that made her heart jump: a flicker of red in one eye.

"Raging on your right!" she cried as Jae-Jin closed the gap, taking a few steps forward.

"No!" Ji-Soo spoke with urgency. "Don't move!"

"But they're trying to—"

"I've got it." Jae-Jin put on a burst of speed as he shot neatly between the two Onyx. The one on the right, whose eyes had burst into flames, leapt out of the way with an angry bellow. Jae-Jin stopped short behind them and threw a fan of skulls out as he turned. They slammed into the Onyx, pelting their chests and faces. Both stumbled backwards but recovered just in time to dodge the swing of his axe. The leftmost beast surged forward and swiped four bloody scratches into Jae-Jin's upper arm.

"Lissa, can you cast Soul Drain from here?"

"On it."

She stepped forward a few paces, swiping her finger upwards on the touch pad to let the spell fly. Both Onyx staggered as it pulled energy from their bodies. Jae-Jin used the precious seconds to his advantage and swung his axe a second time. This time it connected, slicing one beast in half from armpit to hip bone and cutting the legs off the other. Its torso hit the ground with a sickening *thwop* as it screamed in agony, flapping its arms like an injured bird.

"Enter. Now. Lissa and Ray in the lead."

The team sped forward as Jae-Jin stood over his kills, keeping watch. The mini-map swarmed with red dots as they approached the great doors of the church like bees circling their hive, too nervous to stand still. Inside the entrance hall, the colossal stones of the floor had been shattered by huge trees that had broken through to climb towards the skies. Wooden pews lay in disarray. Some of them were broken in half. Ray strafed to the right, always careful to keep an eye on the doorway that led into the next room.

"Clear," he said. "Move forward."

As they drew close to the alcove, a spatter of mud hit Lissa's face. She rolled backward out of pure instinct to get out of the way of whoever had thrown the attack as Ray threw his own handful of mud into the darkness. Another Mender emerged from it with a haphazard grin on her face as her hair danced in the air above her. Zio thrust at her with a great tusk in her arms as the Mender vanished, teleporting to a spot behind them. Lucas just barely managed to divert a seaweed attack that would have taken them all by surprise by extending his wings to block it.

✦FANG HAS BEEN ELIMINATED BY JAEBOMB✦

Lucas retracted his wings to reveal the Mender slumped over one of the edges of Jae-Jin's axe. He gave it a shake to throw off the body and stepped forward to join them.

"Nice."

Lissa cast The God's Theft to steal the last of the lifeforce from the corpse on the floor, replenishing her team's reserves. They moved back towards the doorway and slipped into the silence of the next room, where more towering oaks had broken through the ground. Between each were dozens of wooden tables of varying shapes and sizes. Some were crammed right next to one another. Atop each table was a metal stand that held about two dozen plain white candles. Most of them were lit, giving the room around them a warm glow. As their eyes adjusted to the darkness a figure became visible near the back wall.

"Is that—"

Ji-Soo cut off Zio's words.

"Wait. This looks like a trap. Jae-Jin and Lissa, move left and stay close to the walls. Ray, Zio, cover the right."

They moved to their positions, all watching the figure. It stood perfectly still. In the shadows it was unclear what they were facing, but the dot on the mini-map told them it was another player. Lucas glanced up at the ceiling to make sure they weren't in for another ambush.

"Nothing up above."

"I don't like this," Zio said as she inched along behind Ray. "They should just come out and fight!"

"That's not—"

Jae-Jin's remark was lost as two more enemy players appeared on each side of the figure out of nowhere. They all began to glow, revealing their identities: two Plunderers and a Weaver. The three huddled together like witches over a cauldron as something bitter and deadly brewed between them. Then the Weaver crouched and sank its fingers into one of the cracks in the tile where a tree root had burst through.

"Defensive positions!" Jae-Jin yelled. "Now!"

Ray and Zio rolled to the floor and crouched behind a table just before the ground started to shake beneath them. From the place where the Weaver's fingers were buried in the dirt, a great crack appeared, splitting the ground as it ran across the church floor fast in Jae-Jin and Lissa's direction. They both leapt out of the way as the earth opened under their feet while Lucas spread his wings and rose in the air above their heads.

"Keep jumping, folks," he said as he hovered above the room. "Keep their eyes on you."

The Plunderers were advancing on Ray and Zio's hiding spot with their scimitars drawn. Zio's avatar trembled as it hurled leeches in their direction. They fastened to their hosts' bare chests and arms hungrily and the Plunderers stopped to slash at them with their weapons as they grew fat with blood. Enemy life started to trickle into all their health bars.

As the Weaver held fast in its crouching position, Lucas floated to the ground behind it and landed on the floor without a sound. It was about to stand when Lucas reached forward and sliced its throat from ear to ear. He pushed it to the ground in a pool of its own blood and leapt over the body as he moved towards the Plunderers standing between himself and his teammates. They were all vaguely aware of the cry of the crowd just outside their headsets.

✦VULTURE HAS BEEN ELIMINATED BY IMPACT✦

"Great move, Lucas!" Ji-Soo sounded pleased. "Only four to go. You taking out those Plunderers, too?"

"You bet I am." He crept up on the enemies in his line of sight as they continued to struggle to claw leeches off their bodies. When he was within six feet he stopped and stood still. His head bowed as his wings stretched out and drew back. As they moved forward the wind they carried knocked the struggling Plunderers to the ground. They looked up just in time to see the bundled blades in his hands. One tried to cast Sail the Styx but the spell was interrupted. Lucas was too fast. He cried out with delight as he struck them both down.

✦SEAR HAS BEEN ELIMINATED BY IMPACT✦

✦IKONIK HAS BEEN ELIMINATED BY IMPACT✦

"Lucas, you're the real MVP today," Ji-Soo said. "Your dinner's on me tonight."

"No way," he replied. "Devon would never let us pay for our own dinner the night we won our first championship."

"Focus, please." Jae-Jin came in, sounding irritated. "We have five minutes before time penalties, so we need to take out the leader, fast." He paused to glance at the map. "Four are in the vestry. Let's go."

They darted across the room to a door on the left side. It had been ripped off the hinges. They crossed the threshold to find a cluster of Onyx waiting for them. Jae-Jin cut them down with his axe, taking out all but one. Lissa leapt towards the survivor, trading a few blows back and forth. The Onyx dodged her swipes well. One attack connected as its claws made contact with her Plunderer's naked chest and clawed into the flesh of her clavicle. Her breath hitched as a hook of fear caught in the meat of her throat. She stared at her attacker's empty eyes. Would she be killed by this thing?

Her question was answered as a long tendril of seaweed wrapped around its neck before her eyes. Seconds later it gagged its captive, choking its life away. Lissa got her bearings just in time to see Ray giving it a stomp to ensure that there wasn't a scrap of life left.

"Thanks, friend."

"My pleasure."

The room, at a glance, appeared empty. It was lined with simple wooden wardrobes that looked as if they had been made by hand. Several stood open to show their contents, which were mostly vestments on carved wooden hangers. One held only black capes.

"They're not here anymore." Jae-Jin turned back towards the door. "Must have slipped past while we had our hands full with the Onyx."

They looked at the mini-map to find only two red dots left. All Onyx had been cleared, and only their human enemies remained. They fled towards the door of the church. The team dashed after them, eager to finish the fight. As they passed back into the chapel, they caught sight of them: a Brutalist and a Mender.

"There they are!" Ray sounded excited. "Go out defensive!"

Their prey vanished through the archway just in time to escape them. As they emerged into the light, Jae-Jin and Ji-Soo dropped to a roll while Ray, Lissa, and Zio took protective stances. The Mender was already casting Mud Breath, but the spell faltered, unable to find an open mouth to enter. Lucas took the opportunity to fly into the air over the battle to watch it unfold from above and keep a close eye on weak spots to strike.

Ji-Soo came out of her roll and unfurled both wings as she spun her body to the right. One slammed into the Mender and interrupted her as she attempted to cast another spell. As she stumbled Ji-Soo rolled again and rose mere inches in front of her opponent's face. She relished the expression of surprise she saw there as she drove a crossblade deep into its guts, killing it instantly.

✦HIGHPRIESTESS HAS BEEN
ELIMINATED BY SHOUJO✦

"Guys! Look up!"

At the sound of Zio's voice they finally noticed what was happening above their heads. The remaining Brutalist was in the sky above their heads. It grappled with Lucas, both flapping their wings wildly to try to gain some footing in the air.

"That's Hawkeye," Jae-Jin said in a dark voice. "We need to get him out of there."

Lissa grew still, stroking both thumbs up her Orb's centre buttons with a perfectly timed flick and closed her eyes as the map went black around them and the river of death appeared. She stood at the hull and watched as the other Brutalist—Hawkeye—surfaced in the waters, choking. In her last few moments alive Lissa could have sworn she saw rage on her face. Then she was pulled below the surface and did not rise again.

✦HAWKEYE HAS BEEN ELIMINATED BY NAGIKO✦

"We did it!" Ray cried, ecstatic. "We did it!" He jumped up from his chair and pulled off his headset. The roar of the crowd surged in with such force it disoriented him, but he quickly gained his footing and hugged Zio to his side as she stood up, too. Her eyes went wide as she took off her own headset and heard the sound of the cheers.

"That's for us," she said in an awed voice.

"Yes. And also for Mastermind," Jae-Jin said, gesturing towards the screen behind him. They all turned to see the brackets for the night pictured on the screen. Of the six teams that competed, two remained. Lissa glanced over at the booth next to them to find the members of Fallen Angel staring up at the results with angry faces. Hawkeye looked in their direction with a sour expression.

"Uh, did we just make an enemy?" Lucas asked as he caught sight of her.

"Maybe a few." Jae-Jin was switching off his Orb, not bothering to look up. "Can't say I care. There may be a lot more along the way."

CHAPTER TWENTY-NINE
HOW FAR WE'VE COME

WHEN LISSA REFLECTED back on the evening (as she would many, many times as the journey of her life unrolled before her and she glanced back over her shoulder at where she'd been), she found that her memories of being in the green room after the first match were the most dreamlike of everything that happened that night.

Being on stage in front of thousands of fans, feeling the energy of their anticipation and the roar of their approval, was an electrical high, both real and unreal at the same time. Their second match pitted them against Sleight, a match that felt tenuously close but left her in admiration of them all, especially Rogue, the leader. They had all been impressively calm, even when Lucas finished them off with a well-timed Transcendence that just barely interrupted a strategy that could easily have finished them off. After the match, they'd also come to shake hands, which Lissa admired. Fallen Angel had not done that.

For a while she'd chatted back and forth with her teammates after the second win, but eventually she found her mind drifting in and out of reality, constantly trying to grasp that all this was really happening. Her chest thrummed, excitement and fear intertwining there like thunder and lightning.

Mastermind was next.

"Lissa."

Lissa blinked twice as she realised Jae-Jin's hand was resting on her shoulder, then looked up to find him standing over her. The others were standing a few feet away in a cluster, chatting with two of the girls from GDA.

"You okay?"

"Yeah."

He nodded, looking as if he was deciding whether or not to believe her as her eyes wandered around the plain walls of the room, the tables, the bowls of snacks atop each. A tall, chubby guy polished off an energy drink in their vicinity and chucked it into a nearby trash can as he burped aloud.

Lissa opened her mouth to say more, but she was interrupted as Devon's voice boomed across the room.

"Look at these firebirds!"

They looked up as he entered, as did many of the other players in the room. He'd been absent for a while after taking a phone call right after the win against Sleight, but his glow of pride had not faded. He strode past their huddle and gathered Jae-Jin into a bear hug so fierce his feet lifted off the floor. Zio giggled and snapped a quick photo with her phone.

"Jae-Jin's first time being hugged, ever. Gotta capture this for posterity."

He tried to give her a terse look as Devon returned him to the ground but the little smile the hug left him with ruined the effort. Meanwhile, Devon embraced the rest of them with hearty pats on the back.

"Now, come on, get in! Let's do this as a group thing!"

They huddled close, arms around one another's shoulders. Jae-Jin groaned.

"You guys are squishing me."

"Learn to love it!" Devon growled with emphasis at the end, eliciting more giggles from Ray and Lissa. He plopped down on the arm of the sofa as they took their seats. Lissa briefly noticed a skinny kid with dark hair and eyes—one of the members of SharD—staring at them from across the room with a furrowed brow.

"Sorry I got interrupted at a prime moment there, but firstly, congratulations. You all played that second match beautifully."

"They were good, right?" Lucas looked to the rest of the group for confirmation before going on. "I've admired them for a long time. It was crazy to finally play against them."

"They impressed me," Jae-Jin said. "Their play was clean and strong, and I appreciated that they came by afterwards."

Devon nodded emphatically. "Don't be surprised if you see them again down the line. They have the makings of a great team. But so do you—and I'm very proud of how it went. You did *not* need my help in that one."

"Or we already learned to use your help, which is why it went well in the first place," Ji-Soo said. "Don't play it down."

"All right, all right. Still, that was damn near perfection. What were your takeaways?"

Ray was first to speak up.

"Expect the unexpected, always."

"Good. What else?"

"Lucas is apparently in boss mode when we compete." Lissa grinned as she looked at the subject of her comment. Lucas barked laughter, then looked around as he realised how much of the room was looking in his direction.

"Yeah, I'm hyped. I can't help it."

"We can still lose," Jae-Jin said calmly. Devon snapped his fingers, a man having a long-sought-after eureka moment.

"Yes," he said in a strong voice. "And that may sound like a total downer right now. But why is it important?"

"So we don't get high on the rush and lose our focus."

Devon's eyes darted around the room before he went on, his voice a bit lower than before.

"I know some of you have been watching and already expect this. Mastermind is appearing very solid so far. But I still see Logan Peterson skating the very edge of fighting fair, pulling little dirty things here and there he thinks he can get away with. And he's lucky he hasn't been called out on any of them yet."

"He's the worst kind of player," Jae-Jin said. "I noticed too."

Lissa felt her anxiety rising as she looked at both their faces. They could still lose to Mastermind. All the effort they poured in could be erased.

"You can still win," Devon said, looking at all of them with an earnest expression. "But you don't need me to tell you that anymore."

"We always need you." Jae-Jin still looked serious as

he spoke, but something in his eyes was softer than ever before. Devon clapped a firm hand on his shoulder. No more was said, but something passed between the two men that was all the more precious for being unspoken.

A moment of silence passed in which several members of the team suppressed their smiles as Ji-Soo traded spots on the long couch with Ray so she could sit next to Jae-Jin.

"Lissa, are you remembering the breathing I taught you?"

She nodded with emphasis.

"What breathing? I wanna learn your ancient secrets," Zio said.

"Ah, well, it's simple," Devon replied. "It's called 4-7-8 breathing, but it stimulates the parasympathetic nervous system and helps to slow down the fight or flight response. So first, you inhale through your nose with your mouth closed for four seconds. Then you hold your breath for seven. Lastly you exhale through your nose for the count of eight. If you're in a match, for instance, and you can't afford the focus to count, you fill your belly up like a balloon. When it feels full, you hold your breath, then let it go slowly when the moment feels right to you."

Zio put a hand on her belly, practising a few rounds. Devon and Lissa watched her close her eyes as she fell into the rhythm. After a few cycles, she opened them again and smiled.

"It works! I can feel myself getting calmer."

"Breathing is powerful stuff. Don't forget it—it might come in handy at just the right moment."

Devon trailed off as a familiar figure walked up to their little huddle. No one greeted him.

"So, this is Team Phoenix," Logan Williams said, enunciating the team's name in a mocking tone. "The nobodies who climbed the leaderboards in a couple of months. Impressive."

The silence continued. Lissa felt her heart begin to hammer. Instinctively, she took a deep breath through her nose, imagining a balloon filling inside her belly.

Logan folded his arms as he regarded each of them.

"Still never climbed over us, though."

"Yet."

Logan looked sharply at Jae-Jin, who returned his gaze with every bit of the ice he was known for.

"You the leader of this motley crew?"

"One of them."

Logan walked up to Jae-Jin until their faces were a few inches apart. His teeth were slightly bared, a dog considering whether or not to strike.

"We'll wipe the floor with you tonight."

"Will you? You barely survived the last time we faced off against you."

Lissa watched Jae-Jin's reply with perfect calm and felt a flash of envy. She could never handle a situation like this with such grace.

Logan snorted.

"I killed you all in the end. And if I have to, I'll do it again."

He turned around to face the rest of them, glaring like an angry little gremlin. And it hit Lissa all at once what she was looking at: the little monster in the flesh. Exactly what Devon had told them about. Logan was here making threats because he was afraid to lose everything they'd worked so hard for. She felt a stab of compassion, surprising and unlikely and warm.

Lissa found herself speaking before she knew what she was about to say.

"Good luck. It'll be a great match either way."

She watched as his petulant expression melted into confusion. He opened his mouth, closed it, and opened it again. Then he shook his head and stalked away.

"Wow, Lissa," Zio said, shaking her head. "Were you just... nice to him?"

"I'd call it cordial. But I suppose I was, in a way."

Lissa looked up at her coach. Devon looked back at her without speaking, but his eyes confirmed that he'd seen the same thing she had. They exchanged a barely perceptible nod as the same voice that spoke in their headsets during the match came over the loudspeakers.

"Finalists, the last match will begin in ten minutes. A staff member will be there shortly to escort you to the stage."

"OK, this is it," Lucas said, as much to himself as to the rest of them.

Devon motioned for them to gather in a circle again.

"Put your hands in, Phoenix."

As Lissa felt the warmth of the others' palms, a spark of perfect happiness fired inside her chest. Calm draped over her shoulders and spilled over her body. They were here, now. That was all that mattered.

As he'd done before, Devon laid his hand on top.

"Lucas, do the honours."

"Phoenix, what do we do?" Lucas said in a powerful voice.

"Rise!"

"What will we do today?"

"Rise!"

"What will we do, always?"

"Rise!"

A small hand touched Devon's arm. He looked up to find Charlie there waiting. The circle broke apart as they stepped back.

"Please follow me," she said.

CHAPTER THIRTY
REGIONALS:
FINAL MATCH

CHARLIE LED THE team back to a stage that had been completely transformed from the one they'd seen only half an hour before. The booths they'd previously played in had been cleared away. The stage was bare except for three long curved tables. Each faced inward to form a circular shape in the centre of the stage. In the middle of these hung an enormous vertical banner that flapped in an invisible wind. As they watched, the game's races appeared on it, striking confident poses similar to the ones they'd shown off during the opening ceremony.

"This way," Charlie said, extending her hand in the direction of the staircase. Devon stepped aside as they reached the base. He high-fived each of them as they walked past to make their way up to the stage.

"You got this," he said, flashing his million-dollar smile.

As she drew close Lissa noticed the chairs were the same as the ones they'd sat in for the prior round. The monitors, however, had been swapped out. These were silver rather than black and much broader than the ones they'd previously played on. They were also curved, mirroring the shape of the table they sat at.

"These are *expensive* monitors," Lucas said on her right. "4K, too. It's gonna look sick."

"On the other hand, our old ones might look like crap when we get home," Ray said from Lucas's far side. "Like when you go back to watch stuff you loved as a kid and wonder how you ever watched it looking like that."

"If we win this, we might be playing on these sweet babies before you know it." Lucas powered his on with what looked like a caress.

Lissa pressed the power button and waited. The monitor came to life in less than three seconds on the *Ancestral* start screen. Lucas was right—the reds and golds of the logo were crazy vivid.

"Omari's coming out," Ji-Soo said.

They all glanced up to see Omari Badu standing on the walkway that connected their stage to the one at the back of the room. He checked out the tables to make sure everyone was in their seats before raising the mic back to his mouth.

"*Ancestral* fans... are you ready for the grand finale?"

The cacophony from the crowd was deafening. He let them scream it out a while longer before he went on.

"But in the end, only one thing matters: what team is left standing. That team will take home the regional cup tonight and clear the way to start their journey towards the next landmark: the first ever national championships, which will be coming next year!"

Omari cupped a hand to his ear and nodded,

drinking in the uproar. He looked to be enjoying every moment of it.

"This guy was born to be on the mic," Lissa remarked.

"For real," Zio said.

"Also, we have a surprise for you that's been in the making for a long time. Tonight, we are thrilled to debut the first new *Ancestral* map since the game's release. It'll be in our next update, but tonight, you get to see it for the very first time as our competitors will play out the match in it! Are you ready?"

"A new map." Lucas took a deep, shaky breath. "Oh, man."

Fear shot through Lissa's chest as this information registered. No one else spoke, but she guessed they were all feeling it. They'd memorised every map; knew all its nooks and crannies and weak spots, and most important of all, they knew what to do to hold back the enemy from reaching the graveyards. In this map they'd have to defend themselves while figuring out where the burial grounds were and how to protect them. Mild anger flickered in her belly. How was that fair?

"Team Mastermind and Team Phoenix: best of luck to you both. And now may I introduce you to a world that may change the way you play for good: Arctic Falls!"

As the map loaded, they found themselves facing walls of stone cloaked in darkness on every side. At a glance, it appeared that the new map was set in a valley with no signs of life. Not even a bug flew through the air. But then Ji-Soo figured it out.

"Hey. Look up."

Above their heads a vast waterfall poured down from the rock face. Or rather, it once had, because now it was frozen into pointed white spires that glowed from within with a mysterious light. Above it, a clear night sky showed the winking eyes of hundreds of thousands of stars. It was such a beautiful sight they all paused despite the threat of their new surroundings. Jae-Jin was the first to speak again.

"We can't scale this. There's no way around."

"I see something." Ji-Soo jumped down to a platform of rocks beneath them, then another. "There's a cave entrance over here. Or a break in the rock wall. I can't tell yet." Her tone lit up as she drew close.

"Guys! Come here!"

Lissa bounded in her direction as she kept an eye on the mini-map for their enemies. Dots swarmed over it, but there were hardly any in their direct vicinity. As she moved closer to Ji-Soo's position, she saw a few drawing closer, but she lost her focus a second time as she saw through the alcove in the rock wall to what waited on the other side.

A still black lake stood before them, the tracks of animals that had once visited framing its snowy shores. Beyond it, mountains sloped lazily in their white robes of ice. A galaxy wiped its fingers across the skies above them, leaving streaks of black, blue and white. The full moon hung in the sky off to their right as it watched the scene with impassive silence.

"This is—" Ray started as he moved towards the shores. His words cut off as he slid in the ice and thumped to the ground on his bottom. His avatar was quite a sight sitting there in her mossy robes and muddy arms and legs.

"You can slip in it," Lissa said as she walked around slowly to test her movement. She tried a dash, nearly fell, and caught herself by going into a forward roll. "Wow. They're really pulling out all the stops, aren't they?"

"Just be careful. There's a few over there by the mountains, but I can't see them yet. I know it seems counterintuitive to what we know, but we should move slowly."

They fell into line behind Jae-Jin as he made his way along the edge of the lake. As they drew closer to the foot of the mountains, Zio ran a few steps ahead.

"A path! There!"

"And there's Onyx on it," Lissa said. "Or something."

Sure enough, the red dots on the mini-map showed two enemies waiting for them at the first bend of the path. As they watched, another two joined them.

"Interesting," Jae-Jin said. "Let's prepare for heavy damage in the front, just in case. Zio, come up here with me."

"Let's have Brutalists take the back as well," Ji-Soo said as she moved to the rear of the party. "We can shield if we need to."

She fell into step with him, the great tusk strapped on her back twitching back and forth. Jae-Jin hefted his axe as they approached the entrance to the path, ready to swing at a moment's notice. The red dots on the map were still. And then, as they drew right up to the curve nearest where they waited, all four dots started to pull back and move in the other direction. Lissa watched, bewildered.

"Where are they going?" Ray sounded just as confused.

"Probably setting up some kind of trap. We'll follow at a distance."

The dots were moving towards the end of the path. Jae-Jin took a few careful steps at a slower pace before picking up speed to close the gap between them. The other five were following close behind when he suddenly stopped in his tracks. Ray and Zio skidded to a halt behind him just in time to save the rest from a collision.

"It is a trap. All four vanished."

Ji-Soo stared at the map. "You're right. What the hell?"

Lissa's mind flashed back to that one match that had stuck with her ever since the day she played it. The first time she'd met Logan Williams in-game. And even though she knew she and her teammates had grown strong, that flicker of unease reappeared in her heart.

"They can't be cloaking. That's illegal."

"Let's move. The clock is ticking." Jae-Jin sounded terse.

As they approached the end of the path something glistened in the distance beyond the doorway. Lissa was unable to identify it because of the sun's glare, but it looked dazzling. She narrowed her eyes to try to make it out. She'd just identified the shape of a castle when Jae-Jin cried out as an Onyx appeared out of thin air inches from his face and surged towards his throat with its teeth bared.

"Cloaked!" he yelled as it knocked him to the ground. "They're all—"

"But that's cheating!" Anger was bright in Ji-Soo's voice.

The other three winked into existence, accompanied by a Plunderer with both scimitars drawn back, ready to pierce flesh. Zio shot her vines to try to pull Jae-Jin's attacker off but the three Onyx trampled over them as they trundled forward. Lissa rolled forward and came out in a crouch as she slashed at the legs of their attackers with her crossblades. She made contact with two of them as they howled and stumbled forward, then took the opportunity to slice the off-balance ones from gut to throat. They almost fell dead on top of Ray, who was in the middle of casting Mud Breath behind her, but he saw them just in time to hit interrupt on his spell and step back.

"Get out of this bottleneck as soon as you can," Ji-Soo said as she plunged a crossblade upwards into an Onyx's chin. Its mouth fell open to show her weapon piercing its rotting tongue. "They're trying to use it against us." She shoved the body away and rolled in the direction of the exit that led to the white structures in the distance.

"But Jae-Jin—"

"He can handle it." Her voice sounded even, calm. Lissa had a split second to envy her steadiness before the Plunderer was bearing down on her. Its death mask drew close as if to kiss her face. She watched as its jaw dropped open and the blue mist of Soul Drain began to twist forth from it. It gave her the surreal feeling of being attacked by herself, a strange and intimate glance into a mirror. That moment of fascination could have cost her life. But the illusion was broken as a huge tusk pierced her twin through the chest from behind, its tip only inches from her own chest. Zio stood behind the creature holding it, her teeth bared.

✦JAGUAR HAS BEEN ELIMINATED BY ZIO2GO✦

"Thanks." Lissa's heartbeat sped up as she realised how close she'd been to dying in the most important match she'd ever played.

"My pleasure," Zio replied.

Lissa shoved the Plunderer's body off her to find Jae-Jin had broken free of his attacker. Hundreds of tiny skulls flew from his palms to meet the Onyx that had pinned him down moments before. It turned to run, but not quickly enough. The skulls found their places and dropped their jaws wide before it could get two steps in. The Onyx flailed as the attack made contact and its head went at a funny angle on its shoulders. A moment later, it crumpled dead against the wall.

"I found the graveyard!" Ji-Soo sounded breathless and excited. "Come see!"

Lissa, Ray, Zio, and Jae-Jin crossed the threshold of the path to find a stunning scene before them. The thing in the distance that had blinded Lissa to look at was the sun glinting off the ice of a frozen city that stretched away from them for miles. Near the entrance stood a garden of more than a dozen magnificent sculptures glistening in frost. Behind this, mighty walls and archways reached towards the sky above, and even further back in the distance the spires of tall buildings could be seen.

"Here!"

Ji-Soo was off to the far left of the area. She waved at them and pointed to an entryway in the wall she stood near. Lissa couldn't make out what was beyond it from where they stood.

"This map is wild." Lucas sounded awed.

"I'm surprised there's no one in there."

Ray double-checked the map. "Maybe no one else has found it yet. The rest of them are up north in the city. Some are moving this way."

"We think. But the last attackers were cloaked. And no one stopped the match. They should have, but they didn't." Lissa heard a note of anger creeping into her own voice. She inhaled deeply through her nose in hopes of calming herself, but a pulse ticked in her neck, steady and fast.

"We discuss after. Not now." Jae-Jin stepped inside the sculpture garden, glancing at a carving of a powerful horse galloping with a knight on its back. The knight brandished a pike that came to a sparkling blue point. "Everyone keep the graveyard location in mind as we move forward."

"Onyx! Far side of the garden."

As Ray called out the ground beneath them started to tremble. A mass of Onyx came into view a few hundred feet away through the largest of the archways, but instead of heading straight for them, they pivoted to the right and poured through the sculpture garden. Jae-Jin ran after them in Ji-Soo's direction.

"They're rushing the graveyard! Who can—"

"I can," Zio said as she dashed after him. "Just let me get a little bit closer."

The horde closed the distance to Ji-Soo before they could reach her, but luckily, she was ready for them. She cast Wings of Fury as they got within a few feet of her, killing the three in the front instantly with one wing while she extended the other to block the entrance to the graveyard. The bodies fell on the beasts behind them, slowing their progress as the rest of the team closed the distance.

Just before they gained their footing Zio's avatar stopped and came to a crouch. Raising its muscled arms above its head, it brought its fingers down into the icy soil beneath its feet and gave a powerful howl. The forest animals galloped out of the distance and bore down on the half-dozen Onyx that remained in the fight. As their hooves crushed the bodies beneath them, Lissa heard Ji-Soo cry out.

"One's in there," Jae-Jin said.

"An Onyx?"

"No. A player." He was already through the doorway as Zio's spell was resolving. "We have to save her. Now."

Lissa took off running through the archway, keeping a close eye on Jae-Jin's back as he ran. She quickly caught sight of Ji-Soo shoved against the fences that marked off the gravesite. A Mender had her by the neck with its seaweed and glowered down at her as it continued to wrap more layers of it around her throat. She was also a mere ten paces from the graveyard itself, meaning the match was dangerously close to an end in their enemy's favour.

She leapt into the air as her skirts twirled long around her legs. Her eyes flicked to her stats as her fingers moved, casting Soul Drain at the moment she recognised she had the energy to do so. The Mender stumbled as the spell made contact. Ji-Soo clawed at her neck, struggling to get free of the seaweed that pressed down on her windpipe.

Lissa took advantage of the Weaver's weakness and descended on it at full speed, a smile spreading on her face. Vengeance. She had learned to be wary of anger.

But weren't there also moments like this, where she could use it to her advantage?

The thoughts still wandered through her mind as both scimitars pierced the Weaver's belly. Lissa had a moment to look into her face with its blackened lips and eyes before she ripped upward with all her might, slicing it into three pieces. The Mender's face went slack as she kicked it to the ground. Lissa's fury boiled bright and true in her chest as she looked at the helpless corpse, thinking: *No one can beat me! No one!*

✦CHAOSRING HAS BEEN ELIMINATED BY NAGIKO✦

"Nice, Lissa," Lucas said. "That was their superstar."

"I'm not worried about him," she replied. "Logan Williams is the one I want to see go down. Ji-Soo, you good?"

"Yep, fine. Thanks for jumping in." Ji-Soo was jogging up to meet the rest of them. The red marks the seaweed had left behind still crisscrossed her neck. "I see three coming down where the Onyx came from. Let's go cut them off."

They made their way back, heading for the towering archway. As they passed through it, five new enemies came into view some hundred feet in front of them: three Onyx in the middle and two Morteists, one flanking each side with their axes slung over their shoulders.

"This makes no sense." Ray sounded confused. "If we kill these two, it'll be all of us against Logan a second time."

"He wants revenge." Lucas sounded sure of

himself. "But it's foolish. It's that anger we saw in the green room."

The little monster, Lissa thought with a flush of shame. *The same one that's inside me right now.*

The two Morteists broke away to the right and left, leaving the three Onyx to meet them face to face. Ray cast Mud Breath before they could close the distance, but the creatures ducked and managed to evade the spell.

"They're gonna flank. Watch the back."

"I'll stay on these," Ray said as he rolled between the Onyx's legs, causing them to grunt in alarm. He stood behind them and cast Seaweed Bind, collaring them both in place as they started to choke. Zio struck them with her great tusk while Ray pulled them backwards.

"Why aren't they dying? Are they Raging?"

"The eyes aren't red—"

Both Onyx reached up and ripped the seaweed off their necks in perfect sync. As they did, their gazes burst into flame. They screamed with rage as their forms doubled in size.

"What the hell is this?" Ray cried out as he rolled backwards. "Did they just... grow?"

"Lissa! Help!"

Her fingers performed the combination for Dark Rush without a moment's hesitation just as one of the Onyx wrapped a clawed hand around Zio's neck and lifted her off the ground. She kicked at it helplessly. Lissa's spell started to weave its dark magic in the direction of the struggle, but lost the battle as the Onyx used its free hand to claw Zio's exposed torso. Blood spilled from the wounds as the beast dropped her corpse unceremoniously onto the ground.

✦ZIO2GO HAS BEEN ELIMINATED BY ONYX✦

"Ugh!" Zio yelled into the mic. "No no no!"

Lissa sped towards the creature with her scimitars drawn and drove both into its gut. It sputtered forth a bloody, boiling liquid onto the ground before collapsing atop Zio's body.

Lissa felt a hard resolve crystallising inside her, one she couldn't quite reach until this moment in the match. She felt anger swirling at its core, along with determination, confidence, and even a hint of sadness. The sadness, she guessed, that she carried all along. But she also felt the power of all those emotions strong inside her. For a second, she knew exactly how strong she was.

And maybe I can use that to my advantage.

"Don't worry, Zio," Lissa said. "We're going to win this one for you."

"Coming up the back now!" Ji-Soo yelled. "All hands here!"

Lissa turned to see one of the Morteists summoning a cloud of death masks to assemble Skull Shatter. They had two seconds to protect themselves before the whole team was dead.

"Defend! Now!"

Lissa clapped her hands to her ears as her teammates did the same. This was the only protective posture that could save them from the attack. Jae-Jin and Ji-Soo moved into position with the precision of synchronised dancers. Lucas and Lissa were a split second later but still managed just in time. As they waited for the attack to end, an unpleasant message scrolled across the screen.

✦DYNAMIX HAS BEEN ELIMINATED BY JOKER✦

"It's my fault." Ray sounded miserable when he spoke. "I was too slow."

No one responded to him as they came out of their defensive poses. Jae-Jin was already swinging at his twins. One blocked him with the flat part of his axe with a mighty clang, shoving him off. Jae-Jin backflipped to his feet as Ji-Soo's wings swept back and her hands drew close to her face. Lissa saw what she was doing and felt a flood of relief. Death Flight was one of few Transcendences that couldn't be interrupted or blocked. Her heart rate slowed as she watched her friend's wings split into swords. Surely, there was no way they could survive this.

Lissa was right: their opponents did not sustain. What she did not account for was the bomb one of them threw in the split second before Ji-Soo sliced their heads off their necks. She threw herself at Ji-Soo to knock her out of the way without calling out her move, but she knew there was no time, not even to warn Jae-Jin. Ji-Soo was saying something but the din of the bomb going off blew her words into pieces.

✦JOKERS_HAND HAS BEEN
ELIMINATED BY SHOUJO✦

✦SABERZ HAS BEEN ELIMINATED BY SHOUJO✦

"That was too close." Jae-Jin sounded shaken. "Ray, are you OK?"

"Yeah, just disappointed."

"Hang in there. This isn't over yet." Ji-Soo stared

at the mini-map. "There's no more enemies on this screen."

"Logan Williams is cheesing this. He's using cloaking." Zio's anger leaked through her words.

"That's cheating. He'll be disqualified."

"Why haven't they called it, then?"

A few seconds ticked by before Jae-Jin spoke. His voice was more determined—and emotional—than any of them had ever heard it.

"We can still win. Will we rise, Phoenix?"

"Yes!" Lucas cried passionately.

"Absolutely."

"Yes," Lissa said without hesitation. "We will."

"Now let's hunt him down. Move forward as a group through the entryway. When we get to the town we'll split up: me and Lucas left, Ji-Soo and Lissa right. Be careful and stay close. Got it?"

"Copy."

"Yep."

"OK."

Lissa's heart was thumping so hard she felt a pounding in her ears. Once again, they had clawed their way to the very end of the match. And again, they were facing the same enemy. An angry player who let his rage drive him forward.

Just like you, her thoughts whispered as her team ran forward, their boots pounding the snow.

How can I be different? she whispered back to herself.

He's willing to cheat to win. You would never do that.

She nodded to herself as her resolve hardened like a rock inside her soul. No, she would never cheat.

Because cheating meant she would never know just how strong she really was. And today, on this icy battlefield, she would find out.

Once through the passageway buildings of all shapes and sizes towered above them, all carved in ice down to the finest detail. Lissa recognised they were all recreations of different architectural styles throughout history. A neoclassical structure with a dozen columns stood off to their left. Her eye caught the pointed spires of an ornate Gothic building a few hundred feet in the distance. A few Italian villas stood directly in front of them in a cluster. They were taking their first steps towards them when Ji-Soo cried out.

"He's heading for the graveyard! I just saw it!"

Fear threatened to pour into Lissa's brain as she turned and ran, pressing her anger down. She inhaled deeply through her nostrils. Feeling her focus grow sharper as the breath filled her lungs, she held her breath as Devon's face rose in her mind.

So first, you inhale for four seconds...

Her fear hammered at her in desperation. She let it clamour as she ran, focusing on nothing else but the destination and the breath. Releasing it. Feeling the slow passage of it leaving her body. Drawing it back in slowly as her lungs filled with blessed, perfect air.

"There!" Jae-Jin cried as he strafed to the right. "Lissa, cut to—"

He would have commanded her to go down and to the left, but somehow she already knew. The answer was in the breath, although never implicitly spoken. Lissa marvelled as she realised this was the place inside herself where she could sense what to do without words. As she exhaled, she felt a sparkle of magic pass through her, twinkling down the skin of her arms.

Dark Rush.

Logan was nowhere in sight, but she trusted this new whisper coming from inside her. So she cast the spell. A split second later Logan's Mender appeared a few dozen paces from the graveyard entrance, the swirls of Lissa's spell rendering him helpless. He shot seaweed from his palms haphazardly to try to break free. Ji-Soo and Jae-Jin were both coming at him at top speed, closing the distance as fast as they could.

"Yes, Lissa!" Lucas shouted.

Logan shook off the last vestiges of the spell and spewed mud in Lissa's direction. She rolled out of the way with ease, timing it with a long exhale. The feeling of being perfectly in sync awed her. She and her friends were fighting for the highest stakes. Just a few minutes ago, she felt terrified. But now the fear had transformed into something else: power.

Lana's words rose in her mind, glowing on her phone screen in the darkness of a long, lonely night.

You have what it takes to win.

Ji-Soo and Jae-Jin had closed the distance as Logan cast his last spell. They were mere feet away when he whirled on them, slinging seaweed in their faces. It caught Ji-Soo's arm and wrapped around it with terrifying speed. She slashed at it with a crossblade as it jerked Ji-Soo off the ground but was unable to slice it away. Lucas dashed in to try to help her. Lissa stood watching the scene, unmoving. The new whisper inside her said not to rush in. Wait. Just wait.

Jae-Jin hit Logan with the flat side of his axe and knocked him hard to the ground. He leapt atop the body as Logan struggled, and for that quick inhale of time, it looked like it would be over. But in the next second Jae-Jin was rolling backwards and flailing to scrape leeches off his robes as they crawled with terrible quickness towards his face. Logan had managed to throw Thirst of the Leech just in time—which meant that his Transcendence bar was empty.

Now.

Lissa moved in his direction, each step feeling like the slow syrup of a dream. She saw Jae-Jin, struggling on the ground to claw the bloodsucking bugs away, Lucas helping Ji-Soo to her feet. Logan was starting to sit up, but the daze the Transcendence left behind was still heavy on him. She had three seconds at most.

It took her two to close the distance and a third to crouch behind him and plunge her scimitars into his skull, one on each side.

✦WRAITHX HAS BEEN ELIMINATED BY NAGIKO✦

"We did it!" Lucas yelled into the mic. "Oh my god, we did it!"

A deafening roar thundered just outside their headsets. One by one, they removed them to find a wild cacophony had descended on the dome. People clapped and screamed from their seats, waving their signs and lightsticks wildly as the excited voices of the shoutcasters blared throughout the space. Lissa looked at her teammates just as Lucas was pulling her out of her chair and crushing her in a hug. Over his shoulder she saw Jae-Jin embracing Ji-Soo, smiling down at her.

"—have a new champion! And the way Team Phoenix handled those last few minutes was an absolute triumph—"

"Lissa Walker played that final kill to perfection! I can tell you one thing for sure—after this night, sponsors will be beating down the door to get to Team Phoenix first! You know, Greta, their story is remarkable. They truly rose from the ashes!"

"And now the world will know it," Greta replied with a sparkle in her voice. "We got to see history tonight. Congratulations to Team Phoenix, our new regional champions!"

CHAPTER THIRTY-ONE
AFTER A VICTORY

"SO... HAS IT sunk in yet?"

The six of them considered the question as Devon waited. He was in no hurry for an answer, and they all knew it. He was a patient man. He also knew exactly how overwhelming it was to be where they were right this very second, and how delight flooded your senses and surged through every pore of your skin. But with it came fear, too: fear of loss, and the feeling of standing atop a tall building that is growing underneath your feet as the street below hurtles away from you, and the people you knew shrink into specks and then vanish altogether, glorious and lonely all at the same time.

"I guess not, because it feels like I'm in shock."

Their eyes followed the sound of Ray's voice. He sat curled up in one of the white upholstered chairs in the gaming station nearest the front door. As late as it was after the long drive home, Devon had driven them directly to PlaySpace. It was the place they all felt the most safe, and despite the excitement of the idea of a victory dinner, it was where they had all wanted to go in the end.

"Yeah," Zio said. "It doesn't feel real. But I still feel high as a kite, even though a part of me wants to sleep for a week."

"I don't feel much shock at all." Ji-Soo and Jae-Jin sat together on the white sofa from the next station over, which they'd pulled over to make enough room for all of them to sit close together. Jae-Jin watched her as she spoke. "Is that weird? I just feel accomplished. Like, the deepest, most rewarding sense of accomplishment I've ever had."

"You worked hard for it, so you should," Jae-Jin said.

She gave him an incredulous look.

"So did you! Everyone in this room did."

"You're right. But no one has worked as closely with you as I have. I've seen you change so much as we worked together to lead the team."

They looked at each other as if they were the only ones in the room, their faces heavy with unexpressed words. After a few moments, Devon broke the silence.

"Just date already," he said, laughing through his words. "You two are the last ones to see what's staring the rest of us in the face."

Jae-Jin looked around at his friends with wide eyes. Ray and Zio giggled like schoolgirls passing notes, while Lucas covered his laugh with a hand. Lissa simply smiled.

When he turned back to Ji-Soo, her face was soft and patient. A flash of the old Ji-Soo passed through Lissa's mind as she looked at her. Jae-Jin was right. Her friend *had* changed, and she respected and loved her more than ever because of how far she'd come.

Jae-Jin reached out and took Ji-Soo's hand, their

fingers intertwining as if they'd found their perfect resting place. She had a moment to smile back at him before the room exploded in applause. Ray and Zio exchanged a passionate high five as they cheered for their leaders.

"YES!" Lucas yelled as he clapped his hands like a man at the opera giving an ardent standing ovation. "More rewarding than winning the cup!"

"Oh, shut up," Jae-Jin said as a blush crept out from beneath his jersey and started its way up his neck.

"Seriously," Lissa said. "I'm really happy for you two. You're great leaders. Without you, I don't know if we could have done what we did tonight." She looked across at Devon, taking a deep breath. He nodded back at her. She could see in his face he knew what she meant to say. She swallowed the nervous twinge in her throat and continued.

"For me, finding this team and winning this not only gave me amazing friends that helped me achieve a dream, but it also helped to heal something in me. Some of you I have never told about this—except Ji-Soo and Devon—but I had a younger brother who died not long ago. It left me lost and I didn't know how to find my way through it. But tonight, after we won, I felt peace for the first time since he passed. I know he'd be so proud of me—of us—tonight. Phoenix is so much more than just a team to me. You're family."

Lucas and Ray ran to her before she could finish, hugging her from behind. She looked up at Ji-Soo to find pride shining from her friend's face.

"We love you, Lissa," Zio said. "I'm so sorry about what happened to your brother. But I'm also glad that we could help you find your way through it."

Devon reached out and took Lissa's hand as Lucas and Ray continued to cuddle her. When some time had drifted by, he stood up and walked over to the drink machine, fished in his pockets, and deposited a few quarters into the machine, then returned to them with a soda in hand.

"You know, some things will change now that you've won. Sponsors will start to call. Your public persona is going to go nuts for a while. Everyone will want to know about the scrappy kids who unseated Mastermind. It'll be exciting and overwhelming. And you'll need someone to manage it."

Ji-Soo sat up straight in her seat, her face alert. Her hand was still clasped in Jae-Jin's.

"Will you be our coach, Devon?"

He laughed. "Of course I will. I can't imagine not being there. Although I have to admit it's the most interesting feeling to find myself a coach all these years later. I always felt I didn't succeed as a competitive player in the end. But here I am using that experience in a whole new way."

"Life is strange and wonderful," Zio piped up. "If I've learned anything from these last few months, it's that. Things that seem impossible are possible. Your mind really steers the direction of the boat." She looked towards Devon. "Of course, we learned that from you."

"I'm just the messenger. Trust me on that. I can tell you anything, but you're the one that puts it into practice. I just helped along the way."

Zio grinned, looking like the happiest girl in the world.

"So, I have a question," Lucas said. "There's a lot out

there about corrupt sponsorships in the esports world. How do we know what to look for to avoid them?"

"Well, that's another thing that's changed a lot since my time," Devon replied. "We'll need to be aware and learn more about the bad deals that have happened to others. But I think it's something we can handle. I feel sure you'll have more than one offer to choose from, so we'll weigh the options and discuss it as a group."

"Will Mastermind lose their sponsor now?"

"Hard to say. Depends on the sponsor. But they can't play in nationals because they've been defeated at the regional level, so it doesn't look great for them."

"Man, I bet they hate us now." Lucas fidgeted with the keychains on his backpack as he spoke. "Logan Williams probably wants to beat our asses. Literally."

"That's another thing," Devon said. "By winning in this way, you will make enemies. I had them, too. Most of them are all talk but every once in a while you'll run into a bad egg who doesn't see the line between what's OK and what's not. He could very well be one of those. At any rate, be careful and aware. If he sends threats of any kind, let me know."

They nodded quietly as they processed this information.

"It's just hitting me how tired I am," Jae-Jin said, standing up with Ji-Soo at his side. "I want to sleep soon because I have some ideas for how we should progress, and I want to map those out as soon as I can. And I need to take Ji-Soo home."

As if he'd flipped a switch, the others started to gather their things, murmuring about what they had planned the following day.

"So, wait," Lissa said. "Do we practise tomorrow? Leaders?"

"We practise every—" Jae-Jin started, but he trailed away as Ji-Soo squeezed his hand. He looked down at it, then up at her face with a quizzical expression.

"I say we take a break for a day. We've earned it. What do you think, Jae-Jin?" she said, fluttering her eyelashes at him innocently.

"Oh, man," Ray said, laughing at the exchange.

"That's fair. But I won't know what to do with myself. I've played every day since launch."

"I'll take you on a park date. It'll be fun."

"What is this 'fun'?" he said as he slung an arm around her shoulders, and they headed for the door. "Good night, friends."

"Hold it for us!" Lucas cried as he, Ray, and Zio ran to catch up with them. "See you soon, champions!"

The door swung to a close with a tiny creak. Devon and Lissa stood there, watching them go as silence swallowed up the room.

"I'm so proud of you, Lissa," Devon said as they watched their friends walk to their cars down below. "I really am."

Lissa responded by engulfing him in a hug. They stood there for a while, a man with a past and a girl with a future, both feeling happy and safe and right. And when the moment had passed, he opened the door for her with a gentle smile.

"Now go home and enjoy your victory," he said as he waved goodbye to her. "You've earned it."

EPILOGUE

>**hellodearone (12:29 am):** *i know you're probably still upset with me but... i wanted to say congratulations.*

THE MESSAGE CAME as Lissa was sitting at her PC, rereading one of their old conversations on her phone. She started as if she had been caught in the act, imagining Lana looking right at her. And while the tug of fear in her chest was still there, she realised that this person cared about her.

You care about her, too, her mind whispered. *And you know it.*

>**MonoNoAware (12:34 am):** *How did you know we won?*

>**hellodearone (12:34 am):** *its all over the forums. everyone is talking about you being the first woman at regionals to make the final kill. some people that were there even posted pictures.*

>**hellodearone (12:35 am):** *plus i was watching. hoping to see you win.*

>**MonoNoAware (12:36 am):** *So you know what I look like now?*

➤**hellodearone (12:36 am):** *yes. you're the pretty girl with the dark hair.*

Lissa reread the sentence as her heartbeat sped up to a maddening pace, her brain accelerating her thoughts to gibberish.

➤**hellodearone (12:37 am):** *ah, i hope that wasn't too forward.*

➤**hellodearone (12:39 am):** *so did sponsors approach you?*

➤**MonoNoAware (12:40 am):** *Not yet. Devon thinks we'll hear from them soon though. Oh, Devon is our coach, BTW.*

➤**hellodearone (12:41 am):** *the tall Black guy with the big smile, right? he looks so friendly.*

➤**MonoNoAware (12:41 am):** *He is.*

➤**hellodearone (12:42 am):** *i bet he's beyond proud of you tonight*

➤**hellodearone (12:43 am):** *must be hard to sleep after that win*

➤**MonoNoAware (12:44 am):** *Yeah.*

➤**MonoNoAware (12:44 am):** *I've only been home for a little while. My dad was excited about it too, so we talked for a while before I came up to go to bed.*

➤**MonoNoAware (12:45 am):** *It's just... all still running through my head. I feel like my brain is going ten million miles an hour.*

➤**hellodearone (12:46 am):** *its ok. It was inspiring to watch.*

➤**hellodearone (12:46 am):** *and speaking of that, i think seeing you succeed in this championship helped me make a decision.*

➤**MonoNoAware (12:46 am):** *What's that?*

➤**hellodearone (12:47 am):** *i'm going to try to go competitive. i've hid in my shell for long enough, and* *even though i'm scared to death, i'm tired of being afraid and doing nothing about it*

Lissa paused as she stared at the message, trying to find the right words for the feeling she was having.

➤**MonoNoAware (12:47 am):** *I'll be there to cheer for you, Lana.*
➤**hellodearone (12:48 am):** *thank you ∗blush∗*
➤**MonoNoAware (12:48 am):** *But wait. If you wanted to compete in nationals, wouldn't you already have to have ranked in regionals?*
➤**hellodearone (12:48 am):** *yes. but remember i'm in hong kong. so our regionals haven't been announced yet. maybe now that you've had them in the states we'll get them here too*

Lissa felt exhaustion rushing over her now, bringing a light-headedness with it.

➤**MonoNoAware (12:49 am):** *It just hit me how tired I am. There's so much more to come.*
➤**hellodearone (12:49 am):** *yes. for both of us.*
➤**MonoNoAware (12:50 am):** *I'm not mad anymore, Lana.*
➤**hellodearone (12:50 am):** *i'm so glad. the idea of losing you scared me.*
➤**MonoNoAware (12:51 am):** *Me too.*
➤**MonoNoAware (1:00 am):** *Good night. <3*
➤**hellodearone (1:00 am):** *good night, lovely. <3*

Lissa shut off the monitor and got back in bed. Her fingers held fast to the phone close to her face as she imagined Lana somehow far and near at the same time, as her consciousness drifted in and out like the tide. Then it fell to the pillow beside her as she slipped away again, a deeper dive into the sea of sleep.

Her phone screen turned itself off as she floated there, lulled by the current. She came up again one more time, long enough to realise that she needed to plug in the phone on the bedside table or it would die during the night. As she sank back into the pillow and started to spiral back down to blackness, a single conscious thought glowed briefly before the sea of dreams consumed her.

We won.

ACKNOWLEDGEMENTS

THE EXPERIENCE OF writing this book was one of the most rich and challenging of my life so far, and without these people, it never would have happened. Firstly, my friend Cassandra Khaw, who introduced me to Rebellion in the first place—I'm forever grateful for how that small gesture allowed one of my greatest dreams to come true. Thank you with all my heart.

To both David Moore and Amy Borsuk, my editors: Thank you both for your patience and your support. The book would not be what it is today without you. To my dear friend Mario Reid, who planted the seed of the book's title before I started to write it. To my husband Patrick, who urged me on as I fumbled my way through each step of this journey and supported me at every turn. Lastly, to each person in my life who inspired me by being exactly who you are without apology, no matter how difficult that may have been (or still be). Threads of your magnificent color are woven all throughout these characters, and I cannot wait to introduce the rest of the world to them.

ABOUT THE AUTHOR

Colette Bennett is a New Orleans-born writer driven by a love of video games, pop culture, and horror fiction. A journalist since 2007, her work has appeared on national news outlets such as CNN and Yahoo as well as gaming sites Kotaku, Joystiq, Destructoid, Touch Arcade, and GamesIndustry.biz. Her short stories in print can be found in *The Corona Book of Science Fiction* and *The Corona Book of Horror*. She lives in Atlanta with her husband and three extremely needy cats. *Enter the Meta* is her first novel.

FIND US ONLINE!

www.rebellionpublishing.com

/rebellionpub   /rebellionpublishing /rebellionpublishing

SIGN UP TO OUR NEWSLETTER!

rebellionpublishing.com/newsletter

YOUR REVIEWS MATTER!

Enjoy this book? Got something to say?

Leave a review on Amazon, GoodReads or with your favourite bookseller and let the world know!